Claim Me Forever

A.L. Jackson
www.aljacksonauthor.com
Cover Design by RBA Designs
Editing by SS Stylistic Editing
Proofreading by Julia Griffis, The Romance Bibliophile
Formatting by Champagne Book Design

More from

A.L. Jackson

NEW YORK TIMES BESTSELLING AUTHOR

Claim Me Forever

NEW YORK TIMES BESTSELLING AUTHOR
A.L. JACKSON

Prologue

HE STARED AT ME FROM WHERE HE STOOD TWO FEET AWAY. I could almost see the intensity he'd watched me with since the first time we'd met break free and become something palpable.

Become something alive and real.

How, when we were little more than strangers? I fought for the walls that I'd kept like a fortress for my entire life.

"Why, Ezra? Why? You don't know me or owe me or care for me—"

"Bullshit." He moved so fast that I didn't even realize what had happened before he had my back pressed to the counter and his hand in my hair.

"Bullshit." He whispered it that time, so quiet, but it still boomed between us.

"I might not know all the details about you, but there's something about you that I recognize here." He gathered up my hand and pressed my palm flat to the ravaging at his chest. "Something I feel. Something I know. And the problem is, I care too fucking much."

My chin quivered as I gazed up at his rugged, masculine face, the atmosphere shifting, greed infiltrating the space.

He grasped me by the back of the neck.

My lips parted and the air trembled around us.

His attention dipped to my mouth before it flicked back up. The honey of his eyes had turned molten.

"Tell me not to kiss you." His words were a gnarl of desperation. Issued in a bid of restraint neither of us seemed able to possess.

My fingers curled into his shirt.

I wavered.

A second.

An eternity.

I knew better than giving in. Knew better than trusting anyone when trusting had only caused me a lifetime of pain.

Still, I whispered, "I don't want to."

Knowing I was the fool who would only bring danger to his door...

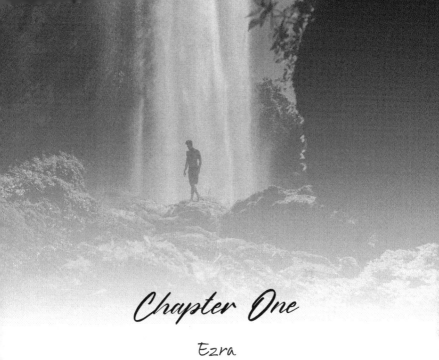

Chapter One

Ezra

I T WAS THE PITCH OF NIGHT AS I SLOWLY EASED MY SUV up the path carved out by tires that cut through the field. High grasses rose on each side, scratching against the metal as I passed over the bumpy terrain. I peered out my windshield through the spray of headlights as I eased deeper into the field, searching for anything that might be amiss.

Mr. Landers had called into the station two nights ago saying he kept seeing lights coming on up this way on his property at all times of the night, but considering the old buzzard was continually paranoid someone was trying to steal from him, sending my deputies on constant goose chases that led to absolutely nothing, I hadn't given it much thought.

He'd called in again an hour ago, though, and since I was patrolling out this direction, I figured I'd swing by to give it a look. The least I could do was offer the man some peace of mind, though I doubted he'd ever find much of that.

My Tahoe bounced over the uneven ground as I followed the path that led to a small copse of soaring trees that surrounded a small

4 | A.L. JACKSON

pond on the Landers' property. The only reason I knew it was there was because we used to sneak out here as teens and use it as party grounds, which I was pretty sure was where the poor guy had gotten his phobia from.

I came up around a bend, and my headlights caught on something up ahead—a flare of light against metal and chrome.

Well shit, there was something out here after all.

A car that sat with the front facing out where it was backed into the cover of the bushes and trees.

My nerves ticked a fraction, and I reached for my radio and pressed the button to speak to my dispatcher. "Hey, Pamela, it looks like we might have an actual trespasser out here on Landers' land near the pond. Newer model Ford sedan. Red. I'm going to check it out."

"You mean he wasn't calling in another false alarm?" Her voice was a tease.

"There is a first for everything," I told her with a chuckle, though I didn't let my attention wander from the vehicle in front of me for a second.

Vigilant.

You could never be too sure about what you were coming up against in this line of work, even though in all likelihood, I was about to get myself an eyeful of two people sneaking off so they could go at it, thinking they were hidden away and wouldn't be discovered.

It would be the most action I'd had in years.

I would have laughed if it wasn't so goddamned painful.

Before Pamela could respond, Samson's voice broke through the shared line. "Do you need backup, boss? Things are quiet on Manchester. Bored as all hell over here, man."

Samson was my only other deputy on tonight, and he was patrolling downtown Time River. I didn't usually work nights, but I was covering for another deputy who'd had a family event she'd wanted to attend.

"What, you think you're on the job for your entertainment?" I let the razzing wind into the question.

"Nah, man, I just don't want your old ass to come up on more than you can handle." He tossed the razzing right back.

Samson was cool as shit. My whole staff was. I felt lucky to have a team as driven, hardworking, and compassionate as the one I did. Ensuring our streets and homes were safe from the depravities people could be so inclined to commit. To the immoralities and sins that ran rampant.

Just because Time River was a small town didn't mean we were immune to those threats.

None of us were.

My chest tightened as thoughts of how those depravities had made their way into my life. Visions of the tragedy warped my mind in a snarl of affliction.

God, the lengths I would go to finally find the monsters who'd spilled innocent blood.

I scrubbed a palm over my face to break up the thoughts. Right then was not the time to be contemplating retribution, not when I needed to focus on the job that was right in front of me.

"Think this *old man* has it handled." I forced easiness into my voice.

"Let me know, and I'll be there." A true kind of care dripped into his tone.

"I know you've always got my back, but I'm sure it's nothing."

"All right then. Just be safe out there, brother."

"Always."

I scanned out the windshield at the car, searching for any movement.

When I found no indication of anyone around, I unlatched my door and slipped out with the engine still running and the headlights cutting through the darkness. I kept my hand on the handle of my gun as I slowly crept forward, and I pulled out my flashlight with the other as I tromped over exposed roots and pitted ground.

I lifted the flashlight and pointed it toward the car, squinting as I crept below the endless web of stars that spun through the heavens, the moon missing tonight and making them all the brighter.

Unable to make out anything through the windshield, I eased along the side.

My blood pounded an extra beat as I felt a small shift in the air. A sense of awareness that the car hadn't been abandoned.

Shining my light against the glass, I peered through the driver's side window. It took me a second to realize the seat was laid all the way back and someone was buried underneath a thick white blanket, completely gone to the world as they slept.

I tapped the glass with the end of my flashlight.

That was all it took to send a commotion of flailing arms and long blonde hair bolting upright, right about the same time as a scream pierced the night. The woman inside scrambled backward even though there was nowhere to go.

Shit.

I'd scared the hell out of her.

I realized she wouldn't be able to make me out at all, and she had no idea who was outside her window in the middle of nowhere, even though I wasn't sure that her finding a 6'5" man who was just about as wide as he was tall lurking on the other side any more comforting.

The fact I had a big SHERIFF stamped across my vest was a toss-up, too.

I took a step back from the door and shined the light on myself, my other hand held up in surrender.

Nah, not protocol, but I couldn't handle the way she kept screaming inside, like she was pretty sure she was about to get chopped to pieces and tossed into the pond.

My movement was enough to clamp off her screams and for the wild clamor on the inside to cease. But her breaths were still so heavy and ragged I thought I could actually hear them through the glass and metal, her fear so profound I could feel it ricocheting across my flesh.

I gave her a whole minute to adjust before I reached out and softly knocked my knuckles against the window. An eternity passed before she finally pushed the button on the locks and popped open the door, so slowly that I had to wonder if she hadn't been contemplating starting her engine and trying to make a getaway.

It lit the cab, but the light was so dim that I couldn't make much of her out.

"Are you okay in there?" I asked, keeping my voice as soft as I could.

She inhaled a jagged breath. "Am I okay? You scared the crap out of me. I bet you love it, don't you? Sneaking up on unsuspecting women? I thought I was going to have to stab you."

A disbelieving chuckle escaped, unable to believe the little trespasser had just tossed that out there.

"Stab me, huh?" I inclined my head.

She seemed to war before she said, "Um, yeah, I have a knife. I'm supposed to like…disclose that, right? That I have a weapon?"

She lifted her chin like she was warning me she'd use it if I were to make the wrong move.

She seemed to be calming down enough that I took a step forward, and I leaned down and shined the flashlight into the cab.

Nearly got knocked onto my ass with the sight of the big blue eyes that stared back. So fucking startling she might as well have gone ahead and stabbed me with that knife right in the chest.

My breath gone.

Punctured.

Wiped away by a flood of aqua that slammed me from out of nowhere.

My stomach was suddenly in a fist as I took in her face.

Defined cheeks and sharp nose, brows and lashes thick, lips so goddamn full I had the urge to reach out and trace them to find out if they were as soft as they looked.

The attraction was as dense and lush as her lips.

Fuck.

What was wrong with me?

That was the type of compulsion that was dangerous.

I sucked it down and focused on doing my job, and I did my best to keep the roughness out of my voice. "Mind if I take a look at that knife?"

Aqua eyes narrowed in speculation. A lithe panther ready to

pounce. "I might mind. I haven't decided if I'm going to have to use it or not."

She was a fiery thing.

My brow arched, and I bit back the chuckle that wanted to break free, liking the way she dared to talk to me a little too much. "I'm also the Sheriff around here, and I think it'd be in your best interest if you cooperated."

"Fine," she huffed like I was the one who'd broken the law, and she dug around in her console and produced the tiniest switchblade I'd ever seen.

A swell of protectiveness rushed me. Did she think she was going to protect herself with that pitiful blade? She wouldn't have even broken skin.

Tuning out the unwanted reaction, I tucked the knife into my pocket and studied her where she itched in the seat. "Do you want to tell me what you're doing out here?" I asked.

Uncertainty brimmed in her eyes, and she looked around, hunting for the best lie. "Um…camping."

It fully came out like she was the one asking me.

"Camping?" I challenged.

"That's right. There's a really beautiful pond right over there." She pointed toward the blackened pool that rippled with the bare breeze before she turned back and sent me the fakest smile I'd ever seen.

A gorgeous fucking smile, but still fake.

A vise grip of worry clamped down on my heart, and that feeling surged back, bigger than before, sure this woman was in some kind of trouble. Still, I pressed, "A pond that belongs to a Mr. Landers. Did you not see the *Keep Out* signs? You're trespassing."

"Oh my gosh, really? I totally didn't see them." She feigned innocence.

I lifted my brow, and she sighed. "Fine. I saw them, but I didn't mean to cause any problems. I was only…" She paused, agitation running through her as she turned her attention out the passenger-side window. Her tongue swiped across her lips before she said, "…Looking for a private place to sleep where nobody would find me."

"But I found you." I didn't know why it came out like it meant something.

Her brow knitted in frustration. "Uh, yeah, because you're like some kind of bloodhound. I'm in the middle of nowhere and there's not really even a road."

"Not sure that you're as sneaky as you might think you are."

I couldn't tell if it was annoyance or dread that cut into her expression, and she dragged her hand through the matted locks of her blonde hair. "I guess I'm not, am I?"

I was pretty sure she was speaking to herself. Then she sent another one of those smiles my way. "I'll just be going on my way, then, if you'd kindly move your SUV so I can get by."

She waved a hand in the direction of my headlights.

All kinds of daring and confident.

"You're getting a little ahead of yourself, don't you think?"

She bit down on her bottom lip. "Am I in trouble?"

I didn't know what it was that made me stall. Normally, I'd give a warning and send the trespasser on their way. No harm, no foul. But there was something about her that told me I needed to look closer.

Unable to shake that feeling that maybe she was *in trouble*, but not in the way she was implying.

"How about we take a little ride down to the station and then we can decide."

Then I widened her door because I wasn't offering it as a suggestion.

Chapter Two

Savannah

SHIT, SHIT, SHIT.

My attention darted around, searching for a way to get out of this. Three days here, and I'd already found myself a hulking mountain of trouble with a giant *Sheriff* stamped across his chest.

It wasn't like I didn't think I'd run into trouble, coming here, doing what I was doing, but I hadn't really imagined it would look quite like this.

This brute of a man who filled up the entire door of my car.

Every inch of him bulky, corded, and ripped.

The short sleeves of the brown uniform he wore stretched so tight over his biceps that I didn't know how the threads didn't bust, and the man was so tall that he blocked out the sight of the stars where he towered over me.

A beautiful, oppressive eclipse.

Hello, Hot Cop.

He had that rugged look. A squared, powerful jaw with scruff beginning to show, skin tanned from spending hours out under the sun. His wavy hair was brown and dappled in blonds, like the sun had had its way with it, too.

Hardness oozed from every rigid line of him, all except for the softness that kept playing at the edge of his lips that were more alluring than any man should ever have the right to. That and the concern that constantly flared in the depths of his honey-kissed eyes.

All things considered, I should probably be terrified of being out in the middle of nowhere with the stranger, but he didn't set off my fight or flight intuition. Which was reckless. I knew better than to think he might actually be a good guy.

He widened my door. "Let's go," he said, his voice as rough as the rest of him.

Fear skittered down my spine. Was I really just going to allow myself to get put into cuffs? There had to be a way to talk myself out of this. It wasn't like driving onto someone's property was that big a deal.

And this guy? He seemed more concerned about my well-being than any code I had broken.

I hated to take advantage of it, but the man *was* trying to arrest me.

I sent him the most dazzling smile I could muster while I stoically ignored the way my stomach twisted in a knot of dread. "Is that really necessary, Officer?"

Awareness swam in those eyes that were the warmest brown that I'd ever seen, like he could see straight through to my intentions.

"I think it is." His lips hitched up farther at the side in some kind of smirk I didn't know how to read.

I got lost staring, trying to decipher it.

It took it stretching into a full, arrogant smile for me to realize he knew exactly what I was trying to do.

I wanted to smack myself across my own stupid face for being so blatant.

"Get your purse and keys and leave the rest of your things."

Panic welled. "But my car—"

"Will be just fine. I'll have someone bring it in."

"Can't I just—"

"No."

I had the urge to scream. To scream in frustration because this guy wasn't giving me an inch. I had important things in the trunk. Things I couldn't stomach the idea of losing. The journal that had brought me here. It had to mean something. Had to mean I was on the right track.

I pasted on that bedazzling smile again. I'd had to use it so many times over the years to get my way. To make it. To survive. "At least let me follow you with my car. I promise to stay within the speed limit."

"Come on, Little Trespasser. Get out of the car. You don't want to make this harder than it has to be."

I scowled at him because the brute wasn't budging. "You act like I committed murder," I mumbled under my breath.

I shuffled out from under the comforter and slipped out to stand. Irritation blistered through me. I couldn't believe I'd actually fallen asleep when I was supposed to be on watch, scoping out the area to see if there was any activity around that pond.

Any hint or indication.

What the hell was the point of a stakeout if I slept through it?

But I wasn't exactly a professional.

I was just…desperate.

Hot Cop curled his hand around my upper arm. I jolted at the contact. At the warmth that streaked beneath the surface of my skin.

"Maybe I need to make sure you didn't. You *were* wielding a knife." The man had the audacity to chuckle.

"That was for protection."

Something passed through his enormous body. A ripple of unease shifting his demeanor as if he'd been blown through by a ghost.

"You shouldn't have been out here alone," he grated.

"I can take care of myself."

"And what if I was a bad guy?" The words flowed low like a threat. He was standing so close to me I couldn't think straight. "Someone who was out here with the intention of hurting you? What would you have done then?"

"I'm not your problem to worry about." I couldn't help but spit it. As if anyone really cared? I'd learned a long time ago that the only person I could rely on was myself. The one exception was Jessica, and right now she was relying on me.

Turning my back to him, I leaned into my car so I could reach my purse from the passenger seat. When I turned back around, he'd somehow moved even closer. Boxing me in.

A shiver rolled down my spine.

"If you're here? In my town?" His voice was close to a growl. "Then you are my problem."

He finally released me from the trap of his presence by taking a step back. He pushed his fingers through the wavy, longer pieces of his hair, suddenly irritated. "Shut the door and lock it."

I did as he said, unable to resist the weight of the command he'd given. I pushed the button on the fob, and the horn blipped and the lights flashed.

"Let's go," he grunted.

He started back toward the glare of headlights just up the path.

In confusion, I clambered along the rutted ground behind him. "Aren't you going to put me in cuffs? Pat me down? Read me my rights?"

I had rights, didn't I?

A phone call?

I almost laughed. Who the hell was I going to call?

"Do you want me to?" He tossed it out from over his shoulder as he trampled up the path.

"No."

"I think we have an understanding then."

The scoff of a laugh left me.

No, we most definitely didn't have an understanding.

He opened the rear passenger door. "In you go."

I obeyed because I *really* didn't want him to put me in cuffs, even though he basically locked me in a cell with all the bars and plastic that were happening in the backseat.

He shut the door then climbed into the front. He put it into reverse, and the tires of the SUV spun and the engine revved as he backed into the high grasses before he shifted and headed back down what I'd been so sure was an invisible path.

He didn't say anything as he drove us back down the bumpy trail. We finally hit a regular dirt road that went on for about a mile before we turned onto one that was two-lane and paved. From there, it took us about ten minutes to get into Time River.

A speck of nowhere in Colorado.

Except it was the one place where I'd had to come.

There didn't seem to be a single car on any of the streets in the small town, the windowfronts of the shops and businesses darkened in the deep, slumbering night. We wound down Manchester, the main street that cut through and seemed to tie the entire community together.

The Sheriff slowed and made a left at one of the few stoplights, and a moment later we were pulling in front of a low-roofed brick building. Dingy lights covered the parking lot in a dull glow.

He parked in a reserved spot that said SHERIFF—one with a capital "S".

Awesome.

Hot Cop was *the* Sheriff.

He killed the engine, and a second later, he opened my door and extended his hand to help me out.

I took it, my hand dominated in his massive grip, and I basically had to hop out of the elevated backseat and hold onto him for support. I landed on my feet, so close to him that I was inundated in a swath of his scent.

Pine and citrus and laundry detergent. So distinctly man that I inhaled on instinct. Letting him glide into my senses for the barest flash of a moment. And I wondered if I'd forced myself to go it alone for so long that my body was staging a revolt. Because on all things holy, I didn't have reactions like this.

"Let's get you inside." He said it like he might be doing me a favor.

"Is camping out on someone's property even a crime?" I grumbled as he began to guide me across the lot.

"I think you already know the answer to that," he said, so cool and casual with his whiskey-scuffed voice.

The hand he guided me toward the front door with wasn't quite touching the small of my back, but that didn't mean I couldn't feel the heat of it as he ushered me forward, his giant body lumbering along, all those hulking muscles flexing and bowing with each step.

He leaned around me to open the swinging-glass door, and I held my breath since I'd learned my lesson the last time he'd gotten too close.

Stay as far away from the hypnotizing effects of Hot Cop as possible.

I squinted as we stepped into the blinding lights of the Sheriff's office, doing a cursory scan of the place. The lobby was furnished with a few plastic chairs and an artificial fern that sat next to a water cooler on the far-right wall. Ahead of us was a counter, and the chair behind it was vacant. The walls and floors were stark white and bare.

Super homey.

He guided me toward a door to the left of the counter. "This way."

He punched in a code, and the door buzzed and popped open. It led into a big open room that had six desks. Only one was occupied, one at the far side where a woman who was probably in her early forties sat with a headset in front of a computer.

She swiveled around when she heard us come in with a welcoming smile stretched across her face. "Well, this must be our trespasser."

"Yup," he said.

"She looks dangerous." The woman was all grins.

Hot Cop chuckled. So low that I felt it vibrate across my flesh. "Knife wielder and all, this one."

Did they think this was a joke?

But then I guessed not because he was punching in another code and a larger door was popping open. One that led into a short hallway with two holding cells on each side.

All of them were empty, but not for long because he opened the first one, the metal bars sliding open.

Sweat suddenly slicked my skin.

"In you go."

Shivers raced, and nausea rolled in my stomach. "I thought you were just bringing me in to ask me some questions?"

"Oh, we're going to have some of those. Now have a seat."

My fight or flight finally kicked in, and I had to ignore the sudden vision of pummeling the guy in the stomach so I could race out the door while he was doubled over.

Bad idea, Savannah.

Hitting that slab of rock-hard abs would likely only break a wrist.

I shuffled to the bench that hung low on the wall. I'd watched enough movies and shows to know it was often used for a bed, and I cringed at the thought of being stuck in here for too long. Warily, I sat down, shoving my hands under my thighs to keep them from trembling while the giant of a man stood in the doorway just staring at me.

God, did he have to be so stupid hot?

It was distracting.

Disorienting.

I just needed to cooperate. Answer his dumb questions and get out of here. Pay a fine or whatever was required. Because I had far more important things to do than being behind bars.

He ambled forward, shoulders so wide he nearly took up the entire cell.

Eyes that dripped with honey washed over me, his aura so thick I thought I could taste it. Potent and powerful and somehow comforting.

Do not let this guy fool you, Savannah.

He angled his head, and his words scraped through the tense air. "I'm going to need to see your ID."

ID.

Right.

I fumbled into my purse for my wallet and dug out my license.

He looked at it for a long minute before that gaze was back on my face. "It's nice to meet you, Savannah Ward. I'm Ezra. Ezra Patterson."

Then he stood and walked out, leaving me sitting in an open cell, having no idea what the hell to make of him.

Chapter Three

Ezra

I RAN HER ID THROUGH THE SYSTEM.

Savannah Iliana Ward from Houston, Texas.

Twenty-five years old.

Blue eyes.

Yeah, already noted.

I tried to skim over height and weight since that seemed like a blatant invasion of privacy, but I'd noted all on my own that she was so tiny she could probably fit in the palm of my hand.

The only thing that mattered was she had no warrants or record.

She was clear.

Relief churned through my guts, thankful I didn't have a reason to hold her or lock her up.

A tiny bolt of guilt zapped me considering I could have run her information out in the field. It didn't last long. If I had and sent her on her way, she would have disappeared. Gone in the fiery blaze of her personality.

The thing was, I'd learned to trust my gut, and I was sure I wasn't mistaken that she was in some sort of trouble, and that gnawing wouldn't allow me to cut her loose to face whatever it was on her own.

If she was sleeping in her car, she was doing it for a reason.

Out of necessity or fear. Out of hiding or surviving.

Didn't know which, but I knew it was something.

The woman was cut in this sassy ferocity that promised she was a fighter.

A survivor.

And maybe…maybe she needed a hand. A break. A bit of help to see her through her struggle to wherever she was going.

I wasn't so sure that she was going to be all that keen on sharing that information, though, and I had a hunch she would be resistant to accepting a hand.

A little hellcat ready to claw her own way out of whatever situation she was in.

My heart panged in a beat of determination.

I wanted to show her we didn't have to always do everything on our own. Show her there were people we could rely on and not everyone was out to take.

Maybe I only wanted to prove it to myself. Make amends for the times I'd fallen short. Maybe I was looking for a way to bury the guilt. Cover the bad with some form of good.

I didn't know. The only thing I was sure of was I wanted to be there for her in some way.

With a sigh, I pushed from my desk, grabbed Savannah's driver's license, and headed from my office and back into the main room where Pamela was brewing a fresh pot of coffee.

"I thought we might need a little bit of this to get us through the night," she said.

Pamela used to be a deputy until she'd gotten hurt in the line of duty seven years back. She'd been in a high-speed chase against some bastard who'd held up the 24-hour gas station on the far side of town. She'd crashed and had sustained a severe crush injury to her right upper leg. They'd said she would likely not walk again, but she'd refused that fate and had fought with everything she had through the surgeries and rehab. She was left with a profound limp on that side, but she was standing.

Another survivor who'd refused to give up.

"I think that might be in order."

She lifted her chin to the ID in my hand. "Did anything come back?"

"Not a lick."

Relieved satisfaction brimmed in her expression. "Good. She seems sweet."

Incredulity huffed from my nose. "Sweet, huh? I thought she might claw my eyes out when I first walked up on her. Nearly scared the pants off her."

"You wouldn't have minded that a bit, now, would have you?" Her brown eyes gleamed.

Images flash-fired through my mind before I had the chance to stop them. What that would be like. Seeing her that way. Her body bare, her lips parted, those eyes on me as I touched her.

I clenched my teeth with the dishonor of even thinking it, and on instinct, I fisted my hand with the black band that I still wore around my finger. Unable to remove it. I kept it on as a reminder of how I'd failed.

I swallowed around the rock in my throat and forced myself to give Pamela an unfazed scowl. "You're going to get yourself into trouble one of these days with those suggestions. How's it my young deputies know what subjects are off limits, yet you go tossing them around like appropriate work conversation?"

She poured herself a mug of coffee, continuing like she hadn't even heard the warning, "Don't act like you didn't notice she's a pretty little thing."

Another stab of guilt, knowing I deserved no pleasure after what I had done.

But it didn't stop the lust that tied my stomach in a knot when I thought of the little trespasser currently sitting in the cell.

"The only thing I noticed is she might need a leg up," I corrected because it was the one thing that mattered.

"She might need that, too. Plus, this and a good night's sleep." Pamela drew attention to the mug of hot tea she'd made for her.

Pamela might have a whole lot to say about everything, but her heart was gold.

"I'm sure she'll appreciate that," I told her as I took the mug and went to punch in the code to the holding block. It gave, and I ambled up to the open cell and leaned my shoulder against the doorway as I stared at the woman who was gnawing at the edge of her nail.

Nerves rattling around her.

Anxious and antsy.

Dark-blonde hair threaded with browns a mess and those aqua eyes so wide.

I blinked before I fell into the stupor of it, and I tossed her a casual smile. "Good news, Ms. Ward. You have a clean bill of health."

Those eyes narrowed. "I wasn't aware this was a medical examination."

"Oh, but it is. It's all about keeping your nose clean."

She snorted then tipped up her chin, so goddamn pretty it was difficult to keep my breath from hitching. "So, am I free to go or do I need to pay a fine or something? I really was just camping, but I fully learned my lesson. I promise I'll be a good girl."

She raised her right hand in a Scout's honor.

Good girl, my ass.

I got the sense she was playing dirty.

Knowing exactly how to wrap a man around her finger.

Dangerous.

Or maybe I was just the fucking fool who kept taking every word from her mouth as seduction. All the wires running between my body and brain getting crossed.

What I needed to remember was she had been out in that field for a reason, and the whole purpose I'd brought her down here was to offer some help.

"But I'm guessing you weren't camping because of your love of the great outdoors, but because you didn't have anywhere else to stay."

I approached her when she started chewing at the edge of her nail again, her knee bouncing, like the confession might be on the tip of her tongue but she felt compelled to hold it back. The bench creaked with my weight when I sat beside her, and I pushed the mug into her line of vision. "Here."

Speculation narrowed her gaze as she accepted it. "You aren't trying to drug me now, are you, Officer Patterson?"

Her brow quirked with the tease, and I scrubbed a palm over my face as I chuckled. "That would be a negative."

"Are you sure?"

"Positive."

I saw her fighting a grin as she took a sip. A small groan of pleasure rumbled through her. "Thank you," she whispered.

"You can thank Pamela. She's more thoughtful than me."

We sat in a strangely comfortable silence as she sipped at her tea before I finally broached a subject that made my insides quake in that same protectiveness I'd felt earlier, though I tried to keep the rage from sounding in the words that scraped from my throat.

"Are you in danger? Running from someone?" The question seemed to clang against the stark-white brick walls.

She laughed a surprised sound and shook her head. "No."

"Then what were you doing out in that field?"

What are you doing in Time River?

She hesitated, warred, and her attention remained on her lap when she finally mumbled, "I was just trying to save a few bucks until I find a job here. I was driving through on vacation…and I…loved it so much that I decided to stay."

There was something about the way she said it, the way she stumbled and started before she rushed the explanation at the end that told me there was more to her story than she was letting on.

But still, that suffocating fury loosened inside.

"How long do you plan on being around here?" I asked.

"I don't know." Sitting back, she leaned against the white bricks, her words turning into a wistful murmur. "Until I find what I'm looking for."

"I guess we all are looking for something, aren't we?"

"Yeah," she whispered.

Silence covered us for a few beats before the offer was getting free. "I might know of a place that's hiring."

Confusion twisted through her features before she seemed to remember what we'd been talking about. "Oh. Really? That's not necessary."

"You just said you needed a job."

Her lips pressed into a thin line. "I don't want to be a burden."

"Not a burden. I'll call in the morning and make sure they're still hiring. In the meantime, let's find you a place to sleep."

A frown knitted her brow. "What do you mean?"

"You didn't think I was going to cut you loose in the middle of the night when you already didn't have a place to stay, did you?"

I couldn't tell if it was relief or distrust that carved through her expression. The way those eyes slipped over me like she was trying to discern my true intention.

The energy she compelled tugged, pulling at a place I couldn't let it. I pushed to standing to escape it, and I roughed a hand through my hair to chase away the agitation. I strode back for the door. "Come on."

She hesitated for only a second before she scrambled to her feet, and she followed me out into the main office where Pamela was watching me with all that knowing speculation that she loved to watch me with, and I led Savannah into my personal office.

I gestured to the worn beige couch on the left wall. "It's not much to look at, but it's comfortable."

I went to the cabinet on the opposite wall to pull out a pillow and blanket.

"Wait, you want me to sleep here?"

"Yup."

"In your office?"

"That's right."

"After you took my knife from me? How am I supposed to protect myself?"

I turned around, taking in the woman who stood across the room glaring at me in disbelief and distrust. She was probably too thin beneath the bulky sweatshirt she wore, but there was no missing the strength she radiated.

A fighter.

A survivor.

"And who exactly do you think you're protecting yourself from?" I asked.

Eyes widening, she waved a hand my direction. "Oh, I don't know...maybe you."

I took two steps her direction.

Drawn.

Persuaded.

Unable to stop myself from taking another then another until I was right in front of her.

The air shifted. A sensation pulsing in the space that separated us. A buzz that slipped over the surface of my skin.

"Are you scared of me, Savannah?" It came out too rough. A warning. Maybe it was just a warning for myself.

She stared up at me, the sharp angles of her defined face exposed in the light, her pretty pink lips parted.

"No."

It was a breath.

A whisper.

And I was too fucking close to her, towering over her slight, tiny frame.

I forced myself to take a step back and cleared my throat. "Good. The only person around here you need to worry about is Pamela since she might find it fit to come in here and gab your ear off, but I can't be held responsible for that." I tried to force it into a lightness I wasn't feeling. "I need to get back out on patrol. You'll be safe here. I'll see to it that your car is waiting for you in the morning, and we can talk about that job."

I tossed the blanket and pillow to the couch, and I headed for the door before I said or did anything more idiotic than I already had.

I mean, fuck, I'd brought her down here, and not exactly under her own free will. I was responsible for her, and I was letting whatever this feeling was cloud my judgement. It wasn't like me to let someone get under my skin like this.

But there I was—itching.

Itching to touch.

Itching to explore.

My reaction to her verging on inappropriate.

I turned the doorknob, knowing I had to get the hell out of there. Only her throaty voice hit me from behind and stopped me in my tracks. "Why are you being so nice to me?"

Reluctantly, I looked back at her, my throat thick. "Everyone needs a little extra help once in a while, Savannah."

She blinked like she wasn't sure she could accept it. "Thank you," she finally said.

I gave her a tight nod, the words gruff, "Get some rest."

Then I walked out the door, flicking off the light as I went.

Chapter Four

Savannah

"**S**AVANNAH. WAKE UP."

I struggled to blink my eyes open at the low, grumbly voice that prodded me from sleep. Confusion rolled through me as I tried to discern where I was at. It only took my sight landing on the rugged face peering down at me to send the events of last night careening back through my brain.

Hot Cop finding me out in the field.

My quasi-arrest.

Sleeping on this couch that should have been the most uncomfortable thing on the planet but instead had felt like I'd splurged and rented myself a room at The Four Seasons.

Waking up to this…

Ezra Patterson leaning in close, brown eyes washing over me in a vat of warmth and concern that appeared way too genuine for my own good.

Because on all things holy, he looked so good in the morning. Lit up in the bare rays of sunlight that slanted in through the slats that covered the window. His scruff coming in thicker than it'd been since the last time I'd seen him.

How was it possible his face was even more handsome than I'd thought last night?

It took me until then to realize I'd been staring up at him like I was coming out of a dream, and I shot upright to break myself out of whatever trance the man had me under.

It sent him reeling back where he was sitting on the coffee table, and he rubbed a gigantic palm over his face like he needed waking, too.

Maybe we both were suffering the same affliction.

"What time is it?" My voice sounded groggy, eyes squinting as I tried to adjust to the dimness that filled the room.

"Early."

Groaning, I stretched my arms overhead and yawned. "I don't do early."

"Well, you do now if you want this job. I have you an interview at eight."

A disorder billowed through me.

Right.

He thought I was broke. Sleeping in my car because it was my only option. Honestly, I was surprised he'd bought the lie.

But the truth was, I wasn't exactly loaded. My whole life had been spent trying to keep afloat. Caring for my sister and myself the best that I could, but it'd always been an uphill battle.

And when I'd finally risen above my circumstances, believed in myself enough to chase a dream, that had been snatched away from me, too.

I had a small savings that I'd stashed away for a rainy day, but it wasn't going to last forever. And if I was going to stick around here for any amount of time…?

"How long do I have?" I asked.

"An hour."

My eyes popped open. "Wait, what? I'm supposed to be ready in an hour, and I don't even have a place *to* get ready."

I'd checked out of the motel where I had been staying yesterday morning since I'd decided a hunt was in order, desperate to find a thread, a hint, an innuendo…anything.

But my clues were few, and I was terrified I was only going to continue running into dead ends.

Ezra climbed to his feet, a freaking mountain that towered over me where I sat on the couch wrapped up in a blanket that smelled far too much like him.

Pine and citrus and all things man.

"There's a shower here where you can get ready." He dug into his pocket and dangled my keys in my face. "Your car is here, as promised. You can grab your things, and I'll show you to the locker room."

He turned on his heel and started for the door, calling, "You'd better get at it, Little Trespasser. Time's ticking, and I'm guessing you might not want to go into your interview with your hair looking like that."

The nerve of this guy to look back at me with a smirk.

My hands flew to the matted mass, and I patted it down like I could cover up the bedhead.

I scowled at him. "You're kind of overbearing, do you know that?"

Okay. Sweetly overbearing. Like a big, burly, grumpy teddy bear who probably just needed a good snuggle.

But still, he hadn't even given me a single detail about the job. What I'd be doing and what I would be getting paid, not that I really cared since I was only in this town for one purpose, but he could at least fill me in on wherever he was dragging me to.

A rough chuckle scraped the air. I swore, it zinged across my skin. Damn him.

"I don't think you know the meaning of overbearing, Ms. Ward."

He strode out the door, simply expecting me to follow. Part of me wanted to pout and protest and perch myself on that couch for the rest of the day, but I at least had to give the guy a little credit.

He hadn't charged me or even given me a fine.

I mean, I could be headed to the courthouse right about now rather than for a job interview, so I scrambled to stand, shoving my feet into my shoes as I went chasing after him, hopping on one foot while I dragged one on then doing the same with the other.

He was halfway across the room filled with desks by the time I'd made it out the door. "Can't a woman even get her shoes on before you go stalking off expecting her to follow?" I grumbled.

"I've got things to do," he said, heading for the same door he'd led me through last night. He tossed it open, and I barely caught the handle in time to pull it back open. I rushed across the lobby and out the front door and into the morning light that had begun to soak the crisp October sky.

The sky was strewn in pinks and purples and blues, and the mountains that hugged the little town jutted into the horizon.

It was so gorgeous that I almost skidded to a stop to take in the beauty.

But Ezra Patterson was already down the steps and across the parking lot where my car was parked, and he reached into the driver's side and pushed the button to pop the trunk.

Fear sank like a stone into the pit of my stomach, that living, thriving thing that promised I couldn't trust anyone. I'd tried. I'd taken the risk, had gone against my better judgement, and had contacted the authorities in Houston. Pain lanced through my heart as I thought about what had happened. I couldn't take that chance again.

Racing for my car, I nabbed my bag from the trunk before Officer Patterson had the chance to get there.

That strong brow tightened, and his steps slowed in caution as he approached where I lingered behind the trunk. "Why's it that you're looking like you have something to hide?"

Forcing my best scowl, I hugged the bag closer. "Maybe I don't want you rummaging around in my private things. My *lacy*, private things."

I lifted my chin, daring him to invade my privacy.

In exasperation, he scrubbed a hand over his face like he didn't know what to do with me.

Good.

He'd get annoyed or bored and forget that he'd stumbled on me.

Only my molars suddenly ground and that ball in my stomach dropped for entirely different reasons. Reasons that were so foolish and ridiculous that I couldn't comprehend the knee-jerk reaction.

But it was the first time that I noticed that Ezra was wearing a ring around his left ring finger.

Hot Cop was married.

My teeth clamped down on my bottom lip to squelch the feeling that came a little too close to disappointment.

I didn't do relationships or flings or even one-night stands. Not anymore. Getting that close to someone was not an option.

But there was something that twisted through my insides at the thought of him being with someone else.

Jealousy, I guessed.

Which was just plain stupid.

Swallowing it down, I plastered a bright smile on my face. "Are you going to show me that locker room or leave me standing out here all day?"

I didn't have time to prepare myself before he reached out and snatched the bag from my arms. He turned on his heel and started back up the walk.

I hurried behind him. "Hey. That's mine."

He threw open the lobby door, and I followed him inside. "You already made that abundantly clear."

He strode to the office door and punched in the code. I was right behind him. "So give it back."

"Have you ever heard of a little thing called chivalry?" His words were gruff as ever.

I scoffed. "And haven't you heard that chivalry is dead? Do you think I'm not capable of carrying my own bag?"

I hated the panic that locked in my chest. The feeling that I might lose something important. That he held it in his hands and there was nothing I could do about it.

He whirled on me just as I was stepping through the door. "I think you're capable of many things, Savannah, but maybe you need to realize that just because you can do it all yourself, you don't have to."

I froze beneath the weight of him. His big body and that honey stare.

Then I bit down on my bottom lip when I realized Pamela was right across the room, trying to go incognito where she had been packing up her things to leave but suddenly found our interaction much more interesting.

Ezra fumbled back a step when he realized it, too, and he refused to look at either of us as he turned and strode for a hallway to the left of his office. I sent her a furtive glance, lifting my shoulder in an *I have no idea what that was about* gesture. I didn't want to contemplate it, either. Then I bolted along to catch up to the man whose legs were so freaking long he took the entire room in like four steps.

Apparently, he really did have places to be.

He moved down the hall before he tossed open a door to the left.

It was a typical locker room, the floors and walls tiled in the same drab beige tiles. A row of tall lockers were attached to the wall on the right with different last names carved into plates. On the opposite side were three shower stalls, and a mirror and sinks were straight ahead.

He set my bag on a bench next to a fresh towel that had been placed there.

My stomach tightened in a fist.

Had he already been in there getting it ready for me?

I knew better than to believe any person could be this kind. But God, he seemed it.

Sweetly overbearing.

Harshly considerate.

Like it was his God-given duty to care for those around him. I wondered if it was really out of kindness or if he believed it was his responsibility. Or maybe he was just a master manipulator like the rest.

"Here." He dug into his pocket and pulled out a scrap of paper. "That's my favorite restaurant in town. I talked to the owner. She's a lifelong friend and is dating my cousin. She is about the nicest thing around. She was excited to hear I had someone who might be interested in a job because she's definitely in need of some help."

I scanned the note.

Time River Market & Café
245 E. Manchester
8 a.m.
Ask for Dakota

Below it was a second address with 6:00 p.m. written next to it.

"What's this?" I asked, pointing at the extra line.

He hesitated for a beat before he said, "A safe place for you to stay." Then he quirked a brow. "You know, because I don't want to have to haul you in for trespassing again."

"Ha ha." I rolled my eyes and tried to ignore the way my chest squeezed tight.

He's married. He's married. He's married.

Silently chanting the reminder seemed prudent.

My self-preservation whispered that it shouldn't matter if he wasn't. It wouldn't have changed anything.

He already had the door open and was heading out when I managed to call, "Why are you doing this for me?"

Uncertainty flashed through his rough features. "Like I said before, everyone needs some help every once in a while, Savannah."

"And do you give it to everyone who stumbles into your path?"

Those eyes both flared and softened. "Only to the ones who deserve it."

Chapter Five

Savannah

I T WAS 7:45 WHEN I PULLED INTO THE PARKING LOT OF TIME River Market & Café. Refreshed from the shower and wearing a cute sundress that I'd paired with a thin cardigan since the mornings and evenings were cool.

My hands tightened on the steering wheel as I scanned the lot. Searching. Sifting through the faces of the few people who were either leaving or entering the restaurant. Wondering if they knew anything. If they'd seen her. If she was near.

If I was only being paranoid, jumping to conclusions that were foolish to be made. If my gut that promised that she was in trouble and needed help was correct or if she was actually fine.

It was funny that both scenarios would shatter the last piece of my battered heart.

Because I'd been unable to accept the last thing that she'd said to me—when she'd told me that she didn't need me anymore.

Inhaling a steadying breath, I climbed from my car and headed to the entrance of the cute restaurant that sat on the main drag of Time River.

A bell dinged overhead, and my mouth watered as I was inundated with the most delectable scents.

Freshly baked pastries, coffee and cream, bacon and syrup.

The front portion of the restaurant was a country store. Displays full of jewelry and handmade soaps and every other bauble and trinket you could imagine were set up throughout the room, but it was the forty or so people milling around waiting on a table that made me sure that Ezra hadn't been exaggerating the owner's need for help just for my sake.

Hope swelled. This was exactly the type of place I needed to be. Where I could watch and listen.

I glanced behind me, half expecting to see Jessica walk through the door.

"Hi, can I help you?" a voice called, jarring me from the dream. I turned to find a woman calling to me from behind a high counter with two registers that sat on the left.

Clearing the emotion from my throat, I gave her a small wave. "Hi. My name's Savannah, and I have an interview at eight. I'm supposed to ask for Dakota."

The woman's face lit, her smile stretching wide as she came around the counter. "Ah, you must be our new favorite person. I heard that Ezra was sending someone over, and let me tell you, we were happy to hear it. We've been absolutely slammed since two of our servers left for college a couple weeks ago. I'm Beth, the general manager, and one of Dakota's besties." She stretched out her hand. "It's great to meet you."

"It's nice to meet you, too," I said as I returned her handshake.

She started in the direction of the double doors that sat propped open and led into the dining area, gesturing for me to follow. "You are going to love working here. It's crazy busy, but the people are crazy awesome."

She tossed me a grin from over her shoulder. "Including myself."

A giggle rolled up my throat at her easy confidence.

She was tall and willowy, her skin just a shade lighter than her black hair that she wore in a floral fabric headband that tied at the base of her head and flowed down her back.

"Well, I do have to say that I approve of awesome," I told her as casually as I could, fighting the wobbling emotion in my voice.

I didn't get a whole lot of it. But maybe…maybe this would be the place where I'd find it. Where my luck would finally turn, and I'd find the one person in this world who meant anything to me.

"It's a good thing. There's plenty of it around here." She waved a hand at the packed dining room that buzzed with activity.

Servers rushed around. Dishes clattered and voices droned, filling the place with both a casual and hectic vibe.

The scent was almost overwhelming, and my stomach twisted with how delicious everything smelled. I hadn't taken the time to eat last night before I'd gone searching, trying to follow the clues that were so few that I hadn't really known where to start.

The café had a rustic, chic vibe. Trendy but cozy at the same time. The booths that lined the three walls to the left were gray wood with cream and light-blue checked cushions. There were a bunch of long tables done community-style that took up the open section in the middle.

All the tables and booths were decorated with sprays of baby's breath that sat in small buckets.

To the right was a long counter. At the far side of it was a coffee bar and a glass display for the bakery that was stocked with every kind of deliciousness. High stools took up the other half, each currently occupied by a trio of old men sipping from mugs of coffee and clearly embroiled in tales from the past.

There wasn't an empty seat in the restaurant.

"I see this is the place," I said.

"Once you taste the food, you'll see why."

"I don't doubt that."

"All your meals are included, which is pretty much the whipped cream *and* the cherry on top of a pretty incredible job. I mean, I'm not biased or anything."

Beth led me through a swinging door behind the counter and into the chaos that was the kitchen on the other side. Several servers were darting around, carrying orders and filling drinks, and cooks called instructions through the long window lined with heat lamps where they set orders to be picked up.

A woman with a brown ponytail leaned toward the window and hollered, "Thanks for that, Will."

"Anything for you, Dakota."

Beth shook her head with a grin as she approached her. "You have all those boys wrapped around your cute little finger, don't you?" she teased.

The woman at the counter straightened. "I'm pretty sure it's the other way around. I don't know what I would do without them," she said. Then her mouth split into a full smile when she noticed me trailing behind Beth. "Tell me you're Savannah and you're here to save my life."

Easiness glided from her, this comfort and welcome that I wasn't quite sure what to do with.

I went for light. If I was going to work here, then I needed to fit in. Not come across like I was here for any other reason than needing to make some extra cash. "Well, I might not be able to pull you fully from the deep end, but I think I might be able to help get you closer to the top."

"A breath is all I'm asking for. I'm Dakota." She didn't stretch out her hand for me to shake. Nope. She hugged me, instead. I couldn't stop the surprised laugh that choked out as she rocked me back and forth. "It's really great to meet you, Savannah."

She stepped back, holding onto the outside of my shoulders as she gave me a once-over. It didn't feel judgy, but like her only intent was to get to know me.

"Welcome to Time River," she continued. "The best little town in the entire country, in my humble opinion. Ezra told me you had come through visiting and loved it so much that you decided to stick around a bit and might be interested in helping out here."

She was gorgeous.

Dark, dark brown eyes.

Cheeks full and pink.

Tall and curvy.

I'd put her at maybe twenty-six or twenty-seven, a year or two older than me.

"I used to work at a breakfast place, so I should be able to catch on quickly," I told her.

"Well thank God for that. Grab yourself a tray and get busy," Beth tossed out, so casual.

Dakota swatted at her. "We need to at least let the poor girl decide if she wants to work here or not. An application might be in order, too. Let's go back to my office so we can get that taken care of."

She waved at me to follow.

"I'm going to head back out front," Beth said as she moved toward the swinging door. "I'm sure customers are piling up. Shout if you need anything. It was really great to meet you, Savannah."

Dakota laughed under her breath before she returned her attention to me. "We can be a lot to handle around here, but I don't think I'm biased when I say I think you'll like it. Plus, the tips are great, and you get an hourly wage on top of it."

"That sounds fantastic."

"We're family around here." Her voice lowered with emphasis. Like what she was saying actually meant something and she wanted me to know it.

My throat thickened, and I followed her into her office. The emotion I'd been trying to keep down crested, confusion and comfort, and the words came out a little softer than I wanted them to. "This is all very kind of you."

She glanced back at me. "If Ezra vouches for you? Then I know you're a good one."

I bit my tongue, refusing to tell her that he didn't even know me. That he'd all but arrested me last night. Our first interaction close to criminal.

"He seems like a nice guy," I mumbled. It came out sounding like I was trying to suppress some kind of truth.

Dakota paused, gaze taking me in from over her shoulder as some kind of sadness quieted her tongue. "He's the best, Savannah. Through and through." Then her mouth tweaked up at the side. "Grumpy as all get out, but the best."

My stomach tightened, and I was too much of a coward to ask her what that meant. Instead, I grumbled, "Tell me about it."

Giggling, she rounded a cluttered desk that faced out, and she grabbed a tablet and punched a few things into it before she handed it to me. "Here. Fill this out. The job is yours if you'd like it. We'd love to have you here."

I scanned the questions, and I nervously raked my teeth on my bottom lip when I saw one of the first questions was asking for my address.

"Um…I only decided I was staying yesterday."

Dakota laughed again, like she truly didn't have any reservations about hiring me. "Don't worry about it. Leave that spot blank, and once you find a place of your own, we'll get you updated."

So, I filled out the information that I could, and twenty minutes later, I was picking up a tray like Beth had joked.

And just like that, I worked at Time River Market & Café.

I fought the wave of satisfaction I found in it, and I reminded myself not to be a fool and get comfortable.

This was temporary.

I was here for one reason and one reason only. I was going to find my sister…then we were going to get the hell out of here.

And we were never looking back.

Chapter Six

Ezra

"**D**ADDY, DADDY, DADDY!"
I'd not even fully stepped out of my truck before I was hit with a barrage of little voices calling me by my favorite name. The three of them ran my direction where I'd pulled up to the curb to pick them up from their after-school program.

My mother had stayed with them last night, then had dropped them off this morning since I'd been on duty. The woman was a saint, the way she'd stepped up to help me in my greatest time of need. I had no idea what I would do without her.

Relief flooded me as the kids approached.

I knew they were safe with my mother when I had to be away, but it still was a bitch letting them out of my sight. Giving them space when it felt like instinct to wrap them in my arms, guard them from the evils and atrocities, and ensure nothing bad could ever touch them.

It was bad enough, being a cop and seeing all the horrible shit that went down. And after what had happened to Brianna? It was a million times worse.

The fear.

The feeling like I needed to watch over them every second.

Protect them the way I should have protected their mother.

But I knew I couldn't keep the reins cinched that tight. The only thing that would do was suffocate them.

Stifle their growth.

Make them even more fearful than they already were.

They needed to spread their wings, and they needed their dad there to support them as they prepared to fly.

Owen and Oliver broke out ahead of Olivia. There were the most enormous smiles on my four-year-old twins' faces. Their white-blond hair bounced in sync with their backpacks as they ran. So fucking cute it clutched my heart in an agonizing fist.

Both held coloring pages over their heads. "Look it, Daddy, look it!"

I knelt at the same time as they made it to me.

"What do you have?" I made sure to keep a boatload of enthusiasm in my voice.

"Today we learned all about the biggest insects in the whole world, and we had to draw our favorite one, and mine is the Titan Beetle!" Awe filled Oliver's brown eyes. "It is at least six whole inches long. Can you even believe it?"

"No way."

His brow lifted so high it was comical. "Yes, way."

"Holy cow, now that is big. I don't think I'd want to come up on one of those in our backyard."

"Don't even worry, Dad, they only live in the rain forests, so there is no way they're gonna be comin' around here."

"Whew." I dragged my fingers over my forehead like I was wiping up sweat.

Oliver giggled.

I turned my attention to Owen. "And what did you draw, buddy?"

"Phryganistria chinensis…" He sounded it out with his little slur, his *r*'s coming out like *w*'s the way they always did.

"Phryganistria chinensis?" Hell, I probably pronounced it wrong, too.

"A stick *bwug*," he clarified, holding up his drawing that was one long line with four smaller ones coming off it. "It's two feet *wong*, and it *wooks wike* a stick. You can't even see it one bit because it gets all hidden in the *twees*."

Owen's demeanor came across as shier than his big brother's. Oliver was three whole minutes older than him, and they looked nearly identical, except Owen's brown eyes were a tad bit lighter than Oliver's—closer to the color of mine.

"Now that is long. That thing must nearly be as tall as you," I teased, tipping up his chin and making him giggle.

"Even *tawer*, Daddy," he said, so sweet.

My chest squeezed.

"I think he might be exaggerating," Olivia cut in.

Chuckling under my breath, I glanced up at their big sister who hovered behind them. "You think so, huh?"

"Don't you know that all kids do it, Dad?"

My chuckle grew, and I stretched out a hand for her to come closer. "How was school today, Livvie-Loo?"

Her adorable face split into a grin. "It was the best! I got an A+ on my spelling test, and that means I get to go to the library in two weeks to compete against all the grades in the spelling bee, so you have to help me study all night long because you know there are going to be really hard words."

"Like phryganistria chinensis?"

She rolled her eyes, and her blonde hair that was braided into two long pieces swished along her shoulders. "Dad, you are such a dork."

"A dork? Who, me?"

I'd be anything she wanted me to be if it conjured the kind of smile she was watching me with right then. She'd had it the roughest, but she was coming through. Lighting up the room the way she used to before joy had been stripped out from under her.

"Yes, you." She widened her eyes like she was horrified to be standing by me—like she was going on thirteen instead of seven—even though her lips were twitching all over the place.

"Well, let's get you home so we can get some dinner and start that extra studying." Pushing to stand, I opened the back door and the three of them clambered inside. I buckled the boys into their car seats and ensured Olivia was strapped into her booster.

Poor girl was smooshed in the middle, but I couldn't bring myself to purchase a minivan or some shit like that. But I figured the truck gave us the opportunity to hit the wilderness on the weekends, something we'd been doing a ton.

Taking some uncharted dirt road out to the mountains.

Exploring places we'd never been.

There was something about being outdoors here in Time River that was healing.

The fresh air.

The brisk rush of the raging river.

The open space that murmured of possibility.

The whole ride home, the cab was nothing but the chaos of their voices, each of them trying to talk over the other as they told me every minute detail of their day.

I kept glancing at them through the rearview, my spirit full, fucking loving it that they wanted to share everything with me.

It only took five minutes to be pulling up in the driveway of the modest house I'd spent the last year renovating. I'd needed something to do with my hands since sitting idle was the most dangerous thing I could do, doing my best to rein in the fury, to tamp the vengeance and the hate that kept threatening to spill out.

The way I hunted every goddamn day for any sign. For any evidence that had been missed. Constantly watching. Desperate to make up for every pitfall and mistake and betrayal that I'd cast.

My chest tightened as I glanced at my kids as I put the truck into park. Guilt constricted because I knew way down deep there wasn't one goddamn thing I could do to make up for the treachery.

And while I'd never call it justice, I would ferret out those monsters, and I would make them pay.

I helped the kids out, tossing all three backpacks over my forearm before I let them in at the front door. They scrambled inside, footsteps pounding as they headed down the hall to their rooms.

Their excitement was palpable, and the realization that this place had become their home was a balm to my battered soul.

I set their backpacks on the floor next to the door. A smile tugged at my mouth when I saw my mother was in the kitchen.

No surprise since she basically flitted between our two houses. My childhood home was just on the next street over, which was one of the reasons I'd picked this house when I'd been looking.

Unease rolled through me when I thought about how she didn't know that I'd be living here whether the tragedy had happened or not. Mom thought I'd bought this house out of grief, because I couldn't live in the same house where Brianna and I had been raising our family, no clue that life had already fallen apart. That we'd suffered a collapse and there'd been no chance of rebuilding.

She'd loved Brianna so fucking much, like she was her own daughter, that I'd never had the heart to tell her the truth, but that didn't mean that truth didn't weigh on me like ten-thousand pounds of rubble.

Mom was bent in two at the oven and removing a casserole dish. The scent of red sauce and garlic filled the air.

"What do you think you're doing, Mom?"

She sent me a smile as she set the hot dish on a pad. "Well, I am bored out of my mind now that the kids are back in school, so I figured I'd be of use and make my favorite people in the world something to eat."

Gratitude expanded my chest. "You didn't have to do that. You already do too much."

She shrugged like she hadn't basically saved my life over the last year and a half. "I wanted to. Besides, you were up all night and then had to go back in this afternoon. I don't want you running yourself ragged."

I'd come home after dropping off Savannah's car and slept for a few hours, but I'd gotten a call that there'd been a break-in at the library overnight, likely some kids out destroying property for the fun of it, but I'd still wanted to take a look for myself.

"I don't mind it so much, and you know I'm plenty capable of making dinner," I told her.

"Are you trying to tell me you don't like my cooking? Eating at Dakota's café for half your meals has spoiled you. Like any of us could compare with what comes out of her oven." Mom tsked the tease.

A chuckle rolled out as I ambled into the kitchen. I'd remodeled this place from top to bottom, and if I was telling the truth, I'd admit I was proud of it, and the kitchen was no exception. The cupboards were a sea blue and the countertops a white, cracked granite.

It felt both upscale yet easy to live in, and with three kids, that was what was important to me.

I moved to my mom and pecked a kiss to the crown of her graying head, which wasn't hard to do considering she was about a foot shorter than me. "Not gonna lie, she's pretty good, but no match to you."

Mom patted my cheek. "Charmer."

"Mean every word of it."

She stirred the vegetables that simmered in a saucepan, her grin wry. "Like I said...charmer. You always knew how to get your way when it came to your mom."

Leaning back against the counter, I crossed my arms over my chest. "Hey, I was a good kid."

Disbelief filled her chuckle. "You, Ryder, and Cody were nothing but a handful. That's all I've got to say about that."

Growing up with my cousin, Ryder, and his best friend, Cody, had been a blast. We were always out running amok, riding our bikes and exploring. Forever covered in dirt and up to all kinds of adolescent shenanigans, even though they were always in good fun and never meant to hurt anyone.

Ryder had run into a rough patch, though, and had lost his way for a bit, but at the root of it, he'd known where he belonged. Had known we would always be here for him, no matter what he was dealing with.

"We weren't so bad." The chuckle that came out with it sounded like I was feeding her line.

"That laugh right there should tell you everything you need to know. Now, go get washed up, dinner is about ready."

I didn't call her out on treating me like I was twelve instead of thirty-one since I was too busy glancing at the clock.

Anticipation and uncertainty rolled.

Five forty-five.

My chest tightened, and my thoughts were instantly back on the woman who I had no business letting infiltrate my mind. But she'd been there all day, slipping over me and threatening to sink in.

Savannah Ward.

I couldn't help but wonder how she'd fared at the café. Wonder what Dakota had thought about her. If she'd had reservations or if she'd hired her on the spot.

Only those thoughts had kept straying farther, deviating into territory they shouldn't. Wondering who she was. Why she was here. What that hint of darkness that had flared in her aqua eyes had been about. Why it seemed like she was always at the ready to pull out her claws and fight, all while doing it with a smart, sassy mouth.

If I'd kept those thoughts barricaded there, that would have been all good. On the up and up.

But I'd be a liar if I denied it'd gone farther.

Deeper.

Unable to stop myself from imagining what *that* mouth would feel like on me. What it would be like to touch her. Take her. Fuck her.

If she felt the churn in the air when we came near or if that shiver of lust was all on me.

In discomfort, I cleared my throat. "I actually have a favor to ask."

Mom picked up the casserole dish and placed it on the table. Her eyes that were the same color as mine sparked in curiosity. "What's that?"

"I might have someone interested in renting the guest house. I have an appointment with them at six. If you wouldn't mind staying with the kids while we meet?"

No doubt, she'd caught the wobble in my voice, the way her brows tugged inward a fraction. "Of course, I don't mind. That would be great if you found a reliable renter."

Only her voice didn't match, like she'd tapped into my uncertainty.

Because I had no idea what I was doing, or more importantly why. The only thing I knew was beyond the attraction, beyond the need that sparked at the sight of her, I couldn't stomach the idea of Savannah not having a safe place to stay.

There was something about her that twisted deep.

Drew me in.

This woman there was no way I could allow myself to have, but one I somehow couldn't let go.

Chapter Seven

Savannah

"**G**OODNIGHT, SEE YOU IN THE MORNING!" DAKOTA called it from where she was sitting at her desk typing something on her computer.

Slinging the strap of my purse over my shoulder, I slowed so I could pop my head through her doorway. "Thank you again for everything."

"Um, are you thanking me? I asked you this morning if you were here to save my life—and life saved." Lifting her hands in praise, she smiled her kind smile, the woman so adorable that I had the stupid urge to round her desk and hug the crap out of her.

An impulse that was highly dangerous since I knew better than getting close to anyone.

It was really hard hanging onto it when she was basically the nicest person I'd ever met, like Ezra had promised she would be, and if I trusted my gut at all, it would have told me that it wasn't a façade she wore. But I'd met plenty of people who'd seemed nice at the beginning before their own selfishness and greed exposed their true colors.

I just needed to be careful, guard myself, but also get close enough that it might help me in the end.

Working at a busy café was pretty much the best scenario. It would give me the opportunity to watch. To overhear. To maybe get lucky enough to pick up a trace of Jessica. Someone who had known her or met her or maybe just recognized her face. Someone who could confirm that she had been here. That she *still* was.

My stomach tumbled over with the urge to ask Dakota.

Not yet.

It would be stupid to put my trust in her so easily.

Forcing the easy smile I'd been wearing back onto my face, I did my best to keep my composure. "I think the stack of cash sitting in my pocket right now would dispute that claim."

I couldn't stop the swell of gratitude that pressed at the empty hollow of my chest. Weighty and full. She'd hired me without reservation. Given me a chance.

And maybe it made me a fool, but that counted for something.

"How about we just agree that we're both getting mad benefits from the arrangement?" she said.

"Deal." A soft chuckle slid out with it.

I went to leave when she called out again, "It is really great to have you here, Savannah. I truly hope you love it."

The problem was, I thought I might.

"And I hope you have a great night with that man of yours," I told her, changing the subject to the one I knew would distract her. I'd heard *all* about Ryder Nash. It was safe to say Dakota was crazy in love.

Giggling, she flushed. "I plan to."

Without saying anything else, I turned and headed from the kitchen and back through the store. Beth had gotten off an hour ago, and it was fairly slow at the moment during the shift change, a lull right before there apparently would be another rush for dinner.

I was out the door and climbing into my car by five-forty, my attention skating the lot like I might lift my head and catch sight of Jessica.

Ridiculous, but finding her was the only hope that I had, and if I lost that…?

I dug into my bag and pulled out the note Ezra had given me. Such a senseless, imprudent girl with the way my heart squeezed. I stared at his strong print inscribed on the paper, as if details about the man might be hidden in the script.

I had no idea where he was sending me or why he cared. I mean, it wasn't normal, right? Someone being that thoughtful? Finding me a job and a place to stay?

But maybe as the Sheriff, he really was concerned about me trespassing or loitering or just in general mucking up the peace of the gorgeous town.

That had to be it.

And if I was going to stay here, I would need an actual place of my own because the run-down motel where I had been staying wasn't going to cut it, and thanks to Hot Cop, sleeping in my car had quickly become an unviable option.

So I plugged the address into Maps and followed the directions through town.

My attention wandered as I traveled beneath the endless sky that had just begun to gray and pink.

Time River seemed a million miles away from Houston.

A different plane.

A different universe.

Quaint shops and restaurants lined each side of Manchester. People strolled, their paces slowed and smiles on their faces, as if they all might know each other, and if they didn't, they would be happy for the introduction.

An alternate reality from what I knew.

The entire time, I scanned, clinging to that hope.

I had made it to the opposite side of town when I was instructed to make a left into what appeared a family neighborhood. The houses were all one-story and well-kept, far from flashy, but cozy and comfortable. Each were surrounded by soaring trees and fronted by green, manicured lawns.

I made the next right before *You've arrived* echoed through my speakers.

Confusion knit my brow.

It wasn't more than an alley that ran behind a house enclosed by a high, white wooden fence. I'd been expecting some sort of apartment building or duplex, though I noticed a small sign staked at the side of the drive that confirmed the address.

Making the left on the dirt alleyway, I inched behind the fence that ran along the backside of the property before a tiny house facing out into the alley came into view.

A guest house, I realized, situated behind a larger house with a big yard separating them. A really freaking cute guest house that was painted white with blue trim and had a pitched roof and a miniature porch out front.

It even had a rocking chair.

So adorable and welcoming that my chest panged. It was funny that I'd always imagined a place like this. A place that whispered of home.

I used to murmur stories to Jessica at night, in the times when we'd lie there awake, shaking and afraid. I'd plant dreams in her ear that one day we would find a place to call home. A home like the ones we'd sometimes see in movies and TV.

Shutting off the engine, I cranked open the door and stepped out. The soles of my shoes crunched on the loose gravel as I moved a couple steps closer so I could take in everything. The front of the guest house was situated out toward the alley, and even though I couldn't see over the high fence that surrounded it, it seemed the small house shared its backyard with the main house, their back porches directly facing each other.

A massive tree rose behind the guest house, and its thick, twisted branches stretched wide. The leaves were lush and dense and cast a giant wedge of shade over the yard. Those branches waved in the cool breeze as birds flitted through, while the last of the sun broke through and dappled the ground in splotches of light.

"What do you think?" A gruff voice suddenly grazed over my nape, not more than a foot away.

Startled, I whirled around, and my fist flew out in a pathetic attempt at protecting myself. I'd been so wrapped up in studying the little house that I hadn't noticed that I had been sneaked up on.

My guard down.

Only my fist whacked into a chest. A chest so solid and hard that I would have cried out in pain if my breath hadn't gotten snatched from my lungs by the big hand that grabbed me by the wrist to prevent a further attack.

Warm brown eyes glinted, and amusement danced across Ezra's rugged face. "You really are dangerous, aren't you?"

Heat burned from the connection where he held me and left me on unsteady feet.

I jerked my wrist free of his hold, and I scowled at the man who stood there as casual as could be. "Me, dangerous? You scared the crap out of me."

"That seems to be awful easy to do," he drawled in that low, grumbly way. I wondered if he had any idea that it sounded so nice. If he used it on all unsuspecting women because God knew my belly was tipping at the sound.

"Maybe you just keep creeping up on me." I shook out my hand, not sure if I was trying to slough off the sting from hitting him or the burn that still encircled my wrist.

One thousand percent, I needed not to be crushing on this guy. He was married, for God's sake, and that was territory I never stepped into.

Ever.

Honestly, though, I didn't think that he was the type. He seemed too loyal. Too genuine. But I couldn't help but sense that something was there. Something simmering between us, deep and alive.

Attraction.

And that kind of attraction was bad, bad news.

"And maybe you need to be more aware of your surroundings." I couldn't tell if he was teasing or serious. Because I was sure I felt it. A flare of concern. A rumble of aggression. Like he would single-handedly take out any threat that might come my way.

It was gone before I could process it, and the burly brute stuffed his hands into his pockets and rocked back on his heels in pure nonchalance.

Only nothing about it felt nonchalant considering the action caused my gaze to drift, dragging down on its own accord, without permission.

My breaths turned shallow.

The man had changed out of his uniform and was wearing black sweats and a tight, plain-white tee. The thin fabric stretched over his muscled frame, his arms bulging and his thighs pressing against his sweats.

My stomach tightened, and I took a step back and forced myself to stop ogling him.

Safety measures and all.

The man was far too appealing for his own good.

I bet he had half the town salivating over him. Committing crimes just for the sake of him putting them in cuffs.

He must not have been immune to the tension that curled through the dense air because he cleared his throat, and he also stepped back as he roughed one of those massive hands through the longer pieces of his hair. "How was the café?"

"Good. Dakota is every bit as awesome as you said." I hoped I wasn't panting when I said it.

"Good, good," he muttered. "You think it's going to work out?"

I didn't know if anything was going to work out. How this was going to end. But I forced myself to speak. "Yeah, it's great. Thank you for setting me up with that. I know you were putting your neck out there for a stranger, so I appreciate it."

I did. Truly. It was rare that anyone had ever stepped out for me.

"Don't make me regret it." He smirked.

I rolled my eyes. God, I didn't know what to make of him. So rough and hard and unbearably sweet.

"I'll do my best." I fought my own smile.

"Come on, let's check this place out."

He didn't wait for me to answer. He strode up the single step onto the porch and headed for the front door.

I finally gathered my senses enough to scramble after him. "Don't we need to wait for the owner?"

Producing a key, he slid it into the lock, not bothering to glance back when he said, "I am the owner."

He swung open the door, and he nearly had to duck as he stepped inside.

I stumbled a step before I hurried to catch up to him, my hands already out in front of me as if I were trying to protect myself from the big bad wolf, except the only thing this guy was trying to kill me with was kindness.

And he thought *I* was dangerous.

"Oh, no, no. You've already done enough for me. I can find my own place to stay."

I rushed in behind him when he didn't slow. Then I was slamming to a stop, my jaw unhinging at the sight.

If I'd been awed by the outside, I was dumbstruck by the interior.

It'd been completely redone. Both sleek and homey, the furnishings velvet and plush. Comfortable and stylish.

There was a living area straight ahead with a wall of French doors and windows that overlooked the big backyard that separated the main house from the guest.

There was a complete kitchen with white-cracked granite and matching sea-blue cabinets, and there was a door to my right that I could see led into a bedroom.

But what held my attention was the playset and the children's toys out in the backyard.

A frown pulled to my brow, and I pointed out the wall of windows toward the larger home across the rambling lawn. "Do you...live there...with your family?"

Obviously, Savannah.

But I couldn't help asking it. Couldn't help but question everything because I was not getting Officer Patterson at all.

"Yup." He went into the kitchen and flipped on the light, seeming to ignore the reservations spiraling through me. "This isn't the biggest place in the world, but I think it's a bit better than sleeping in your car."

My jaw dropped. "A bit better? This place is ridiculous." Beautiful and perfect and absolutely the last place I could rent. My head shook as I tried to gather my senses. To understand why he would offer this. To discern his intentions.

Was he some weirdo psychopath?

A control freak?

Did he want some kind of tryst?

Or was he truly just kind?

I swallowed the disorder of questions down, realizing his reasoning didn't matter. The only thing I was certain of? I needed to end whatever this was between us.

"Thanks for the offer, Officer Patterson, but I can't afford this."

It was an easy excuse.

One he was sure to buy.

Because with the reaction he evoked in me, the last thing I needed was to have to watch him through the back windows with his family.

No thank you.

"You don't need to worry about the money."

Air huffed from my nose. Was he kidding me? "Don't need to worry about it? I am not here for you to take care of me. I already told you I'm not your responsibility, and I can take care of myself."

Intensity deepened every line in his powerful brow, and he took a step toward me. I wished he wouldn't. Because the ground shook beneath my feet, rolling up my legs like thunder. His presence dominating and profound.

"I thought we already established that I don't think that?" he growled, the burly bear coming out to play.

"Then why do you keep doing all this for me?" It was a huff and a plea, and I hadn't realized I'd kept stumbling away until my back knocked into the wall.

He was right there, his aura smacking me in the face again, making me dizzy.

Citrus and pine.

Severity filled his voice. "Because I consider myself a good judge of character. Because I can see there's something going on in your life. Because there's something about you that makes me want to be there for you."

"Don't you think your wife might have something to say about that?" It shot out with a whole ton of force.

A pure accusation.

Because I felt *this*, and I knew he did, too, and it really pissed me off that he was stepping into it.

Here he was, already showing his true colors.

I shouldn't have been foolish enough to think for a second that him helping me came from good intentions.

He reeled back like he'd been punched in the gut, stumbling away and fisting his hand with the ring on it like he'd forgotten it was there. His teeth ground so hard that I could hear the grating. There was no missing the pain that scraped through the dense air. "Since she's dead, my wife won't get to *say* anything ever again."

Torment ground through his words, and it was me who got punched in the gut that time. Regret slammed me so hard I nearly buckled in two when I realized how callous my incrimination had been.

I didn't have the chance to tell him I was sorry, that I was wrong for making assumptions before he stormed out the door, leaving a wake of anger in his path.

Anger I was certain wasn't directed at me but at himself.

He left the door gaping open, twilight seeping into the guest house and uncertainty rustling with the wind.

I didn't know how much time passed as I stood there shifting on my feet in the middle of this adorable little home. I was never surer than then that it couldn't be mine.

"Crap," I finally muttered under my breath before I slipped out the door and shut it behind me, Ezra Patterson long gone but his intensity still lingering in the air.

Exhaling, I glanced around. I felt like an enormous jerk, but I also had to remind myself that I'd had no way of knowing that his wife was dead.

That he was a widower, and he was still clearly reeling from it.

I was only standing for what was right, and I hadn't meant to hurt him.

I got into my car and drove away because I needed to get out of there, away from the feeling that had bubbled up from the depths and climbed into my chest.

It was best to end things then.

Before it got messy.

Before I *cared*.

⌒⌒

I checked into the same motel where I'd stayed my first few nights after I'd arrived in Time River before the whole trespassing debacle.

It was on the outskirts of town, an old-style two-story with exterior doors.

Basically a dump, but it didn't bother me much considering I'd spent most of my life living in those.

Freshly showered and dressed in a long-sleeved tee and sleep shorts, my wet hair twisted in a towel, I climbed onto the bed. Sitting cross-legged, I dragged my bag closer.

Hope and dread and anticipation drummed at my ribs.

I drew the zipper down then dug beneath my clothes to where I'd hidden the leather-bound journal at the bottom.

I pulled it out, and my heart slugged in a wave of grief and worry. I ran my fingertips over the imprint on the front before I opened it to the first page. My gaze traced the words that I'd read at least a thousand times, though I still had a hard time discerning what they really meant.

If I was off base.

If I was making a huge mistake, putting hope into something when there was no hope to be found.

But for Jessica, any chance was worth it.

<u>Journal Entry</u>

I know that I was overstepping, but I couldn't help it when I saw her in the store today. She was in line in front of me, and I could just...tell that something was off. Could feel it radiating off her pores like a disease.

I tried to strike up a conversation with her.

She barely smiled in return.

It was brittle.

Nervous.

Afraid.

I followed her out, took a chance, and gave her my card. She seemed almost terrified as she stuffed it into her purse, her attention darting around like she was worried someone might be watching.

She drove away without saying anything else.

I hope she calls, even if she just needs someone to talk to. My heart hurts because I doubt it will happen, but I have to believe that sometimes people are put in our path for a purpose. That there's a reason they're there. It's what this life is about, isn't it?

Helping?

Supporting?

I know it's on others to accept it or not, but I can't help this feeling in my gut. Maybe I'm wrong this time. I wish I was. But unfortunately, I rarely am.

Chapter Eight

Savannah

THE CLATTER OF DISHES AND THE DRONE OF VOICES FILLED the dining room of the café. It'd been crazy busy at breakfast, but we were finally having a lull before we would get hit with the lunch rush.

"Is it always like this?" I asked as I set my tray on the metal counter in the server's station. It might have only been my second day, but since I'd kept up with my three tables yesterday, Beth had promoted me to five tables in my station.

It meant I'd been running.

But I…liked it. I liked the people here. The vibe. The energy.

Everyone seemed genuinely kind, and it felt good to see the smiles on their faces when I set their meals in front of them. Plates piled high with eggs and bacon and toast. French toast topped with fresh fruit and a slew of different flavors of pancakes. Not to mention to-day's special that I'd served at least a hundred times, an Eggs Benedict, done Sonoran-style with green chilis and a side of refried beans.

Dakota knew her stuff, that was for sure.

Beth laughed. "Always. Tell me you aren't complaining." A tease lined her voice, though her dark brow was lifting.

"Definitely, no. I like to keep busy."

"Good. Because if you were considering walking out on me right now, I would have to hunt you down and drag your cute butt back here." Brown eyes gleamed with amusement. "You finally have us with our heads above water. Don't think I won't."

"I have no question about that." There was no keeping the chuckle out of my response.

"Just so we understand each other." She winked.

Tinkling laughter sounded behind us, and Dakota edged in, restocking napkins in the bin as she glanced between us. "Are you giving Savannah a hard time?"

"Who, me?" Beth touched her chest in feigned innocence. "Never. I was simply telling her that she can never leave."

Dakota laughed harder, and her grin slid to me. "Sorry to break it to you, Savannah, but once Beth claims you, that's it. You're ours forever."

"That's right," Beth agreed. "Which means you're coming out with us Saturday night."

Dakota tipped her face toward the ceiling. Excitement rolled up her throat. "Oh my God, yes, I cannot wait. I haven't had a night without my little tornado in months. Not that I mind being at home with Kayden, but every once in a while, this girl likes to cut loose."

She knocked her hip into mine. "And you'll get to meet Paisley. Chloe will be there, too."

Chloe worked the cashiers out front, and I'd already heard about ten different stories of Dakota's wild best friend, Paisley.

"Oh, I'm not—"

"Oh, you definitely are." Beth pointed at me. "Believe me, Savannah, you're going to need it after us running you ragged for the rest of the week."

This was the worst idea in all of bad ideas.

Of course, I needed to get out as much as I could.

Watch.

Listen.

See if I could pick up on any innuendo or trace. I had so little I was going on.

It was just that—I was worried I was starting to like these people. Starting to like being here. Starting to wonder what it might be like to have friends and people that I cared about.

And the only thing *caring* had ever gotten me was a broken heart.

Worst was the knot of regret that laid siege to my stomach after what had happened with Ezra last night.

I couldn't shake the feeling that I should have gone after him.

I should have told him I was there to listen if he needed someone to talk to, and I definitely owed him a giant thank you for everything he had done for me.

I'd contemplated the thousand different ways I would have done it as I'd tossed last night, the restless hours spent warring with the emotions that had conflicted and raved.

I needed to block it off.

Stop this before I wound up in a position that would only hurt me in the end.

Getting close was dangerous.

History had promised me that.

Dakota's expression softened, and she reached out and squeezed my hand. "Don't feel obligated, Savannah, but honestly, we'd really like you to come."

The sincerity in her voice had me speaking before I could stop it. "I'll think about it…that is if I can still walk by the end of the week."

"The only valid reason for you not to be walking is if a fine-ass man made you that way," Beth said with a laugh. "And if you don't have one of those, we'll be happy to help you find one on Saturday."

Then she disappeared out the swinging door, as if the two of them hadn't just given me emotional whiplash.

Amusement shook Dakota's head, and she gave me a shrug. "Like I said yesterday, we're a lot to handle."

"I think we've well established that." The tease was thick, close to soggy.

Beth suddenly popped her head back through the door. "Speaking of fine-ass men, you have one waiting for you at booth eleven, Savannah," she hollered.

My stomach bottomed out.

I didn't need to ask her who it was. I already knew it could only be one person as I pushed out into the dining room. I did my best to keep my cool but my reckless spirit flailed when I saw Ezra Patterson sitting on the far side of the dining room beneath a window.

His big body took up the entirety of the booth, and he was back in uniform which was an unfortunate turn of events considering how delicious he looked in it.

Who knew I could like a man in uniform? My past experiences should have left me repelled.

His long legs were stretched underneath the table, and he had a boot plunked out to the side as if he were too massive to completely fit within the boundaries.

Sunlight poured in through the window, lighting strikes of gold in his brown hair and making his skin glow gold.

Even from across the room, I could see he was bouncing in agitation.

My heart squeezed, and I grabbed a carafe of coffee from the station before I carefully edged forward, unsure of what to say. How in the world was I supposed to apologize? Thank him? All while wanting to tell him he'd been a complete jerk for walking out on me the way he'd done last night, and still completely understanding it at the same time.

He looked at me when I approached, as if he felt me coming, that strange stir in the air vibrating between us. I lifted my chin as I came up to his table, deciding to go professional.

We weren't friends, after all. We were just acquaintances. Two people who'd been randomly tossed together. One person who'd helped another for God knew why, but it was probably best it ended at that.

"Welcome to Time River Market & Café. Would you like to start with coffee?" I lifted the pot.

He roughed a big palm down his face, annoyed or surprised by the introduction, I couldn't say, but those warm brown eyes dimmed with uncertainty. "Can you sit for a minute?"

"I'm on the clock," I told him, filling him a mug even though he hadn't answered my question, needing to do something with my hands since I wasn't sure if I wanted to throttle the man or hug him.

Both seemed highly inappropriate.

"I know the owner. I don't think she'll mind." The smallest smirk hit the edge of his mouth, and it somehow made the rugged man appear adorable. Nothing but a grumbly, soft teddy bear.

"I don't think—"

He blew out a heavy sigh, cutting me off, and he gestured to the spot across from him. "Please sit, Savannah."

Clearly, I had no self-preservation left because I did.

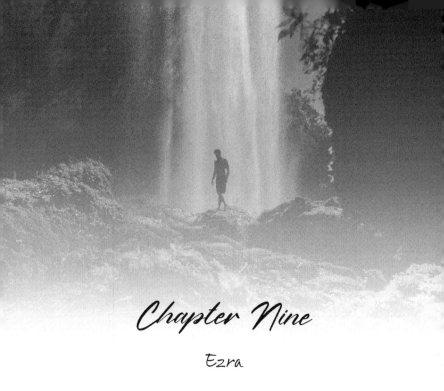

Chapter Nine

Ezra

I DREW MY LEG BACK UNDER THE TABLE THE BEST I COULD AS Savannah Ward slipped into the booth across from me.

I could feel the reservations radiating from her, the way her attention jumped around the café like she was seeking out the nearest escape route.

She had those long locks of wavy, caramel-kissed hair up in a ponytail. It accentuated the sharp curve of her jaw and the full plushness of her lips. But it was the wariness in that aqua gaze that had me shifting in discomfort, and the wood groaned beneath my weight as I sat forward and curled my hands around the steaming mug of coffee that she'd poured.

Silence stretched between us as I stared at her with my heart pounding wild, this feeling I didn't know how to handle or entertain bristling beneath the surface of my skin and making me itch.

"I owe you an apology." How I managed to force it out around the thickness of my throat, I didn't know, the words jagged as they scraped through the atmosphere.

I saw when they landed, the way she barely flinched. "I'm not sure that you do."

My chuckle was raw. "Oh, I beg to differ. Couldn't sleep last night knowing how big of a dick I'd been to you. Wondering where you went after I'd offered you a safe place to stay, then turned right around and offered you my back instead."

Her delicate throat tremored as she swallowed, and she glanced away for a beat before she returned that bottomless gaze to me. "I wasn't exactly being kind in the moment."

I didn't want to evaluate why either of us had reacted the way we had. Why I'd been standing so close, pushing into her space, and why she'd tossed what she'd believed was obvious back in my face.

I couldn't go there.

There was too much going on in my life to stumble that direction. To get distracted by a beautiful woman. I owed it to Brianna, to my children, to see this through.

Still, it was there, humming in the atmosphere. The type of attraction I wasn't sure I'd ever experienced before.

"Nah, it was all on me. You caught me off guard." I ran circles with the pad of my thumb over the smooth ceramic of the mug while my knee bounced a million miles a minute under the table, lungs and heart getting choked out.

"How long has she been gone?" Savannah whispered, the irreverent, cheeky demeanor nowhere to be found.

"Close to two years now."

Sympathy swam deep in those aqua eyes, an endless ocean where it'd be so easy to drown. And I felt like a piece of shit that I couldn't just fucking be honest. Here she was, sitting there thinking I'd lost the love of my life when I'd pretty much despised Brianna by the time everything had gone down.

That truth had been locked on my tongue for the last two years, unable to tell a soul. It was a secret forever frozen in time. How the fuck could I tell anyone what had actually happened? It felt like another betrayal to Brianna to expose the severing. The fucking war zone that had become our marriage.

Savannah's chin quivered. "I'm very sorry, Ezra."

I kept my gaze steady on her. "Me, too. I'm sorry that life can be unfair. Sorry that things often turn out so different than we planned or wanted them to." My tongue stroked out to wet my lips. "And I'm also sorry that I reacted the way I did yesterday evening. I'd like to start over. Would like us to be friends. Would like you to rent the guest house."

I was likely asking for trouble, inviting this untamed, tempting woman into my life, but I couldn't shake it. The need to help her out, even when I didn't really know her.

Her brow puckered, and God, it was distracting, how fucking gorgeous she was, the way the sight of her had my heart doing that frazzled, thundering thing.

She warred, then whispered, "I'm not sure that's a good idea."

"The friendship or the guest house?" It was a struggle to keep it light with the pressure sitting on my chest.

The slightest hint of a smile ticked at the edge of her pretty mouth.

Dangerous to my resolve. To my discretion. To my sanity.

"I'm thinking the guest house thing," she said, eyeing me like she thought I might have ulterior motives. I wasn't entirely sure I could promise that I didn't.

Savannah dropped her gaze for a second before she fluttered those lashes back up to me. Hesitation clashed with some kind of determination. "But maybe we can consider the friendship thing as time goes along."

It was a bad sign that disappointment cut me through.

"Why would you turn down the guest house? Not high enough for your standards?" I arched my brow, prodding her with the tease. The problem was that below it ran a needy desperation.

That aqua gaze narrowed, sassy vixen back in full force. "It fits my standards just fine. Maybe I just don't want to live by you."

A chuckle scraped my throat. "I'm that bad, huh?"

"I told you that you are too overbearing for my taste."

I had to restrain myself from asking exactly what *tastes* she had.

If she liked to be fucked hard and fast and ruthlessly, or if she wanted it tender and slow and sweet.

A shallow breath left her like maybe she'd plucked the visions right out of my mind before humility filled her voice. "I told you I couldn't afford it."

"I never told you what the rent was."

She let go of a slight huff. "I think I could deduce it just fine."

"Well, maybe it's been sitting empty for too long, and I'm desperate to rent it out."

Doubt filled Savannah's laughter, and she shook her head as she sat back in the booth, staring across at me like she could see straight through me. Not to the other side, but to the middle, like she held the power to forage around in my secrets. In my shame and regret. All the way to the determination of what I was willing to do.

"And maybe what you're really desperate for is to find someone to save, and you've pegged me as someone who needs it." It rolled out a challenge, gaze flashing in a torrent of blue, liquid fire. "And I can assure you, Officer Patterson, that I'm not in the market for someone to look after me. And don't think I'm not grateful for what you've done for me because I am, but I am much stronger than you think."

Pushing from the booth, she started to walk.

I couldn't stop the urge, the compulsion, and one second later, I had her by the wrist, a fool stopping her from leaving.

Surprise left her on a gasp, and my voice was coming out far too low as she shifted to peer down at me. "Maybe I do want to keep an eye on you, Little Trespasser. Maybe I like looking at you."

Disbelief had her frozen while I sat there wondering what the fuck I thought I was doing. Crossing a clear line, that was what.

Because there was no mistaking what I'd meant. Where my mind had gone.

It sent that energy swirling around us, awareness thrumming thick.

I didn't know how much time passed before Savannah finally let go of a throaty, knowing chuckle as she untangled herself from my hold. Only she didn't move away. She leaned in close, her voice pure captivation as she murmured, "I think you need to ask yourself just how closely you want to look, Officer Patterson."

Then she turned and strolled off, her long legs exposed in the denim cut-off skirt that hit her mid-thigh, a blue tank hugging her torso, white tennis shoes on her feet.

Casual.

And to my ultimate demise, the sexiest thing I'd ever seen.

I had no choice but to watch her go, attention tracking her as she moved around the café checking on her tables.

I jolted when Ryder suddenly slipped into the booth opposite me like I'd had my hand dipped way down deep in the cookie jar.

Perfect-fucking-timing.

I'd been too caught up to even realize he'd shown. I was meeting him, our other cousin Caleb, and our best friend Cody for lunch. I'd come early so I could get a chance to talk to Savannah alone, which of course I'd had to go and take that conversation fifteen steps too far.

Ryder nudged my shin under the table with the tip of his shoe as he ran a tatted hand through his jet-black hair. He was tall and lean but packed with muscle, covered head to toe in ink. Dude oozed mayhem, but luckily, he'd put that sordid period of his life behind him.

"Ah, I see Dakota isn't the only one who's enamored with the town's newest resident." The words were filled with insinuation.

I scrubbed a palm over my face to break up the trance Savannah had me under. "Don't know what you're talking about."

He laughed, totally at my expense, appraising me like he could read every thought in my mind. "Sure, brother. Don't act like you're not over there salivating. You should have seen what you looked like when I walked up. Vibrating like some kind of barely hinged beast. Half a second from getting up from that booth and stalking over to her to make a claim."

"I wasn't about to make a fucking claim." I scoffed the dismissal.

"And what are we claiming?" Cody's voice cut in, and my attention whipped up to find Cody and Caleb waltzing up to the booth.

Shit. This just got better and better.

"Nothing," I sighed.

"Our boy here is sweet on the new server." Ryder jutted his chin at me.

"I'm not sweet on the new server." I sent him daggers. He'd been pushing me for a while that I needed to start living again. That it was time and I couldn't spend my life alone.

But he didn't get it. What I had done and what remained. This obligation that burned like a storm in the middle of me. A hurricane of retribution that couldn't remain unfulfilled.

Ryder laughed. "Someone get a mirror so we can show Ezra the bald-faced lie that is written all over him and see if he can continue trying to deny what's going down inside of him right about now."

I stood from the booth so Caleb could slide in beside me. "Just drop it, yeah?" I grumbled.

Cody nudged Ryder's shoulder, and Ryder slipped in farther so Cody could take the spot next to him.

"I think we need to see exactly what it is we're dropping before we make that decision," Cody pushed.

Cody was as big as me, wearing a baseball cap over his brown hair, wavy curls getting free at the sides. His beard was thick, and he was dressed in worn jeans and a ratted tee since he spent most of his time working out in the sun.

Just him mentioning checking out Savannah had a swell of possession riding high. Loved the guy like a brother, but he was the biggest player I knew. The last thing I wanted was him *seeing* anything when it came to her.

Except she was already on her way back, no hesitation in her step when she saw the rest of my crew had arrived. Caramel locks swished around her delicate shoulders as she approached, commanding the windstorm that raged around her.

It pressed at the walls and howled in my ears.

She smiled, pouty lips stretching to reveal a flash of white, straight teeth. "Hey there. Welcome to Time River Market & Café, everyone. I'm Savannah, and I'll be taking care of you today. I heard this table is extra special."

A knowing gleam lit in her eyes, and I wondered just how easily she could fit into this place. Like she might become a permanent fixture.

Cody tossed one of his cocky smirks up her way. "Ah, I see Dakota has already told you who we are, though I know we're hard to miss."

His smile was slow and evaluating, far too interested as he let his gaze wander over her, head to toe.

Irritation buzzed in my chest. I shifted uncomfortably in the seat, and I had to keep from kicking him from under the table.

"I might have heard a story or two," she said in her throaty voice, like she was already in possession of every sordid detail. She pointed at him with the end of the pen she had poised over her notepad. "You must be the brother, Cody."

Cody grinned and tipped the brim of his cap. "That's right, darlin', and it's more than a pleasure to meet you."

A chuckle got free of Savannah, but it was knowing and filled with incredulity. "Well, it's nice to meet you, too. What can I get you to drink today, Cody?"

"I'll have one of my sister's famous strawberry iced teas."

"Make that two," Ryder piped in, though he glanced between me, Cody, and Savannah, clearly concerned that I might come over the table to choke Cody out.

"And you're Ryder," she surmised, her smile slow.

He smirked as he sat back in the booth. "The one and only."

"According to Dakota, that seems to be the truth."

Cody groaned. "I don't need to hear about this one's escapades with my sister, thank you very much."

Ryder laughed. "If you only knew."

"Gross, man. Gross."

"What Dakota and I have is beautiful. Nothing gross about it." Ryder drew it out, rubbing it in.

I quelled a chuckle because Ryder loved throwing his relationship with Cody's sister in his face. Dude deserved it with the way he'd gone all protective big brother when he found out about Ryder and Dakota being together.

He was blind if he hadn't seen they were meant to be. The two of them had been coming for a long, long time.

Like Ryder said—what they had was beautiful, the dude so far gone over Dakota it wasn't funny, even though that wasn't close to what Ryder was insinuating right then.

Savannah giggled. "Well, according to Dakota, it's definitely not gross but maybe the details need to be kept under wraps in public places."

Cody groaned again.

My grin was slow. I probably liked it a little too much that Savannah didn't mind busting his balls. She was only just meeting everyone, and she was acting like she was a part of the crew.

"How about you?" She looked at Caleb. My older cousin was dressed in a thin flannel and jeans, which was a mindfuck considering he used to prance around in five-thousand-dollar suits. His blonde hair was shaggier than it'd been, and there was a casualness to him that had never existed before.

"I'll do an unsweetened iced tea."

It was a huge relief that he was here in Time River permanently, engaged to Dakota's best friend, Paisley. He and his daughter Evelyn were safe, and the three of them had ended up right where they belonged.

Together.

"Got it." Aqua eyes dipped to the mug that I still hadn't taken a sip from. "And how is that coffee treating you?"

"I think I'll switch to a regular iced tea. I already drank a pot of the good stuff at the station this morning. Better cut myself off."

Her gaze raked over me, and a flash of that awareness radiated from her. Both knowing and curious.

Her expression went straight to my cock.

She finally peeled herself from where we'd been stuck, and she cleared the roughness from her throat. "I don't know if you read the specials out front, but we have a five-cheese grilled cheese with tomato soup for the lunch special today. I haven't tasted it yet, but based on the way my stomach growls every time I walk into the kitchen and smell the scent coming from the pot, I'm pretty sure you can't go wrong with it."

"You can't go wrong with anything that comes out of that kitchen." Pride filled Ryder's voice.

"I'm hearing that a lot, and believe me, I plan on partaking." Savannah's smile was soft. "I'll be right back with your drinks."

She strode across the dining room, weaving through the tables on those long, bare legs, light denim stretched over her pert, firm ass.

My stomach twisted, held in a twine of lust.

"Hottest damn thing I've seen in Time River in years." A low whistle rolled from Cody as he watched her round the long counter where she started to make our drinks.

Didn't mean for the growl to get out.

"Down boy." Ryder smirked, fucking smug.

"I didn't say anything," I rumbled.

Caleb laughed from beside me. "No words needed to be said with the sound that came out of you, Ezra. That was pure beast. Goddamn grizzly over here. I'm shaking in my boots."

"Run, brother," Ryder told Caleb, a full razzing.

"Nah, that shouldn't be necessary. Ezra already said he wasn't sweet on her." Cody lifted his chin my direction. "She's fair game. You've got no problem with that, do you, Ezra?"

I didn't even realize my hands were fisted on the table until Ryder cracked up.

"I would say he might have a small problem. A tiny one, maybe? About the size of Cody's dick." Ryder lifted his fingers in a pinch. "But still a problem."

"You wish, asshole." Cody shoved Ryder in the shoulder at the same time as I grumbled, "Screw you all."

It didn't take much to surmise all three of them were ganging up on me. Proving a point. Knew it for sure with the way they went quiet, assessing me through the tension, wondering if they'd pushed me too far.

Wondering if I was going to crack.

"Just messing with you, brother," Cody said. "I won't deny it, though, I am happy to see something different in your eyes." Then his grin split into something salacious. "But she is fucking hot. That was no lie."

A sigh pilfered from my nose. "It's not like that. I just found her sleeping in her car out on Landers' property, and I brought her in because I had a sense that she needed a hand. I want to make sure she gets set up on her feet. That's it."

Now who the fuck was lying?

Because there was something inside me that urged me toward her. This prickling that ran along the length of my spine.

It never faded through the entire meal.

It only grew each time she came to our booth.

When she leaned over the table to place our food in front of us. When the air shifted when she refilled our drinks.

She kept watching me every time she stopped by, gaze raking over me in slow perusal.

Not furtive.

But like she was the one who liked *looking* at me and she didn't care a thing about hiding it.

And maybe I was watching her too closely, too, because there was no mistaking the way she continually scanned the restaurant's occupants, even though I could tell she was trying to keep the action secreted.

It felt like she was searching.

Waiting.

On edge.

Like any one person might be the one to bring on her downfall.

And that was where I was stuck. The fact that I was sure she was in trouble. No question, she could be impulsive. Spontaneous and rash. But my training and gut intuition promised there was something more to her story than she'd just been passing through and had wanted to stay.

And maybe that right there was what made Savannah Ward truly dangerous to me.

The truth that I did want to watch over her. Care for her. Help her.

Not because I believed she needed fixing, the way she'd accused me of, but because I thought she might need someone to stand at her side.

I doubted she'd experienced much of that in her life.

Having someone to rely on.

I could see it in her eyes.

The detachment.

The distrust.

And that need to watch over her came close to unbearable when the mayor and his advisors were led to a booth three down from us.

Jack Harris strode in front, waving at a few of the town's residents and giving some hellos, but it was who followed him in that curled my stomach in a fist.

Hayden Obermeyer and Ruben McCoy slipped into the booth seat opposite the mayor, his chief of staff and senior advisor.

I liked most people in Time River.

Most was the key word.

I'd grown up with Hayden and Ruben, and it was my fair judgement that both were pricks.

There was something seedy about them. Something that left a bad taste in my mouth whenever I had to interact with them, which was far too often considering my position in the department.

I knew Hayden would be all over Savannah, and in this instance, I hated being right.

But there was nothing I could do but sit there and watch him give her his smarmy-fucking-smile that I wanted to knock off his pompous face when she came up to their table and introduced herself.

Ryder swiveled to look over his shoulder when my breaths were coming a little too hard as I watched the asshole talk her up, and I nearly saw red when he passed her his business card.

We all knew what kind of services he wanted to provide.

Ryder turned back around, and that smug smirk cracked across his face. "I take it you're reconsidering making that claim?"

Chapter Ten

Savannah

I STUDIED THE BUSINESS CARD AS THE GUY SAT GRINNING UP at me.

> Hayden Obermeyer
> Chief of Staff to Jack Harris, Time River Elected Mayor

There was a phone number and address below it. But it was the emblem stamped in foil high on the corner that really caught my attention. My stomach tightened. I knew that design.

The Time River logo.

It had been drawn in the middle of a page in the journal and had been the main thing that had led me here. The clues were so vague, but when I'd been researching the internet, I'd managed to find it, and along with the few other clues in the journal, I'd been sure this was the place.

I looked closely at Hayden Obermeyer. He had dark brown hair that was cut short, parted perfectly on the left side, his teeth so white it was blinding. A schmoozer, at least that's what my grandmother would have called him.

Guys like this were loose-lipped. All too eager to impress. And was he ever doing his best to impress.

I had to wonder if it went deeper, though. If the logo represented something more than just the town? If it meant a location or maybe a person?

Unease twisted through my insides.

What if he knew something about Jessica? What if she'd been involved with him? What if he'd…hurt her? This guy was in a position of power, and that was something Jessica had always been drawn to.

I couldn't make assumptions. It was too big a jump to make a true connection. But my gut told me he was definitely someone I should watch.

"Where are you from? Wait…" Hayden held up a finger. "Don't tell me, let me guess."

He used the lame question as an excuse to let his eyes that were the same shade as his hair traipse over me like he had every right to the ogling.

I suppressed a shiver of disgust.

I mean, he wasn't bad to look at, but there was something about him that made my skin crawl. I pinned on the fakest smile, the one I'd learned to use to my advantage. "Alright, you can try, but I like to think of myself as a bit of a chameleon."

The guy I'd been introduced to as Ruben chuckled at his side. "A hundred bucks says he doesn't come within five states. This one has no idea what he's talking about."

"Oh, I'm pretty sure I know the beautiful Savannah here." He tossed me another cocky smirk.

"All right, you two, the last thing we need is Time River's newest resident thinking this town is filled with a bunch of flirts." The mayor's smile was gracious as he looked up at me before he returned his attention to them. "Remember who and what you're representing."

There was only the hint of a reprimand in his voice, as if he was used to dealing with Hayden and Ruben's antics.

Jack Harris was probably in his mid to late fifties, hair salt and peppered, his jaw squared and shaven, though there was a bit of a shadow that covered his face. He had that distinguished look, a tailored suit and keen eyes. There was no question in my mind that he'd won a few votes based solely on the fact that he was incredibly handsome.

He was clearly a town celebrity, affirmed in the way the furor rippled through the restaurant when they'd walked in for lunch.

"We just want to make sure she feels welcome," Hayden said, his attention on me.

"Well, I definitely do," I said with that grin.

Hayden wagged a finger my way. "I got it. Texas…but the city."

I might as well have had *Texan* tattooed across my forehead with the way he nailed it. I cringed that I was so obvious. "Wow, you really are good."

"I can guarantee you I am." His eyes twinkled with greed, and there was no missing what he was alluding to.

"Hayden." That time it was a distinct rebuke from the mayor.

But it was the fiery darts I could feel flying from the booth three down that truly penetrated. I peeked that way to find Hot Cop staring over at us, his jaw clenched so tight I thought there was a chance that he might jump out of the booth and come storming our way, like he'd heard every suggestion come out of Hayden and he had a massive problem with it.

Talk about a massive problem.

My wrist tingled where he'd held me, and the memory of the way I couldn't help but play into the attraction came back at me full force.

"Maybe I do want to keep an eye on you, Little Trespasser. Maybe I like looking at you."

"I think you need to ask yourself just how closely you want to look, Officer Patterson."

God, I wasn't supposed to feel *this.*

This well of interest that had sprung in the pit of my stomach.

I wasn't supposed to care or get involved. Putting yourself on the line like that only got you hurt. Left your heart on the chopping block. Mine had been flayed enough by betrayal after betrayal that I knew I had to guard those last tattered pieces with everything I had left.

But I guessed maybe it was his heart—his pain and his grief and his own tattered pieces—that he'd put out there for me to see that had touched in a place that I shouldn't let them.

The man was a widower, for God's sake, and I was still shivering from the tension that had curled around us like an unstoppable force.

It was something that could get way down deep in my veins if I was foolish enough to let it.

I had to be careful. Ignore everything but my single purpose.

I turned back to the men at the table, reminding myself that I couldn't trust anyone in this town, but also remembering that any one of them could have information on Jessica. I just had to wait to act. Be smart about it.

Because if the journal was legitimate? If it was about Jessica and she was afraid? If she was in trouble and the last text she'd sent me was a lie? Then if I started asking questions and the wrong person caught wind of it, any information on Jessica would get locked down tight before I had the chance to really start.

"Well, it's great to meet you all, and I can't wait to get to know you better."

I made sure to keep my focus on Hayden when I said it.

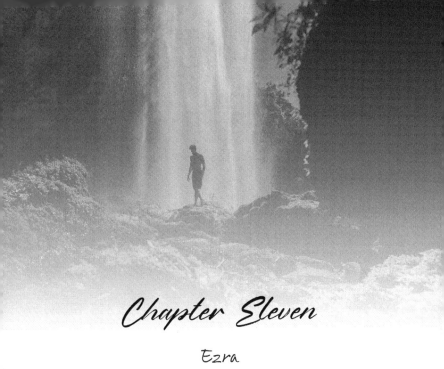

Chapter Eleven

Ezra

SUNLIGHT PUSHED AT THE BLINDS THAT COVERED MY OFFICE window, a few rays breaking through the generic slats and cutting into the murky dimness of the room. Motes danced in them, playing through the quiet and the peace.

Only I wasn't sure there would ever really be any peace.

Not with the way my stomach was a gnarl of knots and my chest was a riot of hate and animosity.

It was funny how it took one moment in time…one incidence… one atrocity to reconfigure who we were. I'd always been a firm believer in mercy. In second chances. Hoping to reform those who'd gone astray because it wasn't like a single one of us could claim that we hadn't made mistakes.

I supposed it was why I went into law enforcement. Hoping to make a difference. To show those struggling that there was a better way.

My teeth ground as I forced myself to open the file folder sitting on my desk.

Grief slammed me.

Sweeping me off my feet and dragging me out into a torrid, violent sea. Consumed by dark, dark waters.

When I finally ferreted the monsters out, there would be no mercy or compassion for the ones who'd committed this abhorrent crime. Not when I thirsted for retribution, my spirit gnawing with the ache for revenge.

The thirst for blood might have been foreign, but somehow, it seemed undeniably right.

I might have fallen out of love with Brianna, but that didn't mean her death hadn't ripped me open wide. I'd failed her. Failed my kids because I hadn't protected her. And I wouldn't fail them in this.

I nudged at the stack of glossy photos, spreading them out so I could see each one.

Blood.

So much fucking blood.

I swallowed down the sickness and forced myself to dig through, riffling through for any evidence that might have been missed.

Studying.

Hunting.

Searching for anything that had been overlooked.

It was protocol that I hadn't been allowed on the case. A conflict of interest. Worry that emotions might get in the way and cloud judgement. Suffice it to say there was conflict and my judgement was definitely clouded.

The department in Poplar about an hour away had been sent to investigate. It'd been labeled a robbery gone bad, and an innocent had gotten in the way. The perpetrators never caught. Only I'd refused to believe it. Had known all along that it was bullshit.

"I think I'm in trouble, Ezra. Please, pick up the phone. I really need your help. Call me."

I would never get those words out of my head. Would never forget the desperation. The panicked voicemail she'd left me after I'd ignored her phone call because I'd been done at that point. I'd given up on her—the moment she'd actually needed me, thinking it was only another bullshit call that was going to drag me back into the chaos that she was.

Chaos I couldn't handle any longer.

Guilt burned in my chest, and I forced myself to study the images.

Nausea crawled up my throat.

There'd been no evidence found at the scene. Not one fucking thing that had led to any suspects. Only the bullets that belonged to a gun that had never been found and the grainy image of a white van speeding away that had been captured on the camera footage.

There'd been nothing else.

No connection to the bullets.

No trace of the fucking van.

It was like none of it had existed.

I jolted when my office door suddenly popped open.

Samson froze halfway through, his hand on the doorknob and an apology on his face like he was remembering he should have knocked before he barged into my office. I tried to shove everything on my desk back into the file before he noticed what I was looking at.

Except he knew. He'd known all along where I'd disappear to. He knew I was hunting. Digging around and asking questions. Knew I was searching. Knew I was stepping out of bounds because I would either get this case reopened or seek justice for Brianna myself.

Pity flashed through his expression before he schooled it, and he played it off like he hadn't caught me going through files I wasn't even supposed to possess.

He sent me a giant grin that didn't quite land. "Lanie and Bryant are both here. That's our cue to get the hell out of here before we get stuck listening to Bryant go on about whatever poor chick he hooked up with last night. Shift's over, boss."

I roughed both hands over the top of my head to break up the disorder. "Thanks, Samson."

He hesitated, and awareness slipped back over his features, that same pity twisting his mouth at the edges. "It's in the past, brother. It's time you let it go."

There was no letting it go.

No stopping until vengeance had been found.

"I know. I just had a thought that...maybe I'd missed something obvious. That enough time had gone by that it might stand out now."

He nodded in understanding. "I get that. But your kids need your focus on them, not on what can't be changed. You should go home to them."

"Yeah, you're right," I told him like I was giving it up, and I tucked the file back into the bottom drawer of my desk and locked it. "You should head out, too, then. Just make sure you don't get into too much trouble tonight."

I arched him a playful brow.

"Never."

"Sure," I told him, chuckling low.

Then he softened again. "Have a good night, Ezra. Take care of those kids and take care of yourself."

Then he rapped his knuckles on my door and walked out.

Chapter Twelve

Ezra

Three Years Ago

IN THE DARK, EZRA PACED BY THE FRONT DOOR, CONTINUALLY roughing his hands over his head as worry clutched his chest. He looked at the clock that hung on the wall for what had to have been the thousandth time that night. It was after eleven, and his stomach was sick.

Hell, every organ in his body was sick. Twisted up and sitting in different spots than they were supposed to. As if his makeup was getting mangled.

Brianna would have gotten off at six where she worked as a receptionist at a doctor's office.

Fucking hours ago.

And he hadn't gotten one single word other than she was going to swing by the grocery store on her way home.

Panic impaled him, darts coming at him from every direction, but it was a different kind of panic than when this had happened for the first time.

That night? He'd driven every fucking street in Time River looking for her. Terrified she'd been hurt. Dread soaking him through that she was in trouble. She'd come in at two, drunk off her ass, wielding the most bullshit excuse he'd ever heard.

She'd promised it'd never happen again, but it'd happened three more times over the past six months.

And now?

Now he was pissed. Angry that she would pull this. Do this to him and their kids.

That anger roiled when he heard the quiet purr of her engine before headlights brightened against the window.

He didn't know how to process the outright disgust that mixed with the overwhelming relief that she was okay.

He hated it—this feeling like he was out of control. Like there was nothing he could do to stop the spiral.

A couple minutes later, a key slid into the lock and the door creaked open slowly, like she thought he might not hear her slinking in hours after she was supposed to be home.

She froze in the doorway like she'd actually believed he wouldn't notice.

Her breaths were shallow and ragged, and she quietly latched the door closed before she turned to face him in the gloomy shadows that crawled along the walls.

Silence stretched between them for the longest time before he finally gritted between clenched teeth, "Where the hell were you?"

She exhaled a shaky sound. "Oh…I ran into a friend who was having a bad day and she needed some company, so I hung out with her for a little while."

Disbelief stoked the fury, and he shook his head. "And you didn't think to send me a text to let me know?"

"Time just got away from me. I meant to."

She meant to.

What bullshit.

He could smell the alcohol on her breath. Could taste her lies. He was so fucking sick of it.

"I'm finished making excuses to our kids for you."

He could feel the disorder blow through her senses, and she took a desperate step forward and grabbed him by the wrist. "Please, don't give up on me. I just…it was a rough day at work, and I needed some time to myself. You know what it's like."

"I would never leave you to worry about me."

Even in the darkness, he saw her blink, her eyes the brightest green. "You think I don't worry about you every day? That every time you walk out that door in your uniform, I don't worry that you might not come back?"

"Don't turn this around on me, Brianna." The words slashed from his mouth. Razors that cut.

She clutched him with both hands, and despair rushed from her voice. "I don't know how to handle the pressure, Ezra. It's so much. Don't you understand? Don't you understand what I deal with every day?"

Sympathy edged into his consciousness, and he pulled her into his shaking arms. Shaking and shaking as he held her tight, praying that it would be enough to keep her demons at bay. He pressed his lips to her crown. "Baby, you can't keep doing this. You can't. You're going to rip this family apart, and I can't stand the idea of that. You need help."

Because when she did this, he felt the strands of his love and devotion being snipped away, and that terrified him. Because each time, he didn't hold her quite as tight.

She nodded against his chest with her fingers curled into the fabric of his shirt. "I'll be better. I promise."

I promise.

Chapter Thirteen

Savannah

I INCHED MY CAR ALONG THE ALLEY BEHIND THE APARTMENT building on the farthest side of Time River, opposite from the motel where I was staying. A pitchy darkness clung to the sky since the moon was completely missing. Even with the few streetlamps that burned, a gazillion stars shone bright, like a vat of them had been poured out from somewhere deep in the heavens and they cascaded and weaved across the canopy in a river of surreality.

I peered at them through the windshield as I came to a stop, wishing upon all of them that this might finally be the break I was looking for.

I'd spent the last two evenings driving around town, trying to piece the few clues I had together, roaming the streets for anything that might strike a chord. I'd driven by this place after I'd gotten off my shift and was struck with a bolt of recognition.

The name of the complex was the exact same thing as I'd seen sketched into one of the latter pages in the journal.

Glenstone Ridge.

When I'd returned to my motel room and looked through the journal, I'd found a scribble of numbers right below.

17a.

So I'd decided to come back and check it out under the cover of night.

I'd made four passes around the block before I'd finally decided to approach it from the back.

I glanced over at the camera sitting on the passenger seat that I'd brought along in case I needed to snap some pictures from a distance.

I almost laughed at the ludicrousness of what I was doing. Did I really think I was some kind of detective? A private investigator?

Photography was my passion. The one thing I'd ever gone after for myself. A dream that had sparked in the middle of the war zone that had been mine and Jessica's lives.

Sadness squeezed my chest as I thought of the way that dream had been ripped right out from under me, too.

It seemed appropriate that I'd use the camera as a tool to fight for the one person in this world who meant anything. Everyone else in my life might have abandoned me, but I knew in my soul Jessica never would.

"We might not be able to rely on anyone else in this world, but we rely on each other. It's just you and me. Always and forever," I whispered to her.

Jessica twisted her pinky finger around mine. "You and me, always and forever."

I sucked in a steeling breath before I grabbed my camera and murmured beneath my breath, "Always and forever."

I snapped open my door then quietly latched it behind me, and I placed the camera strap around my neck as my attention darted each direction in the deserted alley.

My heart thundered in my chest, and when I sensed no movement, I ran on my tiptoes across the alley to the high fence that backed the apartment on the other side.

All stealth-like as I pressed my back against it and made myself invisible.

I almost grinned. Maybe I really was good at this investigating thing.

Okay, probably not considering my breaths were jutting so harsh and loud that I was likely waking every resident in the complex, and I tried to quiet them as I crept forward until I made it to the gate that opened to the back parking lot. It wasn't locked, and I lifted the latch, nudged it open, and peered inside.

A warm glow covered the lot, and cars took up most every spot of the small complex.

The apartment building was super nice, verging on luxury. Unrest churned through my consciousness. How the hell could Jessica have afforded this place?

Not when I was the one who'd always taken care of her—supported her the best that I could.

I had to admit, though, that this definitely would have fit her tastes.

She'd spent her whole life telling me she was going to be rich when she grew up, whatever it took, and those ideas had turned into her own dreams of being a fashion and makeup influencer as she'd gotten older.

And she'd been right there...*right there*...before she'd disappeared, leaving behind that single text that I could never accept.

Ignoring the disturbance that tugged at my spirit, I pressed forward because I wasn't about to give up, and I hurried under the cover of night toward the two-story building, ducking behind cars and trees before I found the sidewalk that cut through the middle of the building. It opened up to a big courtyard in the middle, and at the center of it was a pool surrounded by trees. A bunch of loungers and tables were situated all around.

Oh yeah, Jess would have loved this place, and I hoped to God that maybe I would just find her here, living her life the way she wanted to—even if it meant she wanted to live it without me in it.

I would accept it if that's what truly made her happy.

I glanced at my palm where I'd written the numbers in Sharpie. *17a*

Lights were hung beside each door, and I could see that the

numbers to my left started at one on the front side and ended at 10 right near me, and continued counting up from there.

Seventeen would be to my right.

I moved that direction, creeping past each door, silently counting under my breath as I went.

Thirteen, fourteen, fifteen…

My heart was beating so erratically by the time I got to sixteen that I couldn't breathe, and I was shaking like a jackhammer by the time I got to 17a. Hands quivering out of control. This had to be it. There had to be something.

I could feel it.

Swallowing around the lump in my throat, I quickly peeked around me to make sure no one was around, then I sucked in a deep breath and pushed up to the window, my nose touching the glass as I tried to peer inside.

Crap.

The drapes were drawn.

I warred, fidgeted, and glanced around again before I moved up to the door. Nerves rattled me through.

And I knew it was fear and dread that I felt. What was holding me back and making me skittish. Not fear for myself. But fear that I might just be hitting another dead end.

But I would never know unless I tried, so I lifted my hand and knocked on the door. It echoed through the silence of the night, and that disappointment hit me tenfold when there was no movement on the other side.

I knocked again, a little louder that time, then waited with my ear pressed to the door.

Nothing.

Discontent squeezed my spirit, and I bit down on my bottom lip, contemplating through the disorder, before I came to a quick decision. There wasn't another one to make.

I dug into my pocket and pulled out the tool I'd brought, and I worked it into the lock, trying to keep as quiet as I could as I trudged right into the illegal.

I wondered how condemning it was that I'd watched a YouTube tutorial on picking locks right before I'd come here. I doubted I could even jimmy it, anyway, but my breath hitched when I felt the lock give.

Holy crap.

I did it.

Carefully, I turned the knob and stuck my head inside.

And that was one second before the alarm started going off.

Chapter Fourteen

Ezra

WAS SHE FUCKING KIDDING ME?

I eased up behind her where she stood at the apartment door looking guilty as all get out and every damned bit as gorgeous as she always did.

Completely clad in black like she thought she was some kind of jewel thief breaking into a Harry Winston. Hands fumbling as she tried to close the door like that was going to be enough to shut off the alarm that was thankfully not loud enough to wake every tenant in the place.

Savannah was too busy trying to shove the tool I'd just watched her jimmy the lock with into her pocket for her to notice when I eased up and rested one shoulder on the wall.

"Do you mind telling me what you're doing, Little Trespasser?" I stuffed my hands into my pockets as I asked it considering I was off duty and wearing jeans.

Gasping, she whirled my direction, surprise so stark on her face that I had to hold back a chuckle from tumbling out. She pinned on the same fake smile she'd worn the first night I'd run into her, and she reached up and touched her chest right above the camera that hung there. "You scared the crap out of me."

It seemed I was always doing that.

I arched a brow. "I scared you, huh?"

"Um, yes. I thought you were overbearing, but this whole stalking bit is a little much. Do you always go sneaking up on unsuspecting females at night?"

My brow arched farther, so high I was pretty sure it had to have disappeared into my hairline. "Only the ones trying to break into apartments."

Her mouth dropped open like what I was implying was completely absurd, and she laughed a sound so counterfeit it cracked. "Who, me? Trying to break into this apartment? Pssh."

She was a terrible actress, and she kept biting down on her bottom lip and glancing around like she was looking for an escape route. Nerves vibrated her to the bone, and I had the stupid impulse to wrap her in my arms and tell her whatever was going on would be just fine.

Beg her to tell me what the hell was going on in her life that had her sneaking around.

Promise we'd figure it out.

But the alarm system was still going off, and I grabbed my cell and made a call to the station, eye on Savannah the whole time, keeping her pinned with my stare.

Pam finally answered on the third ring. "Everything okay, boss?"

"Yeah, there was an alarm at Glenstone Ridge, apartment 17a. Call the alarm provider and let them know it's clear."

"Will do."

"Thank you." I ended the call, and I rested more of my weight on the wall as I looked at Savannah.

The alarm shut off a minute later, and I reached into the apartment, relocked the door, and pulled it shut. A sliver of guilt hit me that I was covering this woman's tracks, but I tucked it down because my gut told me her actions weren't malicious.

"So, if you weren't trying to break into this apartment, then what were you doing?" I kept my voice mild.

"Oh, I was looking for an apartment that is supposed to be for rent, and I thought this was the one, and I think I accidentally got too close checking it out and set off the alarm."

"Is that so?"

"Mmmhmm." She hummed it like a solemn oath.

"And you're looking for an apartment, at eleven at night?"

She lifted her chin. "That's right."

Then her eyes narrowed. "And how did you get here so fast?" Aqua raked over me, and her voice shifted into an accusation like I was the one who was in the wrong. "You're not even in uniform."

"Not that I owe you an explanation, but a friend of mine who lives up the street noticed some suspicious activity, and since I live on the next street over, he gave me a call, so I decided I'd come check it out myself. He told me he'd spotted a late model red Ford doing circuits around the neighborhood before it disappeared down the alley. Sound familiar?"

Savannah itched, and her gaze dipped to her feet before she looked back at me with a hike of her shoulder. "Yeah, I was driving around making sure I liked the neighborhood."

"Mmm," I hummed.

She waved a hand around her. "But this place isn't quite what I was looking for, so I'm just gonna go."

She started to turn and walk, and I snatched her by the wrist and pulled her close. "Not so fast, Little Trespasser."

Heat blazed in the inch of space that separated us. Fathomless eyes went wide, and I wondered if I could see all the way to the depths of them to what she was hiding.

To whatever made her skittish and had her constantly looking over her shoulder like she was terrified of her ghosts catching up. Or maybe she was just running headlong into them.

"You can tell me, you know." My mouth was too close to hers, and that feeling that kept sweeping through me every time she was near almost knocked me from my goddamn feet. My stomach in knots and my heart clattering at my ribs.

Her breaths were shallow, and the woman was filling my senses. Mango and cream.

"And what would I tell you, Officer Patterson?" The words came as a whispered challenge.

"What you're in. You can tell me if you need help. What you're afraid of." I still held her around the wrist, and I smoothed my thumb over the spot on her palm that had the number of the apartment written in black ink. "What you're looking for."

Shivers raced her flesh, and I knew I was so out of bounds that I needed to step away. But right that second, I was stuck, needing her to know that I meant it. "I'm here for you if you need someone."

She swayed for a beat, like maybe she was disoriented, falling, before every muscle in her slight body tightened in restraint.

"I don't need anyone's help," she said, and her jaw ticked in something that looked too close to grief. "I can handle things on my own."

"Of course, you can, but you shouldn't have to."

Her gaze fluttered over my face, a severity crackling through the heavens that covered us from above. Then she steeled herself and stepped back, and she tugged her wrist from my hold.

Reluctantly, I let her go.

"Am I free to leave?" she asked with a jut of that sharp, defiant chin.

I wavered for a moment before I muttered, "Yeah."

Nodding, she dipped around me to head in the direction of where I'd seen she'd left her car in the alley.

"But I'm going to be watching you, Little Trespasser," I called behind her.

She spun where she was about twenty feet down the walkway, a sadness in her demeanor that cut me through like a knife. "Don't look too close, Officer Patterson."

Then she turned and disappeared through the opening that led to the back parking lot.

And I stood there wondering what it was about her that made me want to look closer than I had anyone before.

⌒◦⌒

"Daddy, *wook* it!" Owen called as he scrambled up the steps to the slide at the top of their play fort.

"I'm watching you," I called from where I sat on a rocker on the back porch watching over my kids while they played in the twilight that covered the yard.

"Watch me, too!" Oliver shouted, chasing after his twin.

Olivia had retreated to the spot where she had some play horses set up on the lawn—her latest obsession since her cousin Evelyn lived out on a ranch and had her own horse—the little girl getting lost in her own imagination after I'd spent the last hour and a half playing games with them in our backyard.

I'd called it and said I needed a break, but the twins had begged me to stay out here and watch them for a while longer, and there was no chance I could deny their sweet little faces something so simple.

So I rocked in the wooden chair as I watched them play, half content, half itching in my seat.

It wasn't like I had gotten Savannah Ward off my mind since I'd met her, but it was tenfold since I'd found her trying to break and enter that apartment last night.

An apartment that was in fact empty but was not for rent, something I'd found when I'd done a little background check while I was at the station today. It was owned by an out-of-state corporation, likely used for summer vacations or winter ski trips to the nearby resort.

Neighbors said it was almost always quiet and they never noticed anyone coming or going—all except for the ruckus caused by one little trespasser last night.

"Here we go!" Owen and Oliver threw their arms over their heads as they both went down the slide at the same time, holding onto each other as they made the little spiral before they dumped out onto the grass at the bottom. The two of them were giggling like crazy and rolling around before they climbed back to their feet and scampered right back up the steps.

A smile touched my face, love pressing full force at my chest, then I got distracted all over again by my phone that I had rested on my thigh as I rocked.

It was probably a bad idea when I'd texted Dakota earlier and asked for Savannah's number, but I'd figured it might come in handy if I needed to ask her some questions. I ignored that what I was contemplating was clearly gross misuse of information.

I hesitated for a second, staring at the blackened screen.

Screw it.

I tapped out a message and hit send.

Me: Are you staying out of trouble, Little Trespasser?

I told myself I sent it as a warning. As a way to let her know I was watching her. The problem was the whole reason I couldn't look away.

But was it really all that bad to check in?

I'd offered for us to start over. To be friends.

But I was pretty sure any ideas of us being *friends* had been shot to shit the second I'd grabbed her by the wrist that day in the café. And here I was again, treading into territory where I shouldn't go.

I needed to focus on my kids. On finding the monsters responsible for stealing their mother from their lives.

I didn't need to be preoccupied by a woman who was doing little more than passing through town, causing her own sort of destruction as she went.

My knee bounced out of control while I waited, and I should have taken it as my own warning when relief clamored through me when she finally responded about ten minutes later.

Savannah: Are you worried I'm wreaking havoc on your town, Officer Patterson?

My mouth tweaked up at the side. Damn, I liked her sass too much.

Me: Just making sure you aren't making yourself at home on someone else's property, is all.

Savannah: You can rest assured I haven't broken any laws in at least the last five minutes.

A chuckle rolled out, and I shook my head as I tapped at my phone.

Me: Five minutes, huh? Don't make me haul you back down to the station.

Savannah: I think you really just want me in cuffs.

Want fisted my guts.
Dangerous.
I knew she was.
To my sanity.
To my resolve.
But I played right into it, anyway.

Me: I think it's you who's begging to be bound.

It took forever for her response to come through.

Savannah: Don't worry, I won't give you a reason to arrest me again.

She was clearly shutting down the direction the conversation had gone. Wisely diverging paths because it was clear neither of us could go there, but I wasn't sure that she'd treaded onto any safer ground.

I deliberated on what to say before I finally typed out:

Me: Is that an admission of guilt?

Savannah: I told you before I wasn't trying to cause any trouble.

Maybe I was blinded by this attraction, but I believed her, which kept leading me back to one thing. She was in trouble.

Me: Did you find a place to rent?

At least thirty seconds passed before she responded again.

Savannah: I'm just fine, Ezra. You don't have to worry about me.

That was the whole fucking problem. I wasn't sure I could stop myself.

Me: Just…be careful, okay? And if you need me, use this number. I'm right here.

Olivia suddenly came galloping across the yard, white hair flying behind her like a horse's mane. "It's time for dinner, Dad!"

A low chuckle got free. My sweet little caretaker. "Is that so?"

"Yep. The sun is already almost all the way set, and that means it's almost six, and we need to eat fast so we can do more studying for my spelling bee."

I stood, shucking thoughts of the woman I wasn't entirely sure I could get off my mind, and I placed my attention on what was important. "Good thing we have a roast in the crockpot, then. It should be ready."

Taking my hand, Olivia tipped her sweet face up to me. "You did a really good job, Dad. Grandma didn't even have to help you this time."

Affection blistered, and I grinned. "I'm getting there."

Olivia squeezed my hand. "I think you already made it."

Devotion thudded, thick and steady, thankful that my daughter might actually look at me that way.

Through the heaviness, I called out to the boys, "Let's go, yahoos. It's time for dinner."

"Yes!" Oliver fist-pumped the air as he came down the slide.

"I hungee!" Owen slurred as he hustled back down from where he was halfway up the steps, and my twins came barreling for us.

My little family went inside, and I spent the rest of the evening solely focused on my kids, knowing they were my purpose. I couldn't get sidelined or distracted.

None of us were ready for that.

And I went to bed pretending I wasn't thinking about the woman who I was afraid had already gotten under my skin.

Chapter Fifteen

Savannah

I GLANCED AT THE TEXT THAT PINGED MY PHONE WHERE IT SAT on the small bed in my hotel room.

Dakota: Are you ready? Get your cute butt downstairs. It's time for you to have some fun—Time River style.

Yep, I'd done it.

Saturday night had rolled around, and I'd let myself be wrangled into going out with Beth, Dakota, and the rest of their friends.

Anxiety tumbled through me as I stared at Dakota's message.

I couldn't shake the worry that I was making a huge mistake agreeing to this.

Not the going out part since I needed to scope out every place that I could, but the real reason I was doing it.

Because I knew by the shiver of excitement that slicked down my spine that I wasn't doing this as a task, but rather because I wanted to.

Because I'd put myself in the precarious position of really liking Dakota, Beth, and Chloe.

Because I really did need to unwind after a long week at the café, exactly like Beth had said.

Because I'd spent the rest of the week after Ezra had caught me trying to break into that apartment hidden in my motel room in the times that I wasn't working, realizing I needed to figure out how to actually handle this before I did something stupid and got myself into real trouble.

Slinking around in the night wasn't cutting it.

Especially since Hot Cop had a knack of sniffing me out every time that I attempted it.

My stomach twisted again.

I refused to even consider my decision to go out had anything to do with the idea that the surly teddy bear who had come into the café the last two mornings might be there, even though I hadn't dared asked Dakota if he would be.

Each time, he'd give me a sly grin as he sipped at his coffee, his tease so light as he'd tell me he was only there to keep an eye on me.

He'd treated me almost casually during that time, straying away from the questions I could see looming in his thoughts about Tuesday night.

Instead of pushing me on what I'd been doing there, he'd asked me each day how I was. How I liked work. If I'd found a place to stay yet and telling me the offer still stood for his guest house.

Each time, I reiterated that it was a bad idea.

A bad, terrible idea because I liked him too much, and those hard places inside me had begun to soften toward him.

Just like they were softening toward this group who were so kind and wonderful that my stupid heart kept trying to convince me they were genuine.

Another text blipped through.

> **Dakota: Hello? Are you there? Don't make me come upstairs and drag you down here because you know I will.**

Clearing the emotion from my throat, I tapped out a reply.

Me: Apparently, you've been hanging out with Beth too much with those threats 🌑 **On my way down.**

I took a second to peer at myself in the full-length mirror. I had on a tight, red dress that fit me in all the best ways, and I'd paired it with thick-heeled black slides.

Affection bound my chest as I thought of the way Jessica would have narrated my getting ready. Telling me to try this or that before she would have finally found my choices lacking and would have dug through my closet to find the perfect accessories.

Shoes and jewelry and bags.

"I think you would approve, Jess, even though I'm not sure how well I'm going to fit in at a country bar," I whispered as I leaned close to the mirror and swiped some pink gloss onto my lips. I tucked a rogue lock of hair that I'd curled into fat waves back into order, then I grabbed my little black bag and made sure I had my keycard.

Then I slipped out the door into the brisk night air and hurried downstairs, walking beneath the canopy of stars slung low across the heavens as I strode for the muscle car sitting at the curb, its brake lights lit as the powerful engine grumbled where it idled.

The passenger door swung open, and Dakota climbed out. Her lush curves were hugged in the cutest black and pink polka dot dress, and her long brown hair was in the same high ponytail she loved to wear. Throwing her arms over her head, she shimmied her hips. "Savannah! Are you ready to get your party on?"

I couldn't help the giggle that got free. The anticipation. The way this place just felt...different.

Better.

Beyond anything I'd ever hoped to imagine existed.

I didn't want to be the fool who fell for it, but the expression on her face was making it difficult to keep up the doubt.

"You know I am, except I'm afraid I'm going to blur into your shadow. You look crazy hot," I called out as I approached.

She flagrantly rolled her eyes. "Are you kidding me? Tell me hotels still have mirrors because if you saw what you look like walking up the sidewalk right now... I'm afraid this poor town is about to catch fire."

I did feel amazing right then. Sexy. As powerful as the car as I slipped through the small opening into the backseat. I just worried who I thought I was dressing for.

Ryder was in the driver's seat, his tatted hand gripping the gear handle. He glanced back with a smirk on his face. "You look like you're out to break a few hearts tonight, Savannah Ward."

I laughed. "Oh, I might be out for one or two."

Ryder pulled from the curb, and he tossed me a look through the rearview mirror as we were hitting the street. "Just go easy on the soft ones, yeah?"

My stomach twisted into a tight knot. There was no doubt he was referring to Ezra.

Did that mean he was going to be there?

Anticipation spiked.

I did my best to cram it back down where it belonged.

Things were far too complicated in both our lives for us to spend too much time together.

Baggage strewn that neither of us had any control over.

Hurt.

Grief.

Fear.

I mean, the man had lost his wife, for God's sake. Which, hello, it didn't matter anyway since I'd sworn off men.

Absolutely no thank you.

I was done with relationships and attachments.

Better for us to keep our distance before it became the latter.

Because I couldn't shake the words of his last text that had rang like an oath.

I'm right here.

And he might be here right now, but no one ever stayed.

"Soft ones?" I went for light. Carelessness. "I haven't run into any of those yet. Apparently, you breed giants around here."

"Ha, these boys around here might look tough, but they're as sweet as can be." Dakota gave an affectionate shove to Ryder's shoulder.

He reached over and squeezed the inside of her thigh, and his voice dropped with the warning. "I'll show you nice."

"I'm going to hold you to that," she whispered.

Ryder stopped at one of the only lights in town and took the opportunity to bury his face in her neck. I couldn't tell if Dakota was moaning or giggling.

"Would you like me to get out of the car and walk the rest of the way?" I coughed through the tease. "You two clearly need some privacy."

Ryder pulled back, something sly riding on his face. "You might need to unless you're in the business of watching."

Dakota was still giggling when she looked back at me. "Ignore him. The poor baby can go without for a few hours."

Ryder grunted his disagreement.

And I wondered for the first time in years if two people might actually be fated for each other. If they might belong. Because I honestly couldn't imagine these two without the other.

It took us all of ten minutes to pull into a rambling gravel parking lot packed full of trucks and cars. An enormous building that resembled a barn sat at the far back, and it was lit in rope lights that came off the sides, which I assumed were outdoor patios.

Up near the roof, a big, red sign flashed *Mack's*.

Ryder found an open spot at the back, and he was around the car and helping Dakota out by the time she even got her door open. Dakota pushed the seat up for me so I could climb out and offered me a hand. I did my best to keep from flashing the whole town as I got out, and laughter rolled as I tried to angle just right because I was pretty sure poor Ryder was about to get an eyeful.

Dakota stepped more in front of me, blocking the direct view of my panties like the good friend she was. The whole time, she giggled out of control.

It felt good.

Laughing.

Laughing with a friend.

Dakota smiled at me like she'd known me my entire life and

planned to know me for the rest of it, and my chest stretched so tight I thought I might come apart.

"I maybe should have taken this into consideration when I was deciding what to wear," I said, trying to ignore the emotion that ran rampant.

"Absolutely not. You're setting this town on fire tonight, remember? And that dress is perfectly flammable."

I followed them through the doors of the raucous bar. It was packed, bodies wall-to-wall. A dingy haze floated through the air, and the atmosphere was both thick and alive.

Country music blared from the speakers, compliments of the band that played from an elevated stage on the far side of the cavernous room. A dance floor took up the entire middle section, and it was just as jammed as the rest of the bar.

Lights strobed over the faces in a chaotic dance of color.

My attention jumped over each. Searching. Praying for the type of luck I never had that my sister's face would suddenly be one of them. Like she was just going to appear.

Not in the cards, but a girl could hope.

"This way," Ryder said, snapping me out of the hunt. He cut through the crowd that seemed to part in his wake, giving us space to shoulder through the crush. My gaze kept scanning the faces as we wound around the right side, passed by a bar that was surrounded by a horde of people, and weaved through the round, high-top tables that surrounded the dance floor.

Two tables up, a woman was standing on a barstool, waving her arms overhead, her long hair so blonde it was nearly white.

I was pretty sure her shouting wasn't necessary because there was no missing her. She had the attention of every single person in the place. "Doodle Boo, I see you! It's about time your gorgeous ass showed up! It's time to get your drink on."

A giant smile split Dakota's face as she glanced at me. "That would be Paisley."

"I gathered as much."

Paisley hopped off the stool the second we'd fully broken through.

She wore a tight white tank emblazoned with silver beads, cut-off shorts, and red cowgirl boots. She threw her arms around Dakota's neck and squeezed as she rocked her back and forth. "I missed the heck out of you. It's been so busy at the ranch, I haven't had a minute to come into town. I couldn't wait for tonight to get here."

"You better have been missing me," Dakota told her, grinning as she pulled back.

"Always."

I might have stopped believing in it, but I had an inkling this was what real friends meant.

Then Paisley's attention traveled my way. "And you must be Savannah. It's so good to meet you. I've heard *all* about you."

She caught me off guard by throwing her arms around me, too, rocking me around the same way as she'd done Dakota as she whispered in my ear, "My fiancé is a hopeless gossip. Don't tell him I told you because he will deny it to his dying breath since he considers himself the quiet, strong type, but he told me you made quite the impression on the crew at the café this week."

She edged back, her eyes gleaming.

I laughed. "I think that might be an exaggeration."

Was it, though?

Because it was right then that I felt something ripple through the air. An intensity that hadn't been there before. A feeling that washed through me like the gathering of a summer storm.

Hot and tingly and tight.

The same way as it did every time he came within a mile of me.

I looked up.

Hot Cop was there, carrying a pitcher of beer as he broke through the crowd and wound his way to the table.

Big and burly and sporting a day's worth of scruff.

Wearing jeans and a plain white tee.

Looking so damned good that he knocked the breath out of me.

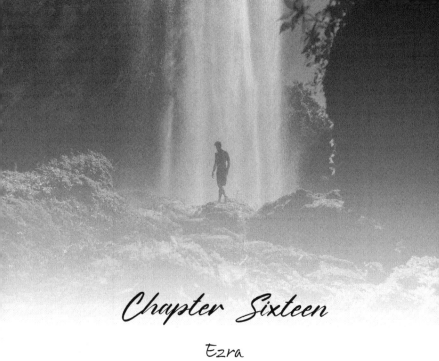

Chapter Sixteen

Ezra

HOW MANY TIMES HAD IT BEEN SAID THAT LIFE WASN'T fair? The proof of it was right there, standing in front of me, Savannah Ward wearing a red dress that was an outright travesty.

I nearly lost hold of my pitcher of beer as I broke through the crowd, coming in just as Paisley was hugging the crap out of the woman whose presence slammed me like a shockwave.

An avalanche.

An earthquake.

I struggled to regain clarity. To remember my duty. What I was supposed to be focused on right then.

Impossible when those aqua eyes snapped up as if she'd felt me staring, a straight sucker-punch to the gut.

That was right about the time Cody was clapping me on the back and making me jump half out of my skin. He cracked up like my reaction was the most hysterical thing he'd ever seen, and he angled in close as he said just loud enough for me to be able to hear over the level of the music, "You might already be too late to make that claim.

Half the bar is already headed this way because that girl is a flame. No woman should ever look that good."

I grunted at him. "Nothing to be late for."

Too bad the denial tasted like sandpaper on my tongue.

Cody only cracked a grin, his curls peeking out from beneath his baseball cap. "You just keep trying to convince yourself of that." He sobered, looking me straight. "It's okay, you know? You don't have to keep going it alone. There's a time for grieving, but there's also a time when it becomes clear your heart might have space for more. None of us are going to judge you for that, Ezra. We want it for you. Support you in every way."

Guilt constricted. I hated keeping the people who meant most to me in the dark. Deluding them into believing a veil of the truth. Because, yeah, there was grief, but it was shaped so different than they thought.

"I'm just living my life a day at a time, Cody. You don't need to worry about me. I'll figure it out."

He squeezed the back of my neck. "Know it, man, but sometimes we just need a little nudge in the right direction. And all I can say is follow your heart…or your dick if that's what's leading."

The dude winked, cracking up again, and he left me standing there shaking my head as he hopped onto a stool next to Ryder. I came the rest of the way over and placed the pitcher and cups in the center of one of the high-top tables that we'd put together to accommodate our group.

As I was leaned over the table, Dakota edged up and slid her arm around my waist to give me a side hug. "Hey, Ezra. How are you tonight?"

"Can't complain."

"I bet you can't since we have something extra special to get you out of your house tonight."

I glanced at her. Her brown eyes gleamed. I swore, the whole bunch of my friends were schemers.

"Cody landing a big landscape job?" I played it off like I didn't know exactly what she was aiming at.

"Oh, we know that my dear brother isn't really what you're here for tonight. I think there's something or *someone* else that has you… interested."

So fucking subtle.

What was even less subtle was the way the air shifted when Savannah slipped onto the stool beside Beth. The way I could feel the heat of those eyes on me again. The way my throat felt achy and raw when she peered at me through the murkiness of the atmosphere. She sent me this pink-kissed smile that was both sly and questioning, those shiny lips glistening with seduction.

I ignored the kick of greed. The intonation of lust.

"Just like I thought." Dakota was suddenly in my line of sight, pulling my attention from where it'd drifted.

I scowled at her, and she patted me on the cheek as she laughed. "I think it's going to be a really fun night, Ezra. Enjoy."

I grunted as she spun away to talk to Paisley, and I sucked it up and decided not to make things weird since I'd already been ninety-nine percent certain that Savannah was going to be here tonight. And I'd handled myself just fine the last two mornings when I'd slipped into the café to check on her.

To make sure she was safe, playing off my presence like a tease.

I'd offered to be her friend, so that was clearly what I needed to focus on right then rather than standing there acting like some kind of creeper with his tongue tied over a gorgeous woman. So I sucked it down and weaved around to take the open spot next to Savannah.

Heat flashed, a throb of that awareness that had strummed since the moment I'd first taken her in.

"Hey, Savannah. How's it going?"

I concentrated on pouring myself a beer from the pitcher rather than looking at her face. Staring at the woman who was just begging for destruction.

I could feel it, anyway, the intensity that swirled.

"Keeping out of trouble?" I tacked on, doing my best to keep it light.

Savannah giggled, though it was low and throaty and deep.

Every molecule in my body reacted to the sound.

"Are you going to ask me that every time you see me? You know a good criminal would never admit they'd been causing trouble in the first place."

She knocked her shoulder into mine.

I took a sip of my beer, steeling myself to fully turn toward her. It didn't matter that I'd prepared myself. My guts still fisted. "And do you consider yourself a professional?"

There was no stopping the low tease that rumbled free. It seemed Savannah Ward evoked something in me that hadn't been there in a long, long time.

Her head tipped to the side. It sent dark caramel waves tumbling over her delicate, bare shoulder. Something sly and sweet danced along her plush lips. "I have skills, Ezra. Mad skills. It just seems yours are better."

A coarse chuckle rolled out, and I folded an arm on the tabletop, taking a swig of my beer with the other. I swiped my tongue over my bottom lip to gather the moisture as I stared over at her.

The woman was so close. A fire that burned at my side.

"Yeah, I keep finding you, don't I?"

Everything about her softened in a tenuous sort of vulnerability, and she gazed over at me.

Seeking.

Searching.

Before she shifted to face forward, and she fiddled with a napkin on the table, her words drifting out in front of her like she didn't know if they were meant for her or for me. "I honestly have no idea what I'm doing."

"Then maybe you need a friend to help you figure it out."

She tossed her gaze in my direction, and her expression edged right back into playfulness. "You want to be my friend, huh?"

I took another swig of my beer. "It's on the table if you want it."

I was worried there might be a few other *things* on the table, too.

Affected amusement pinked her cheeks, though nothing about it seemed timid. Not when everything about her was bold. She inclined closer, her words little more than a breath near my ear, "We can be friends, Ezra Patterson. As long as you drop those overbearing ways of yours."

One side of my mouth hitched up. "I've been working on that. Someone told me I might have a problem with it."

Her giggle was short and deep, so goddamn tempting my cock tightened in my jeans. "Somehow I'm having a hard time believing you could be reformed."

"The real question is if little trespasser's can be reformed." I quirked a brow at her, unwilling to just drop it when neither excuse she'd given me added up.

Her lips pressed together. "Well, I'm working on that, too."

I knew I couldn't press her too hard without sending her running, so I gestured with my chin to the empty spot on the table in front of her. "Can I get you something to drink?"

"Maybe I was wrong, and chivalry really *isn't* dead," she drew out, her voice cut in the razzing as the smile on her face spread.

And I couldn't help the way everything went soft and heavy, the buzz in the pit of my stomach and the pull in my chest.

"You are something, Savannah Ward." It came out lower than it should have.

Sincerer.

With a meaning I didn't really understand myself.

The humor in her features dimmed, almost darkening, like maybe some ignorant fuck had forgotten to tell her she was amazing. "I think you're something, too, Ezra Patterson."

I got stuck staring for too long, only to jump when Paisley was suddenly at my other side, jostling me when she leaned in to place a tray with a bunch of frilly shot glasses rimmed in sugar in the middle of the table.

"It's lemon drop time, baby," she shouted.

"We really are in trouble tonight," I grumbled.

Paisley shoved at my shoulder. "Don't you start, Mr. Straight-Laced. This girl has on her dancing boots, and she plans to make full use of them."

She leaned around me and plunked one of the shots in front of Savannah. "One down and then we're on the dance floor."

Savannah giggled, this airy sound that still pilfered low. "You aren't going to find me complaining. My new friend Beth here warned me I was going to need to cut loose after the long week at work. Turns out, she's a psychic."

Laughing, Beth slung her arm around Savannah's shoulders and tugged her toward her like they were the oldest friends. "It's not psychic, honey. It's called experience. For all the hard work we do, we need to have just as much fun, and I had a feeling that you might want to have some of that fun with us. I mean, we are awesome, right?"

Beth lifted her shot glass.

Savannah was grinning this…awed smile that struck me somewhere deep, like she couldn't quite process what she was feeling. Where she was or how she'd ended up here. Like she was terrified of a newfound hope. Finally, she lifted her shot glass in return.

"Yeah, you all are really awesome."

"I'll drink to that," Dakota said. She held her glass in the middle of the table. Paisley and Chloe did the same, and Caleb, Ryder, Cody, and I lifted our own drinks to meet them all.

Glasses clinked as everyone shouted, "To Savannah!"

All the girls tossed their shots back.

"And Cody!" Dakota tacked it on as an afterthought as they slammed their empties down.

"I see this celebration is no longer about me." Cody was all grins, no offense.

Dakota waved him off. "Oh, come now, big brother. I think you get plenty of attention, don't you? Look at this place? How many women have you not gone home with before?"

Cody rocked back in his stool, all kinds of cocky and smug. "It's safe to say I'm running out of options."

Dakota curled her nose. "Eww."

He cracked up. "Maybe I'm just searching for my soul mate."

Paisley rolled her eyes. "I'm sure that's it."

Paisley and Dakota both squealed when the band changed songs.

"It's my jam! Get those booties on the dance floor!" Paisley shouted.

Dakota, Beth, and Chloe clambered off their stools.

Savannah seemed bewildered by the sudden spectacle, though she was cracking up when Paisley hauled her off her stool by the hand and dragged her onto the dance floor. Paisley set Savannah up between her and Dakota, getting her into a line that Savannah had clearly never partaken in before.

She stumbled all over the place trying to keep up with the choreographed moves, awkward and goofy and still having the best time.

The apprehension that she seemed to always carry obliterated in the moment.

Laughing and laughing, she had her head thrown back as she fumbled the opposite direction than she was supposed to go, and Paisley righted her, sending her the right way.

That laughter never stopped as her gaze caught on mine, though for a beat, it slowed.

Awareness glided through the air.

A burn that ignited when it reached my skin.

And as I sat there nursing my beer and watching her, I couldn't help but think how happy I was that she was there.

Savannah eyed the third shot that had been set in front of her. The smile that had been pasted on her face the entire night remained unfaltering as she said, "And here I thought you were all supposed to be my friends and it turns out you're just trying to kill me."

Her voice had gone free, inhibitions slayed.

Laughter rang from Dakota where she sat on the stool next to her sipping on her favorite hot pink concoction from a martini glass. "Are you a lightweight, Savannah? Don't worry, we'll take care of that little problem really quick for you."

Savannah scowled at her. "Like I said, trying to kill me."

Dakota clearly didn't take it as an offense. Instead, she petted her hair and cooed, "You're so pretty."

A giggle got free of Savannah. "Nu-uh, you're the prettiest. And my favorite."

"Hey, what about me?" Paisley whined where she was sitting on Caleb's lap, right at the same time as Beth huffed, "Now that's just rude. I saw you first and I already claimed you and you're mine."

A slight chuckle rumbled in my chest.

It was something watching Savannah meshing seamlessly with our crew. I wasn't sure it was entirely what I'd intended when I'd introduced her to Dakota, but how would I have assumed it would go down any other way?

Not when Dakota was as welcoming as they came. Paisley and Beth and Chloe, too. I'd known Savannah would be met with open arms.

A warning nudged at my consciousness.

Maybe that was the whole problem. I'd known it. Had pushed for it. Had *intended* it.

If those would have been honest *intentions*, then that would be all fine and good. But I was pretty sure there wasn't anything honest about whatever I was feeling when yet another fucker came up and asked Savannah to dance.

Jaron, the son of the local barber, the kid barely twenty-one. There'd been a slew of men asking her to dance through the night. Just like Cody had suggested. The woman was a flame that lured.

Captivated and entranced.

"There's an empty spot on that dance floor with our name on it," Jaron said.

I couldn't help but roll my eyes at his cheesy pickup line as I took a sip of my beer. I struggled to keep my cool and not tell him to run off to where he came from since the kid was nice and for the most part kept his nose clean.

That didn't mean I wasn't having a tough time not giving him a swift pop to the mouth with the nonsense that was rolling from it.

Of course, Savannah just giggled a sultry sound. "Is that so? I wasn't even aware that you knew my name."

"Formal names aren't necessary. In this case, it's just *you* and *me*."

I gagged a little. For God's sake. Was he fucking serious? Annoyance clamored through my senses as she let him lead her to the dance floor where a slow song was playing, and he wrapped her in his scrawny arms that I was pretty sure had no goddamn clue how to hold her.

Caleb and Paisley had hit the floor, too, along with Beth and Chloe who had gotten hauled off by a couple regulars. We hadn't seen Cody in an hour, which meant he had disappeared with some chick, clearly off searching for his *soul mate*.

The only other ones remaining at our table were Ryder and Dakota, and right then my cousin laughed that smug chord that promised he had me pegged. He slid his arm around Dakota's waist where she stood next to where he sat, tucking her in close.

"Down, boy." He taunted me with the same thing as he had back at the café earlier in the week.

"Don't even start with me, brother," I grumbled.

"Oh, I'm starting with you. How can I not when you're sitting there looking like you're getting the skin flayed from your bones?"

Dakota's nod was emphatic. "Or getting burned alive. Oh, oh, maybe his skin is peeling off while he's getting burned. That's it." The last was a bit of a slur, the number of those frilly drinks she'd tossed back catching up to her.

I grunted. "You two are so loved up that you have no clue what really exists."

"Ha. What exists?" Dakota shook her head like I was oblivious. "Do you think there's a single person in this bar who can't feel the attraction radiating from you two? It's so strong I'm getting second-hand lust."

"Don't worry, I can take care of that little problem for you, Cookie." Ryder burrowed his face under her chin, and she was giggling again.

I swore, these two were impossible to be around. If Dakota thought she was the one who was suffering from second-hand lust? It was palpable every time they were in the same room.

Combustible.

Always felt like I needed to duck and take cover before the two of them went *boom*.

Except for right then, this didn't feel indirect or derived. This sensation that I was going to bust. The way every cell in my body expanded and pressed and throbbed as I watched Savannah on the dance floor.

Gliding around, all that lush dark-blonde hair swishing around her shoulders. Body hugged in the perfect travesty of that dress. But what had me seeing red was Jaron's hand that was sitting precariously close to her ripe, pert ass.

My hand tightened so hard around my plastic cup that it cracked and beer trickled out.

"Fuck," I spat, and the legs of my stool skidded on the floor as I stood. I dropped the ruined cup into the nearly full pitcher since I'd been sipping on that same drink for the entire night.

Ryder cracked up. "If that wasn't ever a sign, I don't know what one is. You're on your feet. Now do something with them."

I glanced between him and the wasted cup and Savannah.

Fuck it.

He was right.

"Get it, brother," he shouted behind me.

I tossed him a finger over my shoulder as I strode for the dance floor, cutting through the few bodies it took to land me at Savannah's side.

She'd just stepped on Jaron's foot, setting them off beat, and I could feel the weight of her laughter ripple through the air as she tried to right herself.

I tried to hold in the chuckle. The way some twisted contentment expanded my chest when I looked at her fumbling around.

The woman a disorder.

That aqua gaze lit when she noticed me approach, that coy thing she loved to wear playing all over those plush, gorgeous lips.

Let's just say Jaron looked less excited to see me.

"Sorry, Jaron, but I'm gonna have to cut in. Give your father my respects."

"But I—"

I used my body to wall him out, not giving him a chance to respond.

Savannah giggled a sweet, disbelieving sound as I slid an arm around her waist and tucked her close, taking her other hand in mine so I could begin to lead her in an easy two-step. I did my best not to breathe out in relief with the feel of her in my arms, but maybe she could hear it anyway as she edged closer. She tipped her face up so she could meet my eyes. "I see the reformation was a complete failure."

"Pssh…I am only trying to keep you from embarrassing yourself. You stepped on that poor boy's toes so many times I doubt he's going to be able to walk tomorrow."

"And have you no care for your own feet?" Her tease was easy.

"Nah, these feet can handle it. You can stand on them if you need to. I'll take care of the rest."

A low, throaty laugh rippled from her lips. It tumbled through me like a crash of greed. "You like taking care of things yourself, don't you, Officer Patterson? Like being in control?"

Neither were actual questions. They were both a suggestion and an accusation.

My throat tightened a fraction. "I figure if I was in control of everything that went down around here, things would turn out a whole lot better for everyone."

"That's because you're genuinely a good person, aren't you?" Savannah's brow puckered in question, a twine of disbelief, like she couldn't fathom that someone might truly be.

My chest squeezed. Shame bottling thick, and the confession was rumbling out before I could stop it. "I used to be, but it seems I keep falling short."

Aqua eyes creased at the sides as she gazed up at me.

A swilling sea.

A storm.

Paradise.

"I don't believe there's a single bad bone inside of you."

Dangerous.

This woman was dangerous.

Fingers reaching in, searching around in my insides like she might have a tap into who I was. And I wasn't supposed to feel like this. My selfishness had proven that I didn't deserve it.

Instead of giving voice to it, instead of admitting she was wrong and needed to stay far, far away, I lifted my hand and twirled her around twice.

Savannah squealed at the sudden change, shiny locks of her hair whipping around before I pulled her back in to me, closer this time, her tits pressed low on my chest as I led her in a gentle sway that still felt as if the earth was rocking below us.

Guiding her in time. To this rhythm that felt both chaotic and slowed.

My hand splayed across the small of her back, and her heart ravaged against mine.

The scent of mango and cream invaded my senses.

A drug.

A dream.

"Oh, you're good at this, Officer Patterson," she murmured, words infiltrating my senses as her fingers crawled up over the thin fabric of my shirt.

I didn't know if I wanted to push her away or drag her closer.

Closer seemed key, and my mouth moved to her ear. "You just have to listen to the music. Get lost in the beat of it. Let it carry you, and you'll do just fine."

"I think I do just fine when you're carrying me."

A grunt of refusal. A flicker of need.

Angling back a step, I twirled her again, one direction then the other, and Savannah was laughing that sound that washed through me, so light and free, so heavy that I was terrified the resonance of it could form new chains.

Bonds that tethered.

I shouldn't.

I shouldn't.

But I was holding her closer still when I dragged her back against me, her body plastered to mine, one hand low on her back, fingertips drifting down over her ass, my other hand gliding up the back of her neck and into the fall of her lush hair.

Every inch burned where she was welded to me.

I'd had half a drink. But I was intoxicated. Drunk on this feeling. Clearly fucking hammered since I was making no prudent choices.

Savannah moaned as she melted deeper into my arms.

What the hell did I think I was doing?

Going askew, that was what. Tripping. Setting myself up for a brand-new sort of disaster.

Because this girl was chaos. A disorder in the peace I was trying to find for my family.

So, when Dirk Cummings tapped me on the shoulder and asked if I minded if he cut in, I decided it would be best if I let him rather than growling at him like some kind of rabid beast.

Instead of staking my claim the way I wanted to.

Only Savannah stumbled back, confusion furrowing her brow at the sudden disconnect. Disbelief filled her gaze as she squinted at me through the haze, trying to process through the jolting change in the atmosphere.

The break.

The divide.

This time, there was clearly no awe mingled in her expression.

It looked like...hurt.

Like rejection.

Dirk went to step in, only she held up a hand. "I think I've had enough dancing."

Without saying anything else, she turned her back and disappeared into the crowd, her head dropped between her shoulders as she fled.

Chapter Seventeen

Savannah

"**D**AMN IT," I MUTTERED AS I SQUEEZED MY EYES CLOSED. I leaned my back against the interior door of the restroom stall, trying to quiet the thunder of my heart and the rejection that barreled through my senses.

Heart and body and mind.

God, I was stupid enough to even let it touch my soul.

I knew better. I knew better.

I knew better than to get too close. To want. To even allow the tiniest flicker of hope to ignite.

Because I knew full well no one ever truly cared. Knew they would leave me in the end. Knew they would never stay.

And it had become glaringly clear that I had been foolish enough to let my mind wander with the possibility of this place.

With the possibility of these people.

I needed to remember the reason I was here. Hold onto it. It was the only thing that mattered, and I'd let myself get distracted. Carried away in the direction of someplace else. To a place that didn't exist. A place I kept trying to travel to. A road that each time I'd even attempted exploring it had left me with fewer pieces of my tattered, mangled heart.

There was so little left of it, and what remained, I needed to protect.

My eyes squeezed tighter, and I quietly chanted, "Remember, remember, remember."

It's only me and you, Jessica. We're the only ones we can rely on. You have to remember that. Hold it close to who you are, and know when you can trust no one else, you can trust me.

How was it me who had forgotten?

I couldn't do this. I couldn't allow these dangerous fantasies to well inside.

The problem was, I'd been all too happy to hold onto him. To keep him a little too close.

The scent of him overpowering.

The heat of him perfect and too much.

I'd allowed myself to get lost in the feel of his big, big body, and the ravaging of his heart had been the rhythm I'd chased. The beat hadn't had a thing to do with the music.

And ultimately, it was me who'd allowed it to hurt when he'd let someone else cut in. Clearly, I'd been far too comfortable in his arms.

Inhaling a shaky breath, I steeled myself and unlocked the stall, stoically ignoring everyone in the restroom as I went to a sink so I could splash cold water on my face.

Maybe it would be enough to knock me out of the stupor that was Ezra Patterson. I had to blame it on him being so stupid hot. That was it. I was just blinded by all his rippling, masculine glory.

I could handle him.

Block him out.

Do what I came here to do. Protect the piece of my heart that remained. Reclaim it. Set everything that had gone bad right.

Not get all cozy with Hot Cop who could so easily distract me.

Resolved, I grabbed a napkin from the bin and patted my face dry before I flung open the door.

So much for resolutions because they all went toppling out onto the floor in front of his feet when I found Ezra leaned against the opposite wall. A hazy mist surrounded him in the dim-lit hall, those big hands that I liked too much tucked into his jeans' pockets. One massive boot was kicked over the other.

No man had the right to look so delicious.

Steeling myself, I swallowed the unwanted reaction and lifted my chin. "I think you might be lost. Men's restrooms are that way."

I pointed to the opposite end of the hall.

"Not in need of the restroom."

"Well, I guess whatever you are in need of or whatever you want isn't any of my concern, is it?"

Damn it. It came out far too snippy. Like I was upset that he'd been okay with someone cutting in.

Which was just plain ridiculous.

"I need to get out of here," I mumbled, and I turned on my heel and started for the break in the hall that led out into the main part of the bar. Ezra had me by the elbow before I'd made it halfway there. He spun me around to face him. Something I didn't want to decipher curled through his expression.

"You're mad." He issued it almost like a question.

I rolled my eyes. "And what in the world would I be mad about?"

Uncertainty flashed through his features, his warm brown eyes almost black in the shadows that played. "That I let Dirk cut in."

Air huffed from my nose. "It was a dance, Officer Patterson. My feet were starting to hurt since you thought it fit to keep spinning me around like I'm a rag doll, so I was done. And now I'm going home."

I needed to get away from him. Clear him from my head and the feel of his hands from my body.

I went to walk again, and in a split second, he had me pinned to the wall.

What the hell?

"Those overbearing tendencies are spinning out of control." How I managed to get the words out around the lump in my throat, I didn't know. Not with the sudden throbbing in my core.

"And I already told you that as long as you're in my town, you are my concern. And it's Ezra to you, not Officer Patterson." The man freaking growled it, and not in his teddy bear sort of way.

"Right, because we're friends." It was a sarcastic scrape from my lungs. I might not know a whole lot about having *friends*, but I was pretty sure whatever was roiling between us out on that dance floor had been the farthest thing from that.

His expression was doing that uncertain thing again. Those eyes creasing in on the sides like he might not agree.

"Yeah. Because we're friends." He seemed reticent to say it.

I trembled with the exertion it took to keep the barricades erected between us.

"Then you're standing awful close to me for it to be considered *friendly*, Ezra." I drew his name out like it was some kind of evidence.

It was apparent we both were just telling ourselves lies.

Like either of us could be immune to this energy. The attraction that burned through the space, singeing all the spots I couldn't let it.

He eased back, slower than he should, and he roughed one of those hands through his hair. "I'm sorry."

I didn't dare ask him exactly what he was sorry for, worried that apology might go too far and too deep. Both of us were treading waters that could so easily consume us.

I ran my hands down the front of my dress like it could brush off the residual of the man. His heat and his scent and the decadent memory of his hands.

"It's fine," I told him. I glanced to the opening in the hall. "I just…" I looked down, touching my forehead like it might offer some clarity before I returned my attention to him. "I'm just going to go. I'm sure I'll see you around."

I wove out from the small opening he'd been gracious enough to leave between us and beelined back into the mayhem of the bar that had grown rowdy and decadent at the late hour.

I needed to get out of here.

Get some fresh air.

Get back *home* so I could faceplant into my bed and pretend like this night had never happened.

It was a mistake coming here, even though my spirit squeezed at the thought, my heart rejecting my mind's statement, remembering how good it had felt to be with Beth and Dakota and the whole crew.

Like I'd been a part of it.

Important.

Seen.

There I was, letting in foolish ideas again.

Ezra was suddenly there, and his heat flamed up my side. He had his hand near the small of my back again, hovering the way it'd been that first night, like he wasn't going to make the same mistake of touching me the way he had on the dance floor.

Too bad I could feel the outline of his hand tattooed on my backside, anyway.

"Let me take you home," he rumbled near my ear.

"That's not necessary. Ryder and Dakota are supposed to give me a ride."

Except they didn't look ready to leave at all when I broke through the crush and made it to our table. They were wrapped up in each other, kissing and whispering things to each other, oblivious to the rest of the world.

"Crap," I mumbled.

"Come on. I'm taking you home," Ezra said.

"That's not—"

"I said, I'll take you home." It came out hard that time, the man cutting me off as he dug into his wallet and tossed a bunch of twenties onto the table.

I scowled, about to argue, except the words faltered when Ryder broke away from the kiss to send Ezra a grin. It didn't deter Dakota. She simply kissed down the side of his neck.

"It looks like you made good use of your feet," Ryder told him, smirking between us.

I didn't have time to ask what that weird statement meant before Ezra grunted. "I'm taking Savannah home."

That snapped Dakota's head up. "Are you okay with that, Snuggle Muggle? We can head out and drop you off if you'd prefer."

Somewhere through the night I'd earned a new nickname. Even in my buzzed state, I was sure I should refuse the way it made me feel gooey inside.

The way I was falling.

Falling for these people.

"No, that's fine. I'm actually going to grab an Uber."

The last thing my rioting body could handle right then was having to be stuffed into Ryder's car with the two of them. I would likely implode.

"You absolutely are not. I said I was taking you home," Ezra cut in.

"And I said I didn't need your help."

"Fine. Take an Uber. I'll just follow to make sure you get there okay."

My mouth dropped open on a heave of disbelief. "And here I thought you were working on this whole overbearing bit?"

"Not tonight, sweetheart." His breath whisked down the side of my neck as he leaned in close to utter it.

Ryder chuckled like he was enjoying our volleying too much.

Ezra pointed at him. "Shut it."

Ryder laughed harder. "I didn't need to say a word. You said it all yourself."

What the hell were they even talking about?

Ezra ignored him and took me by the elbow. "Let's go."

I grabbed my little purse and slung the strap over my shoulder. "Fine. You can give me a ride home if it will make you happy."

"Very."

My belly tipped at the way he said it. There I went again. Slipping.

Dakota still had both her arms wrapped around Ryder's neck as she grinned in some kind of glee. "It was so fun hanging out with you, Savannah. I'm really glad you came. Call me tomorrow if you need to talk."

Her offer almost stopped me in my tracks. So kind. So thoughtful. But it was the innuendo hidden at the bottom of it that basically had me running. I wound back through the throng, unsurprised that

Ezra tracked me the whole way, the man a step behind but clearly still the one commanding the crowd.

As if the weight of his presence carved us a clear path. People kept glancing our way, most of them friendly, though there were unquestionably a few who were speculative of the town Sheriff.

Ezra stepped closer as we got to the door, and he reached out to open it, his other hand low on my back again.

Barely touching.

Burning me through.

Lurching at the contact, I gasped for the cool air that hit my flesh as we stepped out of the bar, thankful for the reprieve, the almost cold night nipping at my skin. It sent a scatter of chills racing far and wide, and Ezra only stepped closer to shield me from the dipping temperature.

"You should have a jacket."

"I told you that you don't need to worry about me, Ezra." The words barely hit the air around the clot of confusion that weighed a thousand pounds on my chest, and I increased my pace like I could outrun everything that he was.

In my haste, I stepped on a larger loose rock in the dirt lot, and my ankle twisted to the side.

Yelping, I nearly toppled all the way over as pain splintered up my left leg.

Then I was gasping for an entirely different reason when I was suddenly off my feet. Completely in Ezra's arms. It took me a couple of shocked, blissful seconds to come to my senses. "What the heck do you think you're doing? I can walk."

I flailed in his hold.

Ezra only tightened his massive arms. "We can't have you breaking a leg on my watch, now, can we?"

"Ezra. This is ridiculous. Put me down."

"Sure thing, Little Trespasser," he said in that casual, infuriating way. The lights on a truck that was as giant as the man flashed right beside us, and he opened the passenger-side door with one hand without losing his grip and effortlessly plopped me into the front seat. "There you go. As requested."

Frustration collided with the attraction.

He gave it no heed and instead reached in and buckled me, his enormous being leaning in to snap it into place. He grinned as if he'd shoved whatever had happened between us inside into a steel barrel. "Safety first."

He slammed my door shut, jogged around the front, and climbed into the driver's seat. The engine roared to life when he pushed the button.

"You are infuriatingly overbearing, Ezra Patterson." I was close to panting from the conflict that he cast.

He put it in drive, and I almost missed when he mumbled under his breath as he pulled out onto the street, "Apparently, I can't help myself when it comes to you."

Silence rasped around us as he began to travel up the street before he finally cut into the tension. "Where are you staying? Tell me it's not in your car." He attempted to inject some of that lightness into his tone.

It got squashed when I murmured, "Nothing has changed since the last time we talked. I'm still staying at the motel."

His jaw ticked, and his hand flexed on the steering wheel in some kind of restraint, the veins bulging out.

God, why did his hands have to be sexy, too?

He made the next left, weaving us through town. His disapproval was so thick I couldn't do anything but sit there and chew on my bottom lip. He didn't seem to like that very much, either, since he glowered every time he glanced over, his breaths heavy and shallow as he pulled into the motel parking lot.

"You can just drop me right here." I pointed at where Ryder and Dakota had picked me up.

"Not going to happen."

He parked in an open spot, and he put the truck into park but didn't turn it off. I went to climb out, but he reached out to stop me.

Flames leapt up my arm.

If he kept this up, I was going to be completely incinerated by the end of the night.

"I don't like you staying here. I want you to take up my offer and come stay at my guest house."

Conflict rolled through me, and I stared out the windshield at the crummy motel in front of us. "I keep telling you it's a bad idea."

"I don't care. It's a safer place than this."

"Well, I care. You just…pushed me away when we were dancing like you couldn't handle the sight of me, and now you're asking me to come live a hundred feet from you? I don't know what you want from me, Ezra."

Vulnerability seeped out with the admission.

Crap, I was a fool, admitting that it had hurt my feelings that he'd let that other guy cut in, but the alcohol had the words tumbling free before I had the chance to think through their circumstances.

Ezra roughed one of those big hands through his hair, and he was staring out the windshield when he rumbled, "Fuck, I'm sorry, Savannah. I didn't mean to hurt you. I just…freaked out because I don't know how to handle the way you make me feel. My life's…complicated."

I refused that stupid bolt of jealousy that screwed through my consciousness because I had no doubt he was talking about his wife. Mixed in with that unwarranted feeling was this fluttering of hope. The type of hope I'd spent most of my life rejecting since it hurt all the more when you realized there was no use in hoping when life was only going to slap you across the face. Drive another knife into your back.

"So is mine."

He exhaled a long breath before he swiveled to look at me. "I'm afraid you're just going to…disappear."

His expression pierced me. An arrow that staked through my heart.

Despair.

Loyalty.

His own flickering hope.

"One day I will."

Once I found my sister, I'd take her away. Protect her the way she deserved to be.

Ezra flinched like my words caused him physical pain, and I thought I could see a battle go down in those warm brown eyes. He finally seemed to settle on something.

"Everyone deserves a safe place, Savannah. Let me be yours, even if it's only for a little while." His voice was rough when he issued it.

A promise.

I guessed I was a fool because I believed it.

"Friends?" I asked him around the jagged rocks in my throat. Knowing the offer was a lie but knowing I'd tell myself a million of them if it meant I got to experience what this was like, even if it was only for a single moment.

Someone…caring.

Truly caring about me.

Wistfulness tugged at one side of his mouth. "Yeah, Savannah. Friends."

We stayed staring at each other for the longest time before he cleared his throat and shut off the engine. "Let's go get your stuff."

Before I could open my door, he was already there to help me out. I thought he'd offer me his hand, but instead, he hoisted me up around the waist before he settled me on my unsteady feet.

My heart took off in the opposite direction again.

"Thank you," he murmured.

"What are you thanking me for?"

"For giving me this little bit of peace."

God. This man. I didn't know how to process him.

His weight and his aura and the goodness that radiated from his flesh.

I figured it was best to ignore it as much as I could, and I crossed the lot and quickly climbed the stairs.

Ezra was right behind me.

His big body a shadow that covered me.

A fortress.

A shield.

I trembled and thought maybe I should just pull him into my motel room.

Let us burn out this fire that raged.

A terrible idea because I had a hunch it couldn't be doused so easily. A hunch that he wasn't close to being ready for a one-night stand. That his loss was too brittle and raw. And I had a hunch that a fling with him might break me.

I dug into my bag for my keycard as I hit the landing, and I moved to where my door was three down on the left.

Only I froze when I got to it. To the metal that had been smashed and dinged and pried in a bunch of different places with what looked to have been a hammer and crowbar. At the latch that was barely hanging on, keeping the intruder out.

My stomach bottomed out and my heart hit the floor. Just as my knees went weak.

In an instant, massive arms encircled me from behind, Ezra holding me up, his mouth pressed to my ear. "It's okay, Savannah. I'm right here. I've got you."

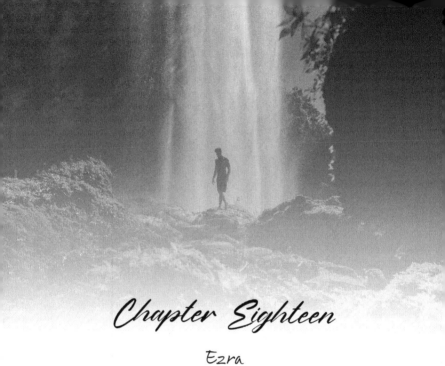

Chapter Eighteen

Ezra

MOTHERFUCKER.

Rage blistered through my being as I held Savannah up, though my attention was darting left and right, ensuring that there wasn't any present danger.

It was bad enough knowing she was still staying at a motel. That she didn't have a safe place to call her own.

But this?

My teeth grated through the disorder that pounded through my being, sickness pooling as I thought of what might have happened had she been dropped off here alone. The what ifs and what could have beens roiling through my mind in a spiral of abhorrence.

The hall was empty, not a soul around, and I kept Savannah close while I dug into my back pocket, pulled out my phone, and dialed the direct number to Pamela. She answered on the first ring.

"Ezra?" Worry laced her voice. It wasn't like she didn't get calls from me when I was off duty, but it was close to two in the morning.

"Hey, Pamela. We have an attempted break-in at the Riverside Motel. Room 227. Get Samson over here."

"Are there any injuries?"

"None that I'm aware of."

"Okay. Good. I'll get him over there right away. He's patrolling about five minutes away."

"Thank you."

"Always. Be safe out there." She ended the call while Savannah released ragged breaths that I could tell she was trying to master.

It didn't matter.

The woman was terrified.

I could feel it. The turmoil tearing through her body and shivering into her spirit. It might as well have been dumping it into mine. The fury that curdled and raced, gasoline in my bloodstream.

I attempted to keep my voice steady when I murmured again, "It's okay."

I carefully peeled her away and shifted her so I could take her by the shoulders. I did my damned best not to lose my cool as I looked down at the horror carved into every gorgeous line of her face.

"It's going to be okay," I promised, hands squeezing for a beat before I nudged her back toward the wall and pried the keycard from her fingers.

I scanned the lot below. Darkness rained from the sky, only cut by the dingy lights that lit the lot. But in it, there was no movement, just the slow sway of the trees that danced in the background.

"Stay right there." The words cut from my throat.

Savannah frowned but nodded.

Never before had I wished that I had my gun more than right then. My stomach was in knots, and I hated that we had no goddamn clue what we were up against.

Whatever it was, I was going to end it.

This wasn't happening.

Not in my town.

Not on my watch.

Not ever again.

Inching up to the door, I pressed my ear to the metal, unsure if the perpetrator had made it inside. The door was thick, but I was ninety-nine percent sure there was no movement on the other side.

Agitation blazed as I edged along the second-story landing, checking to see if any other doors had been tampered with. If some punks had come through looking for a way to get in to steal whatever valuables were inside.

The ball of razors in my gut grew when there wasn't a single one. When I was sure it was only Savannah's.

My spirit howled with the idea that someone might be targeting her.

I was almost back to where she stood when Samson's cruiser came blazing into the lot, and he skidded to a stop at the curb and hopped out, his hand on his holster as he scanned the area before he jogged upstairs.

"What's going on, boss?" he asked when he got within hearing distance.

"Someone tried to break into Savannah's room. Guessing they got interrupted and were scared away before they were able to get inside. The rest of this floor is clear. I'm going to check it out to make sure it's clear inside, then I want prints." The instruction came out like grit.

With the savagery that careened through my veins.

"On it."

I tapped the keycard to the sensor, an upgrade they'd put in about five years back since their previous locks had been easy to pick.

The lock gave, and I had to ram the door with my shoulder to get it open since it was disfigured, metal scraping as I knocked it in.

It swung open to the pitch-black room, and I flicked on the light and stepped inside. Samson was right behind me. My eyes scanned, searching for anything amiss, anything out of place.

It looked like a tornado had hit, but I had a notion that storm was the woman who crept in behind us. Clothes strewn on the floor and the bed, the vanity littered with creams and makeup.

"Is anything out of order from the way you left it?" I asked, trying to keep my cool when I wanted to rant and shout. Fuck me, how desperately I wanted to fly out the door and track down any bastard who might want to hurt her.

She was in trouble.

I knew it, and I wasn't sure I could handle the way it left me reeling.

Savannah's attention jumped everywhere. Categorizing. Her focus landed on the bag that sat open on the bed. "Everything looks the same to me."

Samson pulled back the drape and looked out the window to the back parking lot below before he returned his gaze to me. "No one has been in here who wasn't supposed to be, Ezra. I'm going to scope the rest of the area out, talk to the night manager to see if they noticed anything suspicious, get whatever footage I can. Guessing whoever it was is long gone."

"Thank you."

"No problem. You know I need something to keep me entertained on a Saturday night." He said it casually, joking the way he always did, though his brows kept denting as he studied me, trying to decipher what was going through my mind.

Where my assumptions lay.

If I had a clue who was responsible for this.

Or maybe he was just wondering what I was doing here.

With the woman I'd brought in for trespassing not quite a week before.

Part of me was wondering it myself. The other knew this was right where I belonged. That I couldn't stand the idea of her being in harm's way. That I would destroy anything that threatened it.

He must have felt the ripple of violence skate through the room because he angled his head. "I'm sure it was some asshole looking for anything of value to take. Break-ins like this have happened before. Probably someone passing through. We'll get those prints, though, make sure there isn't something we can dig out of this."

His encouragement did nothing to allay the viciousness that curled my hands into fists.

Samson headed for the door, though he paused to squeeze

Savannah's arm. "Sorry this happened to you in our town. It's rare. But at least you have the best in the business to weed out whoever is responsible."

The dude winked back my way before he ducked out the door.

While I stood there seething in the silence that suddenly filled the room. I could barely look at Savannah when I asked, "Do you have any idea who could have done this?"

Wringing her fingers, her gaze dipped to the floor. "No," she wheezed. "I have no idea. I don't know anyone in this town."

There was something about her answer that hit me all wrong. That feeling taking hold again. A promise that something was out of place when it came to her.

And I had that urge to cross the room and wrap her in my arms.

Tell her I would protect her.

But this time, I wanted to promise that I would never let her go.

So fucking dangerous, but I didn't know how to stop myself when it came to her.

"Let's get your stuff and get out of here." Because I didn't want her exposed for one more second.

<u>Journal Entry</u>

I saw her again today. It'd been three weeks and I'd given up hope that she would call. I nearly stumbled when I walked into the coffee shop, in a hurry the way I always was. I'd even told myself that I didn't have time to stop in, but there was something that compelled me.

I guess it was her.

She was sitting in the corner, almost completely hidden, drinking coffee and reading a book.

I ordered my coffee, and rather than ducking out when they called my name, I moved through the packed coffee shop, through the groups of people who were chatting and others who worked on their laptops, to the small, empty table next to hers.

I sat there sipping my coffee, allowing the tumult of her emotions to wash over me.

Being an empath was hard sometimes. Feeling what others felt.

Their excitement and their love.

Their despondency and their fear.

Hers was convoluted and confused, like she couldn't quite put her finger on what she was supposed to feel.

When she finally made eye contact with me, I quietly told her hi, keeping my voice secreted, hoping to convey that even though she didn't know me, she could trust me.

But it was distrust she was riddled with.

And God, she was beautiful. Striking. Her makeup and hair done to perfection. Dressed in posh clothing that was clearly expensive.

How easy it is for the exterior to shine while the inside decays.

Warily, she returned my hello, but not before she cast another furtive glance around the shop.

We might have been sitting at different tables with silence echoing between us, but I somehow knew that we shared our coffees.

That time.

That understanding.

Are you safe? I finally had asked her, gazing out on the patrons of the coffee shop while I asked it.

She'd chewed at her bottom lip and stared into her coffee as she'd whispered, I really don't know.

I told her I was a therapist and anything she told me was confidential. That I was here for her, whatever she needed.

I could see the doubt and suspicion carved into her features, all while I could feel a piece of her reaching out.

A tendril of her faltering spirit looking for something to hold onto.

A moment later, she got up and left, but not before she whispered, thank you, as she walked by.

Chapter Nineteen

Savannah

MY THROAT TIGHTENED AS I LOOKED AT THE MAN WHO'D begun to pick up my stuff that I'd left strewn about the room. Emotion knitted me in a blanket of a thousand different colors and a million different threads.

Weaving me together or rending me apart, I couldn't tell. There was no making sense of the uproar that crashed through my senses.

No making sense of his care or the brand-new fear that had struck inside me.

All of it blazed through the intensity that rioted in the room. Slamming the walls and radiating back, becoming more and more intense with each fiery pass. I still couldn't believe that I'd agreed to stay in his guest house, but that had been overshadowed by the fact that someone had tried to break into my motel room.

My chest constricted with the impulse to tell him. Lay it out. Why I was here. Let him hold my fears.

How could I fully trust him, though? With the very thing most important to me? This overbearing man who I couldn't discern where his intentions really lay.

A law enforcer, nonetheless.

The last time I'd taken the chance and asked for help haunted me. The face of the police officer who'd come to my house under the guise of taking a report.

Disgust rolled over me as I was hit with the memory of his cologne. A stagnant stench I didn't think I could ever rid from my consciousness. *"I think we could probably help each other out."*

While Ezra was gathering clothes from the floor, I moved to where I'd left my duffle on the bed.

My hand was shaking out of control as I quickly slid it to the bottom under the pretense of stuffing clothes into it. The clump of dread sitting like a tank on my chest lessened a fraction when my fingertips grazed the journal still hidden where I'd left it.

A wash of relief slammed me.

This had to have only been a fluke.

Random.

Coincidence.

I refused to believe what I'd told Ezra had been a lie. I really had no idea who it could have been or even why someone would come looking for me. Unfortunately, claiming it did nothing to eradicate the disturbance that rattled me to the bones.

I zipped the duffle up quickly before I turned to the man who had his arms full of my things.

"You don't need to do that, Ezra."

He grunted. "The faster we get your things together, the faster we can get out of here."

He stood and handed me the pile that consisted of a couple rejected dresses and tops, plus the lacy bottoms to my favorite nightie.

He definitely noticed, the way his masculine jaw clenched as he touched the fabric right before he passed it to me.

Awesome.

I struggled to find some lightness in the middle of this mess, and I quirked a daring brow at him as I protectively balled the pile against my chest. "I already warned you to stay out of my lacy, private things."

How the hell was I supposed to handle him looking at me like that? Not with those honey-kissed eyes that warmed in interest. Or maybe they were just darkening in greed.

"Didn't say anything, Savannah." His voice turned cocky, lowering a decibel, different than it'd been when he'd been searching for an intruder.

Like now that he knew I was safe his mind had turned to different things.

Things that were likely a whole lot more dangerous than whoever had messed with my door.

I went to grab my suitcase from where I'd stored it by the wall, only Ezra was right behind me, grabbing it before I could. "Let me help you."

"Okay, Officer Overbearing."

He smirked as he opened it on the end of the bed. "I thought we established that it is called chivalry."

"I think it's called you being a control freak."

He shocked me when he suddenly turned and dragged his calloused fingers down the side of my face.

A shiver tumbled.

This one made of greed.

His head barely tipped to the side. "It's called me taking care of the ones who mean something to me."

Ruined.

This man was going to ruin me.

I shook myself out of it and angled around him so I could toss the pile into the suitcase, then I went to the vanity where I shoved the rest of my things into my cosmetic bag and tossed that into it, too, before I closed and zipped it shut.

Ezra jostled me out of the way and picked up both the suitcase and duffle.

I all but rolled my eyes, and he chuckled as he headed for the door. "Think you need to get used to having friends, Savannah. Whole point of them is that they carry some of the load," he tossed at me from over his shoulder.

That was exactly what I was worried about.

He paused when he stepped back out onto the landing.

Tension rolled through him again, the man instantly on edge.

Unease skimmed through my senses, but I shoved it down, clinging to what Samson had said.

It was random.

It was random.

Ezra remained on guard the whole way down to the parking lot, even more so as he stood beside me like a sentry as we walked to my car that was parked three spots down from his truck.

A soldier ready to go to war.

He tossed my bags into my trunk, then came to stand in the doorway of the driver's side just as I sat.

My spirit shook. Remembering the first time I'd seen him. The way the sight of him had knocked me senseless. Apparently, I'd gone completely insane along the way. Because I couldn't believe I'd agreed to this. Staying so close to him. More worrisome was the sense of comfort it brought me.

"I'll follow you. Do you still have the address?"

I forced the brightest smile, like this was no big deal. "Yup."

Ezra caught it. "You don't have to be afraid, Savannah. I've got you."

Without saying anything else, he shut my door and strode over to his truck. The engine roared as he started it.

He was hidden behind the darkness of his windows, but it didn't matter. I could still feel the intensity of his vigilance.

I pulled out onto the street and drove in the direction of his house, his headlights glaring through my rearview mirror as he trailed close behind.

The entire ride I fought the sense of being afraid, knowing the whole time that fear didn't have a thing to do with the attempted break-in.

It had every-single-thing to do with the spark Ezra had lit inside me.

Ezra flicked on the light switch, and a warm, buttery glow illuminated the space. My breath hitched. I'd almost forgotten how gorgeous it was. My attention swept over the living room and the kitchen. I suppressed a gulp when my attention was drawn to the French doors and matching windows.

Each of the house's back doors faced the other, and the rambling yard between separated them.

The area was lit in a bare sheen of moonlight.

I stared out at the swing set and toys that littered the lawn and across to his back porch on the far side and his house that sat in stilled silence with the windows blackened.

"My kids are spending the night with my mother tonight." His voice was softly gruff as he issued the explanation, like he'd read every thought and reservation in my mind.

I could only give him a faint nod. I wasn't even sure how to respond. If I was his *friend*, I should know these things, shouldn't I? How many kids he had? Their ages? Their names?

Instead, I stood there fighting the urge to run, overwhelmed by the disorder of it all.

By the things I was never supposed to get too close to.

It wasn't that I didn't like kids. I just had no idea what to do with them. How to act around them or what to say. I'd done my best to care for Jessica growing up, to provide for her, to protect her, though I guessed I hadn't done such a bang-up job, had I?

A surge of grief threatened to clot off the flow of air. Ezra seemed to sense it, and he eased my direction where I continued to linger near the doorway. It was as far as I'd made it inside last time, and he backed me into the very same spot he had that day, his devastating presence sending me fumbling until I was pressed against the white wall.

My breaths were short and shallow as I stared up at the man who watched me like I was an enigma and not the other way around.

He lifted my hand and pressed the key he'd opened the door with into my palm, curled my fingers around it, and squeezed my hand tight.

"I want you to consider this your home, Savannah. Your safe place. For as long as you want it."

"And what if I get in the way?" This was his family we were talking about. His kids. And I was some stranger invading their space.

"You're not going to get in the way," he grumbled.

"Are you sure about that?" I didn't even know how I was breathing, and I nearly passed out when Ezra reached out and traced the pad of his thumb along the line of my jaw.

Pleasure danced in the path of his caress.

Crap. Crap. Crap.

Did I really think I wasn't going to get my heart smashed if I started letting him touch me like this?

Apparently, Hot Cop made me weak, and instead of being smart and pushing him away, I lifted my chin, giving him better access.

Warm brown eyes went impossibly soft. "Positive."

The faintest grin tweaked at the edge of his mouth. "Besides, I already told you I like keeping an eye on you, Little Trespasser."

A minute must have passed with the two of us standing there like that.

Frozen.

Held.

"Get some rest," he finally said. He moved for the door that led to the backyard. "I'll move my truck around to the front in the morning. Lock this door behind me and call if you need anything at all."

"I will." The promise came out too easily.

Opening the door, he stepped out, though he paused to look back over his shoulder. "Thank you, Savannah…for coming here."

"I think it's me who should be thanking you."

That time he did grin. "Let's just call it a mutually beneficial arrangement."

He slipped the rest of the way out and shut the door behind him, and I couldn't do anything but rush to it. My nose nearly touched the glass as I watched him cross the yard and climb his porch steps.

His big body moving through the shadows that played through the night.

And I knew I'd never been in as much trouble as I was right then.

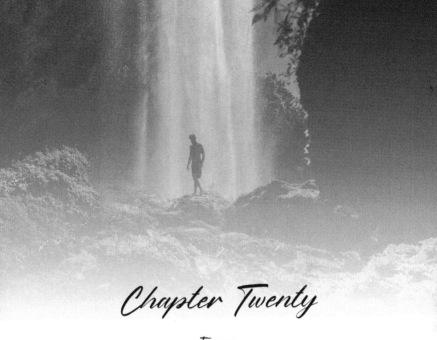

Chapter Twenty

Ezra

"HOW DO YOU SPELL HER NAME, DAD?" OLIVIA ASKED from where she was perched on one of the stools at the island. Her blonde hair was braided into two pleats on either side of her head, each of them a bit messy and uneven, but I was doing the best that I could.

She sat on her knees as she focused on the piece of paper in front of her, and an array of markers and colored pencils and stickers were dumped out around her.

There was no missing the excitement that brimmed from her tiny frame.

I hesitated for a beat, unsure if I'd made the worst decision last night by bringing Savannah back here.

My kids were finally healing.

Figuring out this new life.

It wasn't like when I'd bought this place and fixed it up I hadn't planned on renting the guest house out to generate some extra income.

But I knew I hadn't brought Savannah here to earn a few bucks.

I'd done it because it'd been the only thing I could do.

I'd spent the entire night tossing and turning, unable to sleep as I'd toiled through every scenario of what might have happened at the motel.

My rational mind kept trying to convince me that it was random—no big deal—an attempted robbery.

The problem was, my gut screamed that it was not.

First thing this morning, I'd given the kids the heads up that we had someone living in the guest house. Since then, Olivia hadn't stopped the rapid fire of questions that she'd pelted me with all day.

"Why are you asking?" I quirked a warning brow at my daughter as I planted my hands on the countertop across from her.

She shrugged. "A person needs to know these things, Dad. Don't you know knowledge is power?"

I held back a chuckle. My boys might have been my rough and tumbles, but this one was my handful. Far too smart for me to keep up with.

"What you need to *know* is she's what's called a tenant, which means she rents the guest house, which means you have to leave her alone and give her some privacy. Don't you go being nosy."

Olivia huffed, glancing up at me with those warm brown eyes that slayed me through. Love burned like a flame in my chest every time I looked at the child. "It's not nosy, Dad. It's called being *neighborly*." She drew it out like it was obvious. "Which you should be, too, and not be all grumpy at Savannah because that is really not nice."

Problem was, I wanted to get way too *neighborly* when it came to Savannah.

I gruffed at my daughter. "I'm not grumpy."

She glared at me the way her mom used to do. It never failed to pierce me straight in the heart. "Dad, I really hate to break it to you, but you are the grumpiest. Mindie's mom said you even gave her a ticket. That's rude."

Yeah, because Mindie's mom was going thirty over in a school zone then tried to show me her tits to get out of it.

"I'm a cop, Livvie. It's my job to give out tickets when people are breaking the law."

A flash of sadness filled her eyes, and her words dampened in the kind of caution I never wanted her to feel around me. "But you used to smile a whole lot more."

Air heaved from my lungs. I'd done my best to keep it from my kids.

The strain.

The rage.

This ugly thing that now writhed inside.

I should have known Olivia would be able to see right through it. She'd always had this thing about her. An insight. A deepness that went far beyond her years. Her care so big beneath the sweet sass she always wore.

I edged around the island so I could get to her, and I pressed my lips to the top of her head, my voice soaked in affection. "I'm sorry if I feel different to you, Livvie. If I act different. Losing your mom changed something inside me, but it didn't change how much I love you or care for you. You and your brothers are the happiness inside me, and I want you to know there are a billion smiles inside my heart when I think of you. When I look at you. They're just a little more hidden than they used to be."

She tipped her sweet face back to look at me. "As many as the stars?"

"As many as the stars."

A grin split her face. "I guess I'll let you off the hook then."

Amusement tumbled through me until I caught sight of what she was working on.

An invitation.

One for Savannah, which of course my smart as a whip daughter had figured out how to spell her name all on her own. She didn't need me when she got up to her antics.

To Savannah,
You're invited to dinner.

Olivia had made three check boxes below it.

Yes. ☐
Definitely. ☐
Absolutely. ☐

She'd drawn a bunch of hearts around the boxes and had decorated the letter with pink and green stickers. More hearts and flowers and little colorful strips of tape.

"Livvie." Another warning.

She tucked her shoulder to her ear, all wide-eyed and innocent. "If you're going to be neighborly, you have to see it through. We don't just use our words. We use our actions."

Well, shit, how many times had I told my kids that?

"You also need to ask first."

"But I already knew you'd say yes because you're not grumpy or anything." Another blink of those giant brown eyes.

The kid had mad skills, that was for sure.

Then her demeanor dipped into care. "We should really ask her, Dad. Maybe she's really lonely and needs a friend if she doesn't have anyone to live with."

Setting my palm on the side of her face, I ran the pad of my thumb over the apple of her cheek. "Alright, Livvie, you can ask her, but only to welcome her. From here on out, you need to give her space."

I'd do well to take my own instruction. Tuck it down deep.

God knew I'd had a hell of a time not peeking out the window when I'd heard her car roll up about thirty minutes ago. She'd been gone first thing this morning for her shift at the café, and I was sure the woman had to be dead on her feet.

It'd taken everything I had not to go and check. To make sure she was fine and whole and ensure there hadn't been any incidences at work.

Hell, I'd been half inclined to go into Time River Market & Café and set up shop so I could watch.

But I'd been told I needed to work on that whole overbearing thing. Too bad my daughter was unknowingly feeding into my weakness.

She hurried to fold the letter, even though she was all kinds of meticulous about it, careful to make sure the edges were straight before she sealed it with another sticker. When she was satisfied, she hopped off the stool and darted for the back door.

The boys' heads popped up where they were playing Legos on the floor. "Where you goin', Livvie?" Oliver asked her.

"I'm going to invite Ms. Savannah over for dinner because we really need to welcome her to the neighborhood."

"I want to invite her, too." Owen scrambled to his feet, and Oliver was right behind him, and in an instant, the three of them were scuffling around to make it out the door first.

Each of them trying to outdo the other, like doing it would win them a prize for hospitality.

Sighing, I followed because the last thing Savannah needed was to get bombarded by my yahoos without any supervision. They'd chase the poor girl off before she got the chance to settle. Before she could realize this was a safe place. Maybe freak her out the same way as I'd felt her do last night when she'd peered out into the yard.

Like she couldn't imagine belonging here.

Because she'd promised one day she was going to leave. Disappear. And I was the idiot who kept wanting to beg her to stay.

I traipsed across the backyard behind my kids at a slower pace than their all-out sprint, and a second later, all three of them were hammering at the glass door. I had almost made it to the small patio by the time Savanah was cautiously opening it and peeking out.

Her dark blonde hair was two shades deeper considering it was sopping wet, and it was only then I was realizing she was wrapped in a towel.

Droplets of water twisted and wound down her neck and shoulders before the rivulets disappeared into the cotton she had tucked tight under her arms.

A bolt of lust hit me like a lightning strike.

"Oh," I heard her say in surprise before those aqua eyes were popping up to find me where I shifted on my feet without one fucking clue about what I was supposed to say.

Thankfully, my daughter's manners were much more developed than mine since she stepped forward and reached out her hand. "Hello, Ms. Savannah. I'm Olivia, and this is my brother Oliver and this one is Owen, and we wanted to come and welcome you to your new house, and we would like to invite you to dinner because we knew the cupboards are bare in there and there isn't even one single thing to eat, plus I've been learning to cook just like my auntie Dakota, and I think you'd really like it. I think you already met my dad."

Livvie let go of the words without hardly taking a breath, then she was offering Savannah the folded invitation.

I tried to decipher what was on Savannah's face. The way her gaze kept darting between me and my kids, the panic I could feel welling around her while this emotion I couldn't quite put my finger on brimmed in her eyes.

"Oh." She whispered it that time.

Unsure.

Dumbfounded, maybe.

I finally found my voice. "It looks like we interrupted Savannah. Why don't we all head back to the house and let her finish getting dressed."

Fuck. I didn't want her to get dressed. I wanted to send my kids to my mother's and push through Savannah's door and peel her from the plush towel so I could get to what was underneath.

Revisit whatever was thrumming between us last night.

I felt like a piece of shit, standing there having those thoughts. But it'd been a long damn time since I'd felt anything close to this. Or maybe it was brand-new, this foreign pulse in my chest. The twist in my guts. The need that pummeled through my bloodstream.

One that urged me to step closer.

To pull her against me.

Fuck whatever destruction it would bring because I was pretty sure this woman might possess the power to destroy me.

Olivia scowled at me from over her shoulder. "She didn't even get to look at it, Dad."

"*Wook* at it." Owen beamed at Savannah.

Sorrow lanced through her features.

I saw it.

Felt it.

Through it, she smiled a smile I'd never seen her use before as she looked down at my tiny son. One that was both tender and filled with grief.

"You want me to look at it, huh?"

"Yes," he said through his adorable voice, the single word flooded with a giggle.

She shifted her attention to Olivia. "Did you make this for me?"

"Writing is my favorite thing, so it was no problem. And I think I spelled your name right. I'm going to be in the spelling bee next week."

My chest tightened. A fist of love and worry and the slew of reservations that were battering my mind. There was nothing about this that should feel monumental. Nothing about it that should be anything of significance other than being friendly.

Neighborly, the way Livvie said we should be.

But there was something seeded at the center of it that made me feel like I was at a precipice. A place I'd never ventured to before. A place I wasn't supposed to be.

Or maybe it was Savannah who was the culprit.

The trespasser.

Infiltrating the barriers and seeping through the cracks.

"Wow, this is awesome. I bet you're super smart, aren't you?"

"I'm super smart, too!" Oliver raised his hand as he popped up on his toes.

Savannah choked an affected sound before she somehow managed to loosen the stickers Olivia had used, and she unfolded the note.

"What do you think?" Olivia asked her.

Tenderness billowed across Savannah's face. "I think this is the nicest invitation I've ever received."

Olivia glowed.

I eased closer, and Savannah seemed to be flopping between apprehension and awe, the timid smile kissing the edge of her mouth wistful.

"All right, you kiddos, run on back into the house and give Ms. Savannah a chance to catch her breath. You blitzed her before she even had a chance to finish her shower."

"That's because I'm really, really good at football, right, Daddy?" Oliver asked as he hopped my way.

My chuckle was low.

Yeah, I was pretty sure Savannah had no idea what hit her.

"That's right, buddy. Now run along."

"Here, you can mark your answer on that and give it to my dad." Olivia handed her a pink marker she'd had tucked in her pocket.

"Thank you."

"You can thank me later *after* you eat dinner. It's going to be delicious." Forever the caretaker, Olivia took her brothers by the hands. "Come on so Ms. Savannah can finish getting ready," she said like she was the one who'd come up with the idea.

Amusement played soft in the breeze as the three of them skipped across the lawn, my chest filling with that pride and love that nearly ripped me apart every time I looked at them.

I didn't turn back until the kids had gone inside.

"I'm sorry about that," I said as I swiveled around. I fought the squeezing in my chest when I looked at her.

Afternoon light slanted over the striking angles of her face. Cheeks and nose razor-sharp, and her skin smooth as glass. But it was those eyes that could cut me.

Flay me right down to the middle.

"You don't have to apologize, Ezra. I already told you I didn't want to be the one to get in your way."

Stuffing my hands into my jeans' pockets, I tried not to itch. "I think you should be worried it might be the other way around. Now that they've met you, I doubt much they're going to leave you alone. Take that as your official warning."

Unease flashed through her expression, gone in a beat, her words flooding low. "I don't mind. They seem to come with this place."

"That they do."

"They're…sweet."

Something had shifted once the kids had gone inside. Tension strained between us like the grappling of fingers searching for a place to land. Need stretching like a band that had us tied.

Through it, I huffed my affection. "They're handfuls."

"Like their dad." A soft tease infiltrated the words, and she was looking at me like she was trying to sum up every inch.

My head cocked to the side, and I couldn't hold back the direction my mind went. "Is that what you think I am? A handful?"

I was pushing her. Allowing my tongue to get free. But I couldn't seem to help it when it came to Savannah Ward.

Nearly lost control when her attention dropped to the bulge in my jeans. "I'm imagining you're more than a handful, Ezra Patterson."

"Watch yourself, Little Trespasser, or you're going to find out." My voice turned gruff. Greed saturating my veins. Woman sending me from zero to a thousand degrees.

The air caught in her throat, and I moved without thought.

I dragged my index finger upward along the path of a rivulet that had streaked down her neck.

I could almost see the sparks elicited at my touch.

My mouth went to the shell of her ear. "What is it about you that has me losing my mind? What is it about you that has me wanting to cross every line?"

Jagged breaths jutted her chest, and those eyes flashed up to tangle with mine. "I don't think crossing any of those lines would be safe for either of us, Ezra."

"No. But it doesn't stop me from wanting it." My fingertips moved to her jaw, fluttering gently along the defined angle just as the pad of my thumb barely glanced over that plump bottom lip.

A minute passed between us, both of us just…standing there, held by the force of the energy that swirled and lapped.

Neither of us said anything.

Both refusing to step back.

Maybe we both were just fucking lonely, and it felt good to stand in someone else's space. Someone who might understand in some twisted form.

But it went deeper than that, and I wasn't fool enough not to realize it made her dangerous.

Dangerous to my resolve.

Dangerous to my sanity.

Dangerous to everything I was committed to.

My spirit thrashed as I thought back to my kids who were currently inside excited for this woman to join us, and a thread of unease twined through my senses. Logic making a resurgence.

I couldn't stand the idea of them getting used to having her around only for her to leave one day.

Or maybe I couldn't bear it for myself.

"You really don't have to come," I told her, stepping away before I gave into what I really wanted and carried her into the guest house, shut the door behind us, and peeled her from that towel.

Savannah waved the letter between us, her voice choppy though she tried to play it off like she wasn't affected. "According to this, I do."

"My daughter is a master at getting her way."

"And that's what she really wants? For me to come?" Then her gaze narrowed. "Or did you put her up to this?"

My chuckle was rough. "I told you I was working on my overbearing ways. That was all my daughter."

Savannah cleared her throat, and she turned and pressed the letter to the wall and checked a box before she handed it and the marker back to me. I glanced down at her response.

Absolutely. ☑

"What time?" she asked through the turbulence that still coated her voice.

I should call it off. Tell her to forget it. Instead, I was saying, "Six."

"What can I bring?"

And just like last night, I pushed a little farther, past that boundary I knew I should keep in place, and I told her, "Just bring you."

Chapter Twenty-One

Savannah

I'D VEERED OFF COURSE.

So astronomically off course that I was having a hard time righting myself. Hell, I was having a hard time getting my panties on with the way my legs were still shaking from Ezra being so close.

Blood pounding from the warning that had grunted from his mouth.

"Watch yourself, Little Trespasser, or you're going to find out."

Shivers streaked down my spine.

I was pretty sure the way his honey eyes had turned molten when he'd looked at me was going to hunt me down in my dreams.

The way he'd stared, making me feel like the towel I'd been wrapped in wasn't covering an inch.

The way he'd gobbled up the sight of me standing in the doorway dripping wet.

And then I'd done it. I'd looked. Sure he'd been hard and pressing at his jeans.

Need throbbed at my center. I might have been experiencing a boatload of reservations, but my body was certain of one thing—I really, really wanted to *find* out.

Crap. What had I been thinking, spitting out those inane words, pushing into the energy that wrapped us in chains?

Palpable temptation.

But that was the thing about temptation. Sometimes it was too powerful to resist.

I should have pretended I hadn't heard the clamor at the door, the thousand tiny fists that had banged at the glass. For a split second, I'd been terrified that something had been wrong, so I'd gone running from the bedroom and into the living room, only to grind to a stop when I saw the three eager, smiling faces standing at the door.

Ezra's children.

I'd almost turned right around and escaped back into the safety of the bedroom. But God, they were too adorable out there, bouncing on their toes as they'd peeked inside like they were getting ready to meet their new best friend.

And now I'd been wrangled into dinner.

It wasn't like I wasn't hungry. The café had been extra busy today, and I'd been flat out for all eight hours of my shift. With the little sleep that I'd gotten, I was exhausted…and I'd worked up a mean appetite. I'd planned on heading to the grocery store so I could stock my fridge before that plan had been obliterated by the cute invitation.

One only a monster could refuse.

So here I was, pulling on a cute sundress and a white jean jacket to keep out the cool.

My knees continued to knock as I stepped out the back door of the guest house.

The fall day had almost completely faded away, and it'd tossed pinks and oranges and the deepest blues across the horizon.

I remained on the tiny back porch for a second, trying to get my bearings, to clear my mind and body of the reckless desire that Ezra had hypnotized me with.

This was not a big thing. I was simply meeting my neighbors.

My cute, adorable neighbors who bore a striking resemblance to their father. Without all the gruff burliness, of course.

Resolved, I started across the yard. The soles of my sandals clapped against the wooden steps as I climbed onto their porch, and my heart rate spiked with each step that I took.

It seemed pointless to even try to steady my quivering breaths as I crossed to the French doors that were a match to the ones on the guest house.

Inhaling, I lifted my hand and lightly rapped my knuckles against it. A disorder of pounding feet and screeching voices carried before three little people came skidding up to the glass door, vying to get to the door handle first.

"Me!"

"No, me!"

"I already called it!"

It was Olivia who finally whipped it open, and the tiny twins were peeking out from behind her, each wearing enormous, gap-toothed grins.

I swore, they stole the air just looking at them.

They had the whitest hair I'd ever seen, natural curls soft around their cherub faces, lips so red that they looked like perfect little matching angels.

Olivia was just as adorable, and she had this sweet confidence about her that twisted my consciousness around her little fingers. I could almost remember being that way.

Almost.

Excited for life.

Exuding joy.

Anticipating every next step.

"Welcome to our home." The little girl swept an exaggerated hand over the room before she capped it off with a Plié. A giggle threatened when I saw that she'd changed into a baby blue tutu with a white sequin-emblazoned bodice, tights, and matching white ballet slippers.

I pressed my hand to my chest, dipping into a curtsy to play along. "Oh my, I did not know this was a formal event. I hope I am dressed okay?"

"You are most definitely dressed okay. You don't even have to worry a single bit. But I'm the hostess, so that means I have to make the very best impression, and this is my nicest dress, and I had it from my ballet recital. That's called recycling."

Amusement pulsed. "Well, you definitely made a good impression. You look very pretty."

The little girl beamed and swished her tutu.

I tried to ignore the heated gaze that burned into me from the side, but it was no use. I peeked that way, and I bit down on my bottom lip when I found Ezra staring back.

All six foot five of him. A giant beast standing in the middle of the kitchen, wearing jeans and a fresh white tee, muscles bulging out all over the place.

My stomach rumbled.

"It's a good thing we invited you over because it sounds like you're really very hungry." Olivia took my hand and led me toward the kitchen.

Right.

Hungry.

The problem was, Ezra looked crazy hungry, too.

Positively famished.

It was becoming clear really fast that I should have declined the invitation. Kept those barriers high and wide. Hell, I should have never agreed to come to stay at his guest house in the first place. Should have refused his offer of help to find a job.

Should have refused the offer to be his friend.

I should have just…refused.

Because standing there in his gorgeous house with his adorable children had me wanting to shout a thousand yeses.

And that's how girls like me got their hearts broken. They trusted when they shouldn't. Loved when it hadn't been earned. Hoped when there was nothing to hope for. And I refused to be that girl ever again.

I was here for a reason, to fight for the one thing that I believed in, for the one person who had ever truly loved me.

On top of that, Ezra…Ezra was broken. Wasn't he? He had to be.

Except he didn't look so broken right then. Not when he rippled strength and voracity and looked like he might tear right through the island to get to me.

"You didn't think we'd leave you to starve in the guest house all by yourself, did you?" Olivia's little voice broke me out of the stupor, and I looked down in time to catch her widening her brown eyes like it would have been committing the most atrocious crime.

Then I was getting pulled the other direction as the tiniest hand was suddenly tugging against my left. It was Owen, the one whose voice was softer, his demeanor quieter, a slur twisting his words in a way that yanked directly on my spirit. In his other hand he held a stack of thick, colorful blocks that he had built into some kind of tower. "*Wook* it what I made for you."

My chest squeezed. "Wow, this is the coolest thing I've ever seen."

Pride radiated from him as he handed it to me. "It's a castle in the *fowest* and only *pwincesses* can *wive* there. I fink you're a *pwincess*, right?"

His mispronunciation became more pronounced the faster he talked, excitement winding into the words.

The other little boy was suddenly in front of us, Oliver jumping up and down. "Hey, hey, Miss Savannah, do you want to sit by me? I got a special spot for you."

He raced for a round table that sat beneath a bay window off to the right of the kitchen and overlooked the front yard. He scrambled onto a chair and pounded at the spot on the table next to him. "Right here is for you."

Laughter choked up my throat, emotion squeezing. Overwhelming. Too tight.

"All right, all right, you yahoos, what did I tell you about ambushing her before she even had a chance to get inside? Give her some room." That grumbly voice infiltrated the air.

Providing oxygen.

Taking it.

I didn't know.

The only thing I was sure of was that my lungs rattled at my ribs when I looked at him where he'd gone to stir something in a pot on the stove, those eyes raking over me like a soft confession as he looked at me from over his shoulder.

No apology behind it.

This was who he was. What was important to him. I guessed it was that second that I recognized the full embodiment of his *meaning*. Who he would live and die and breathe for.

A blast of warmth rushed across the space, as if he sensed my understanding. As if he found some kind of satisfaction in knowing that I felt it.

The awareness that thrummed between us grew louder.

Profound.

Anticipation prickled through my senses.

Could I put my faith in him? Could I really trust him?

Before I had the chance to contemplate that slew of disastrous ideas, Ezra angled his head since his hands were occupied with preparing dinner. "Welcome to the madhouse. Make yourself at home."

There was a tease behind it, though I was sure he was giving me another chance to run.

My brows lifted in exaggerated playfulness. "I do, in fact, feel very welcomed."

"That's very good because it was our goal," Olivia peeped at my side.

"You definitely achieved it."

"We aim to please."

I laughed. I couldn't help it. Lost to the sweet mayhem that churned through this house.

Every rigid plane in Ezra's body softened when he looked at his daughter. "Would you do me a big favor, Livvie, and take your brothers to the bathroom and help them wash their hands?"

"On it, Dad."

She hopped into action, and Owen and Oliver didn't seem to mind when she herded them down the hallway.

It gave me the chance to take in my surroundings, and I couldn't help but look around Ezra's private space like I might be able to discover more of him.

To my right was the living area, and at the far end of it was the hall that the kids had disappeared down. On my left were the kitchen and the table, and there was another short hall between the kitchen and dining area with double doors that led to what I assumed was the master bedroom.

I would guess the house had likely been built in the seventies or eighties, but it'd been completely renovated. The color scheme was similar to that of the guest house, though all of it was done on a grander scale.

A stir of questions rambled through my mind.

How long had he lived here? Had he shared it with his wife? Did her presence still linger here, and I was somehow blind to feel it? Was I intruding on it, or in some way, was I truly welcomed?

Clearing my throat, I set the blocks down on the island next to the invitation Ezra must have set there. "What can I help with?"

"I didn't invite you over here for you to help with dinner," he grunted, casting me a quick glance.

Sunlight speared in through the window, lighting him up, his jaw covered in a day's worth of scruff.

My stomach tightened.

Damn him. The man looked so good in the evening, too.

Shucking off the reaction, I quirked him a wry brow. "You didn't invite me. Your daughter did."

A chuckle rumbled the planes of his thick, masculine throat, not that I noticed or anything. "I think the better description was you were coerced."

"She can coerce me any day."

I should have been more worried that it was the truth.

It was warmer inside the house than out, and I peeled myself out of my jacket and draped it on the back of a stool.

Ezra watched me as I did, that warm gaze flaming as I edged into the kitchen and came to stand next to him. He was watching over a skillet of chicken breasts that swam in a bubbly, cheesy sauce. Broccoli was being steamed in a smaller pot behind it.

"It smells good."

He huffed. "Hardly. I know where my skills lie. I'm plenty good at other things, so there's no need to take credit in the areas I'm not."

Why'd that have to come out sounding like seduction? And there I was, playing right into it like this man held me in a fist.

"And what kind of skills might those be?"

He angled down so his mouth dipped close to my ear. "Oh, I don't know, things like…" He dragged it out until he was murmuring, "Sniffing out little trespassers where they hide."

I smacked at his biceps, not expecting the lightness that rushed through my veins at his tease. "Rude."

Ezra laughed. Laughed so low and deep that it seeped beneath my flesh and flooded my bloodstream. The mood shifted and slowed, and that energy pulsed, lulling us into that dream.

We drifted closer.

Drawn.

Compelled.

I jolted back with the clatter of footsteps that came bounding back down the hall, a riot of little voices breaking into the daze.

"Is it weady? I am the stawvingest," Owen said. He raced in to pop up on his toes next to his father so he could see to the top of the stove.

"Careful, it's hot," Ezra warned him. "Go on and get to the table. It's almost ready."

Owen ran to the chair that was closest to the window, and Oliver took my hand. "You gotta sit by me. I already called it, remember?"

"She's not a toy that you take possession of, Oliver." Ezra raised his brows as he went to a high cabinet and pulled out a stack of plates.

"Wrong, Dad, she's mine."

Something that came a little too close to resembling affection skittered through my heart. This feeling like I could slide right in threatening to sink in.

Oliver tugged at my hand and led me to the same spot he'd

claimed before, though this time, he pulled out the chair and patted the seat. "Sit right there."

Emotion squeezed my chest. "The perfect gentleman," I told him.

Maybe Ezra really was right and chivalry wasn't dead.

Olivia took the spot between Owen and Oliver, and she glanced at me with wide eyes. "Gentleman? Pssh. My brothers are nothing but pains in the neck, Miss Savannah. You gotta get used to it if you're gonna be hanging around here."

"I'll give you a massage." Oliver was on his knees, his elbows on the table as he grinned my way.

A tiny giggle made it past my restraints. God, these kids were adorable.

A low, smooth chuckle rang from Ezra and had me shifting in my chair. Honey-kissed eyes played with mischief. "You're never going to step foot in this house again, are you?"

He'd started to place the chicken breasts on the plates.

"Well, it really depends on how good this meal turns out to be," I said, ribbing him.

"We is doomed," Owen said, perfectly serious.

I pressed my hand to my mouth, trying not to sit there and laugh, but I wasn't sure how not to lose it.

How not to get swept up in this sweet, sweet chaos.

I knew better, I did, but for that moment, I didn't care. I gave in, my smile wide as I glanced back at Ezra who was shaking his head with a grin, no anger in his voice when he said, "Apparently my mother has been talking behind my back about my cooking skills. But we already talked about those skills, didn't we, Savannah?"

The man had the audacity to wink as he strode over carrying two plates, his boots thudding heavily on the floor. My insides went haywire. Every synapse misfiring.

He set a plate in front of each of the boys.

"Thank you, Daddy," they both said in unison, though Owen's came out in his precious slur.

Ezra took turns running a hand over both of their heads, dipping down to kiss each of them on the forehead and whispering, "You're welcome."

My chest squeezed. Squeezed so fiercely that I could hardly breathe, could barely say thank you myself when he returned with plates for both me and Olivia.

He pressed his lips to the crown of Olivia's head, so tender, overflowing with care.

I thought I might have choked out loud. Because I'd known somewhere in my mind that there had to be families that were like this, but it'd been difficult to believe.

It was easier to accept that there was little goodness. Little care. That selfishness went directly with survival. Self-preservation the only way.

Only I knew I had it all wrong when Ezra returned with his own plate, the way his attention caressed each child's face, ensuring they were safe and cared for. That they knew they were loved.

Then I straight up whimpered when he reached under the table and set his hand on my knee. He ran his thumb over the sensitive skin, those eyes on me as he murmured, "I'm glad you're here."

"Me, too," Olivia piped in.

"Me, three," Oliver giggled.

"Me *fow*." Owen lifted four fingers, all his little gaped teeth exposed in his grin.

Yeah, me freaking five, the fool who didn't want to be anywhere else.

Chapter Twenty-Two

Ezra

DANGEROUS.

I'd known it all along. Since the second I'd met her. But I'd never felt it so sure than right then as I gazed down from where I stood at the doorway of my sons' room to where she was on the floor.

Her expression was light.

Her eyes brimming.

The boys' beds were these rectangle boxes that rested on the floor and were painted like fire trucks, their bedding red and blue.

Only she was the siren where she sat in the middle of them.

A five-alarm fire raging in the room.

Legs curled beneath her as she sang another silly song to my kids, using her hands to orchestrate. "The itsy-bitsy spider climbed up the waterspout. Down came the rain and washed the spider out."

Her hands swooshed down, and Oliver toppled over onto his mattress like he was the one who was getting washed away.

Like it wasn't me who was getting caught in a flash flood.

Oliver cracked up as he flailed on his back, kicking his chubby legs into the air. "I got washed out!"

Owen bounced on his knees on his own bed, the child wearing a light-blue tee and his sleep undies since he still had accidents, his little hands following along as he sang at the top of his lungs, "Out came *dee* sun and *dwied* up *aww* the *wain...*"

"And the itsy-bitsy spider climbed up the spout again." Savannah used her fingertips to crawl up Owen's belly, and he grabbed her hand in both of his, cackling toward the ceiling. "You get me, Miss S'vannah."

No question, the two of them were so enraptured by the woman's attention they were going to get hooked.

Addicted.

Or maybe I was just worried that was going to be me. That I liked her here too much. Overcome by the sense that it was right, and I wasn't committing a thousand wrongs by inviting her into our home, barring the semantics that Olivia had been the one to do it.

Because I was the one who'd done this. I'd invited her into our lives, and I knew, without a doubt, that I couldn't stomach the idea of her walking.

A part of me recoiled, and my mind tumbled to find logic.

Reason.

Searching around inside of myself to try to put a finger on what this was.

At the heart of it?

I needed to know that she was safe.

Whole.

That we made sure whoever the fuck had tried to break into her motel room last night wasn't a threat. But it went deeper than that. I knew it. This ache to hold her close, an urge I didn't think I'd ever feel again.

As if she felt me staring, she looked my way where I hovered at the doorway. The smile on her face was so real that it nearly knocked me on my ass. I'd seen a lot of faulty smiles out of this woman. Feigned indifference. Brittle joy. But this wasn't one of them.

I didn't miss the way it tipped at the side, either, dipping in her own misgivings as our gazes caught and held.

A moment of vulnerability.

A moment of possibility.

A moment of us.

We were snapped out of it when Owen jumped onto her back, and he curled his little arms around her neck. "I a *kowawa* bear, Miss S'vannah!"

Laughing, Savannah reached around and hauled him to her front, and she tickled his side before she carefully tossed him back onto his bed. "You are a little bear," she said as she poked his belly, making my son squeal.

"A little bear who is going to sleep," I rumbled as I stepped into the room.

I figured it was time for me to come to her aid, to offer her some mercy since she'd gotten wrangled into story-time by Olivia who I'd finally forced to go wash her face and brush her teeth after the three of them had had Savannah ensconced in here for the last thirty-five minutes.

Oliver and Owen had demanded one more song like they were at a concert begging for an encore from their favorite band.

I understood the affliction, but it was time to put Savannah out of her misery.

"Oh, man, do we have to?" Oliver stuck out his bottom lip in a pout.

"Yes, you do. You have school in the morning."

"But it's only preschool that my brothers go to, so it's not even that important so I think it's okay if we stay up past our bedtime since I'm already almost seven." Olivia issued it from where she'd come up behind me.

I sent her a pointed look. "Not gonna happen, Livvie. You might as well drop it."

"Dang it."

I could feel Savannah trying to hide her smile. Could feel the waft of affection. And God, I liked it. I liked it when she carefully climbed to her feet, a bit awkwardly since she was trying to keep the skirt of her dress down. I liked it when she went to Oliver and pressed a kiss to his forehead then turned to do the same to Owen.

"Goodnight, little men," she murmured.

Then she wound around me to stop in front of Olivia who'd changed into her *Moana* pajamas. Savannah tipped up my daughter's chin. "Thank you for making this the best night I've had in a very long time."

Olivia beamed up at her. "It was very much my pleasure."

Tenderness weaved through Savannah's expression, and she cast me a slow glance before she stepped out, assuredly giving us privacy and not wanting to get in the way like she'd been worried she would do.

But she wasn't.

The only thing that caused that alarm to start going off again was the thought of her presence going missing. I was distinctly aware of the vacancy not feeling quite so stark when she was here.

But I didn't bring her here to fill in a gap for my kids.

I tucked the boys in, then followed Olivia to her room where I did the same. "Sleep tight, Livvie-Loo."

She smiled up at me as I pulled her covers up to her chin. "I had a really good day, Daddy."

She only called me Daddy when no one else was around to think her a little girl. It never failed to grip me by the chest. "I had a really good day, too," I said as I wisped a kiss over her forehead.

"We should invite Miss Savannah to eat every day."

I ran my thumb along her cheek, fighting the response that wanted to pop out. One that wholeheartedly agreed. Instead, I prodded her with the arch of my brow. "And what did I say earlier?"

"Yeah, yeah, yeah, we have to give Miss Savannah her privacy, but that sounds like a big mistake if she doesn't even want it, and I think she really likes it here and had the best time ever. Just ask her."

My chuckle was slow. "It was a very nice night, but we have to give her some space to live her own life."

Olivia curled her button nose. "Well, I like her in my life."

She said it so simply. Like it was easy. Like there was nothing else to take into consideration but that one single fact. And I wished it were that way.

Easy.

Wished it wasn't complicated.

Wished I didn't have this shame and regret living so deep inside me.

Wished Savannah didn't plan on leaving.

Because the last thing I could do was allow my kids to grow attached to her and then have them lose her, too.

I had them to think about, even though I couldn't stop from thinking about Savannah, either.

I gathered up Olivia's hand and whispered against her knuckles, "Do you know how much I love you, Olivia?"

"As much as all the stars in the sky."

"That's right. As much as all the stars in the sky. Never, ever forget that."

"Never, Daddy."

"Good," I told her. Leaning down, I swept a kiss to her temple before I walked to her door and flicked out the light. "Sleep tight."

I pulled her door shut, though I left it open an inch so the light from the hall would filter into her room.

I assumed that Savannah would have slipped out the back door and escaped to the guest house, so I ground to a halt at the end of the hall when I found her in the kitchen, at the sink loading dishes into the dishwasher.

My heart skipped a wayward beat.

My approach was slow as I crossed the living room and eased toward the kitchen, voice rough when I muttered, "What do you think you're doing?"

Locks of blonde weaved with every shade of brown tumbled down her back, her delicate shoulders bared by the straps of her dress. Every thought stuttered when she shifted enough to peer back at me. The woman all sharp lines and pouty lips.

Playfulness tweaked at the edge of her mouth. "What does it look like, Officer Patterson? Dishes. And here I thought you were supposed to be an exceptional investigator."

A grunt rumbled out of me, and I inched forward a step, bringing me to within two feet of her. "I think the question is *why* you're doing the dishes."

Her teasing grin dropped, and her demeanor dove into something sincere. "Because you and your kids took care of me all night, and I thought it would only be right to return the favor."

"It's not a favor when it's a gift. That's just what friends do."

Friends.

What bullshit.

Nothing about this was *friendly.*

It felt like hovering at a precipice. Like coming up on an intersection and taking a turn that might change everything you knew about your life. Like staring over a gorgeous valley and finally knowing where you belonged.

Aqua eyes swam, searching me where I towered behind her, so close that I could feel the energy crackle between us. One step closer and I was afraid it would pop. "Maybe I want to give one of those, too," she whispered. "A gift."

"I just don't want you to ever feel like you have to pay me back."

Confusion bound her as she rinsed the last plate and placed it into the dishwasher. Slowly, she turned, drying off her hands with a dishtowel before she set it aside, her gaze full of questions and intent. "Why, Ezra? Why? You don't know me or owe me or care for me—"

"Bullshit." I moved so fast that I didn't even realize I was there. Her back pressed to the counter and my hand in her hair. My fingers kneaded into the base of her skull.

"Bullshit." I whispered it that time, so quiet, but it still boomed between us.

Bullshit to all of it.

"I might not know all the details about you, Savannah, but there's something about you that I recognize here." I gathered up her hand and pressed her palm flat to the ravaging at my chest. "Something I feel. Something I know. And the problem is, I care too fucking much."

Her chin quivered as she stared up at me, and my hand slipped down to grasp her by the back of the neck. Her lips parted and the air trembled around us.

Her tongue stroked across those plump, tempting lips, and my gaze dipped to capture the action before it flicked back up to dive into the endless sea of those aqua eyes.

"Tell me not to kiss you." The words were a gnarl of desperation. The last thread of my restraint.

Her fingers curled into my shirt. Energy thrashed in the inch of space that separated us.

A second.

An eternity.

Before she whispered, "I don't want to."

And that thread snapped.

Chapter Twenty-Three

Savannah

THE HAND AT THE BACK OF MY NECK TIGHTENED AS EZRA swooped down and took my mouth like it'd been his all along. His to possess.

His to command.

Fire zinged down my spine as his lips moved over mine.

Greedily.

Eagerly.

But somehow, the kiss was still soft and sure, and those flames leapt higher when he drew my top lip between both of his, nibbling, tasting, before he stroked his tongue across the bottom.

A needy moan parted my mouth, and my hand fisted tighter in his shirt in a clear invitation.

He took it, and he swept his tongue against mine, deepening the kiss. I could feel the man diving into me.

Feeling me.

Exploring me.

Stroke after decadent stroke, as if he would give anything to seep inside. Know me, inside and out.

One hand cupped my jaw, and the other fisted in my hair as he controlled the kiss.

He tasted of the fresh fruit we'd had for dessert.

Strawberries.

Oranges.

Citrus and pine.

A deep sea breeze. The woods. All man.

Everything I never knew I wanted. Everything I'd craved but hadn't understood what it meant.

On a groan, he pushed in closer, and he pinned me to the counter, his massive body hot and hard against mine.

"Savannah," he rasped through a breath. He took my face in both hands, and he angled back to look into my eyes. It was only a fraction of a second, but in it, time slowed.

Stilled as our spirits cried with possibility. With hope. Like he could see all the way down inside me to every wound that had ever been inflicted.

The next pass of his tongue was a claim.

Dominant.

Desire tumbled, and it spread through every cell and ignited a pool of need deep in the pit of my stomach.

It throbbed, and my thighs trembled as I ached for more of his touch.

"Ezra." I whimpered it at his mouth, the sound lost to the force of the kiss.

Consumed in it.

But I knew that Ezra still felt the urgency that sped through my body. The man was in tune with me the way I didn't think anyone else had ever been. One hand slipped down the column of my neck, making me shake as he ran it down my chest.

He palmed my breast, and the pad of his thumb flicked over the pebbled, sensitive nub of my nipple, before he continued his exploration, and his hand slid all the way around to my bottom.

He yanked me against his hard body.

Every line of him was rigid. Bulging. Brimming with strength and barely held desperation.

His cock pressed against the ache in my belly, making it glow, and my head felt dizzy with the onslaught of lust, just as my knees felt weak with the onslaught of emotion.

This sense that maybe…maybe…

Ezra held me up as he kissed me deeper. With a madness that squandered all thought.

All reason.

Because right then it was just us.

"Little Trespasser, what are you doing to me?" He pulled back an inch as he rasped it.

His mouth parted.

Our lips barely brushing as we panted.

Our bodies swaying in need.

Urging and begging.

His eyes were molten honey as he stared down. Watching me, he took me by the outside of my thigh and hooked my leg over his hip, and he rubbed himself over my drenched core.

Sparks flew, and my fingers sank into his shoulders.

"Exactly what you're doing to me," I whimpered.

"If you could only imagine all the things I want to do to you. How I would take you. The way I would mark myself so deep inside you that you could never erase me." His words were grit.

I had to be delirious. Fevered as I struggled to reach between us to get to the button of his fly.

Because I wanted it.

I wanted him to mark me.

Claim me.

I wanted to know what it would feel like to have this man sliding into me more than anything I'd ever wanted in my life.

It took the little voice echoing from the room down the hall to stop me in my tracks. "Daddy? I need you *weawwy* bad!"

Ezra choked, and the severity that had cocooned us burst.

His forehead dropped to mine, and he wrapped his hand around my wrist.

To stop me or maybe to stop himself, I didn't know, but he held me there for the longest time as we wheezed and tried to orient ourselves.

To come back down to Earth when we'd been soaring someplace outside reality.

"Shit," he grumbled as he edged back another inch. "I'm sorry."

My head shook as I pressed my lips flat like it could put out the fire, but I should have known better than to think it held a chance at dousing the flames that raged inside.

"It's probably for the best."

It was true. It was for the best. That didn't mean it didn't make my heart ache. It didn't mean I didn't want to reach for him and pull him back to me.

"Daddy?" Owen called again.

"I need to go check on him."

"I'll let myself out."

Ezra peeled himself away.

Reluctantly.

Painfully, even.

I couldn't move as I watched him lumber across the living room. I felt speared to the spot when the man glanced back at me right before he disappeared down the hall.

Lust carved into every line of his masculine face.

But there was something more beneath it. Something bigger. Something deeper.

And I let myself dream for one second. Of what it might be like to belong. For someone to care about me as much as I cared about them.

Then I gathered my invitation, blocks, and jacket, and I ran out.

Chapter Twenty-Four

Ezra

Three Years Ago

GLASS SHATTERED FROM THE OTHER SIDE OF THE HOUSE. Ezra had just taken a sip of coffee, and the steaming liquid splashed over the rim of his mug and onto his hand.

"Fuck," he spat beneath his breath, and the porcelain cup clanked as he basically dropped it to the counter and took off down the hall in the direction where the crash had come from, shaking off the sting of his hand as he went.

"Brianna?" he called as he hit their room. He moved toward the small bathroom.

He stalled when he got to the door, and a rustle of anxious nerves slipped beneath the surface of his skin when he heard the sobs echoing from the other side.

Carefully, he nudged open the door. His heart accelerated the way it always did, never knowing what form of tumult he was going to meet. His pounding heart slicked over in ice for a beat when he saw the mirror had been shattered, splintering out from the single impact point in the middle. The decorative vase that had been slammed against it was in a million splintered pieces on the counter and sink.

And his wife…his wife was on the floor with her back pressed to the wall, tearing at the long tresses of her light-blonde hair that she'd just spent the last half hour ironing into curls.

"Shit, Brianna, what the hell happened?"

"I can't take it any longer! I can't take it!"

"What can't you take?" He begged it.

"All of it. Everyone's after me. They're going to get me. They're going to find me."

Terror curdled his blood, seizing everything. This was the part that frightened him most.

The delusions.

What had sent him seeking help, getting her scheduled with a psychiatrist and a therapist. Only he found out she hadn't been going. Her therapist had been concerned and pulled him aside and talked to him. He'd told Ezra that Brianna had missed every appointment for the last two months and she hadn't gotten her meds refilled. He doubted it was protocol, but Ezra had known him his entire life, so there was a trust there. This town was family, each doing their best to support each other.

It made him feel like he was failing because he didn't know how to support Brianna, anymore. Not when she kept making these decisions that hurt her. That hurt him. That hurt their family.

Still, he reached for her like he might be able to be a buoy, a safe place in the storm, only she wailed and writhed out from the wall like a demon had rolled through her body.

"Don't touch me. Don't fucking touch me!" The screams battered the walls, but not even close to how violently they battered his soul.

His worry for her bashed against the frustration. This constant back and forth that he'd been on his knees praying would change.

Thank God his mother had already swung by to pick up the kids to look after them while he and Brianna were at work. He hated it when they were exposed to it. Even though they were too young to understand what was happening, there was no doubt they could feel it.

The way Olivia would go quiet and the boys would cry.

Carefully, he bent at the knees, getting to her level. "Brianna, I can't help you if you don't tell me what's going on. Talk to me. Please."

Sobs spewed from her as she wrapped her arms around her knees and pulled them to her chest. "I don't need your help."

"Brianna, please."

He reached for her again.

Frantic, she smacked his hand away and scrambled back, panting where she was pressed to the tub. "I told you not to touch me," she whimpered, a blanket of tears covering her face.

Barbed wire balled in his throat. "Are you...afraid of me? I would never hurt you."

Scorn filled her cry. "Don't you get it? I don't want you. I don't want you. And I don't need your help. I'm fine!"

Right.

She was fine. She was always *fine*.

Pushing to standing, he swiveled away from her and faced the opposite wall as he scrubbed his palms over his face. He had no goddamn clue how to handle this. How to help her when she kept refusing it. No idea what to do when he felt the threads of their family being ripped apart.

He remained facing away when he started to speak, though his attention dropped to his boots. "I don't know what is going on with you, Brianna, but it's breaking me, and I'm pretty sure whatever it is has already destroyed you. I want to be there for you. Help you. But you have to know this can't keep going on under this roof. Our kids deserve a safe place to grow up, and it's our duty to provide it. You have to make the choice."

He stepped out of the bathroom to her mumbling, "I don't want you. I don't want you. I don't want you."

And he was pretty sure his heart resembled that fucking mirror.

Chapter Twenty-Five

Ezra

MY EYES FLEW OPEN TO THE DIMNESS OF MY ROOM WHILE the blood beat wild in my veins.

Careening.

Crashing.

A thunder of regret and mistakes.

I sat up on the side of the bed and scrubbed both palms over my face.

Shame flayed me into a thousand pieces because while Brianna had *promised*, I'd made a thousand promises, too.

I'd promised to love and keep her.

To protect her and defend her.

To stand with her through thick and thin.

But I hadn't done any of those things.

I didn't know if they'd been pared down by her actions or if they'd been faulty from the beginning.

I'd loved her.

I had.

But looking back over the years, I realized it'd been shallow.

Shaky from the beginning.

Warning signs staked at every turn.

I'd never fully trusted her. Had never let myself fully fall. In the back of my mind, or maybe right smack in the middle of my soul, I'd known she was betraying me.

I eased from the bed and moved through the stillness to the bedroom window. I pushed the drape aside and stared out across at the guest house on the other side of the yard.

A dim light glowed from Savannah's bedroom window.

My stomach clutched in a fist of greed, in the memory of the kiss, in the memory of her touch. It was amplified by the way I'd felt during the dinner we'd shared. With the way she interacted with my kids.

With the way she made me feel.

Yeah, I knew she was keeping secrets herself. But they felt different than the ones Brianna had been keeping.

And maybe the most shameful part of all was I didn't think anything I'd ever felt for Brianna came close to what I was feeling for the woman across my yard.

Chapter Twenty-Six

Ezra

"YOU DIDN'T FIND ANYTHING AT ALL?" I PACED MY OFFICE, looking back at where Samson was slung back in the chair on the opposite side of my desk, his long legs stretched casually out in front of him, though there was no missing the discontent set on his face.

"Not one goddamn thing. If there wasn't the damage to the door, there would be absolutely no evidence that anyone had even been there. No prints. No reports of strange sounds. Nothing on the security footage. And not one person noticed anything strange."

Irritation buzzed beneath my flesh, and I roughed my fingers through my hair, hoping it might give me some clarity. Insight. Any semblance of calm because it was my fucking job to be collected.

To look at each case with discernment.

With logic.

Most of all, I wasn't supposed to let my emotions get in the way.

Too fucking late because the emotions were running rampant.

Rocks lodged at the base of my throat, and my pulse chugged in errant, reckless beats.

I scrubbed a palm over my face to break up the disorder and plopped back into my chair, unable to stop my mind from freewheeling through every scenario.

Three days had passed since we'd found Savannah's motel tampered with. Two days since I'd had her pressed against my kitchen counter.

Dick hard and heavy as I'd come close to going to the place I'd promised myself I wouldn't go.

Since then, we'd played it cool whenever we'd seen each other, though there was a current that ran just under the surface.

Our glances longer and our questions deeper.

Like we both were wondering if we could escape this attraction that had us tied.

Because there was no getting Savannah Ward off my mind. No getting her out of my head or out from under my skin.

The woman present in every thought.

Chasing me through each step of the day and haunting me with every sleepless second of the night.

I should be thankful Owen had interrupted. Should take it as the kid doing his dad a solid. Keeping me out of trouble and focused on what should be important. But I couldn't shake the sense that that was what she was becoming—important.

"How the fuck is there not one piece of evidence?" I asked it toward the ceiling, confusion twined in the exhalation of words.

"Someone's either a professional, or some asshole saw her leaving that evening and took it as his opportunity to bash in her door to see if she had anything of value inside and took off the second he heard someone coming. My bet's on the second."

It didn't sit right.

None of it did.

Samson sat forward, resting his elbows on his knees as he clasped his hands together and peered over at me. His voice lowered in caution. "I know what you're thinking, brother, and I'm worried you're letting yourself get way off base."

My sigh was heavy.

His voice lowered further. "What happened to Brianna was a fucking tragedy, Ezra. Heartbreaking for all of us. But for you? I know it was devastating. Crushing in a way no one can imagine unless they've experienced it for themselves. You lost your wife, man. And you being the Sheriff on top of it? I know the burden you carry. The guilt you wear when there was absolutely nothing you could have done to stop it."

I think I'm in trouble. The memory of Brianna's voice pummeled through my mind like a bludgeoning. My hands curled around the arms of my chair, teeth grinding with the force it took not to fly into a rage.

"You can't look at every crime that happens in this town like it's the same," Samson urged. "And you sure as hell can't hold yourself personally responsible for every person here."

"It's our job to protect the people of Time River," I ground out.

"Yeah, it is, and we do our goddamn best every day, but you told me yourself when you hired me on that we can't take it home at night."

It was what I'd been told when I'd been hired on. What I'd told every officer who'd ever come onto the force after. Passed down through the years from generation to generation.

It was the biggest crock of shit that I'd ever heard.

Samson suddenly rocked back in the chair, elbow on the arm as he leaned his cheek against the heel of his hand and his finger, his deep brown eyes narrowed in teasing speculation. "Except you sure took her *home*, didn't you? You wanna tell me about that?"

"Saw someone in need, and I had something I could do about it." The words came out like shards of glass.

"Oh, I bet you did something about it."

At his insinuation, my brow lifted in warning.

Samson laughed. "Don't get all grumbly with me. I see right through you, brother. I don't even know why you're denying it."

Because it was wrong. Because I didn't deserve to find love when I'd cost so much. Didn't deserve the pleasure I knew I'd find in her.

Plus…she was leaving.

My stomach bottomed out at the thought.

Because, God, I wanted to keep her.

"Can't say I blame you. Girl's wicked hot. Those lips…" Samson groaned, and I fucking growled.

Then he cracked up. "Yeah, I see how it is."

"You don't see anything."

Standing, Samson headed for the door. He paused with it opened to look back at me. "Are you sure about that? Because I'm pretty sure I see a guy who is clinging to the past when his future is calling for him, and I hope to God he doesn't make the mistake of getting stuck searching for something he can never get back."

Without saying anything else, he walked out, letting the door clatter shut behind him.

Chapter Twenty-Seven

Savannah

"WELL, IF IT ISN'T OFFICER OVERBEARING." I poured coffee into the empty mug that rested in front of Ezra. Hot Cop stretched out in the booth, wearing that uniform that his muscles bulged out of in every direction, stealing air as he sat there looking so roughly gorgeous in the morning light.

His jaw was clean-shaven, and those brown eyes were cast in a shade of warmth I had never seen in them before.

Tender but also swimming with a brand-new awareness.

Like that crazy, immaculate thing that had gone down between us two nights ago had become a part of our consciousnesses.

I was doing my absolute best to keep things light. It appeared to be an insurmountable feat when he'd blasted a thousand cracks into the walls surrounding my heart.

Then his children had gone and trampled all over the foundation that I'd built for my life.

And that kiss…that kiss had stolen my resolve and his touch had left me shaken.

But it was the care that continually brimmed in that warm, brown gaze that made me question everything I thought I knew.

What made me wonder.

What made me hope.

Ezra tossed a casual grin my way, though it tumbled through me with the intensity of a 9.0 magnitude earthquake. "How else am I going to keep my eye on my favorite little trespasser?"

"Is that what I am? Yours?"

Crap. It was out before I could stop it. Flagrant and rash.

I bit down on my bottom lip like I could reel it back. At least it'd come out playful.

Ezra didn't seem to take it that way, though, since those eyes tracked me like he never wanted to look away.

"It felt like it…when I kissed you. Like you were mine."

An aftershock rolled through, more powerful than the earthquake from a few moments before. We hadn't acknowledged that kiss in the couple of times I'd seen him in passing.

We'd tiptoed around each other, acting as if it hadn't happened.

I doubted there was a chance either of us would ever forget it.

"I guessed we were both caught up in the moment." How flimsy an excuse.

A challenge filled his expression, and he sat farther back in the booth. It might as well have been a throne with how powerful he looked.

"That's what it was, huh?" His words bristled across my flesh.

"Mmhmm."

It was a good thing Olivia wasn't here because his little girl would be singing, *Liar, liar, pants on fire.*

No question, it was written all over me. That it was more than a moment, and if I wasn't careful, I was going to want it to last forever.

"Weird…I could have sworn it was something else." Seduction wound through his voice, and I cleared my throat when I realized I'd been standing at his booth for an inordinate amount of time and the rest of my section was full except for the table that had just been bussed.

"Have you decided what you'd like to eat for breakfast?"

Those eyes raked over me again.

Me.

He wanted to eat me.

I knew it.

I was terrified that once he chewed me up, he'd spit me out. Or maybe…maybe what I was really terrified of was that he might want to keep me.

"I'll go with the morning special, eggs over medium and an English muffin."

"Great. I'll get that order right in for you."

I went to leave, only this time rather than grabbing me by the wrist the way he seemed to like to do, he grabbed me by the outside of the thigh.

Holy mother, my knees nearly buckled right out from under me. I would have melted into his touch if his expression didn't twist with a dread that stabbed me through the middle of the chest. "Have you noticed anything that has made you uncomfortable? Anything that set you off kilter or just didn't sit right?"

Right.

He was concerned about the near break-in at the motel.

I'd almost allowed myself to forget it. Assign it to chance. I breathed out a sigh. "No. I haven't noticed anything at all."

In worried contemplation, he gnawed at his bottom lip. My attention got stuck there, and I was having a really hard time taking any of this seriously when the only thing that seemed to matter right then was the memory of the way those lips had felt against mine.

"We didn't find any evidence of any kind." It sounded close to an apology. I honestly didn't know whether to be worried or relieved.

"That's good," I settled on.

Ezra frowned in clear disagreement. "I don't know that it is. I would have preferred to have tracked this asshole down to get him off the street." He paused then urged, "I want you to be extra careful, Savannah."

I forced a bright smile, one that came far too easy when I was teasing this sweet teddy bear of a man—this man who kept chipping away at the rubble inside me—and I leaned in close to his ear. "Why would I need to watch my own back when I have an overbearing *friend* to watch over me?"

I pulled back, though our noses were only three inches away.

Ezra released a slow chuckle, as good as a caress that traveled from my head to my toes. He gave a gentle squeeze to my thigh. "You'd better watch out, Savannah…it sounds a whole lot like you're giving me permission."

I leaned even closer to him. "Maybe I am."

Then I turned and walked across the restaurant, injecting a little extra sway into my hips as I went. I didn't have to look behind me to know his stare was devouring me from behind.

I was biting at my own lip when I walked through the swinging door into the bustling kitchen behind it, doing my best to hide my smile when I punched Ezra's order into the tablet next to the server's station.

And God, I could feel the force of it.

This stupid, foolish, gleeful smile.

One I couldn't shake.

Dakota walked past, though she did a double take when she saw me, and she slowly edged back toward me with her head angled to the side. A curious smile was carved into her adorable face. "Why do you look like you just danced with the stars?"

"I don't even know what that means," I told her.

"Oh, I think you do, Snuggle Muggle. You look like you're both dreaming and had your eyes opened for the first time."

My spirit clutched. It felt that way. Like dancing but like there was no weight on my feet.

Floating.

"Oh, Ezra came in for breakfast and was just giving me a hard time the way he likes to do, and I was laughing at a joke he made."

Awareness lifted her brow. "You know he only comes in with Ryder, Cody, and Caleb…that was until he met you."

I forced the roll of my eyes and huffed. "He's just freaking out about the whole motel thing. Don't act like I'm the only one he's protective of." My eyes widened in emphasis. "If it had happened to anyone else, you know he'd be here checking on them, too."

"Yeah, you're right, you're not the only one he's protective of." She leaned closer and lowered her voice. "But you are the only one who makes him look like he's dancing, too."

At that, she walked off without giving me the chance for a rebuttal. It was a good thing because I wasn't sure I could argue, anyway.

Beth popped her head through the swinging door. "Three on table twelve, Savannah. I know the rest of your section is full. Can you handle another table?"

"Yup, I'll be with them in a second."

"And here you said you didn't think you could save this sinking ship." She winked and I laughed, and I tucked my notepad back into the pocket of my apron before I grabbed an order that was ready from the window and walked out into the dining room. I delivered the food and checked on a couple customers before I headed to the new table.

I was trying to ignore Ezra but was failing miserably.

No stopping myself from peeking that way at the booth where he sat. And that glee was gliding free all over again when I found him grinning my way.

God, he made me feel...good.

Giddy, even.

Foolish girl who wanted to get her heart broken.

I cleared my throat as I stepped up to the new table. A ton of faces had become familiar at the café since we had so many regulars, but Hayden, Ruben, and the mayor were some of the more memorable.

There was just something about Hayden that pulled at my intuition, a warning that whispered low at my ear. It was a strange feeling that I should get close to him and a sense that I should run in equal measure.

"Good morning, welcome to Time River Market & Café."

"Ah, I was hoping you were going to be our server this morning." Hayden sent me a grin that was supposed to be appealing but made me feel like I was covered in worms.

Ruben laughed. "Considering he requested we be sat in your section, the chances were good."

Hayden didn't look the least bit humiliated by Ruben's goading. "What can I say, I wanted the best."

"I'm going to have to stop bringing these two out with me," Jack Harris said, shaking his head though there was amusement behind it.

"What, are you embarrassed of us, boss?" Hayden's grin was smug as he looked across the booth at him.

"What else would I be?" the mayor tossed right back.

I swallowed back the unease. "What can I get you this morning?"

Ruben ordered a coffee and the mayor an Americano, and I was jotting it down on my notepad when Hayden said, "Your address so I know where to pick you up for our date tomorrow night."

The worms crawling over me turned into snakes.

I might want to keep an eye on the guy, but not like that. I pasted on a pleasant smile. "I'm going to have to pass, but I would be happy to bring you something to drink."

Ruben knocked his shoulder into Hayden's. "Ouch."

"Don't worry, my friend, I'll win her over." Hayden didn't look away from me when he said it, the man completely undeterred. "But in the meantime, I'll take a mocha. Extra whipped cream."

"Great, I'll be right back."

And Hayden thankfully left me alone for the rest of the meal, and I got a sense that his boss had rebuked him for asking me out while on working hours since he seemed subdued for the rest of the meal.

I didn't mean to be grateful for it, but I was.

I didn't need the added convolution of emotions considering Ezra had me spun up enough. Plus, I was feeling defeated. I'd been here for two weeks, and I hadn't found a trace of Jessica.

I realized I was grasping at straws. Looking for something that might not even be there.

Thoughts of the little clues weaved into my mind. The Time River logo. The matching name of the complex. That had to be something, didn't it? But it was getting harder and harder to believe since I searched the faces of every person I passed, no matter if it was in the café or I was driving down the street, and had found nothing.

Each day that passed without finding her stole more of the hope that I would.

The muddle of feelings grew deeper since Ezra looked like he was a second from coming unglued every time I caught him staring at me any time I'd go to Hayden's table.

I needed a breather from it all, and I finally found a second to steal away, so I headed through the double doors and into the country store and wound around to the hall that led to the restrooms at the back.

I pushed inside, washed my hands, splashed water on my face, looked at my reflection as I whispered, "Where are you?"

I didn't know if I was talking to Jessica or myself.

If I'd gotten lost, too. If I'd stumbled to a place where I was the one who was going to get hurt.

With a paper towel, I patted my face dry and stepped out, though I stumbled when I found a mountain had sprouted up across the wall.

Ezra had his arms crossed over his chest, clearly standing guard.

"Overbearing much?" The razzing left me on little more than a wheeze because I was no longer feeling so light.

He pushed from the wall, so powerful as he crossed to me. At his proximity, my back hit the wall, and he didn't hesitate to box me in.

I should hate it.

Fight it.

Instead, I breathed in his masculine scent.

Citrus and pine.

Warmth glided into my senses.

My fingers buzzed with the impulse to touch him.

He looked both ways to make sure no one was watching us, shielding and covering, and I was sure he was going to kiss me.

Instead, he leaned in and said, "Whatever you do, stay away from that guy, Savannah."

A frown cut into my brow, and I tipped my chin up at him, such a reckless girl when I taunted, "Why? Are you jealous?"

"Call it what you want, but know I fight for the things that mean something to me."

Then he turned and walked out of the hall, disappearing at the end, taking my breath and another mangled piece of my heart with him.

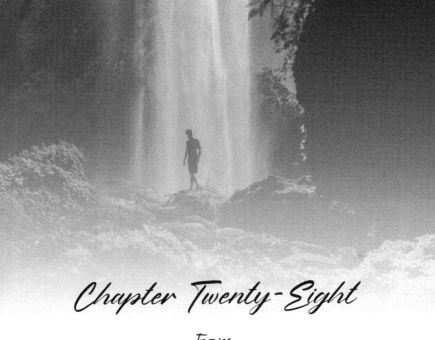

Chapter Twenty-Eight

Ezra

Two Years Ago

TWO DAYS. SHE'D BEEN GONE FOR TWO GODDAMN DAYS. Without a word. Without a trace. While Ezra had gone out of his mind, worry and dread spinning him into a ball of desolation.

Searching every street all while keeping it a secret. Giving Brianna the respect that the therapist had said she needed. Support in the space afforded.

But this?

The lie he'd told his mother when he'd asked her to watch the kids for the next couple days had soured on his tongue.

I got Brianna a two-day getaway at the ski resort for her birthday. Would you mind if we took it together? We could use some time alone.

She'd patted his face, love pouring out. *Of course, I don't mind. The two of you deserve time to yourselves with how hard you work, both at your jobs and taking care of your kids. You're so good together, but to keep relationships strong, you have to nurture it, and I'm so proud of you for taking the time to do that. Besides, you know I'm half bored out of my mind now that I've retired.*

Now the lie that had tasted sour had transfigured to venom, the bitterness so severe he thought he might be foaming at the mouth as he moved back through the house. He'd gotten home after driving every street of Time River again, and when he'd opened the garage, Brianna's car had been inside. He'd nearly come undone with relief, though the anger had immediately spun him into disorder again after he'd stepped inside and heard the shower running from the bathroom in their bedroom.

He'd repaired that fucking mirror, but it might as well have remained shattered.

He crept forward like he was wading through a field of landmines, getting ready to be blown into a billion tiny pieces as he turned the knob and slipped into the bathroom.

Steam filled it, a heated mist that he sloshed through until he was standing two feet from the shower, getting there at the exact same time that Brianna turned off the faucet and pulled back the curtain.

She gasped when she saw him, though a giggle toppled from her when she slurred, "Ezra, you scared the hell out of me."

"I scared the hell out of you? After you've been gone for two days without a word? Are you fucking kidding me, Brianna?"

He choked over the disbelief. Over the worry that had nearly suffocated him. The fear and the dread that had dragged his feet through each step of the day, and the pain that had cut him up and left him bleeding out as he'd been unable to sleep through the last two nights.

And here she was, blitzed out of her mind.

"Where were you?" The demand sliced through the thick mist that clung to the small room.

She stepped out of the shower to grab a towel from the hook. "My therapist told me I should take a couple days to work through some things."

"Without letting me—"

He nearly got knocked flat on his ass when he saw them.

Words clipping off.

Unable to speak.

Handprints.

All over her hips. Her ass. The fronts and backs of her thighs.

Black and purpled where fingertips had burrowed in deep.

Lightheadedness stumbled him back a step, and he gripped his head as shock blasted through his being.

He hadn't wanted to believe it, even though that's where his suspicions had gone, the way she'd act when she'd come stumbling back home at all hours of the night, the way he was sure he could smell someone all over her.

He'd wanted to give her the benefit of the doubt. Support her through whatever she was going through.

Now, there was no fucking question what those prints meant.

The shock wore off to reveal the disgust waiting underneath.

That last speck of love he'd held for her plucked out like a thorn that had infected his heart.

"You're fucking someone?" His voice was a fusion of sharp betrayal and sickened acceptance. He'd known, after all, hadn't he?

Frantic, Brianna wound herself in the towel and took a surging step toward him. She grabbed him by the wrist. "No."

He wrenched his arm from her hold. "Don't lie to me, Brianna. I'm so sick of the lies." A resentful chuckle left him. "You know what, how about you don't say anything to me at all?"

He stormed from the bathroom because he couldn't be in that room with her for one second longer.

She was right behind him. "No, Ezra. No. I...I fell at work...and one of the nurses helped me up. You need to listen to me—"

"Save it, Brianna, because I don't believe a word you say." He headed for the bedroom door.

Needing out.

Away.

Hands fisted in the back of his shirt. "No, Ezra. Please. I need you. I need you. I can't live without you. Please. I'm just...I feel too many things and it's too much. I need you. I can't do this without you."

He tried to wind himself free. To break away.

"Please."

His mind flashed to their wedding day.

To the vows that had been given.

To the ring on his finger.

I'll stand by you, through thick and thin. When things are going good, but more importantly, when things are going rough.

He fisted his hand, the band a glaring reminder of the promise he had made.

"Please," Brianna begged again. "I'll get help. I promise. It will be the last time."

Resigned, he turned to her. "It has to be, Brianna. Because if it happens again, I'm leaving and I'm taking the kids with me."

"I promise."

He wrapped her in his arms and pulled her against him.

Except holding her?

It felt hollow.

Empty.

Like it was no longer what he was supposed to do.

Chapter Twenty-Nine

Ezra

IT WAS CLOSE TO ELEVEN ON SATURDAY NIGHT WHEN I TWISTED the cap off a beer and headed out onto the back porch where I plunked down in a white rocking chair. I figured I'd grab myself a moment to clear my head. Take a fresh breath.

Relax.

The October air was cool and crisp, verging on cold, and filled with the quiet call of the night. The whoosh of the branches as a breeze rustled through the trees. The drone of crickets. The hoot of the owl who'd made himself a home in the eaves of the shed that sat a darkened silhouette on the farthest side of the yard.

I took a long pull of my beer, trying not to itch, laughing under my breath at myself for thinking I'd come out here to actually relax.

That I'd find a moment of it.

Not when I knew the real reason I was out here was because I couldn't get Savannah off my mind, and the only thing I could do was take a few steps in her direction.

The kids were spending the night out at the ranch with Paisley and Caleb, having a sleepover with their cousin Evelyn.

I loved it for them, that they had this extended family that loved them fiercely.

That didn't mean I hadn't been reticent to let them go, that shaky unease that always took me over when they were away rolling through me on a wave of apprehension.

A part of being a parent, I supposed, though I knew a whole ton of it had to do with what had happened with Brianna. I was already crazy protective, but after that…?

Overbearing.

I almost chuckled as my gaze drifted out over the yard, drawn in the direction of the woman who had me in fists.

When I'd dropped the kids off, Paisley had patted me on the cheek and told me to *go have some fun.*

I'd come right back here, not a chance that I felt like hitting a bar, not an ounce of desire to chat up some random girl when the only one I wanted was here.

During that time, I'd done my best at minding my own business because peeking out the window hoping to get a glimpse of Savannah seemed like a creeper move, though that hadn't seemed to matter all that much when I'd given in after I'd heard her car roll up about twenty minutes ago.

I mean, she had all but given me permission.

But I'd felt like I might lose my mind since she'd been gone late. Out of her normal routine, which it really was none of my business what she was doing, but I couldn't help from worrying.

Wondering where she'd been. If she was fine. If she was safe.

If she felt even a modicum of the need I felt every time she got within a hundred yards of me.

It'd taken all my restraint in the hallway at the café not to put my hands all over her. Not to kiss her the way I'd been dying to do. Not to hoist her into my arms and press her into the wall and tell her I couldn't fucking stand the idea of that prick touching her when she'd asked if I was jealous.

She wasn't mine to claim, but fuck, I'd wanted to.

That was the last time I'd seen her, and to say I wasn't dying to catch a glimpse would be a lie.

I didn't feel bad about coming out here, though. Not when I'd caught her peering out of her window about five minutes ago, the barest ripple of movement behind her curtain before she was gone.

But I'd felt it in that flash.

The tugging at my insides that was this woman. A magnetism in the air. Gravity calling me closer.

The light in her bedroom window flipped on before it went out about two minutes later, though a soft glow remained, one that made me assume the bathroom light was on and flooding into her room.

A bolt of need had me shifting uncomfortably in my seat, boots planted on the wooden planks like they could keep me grounded, tension wrenching my muscles as I thought of her tucked behind that wall. Imagining what she was doing right then. If she was changing or maybe stepping under the spray of the shower.

If she wanted her privacy or if she was thinking about me.

Contemplating, I glanced down at my phone that I had rested on my thigh. Maybe I should leave well enough alone because the direction of my thoughts were only going to land me in hot water.

It was the wrong fucking time for me to fall. For me to bring someone into my kids' lives. For me to go putting my heart on the line, but I was afraid it might already be there.

Bottomline, I was going to lose my goddamn mind if I didn't at least talk to her.

My fingers punched awkwardly on the screen, unsure of what the fuck to say.

Me: How are you?

There. Simple. Friendly.

After ten minutes, I'd given up on her texting back, and I started to stand to go back into the house. Only my chest tightened when a text bleeped through, and I dropped back onto the chair so I could read her message.

Savannah: Are you thinking about me, Ezra Patterson? And here I thought you'd forgotten all about me.

Taking a swig of my beer, I stared at the illuminated screen, at the glare that made me feel like I could tumble right into it to get to her.

Me: There is no forgetting you, Little Trespasser.

Savannah: Yet four days have gone by, and I haven't heard a peep from you. That's not very neighborly of you.

Amusement and a shock of need twisted through, and I fought a grin, unimmune to the flirtiness seeded in her words. Loving that she wanted to come out and play. I also knew whatever was brewing between us was far too intense to write it off as inconsequential.

Me: Four days too long for you, Little Trespasser?

Savannah: I think it might be.

I warred between continuing with the taunting and teasing and with sucking up and addressing the obstacles laid out ahead of us.

Me: You told me last Sunday night that it was for the best that we got interrupted, so I thought I should work on that whole giving you space thing.

Too bad I couldn't help going into the café to see her on Tuesday. But at least then there were people around to stop us.

Savannah: It was for the best.

Disappointment kicked. A fucking steel-toed boot to the gut. Air heaved from my lungs when another text popped up behind it.

Savannah: That doesn't mean I didn't want it.

That disappointment got smashed by a streak of desire. By this woman who clouded all judgement. Another message came through before I had the chance to respond.

Savannah: Did you want it? Do you want me?

Fuck, she just laid it out. Pulled no punches. And I had too many things going down in my life to be playing games.

Me: It's not right how fucking bad I want you. Whatever this is? It's bigger than anything I've ever felt.

Savannah: It scares me how bad I want you. But you know I'm not staying here forever.

I bit down on the side of my cheek, unable to fucking swallow her warning, unable to fucking accept that one day she might leave Time River, and I could feel the weight of the vulnerability that hung in both our confessions.

Me: So where does that leave us?

It took her a bit to answer.

Savannah: It leaves me touching myself thinking about you. The way I've been doing every night this week.

Fuck me.

Rocking forward, I set my bottle on the porch and raked a palm down my face, wondering if I was making this shit up. If I'd fallen into a delusion. The best fucking kind of fantasy.

But the words were all right there, a bright, shiny beacon.

My fingers never flew so fast.

Me: Can I watch?

I thought I might die in the time it took her to respond.

Savannah: You did say you wanted to keep an eye on me...

I was on my feet the second her text came through, and I crossed the yard in a blink, prepared to pound on her door to let me in, only it gave when I barely touched it, drifting open on its own.

Protectiveness swelled, a tidal wave that battered my chest, words close to a growl when I prowled through the darkness that hung in the living room toward the short hall that led to the bedroom.

"Why the fuck is your door unlocked?"

I couldn't stop it from slashing off my tongue. Fear sparking in the middle of the mayhem that propelled me forward. Possessiveness rising high.

"Why do you think it was unlocked? Because I saw you out there. Because I wanted you. Because I've been waiting for you."

Her rasping voice floated down the hall, penetrating, luring me forward.

I nudged at the partially closed bedroom door, and it swung open to the dim, muted light of her room.

An arrow of need staked me to the spot, and I was unable to fucking move at the sight in front of me. A growl ripped up my throat. "Oh, Little Trespasser, trying to do me in."

Savannah was on the rumpled sheets of her bed, propped against a stack of pillows that rested on the headboard.

Face so goddamn gorgeous. Lips parted and panting with need.

But what had stopped my heart was her feet were planted on the mattress.

Her panties had been discarded, and I knew she'd been in the middle of it before I'd come, but now her knees were pressed together in an attempt to conceal, like she wasn't quite sure she could expose herself fully.

That didn't mean her hips weren't still moving, the woman writhing in need, and she was clutching a purple vibrator in her hand, those eyes wide and unsure and burning with desire as she stared over at me.

"I think it's you who's done me in, Ezra. I don't…" She trailed off, and my tongue stroked over my parched lips as I forced myself to remain rooted at the doorway.

"Think we're suffering the same, aren't we?"

"Yes," she moaned, full of restraint.

"Let me see what I've been doing to you, Savannah. Let me see the way you've been touching yourself while you thought of me."

She hesitated for only a beat before she spread her knees. I nearly blacked out at the sight of her drenched pussy, and slowly, she pushed in the vibrator.

Her hips rocked from the bed.

"Fuck me, Little Trespasser." I could barely breathe.

She began to drive the vibrator in and out, the little nub hitting her clit every time she thrust it deep.

She was still wearing a white camisole, though one of the straps hung down over one shoulder like she'd been tugging at it, and her tiny tits were pebbled and pressing against the thin fabric.

Aqua eyes pinned me to the spot, and her back arched as she whimpered and drove the toy deeper. "This is what you did to me, Ezra. With that kiss. With those hands. With those eyes. With your care. You made me need something I know better than needing."

Dangerous.

And I was the fool who stepped the rest of the way into her room.

Chapter Thirty

Savannah

I WAS JUST BEGGING FOR THE HEARTBREAK, BUT RIGHT THEN, I couldn't find one molecule inside myself to care.

Not when Ezra stepped from the doorway and into the room as I continued to thrust my toy into my body.

He didn't hesitate to reach to the back of his neck so he could drag his tee over his head.

I went dizzy from the loss of air.

The man was the most magnificent thing I'd ever seen, and I thought I finally understood what being awestruck really meant.

He was a mountain of strength and bristling muscle. A tower that cast a cover of protection over the room.

His shoulders were broad and his chest was wide, and his abdomen was cut in all these grooved, defined ridges that I had the urge to trace with my tongue. His jeans hugged his narrowed waist, and his hip bones jutted out like they were begging for a little of my attention, too.

His skin was sun-kissed and unmarred save for the single tattoo he had imprinted on his left pec.

It was a shattered clock that was kept from falling by butterfly wings, though pieces of the fractured glass fell away at the bottom. There was a green feminine eye in the middle, written there like her soul would for all of time watch over him.

The jagged, gnarled hands were stuck at three twenty-two.

The art was beautiful. Breathtaking. It was also so heartbreaking that I wanted to weep.

I desperately tried to keep it from stinging because I was one-thousand percent certain of what that time stamp meant.

I needed to end this. Stop it before we really got started because it had never been so glaring that I was going to get my heart wrecked. My brain understood it, but my spirit flailed in reproach and my body rejected it altogether.

He took another step deeper into the room.

Energy crashed.

Ricocheting.

Inciting.

He came to stand at the end of the bed, the massive, unrelenting height of him covering me in shadow.

"Look at you, Little Trespasser. Sneaking into all the places I'm not supposed to let you go." His voice was rough and low, and a moan got free at his confession, at the heat of his gaze as he watched me.

I drove my rabbit harder and faster, the buzz humming in the air and the vibrations rocking through my body.

Ezra set one knee on the bed, then the other, and he rose up on them high above me.

Warm brown eyes had gone molten as he stared down.

The man pure heat.

An inferno.

Fire.

It flamed up my legs when he took me by both knees, and he spread me farther, his attention locked on where I thrust the vibrator deep.

"So fucking wet."

An incredulous laugh got free. "One look at you, and I'm soaked, Ezra. Every time. I can't help it. Can't stop it."

Those eyes flicked up to meet my face, and his jaw clenched in steely restraint. "How many times have you fucked yourself thinking about me, Savannah?"

Apparently, we weren't trying to hide this attraction any longer. I didn't know what I'd expected when I'd confessed what I was doing, needing him to know that I hadn't been able to stop thinking about him once through the entire week.

Maybe admitting it had felt safe behind the text. As if it wasn't real. Another barrier separating us.

But this?

I was no longer safe or hidden behind the wall I'd tried to keep erected between us.

I was here, laid out in front of him like an offering.

And God, how desperately I wanted him to take me.

"Nonstop since that kiss. I can't—" I clipped off the admission that I was never fully sated. That I always felt like I was going to burst because a fantasy was never going to be enough.

"I could barely work this week, thinking about you." His words were a grumble. "Spent half of it with my cock in my hand, thinking about you on your knees in front of me, wondering just how good this mouth would feel. But I never allowed myself to fully imagine this. How fucking perfect you would be."

He reached out and pushed two fingers deep into my mouth, making me suck. I whimpered around him, overcome, overtaken.

Then I gasped when I was ripped from where I'd been propped against the headboard and my legs were suddenly wrapped around his waist. My arms flew out to steady myself, curling around his neck, which was hysterical since I'd never been on such unstable ground than I was right then.

Still, I clung to him as he sat up on the side of the bed with me straddling him. My front was pressed to the stony planes of his torso, our lips a breath apart, my heart ravaging against his.

My mouth dropped open when I realized he had one arm wound around my lower back and the other hand had taken possession of my vibrator.

He slowly drove it in. Even slower, he dragged it out. A whimper bled free, and I rose up and sank back down to meet him when he did it again.

"You stole my breath the second I saw you, Savannah Ward. The moment I shined my flashlight into your car and found those eyes staring back. It gutted me, looking at you. And now, seeing you like this? I'm afraid I'm completely wrecked."

Wrecked.

How was it possible he was thinking the exact same thing as I had been?

I gripped his massive shoulders as I began to ride my vibrator like I was riding him.

"Good, it's only fair because I'm pretty sure I'm completely ruined." The tweak of a smile pulled at the edge of my mouth. I nearly came undone when Ezra leaned in and licked it.

A half a beat later, his mouth was fully on mine. This time, his kiss was close to punishing as he continued to thrust my toy. I matched time, chasing the pleasure that sparked in every nerve-ending. Tingles rushed as the need consumed me in a way I'd never been before.

It should be terrifying, but again, I felt like I was floating.

Weightless in his arms.

His mouth explored, leaving mine to kiss a path along my jaw and down my neck, and my head fell back as he lapped a path over my shoulder. He dragged my tank down as he went.

Cool air wisped over my exposed breast before the heat of his mouth covered it, and his tongue stroked over the sensitive peak. A cry rolled my throat, and I began to move faster as desperation took me over.

The need so bright I couldn't see anything else.

Blinding.

Obliterating.

"I want you, Ezra. All of you." I grappled to get to his fly the way I'd done a week ago.

He pressed his lips up under my jaw, and something close to

anguish coated his voice. "I'm not sure I could handle you on my dick, Savannah. Not sure I would ever stop wanting you. Not after that."

In an instant, he had me shifted again, the man picking me up and maneuvering me around like I weighed absolutely nothing.

Putty in his hands.

And that's what I was. Nothing but putty as he laid back on the bed and moved me all the way up so I was straddling his head. He tossed the vibrator aside and drove two fingers into my body.

I rocked and rolled, and a moan curled out of me as I looked down at him, my thighs shaking as he kept driving his big fingers inside me. He wound his free arm around one of my legs, holding me as he growled, "Come here, Little Trespasser, and sit on my face. Let me taste that pretty pussy."

He pulled me down and sucked my engorged clit into his mouth.

Color flashed behind my eyes.

Fireworks.

An explosion.

I came in an instant.

In the first glorious touch.

I was already so worked up that all it took was the pull of his mouth for me to go off. Flames of ecstasy incinerating and leaving me torched.

I gasped and writhed against his face as he languidly licked me, lighting me up in a slew of tiny aftershocks as he led me through the orgasm.

"You think that's going to help in making me stop wanting you?" I couldn't stop it from tumbling out on a ragged breath.

Half tease, half truth.

It made it a million times worse as I edged back and saw the smirk ticking up at one side of his mouth that shined with my arousal. The satisfaction on his face while lust still burned in his eyes. "If I can't keep you, then I at least need to give you something to remember me by."

I was a damned fool because it was that grin that finally cracked through the barrier. What made a bitter part inside me crumble.

I slid down his body, all the way until I was easing off the side of the bed and onto my knees on the floor. I pulled him up to sitting as I went.

Ezra watched me intently, like I was a mystery.

A missing link.

A truth.

I leaned down and undid the laces of his boots, glancing up at him every few seconds, the stupid girl who was letting foolish dreams slide in.

He kicked them off, his attention on me as he did, and this time when I moved to the button of his jeans, he didn't stop me.

He helped me instead, shifting enough to drag off his jeans and underwear.

My entire being clenched, and I was completely caught off guard by the fresh wave of desire that barreled through me.

Ezra's cock was the perfect match to the man.

Long and unbearably thick.

The head was fat and purpled, the slit beaded with precum.

I glanced up at his face and, in an instant, my breath was gone.

Because Ezra was wearing an expression I'd never seen him wear before.

One of sheer, unmitigated possession.

He stood, naked, bold, and towering over me.

I shook where I knelt as he fisted himself and brought his head to my lips, and I knew I was done for when he said, "I like it rough, Little Trespasser. Are you good with that?"

Chapter Thirty-One

Ezra

AQUA EYES FLARED WHERE SHE WAS ON HER KNEES IN FRONT of me. I wondered if she had the first clue how goddamn sexy she was. The temptation she embodied. The truth that she was getting so far under my skin I had no idea how I was ever going to get her out from under it.

I should have ended this with her tight little body trembling and shaking from the orgasm that had torn through her.

Walked and turned my back.

Because the whole intent had just been watching, but the second I'd caught sight of her splayed out on that bed, there was no stopping the madness. No way to keep from touching her when she had so clearly been begging to be touched.

I wouldn't lie. I wanted this. I wanted those plump, full lips wrapped around my cock. I wanted her to have the taste of me scored in her memories the same way the taste of her would forever be scored on mine.

And I hadn't been touched in so fucking long. Not since that un-bearable day. Not since the moment seeking pleasure for myself had revealed my greatest selfishness and I'd failed Brianna in the most brutal way. Failed my kids in the most brutal way.

I never thought I'd really want anyone again. The shame so great, that I'd never even crave it.

Funny since I'd never craved anyone the way I craved Savannah Ward, and I was certain I never would again.

She lifted that fierce chin as she fisted me at the base, right over my own hand.

"I can take it."

She flicked out her tongue to lick across my dripping tip.

Pleasure spiked through the middle of me. "Oh, Little Trespasser, what I would do to you."

Without hesitation, I pulsed into her mouth, so deep that I hit the back of her throat. Her hands shot out to brace herself on my thighs, and Savannah made this moaning, gurgled sound that vibrated around me.

A lust-inducing song.

It sent sparks lighting up my spine.

I stilled with her lips stretched wide around me, her mouth so fucking wet and warm that I nearly lost it right then. I let the pad of my thumb trace along the defined curve of her cheek. "I don't think I've ever seen anything more perfect than this. You on your knees for me with that pretty mouth wrapped around my cock."

I twined a hand up in her hair, fisting a handful as I drew out then pushed back in.

She whimpered and held on tighter to steady herself, and I began to take her mouth in long, deep strokes.

Aqua eyes stared up at me as I drove into her mouth, a severity unlike any other thrashing in the room.

My heart a thunder. Lust racing. Need overpowering.

Fucking her mouth shouldn't feel better than any pleasure I'd ever known. It shouldn't feel like I was being changed. It shouldn't feel like this *mattered*.

But there was no escaping it, gazing down at Savannah, at this woman who was letting me touch her this way.

Long-dead embers flamed with every pass, and it lit in the vacant places inside me that I thought would be forever frozen, and the heat rose higher and higher with each possessive thrust.

"Do you have the first clue, Savannah, how good you feel?" I grunted it, body groaning with the pressure of trying to keep myself from completely snapping.

I wanted her in a way that was hazardous.

The direction I was traveling was careless and hasty.

But I needed it. I needed this. I needed her.

Desire blistered through her all over again as she let me take her mouth like it'd always belonged to me.

Like we'd done this a thousand times.

Like we each got it.

Knew what the other needed.

This connection unfound and unsafe. So intense I didn't know how we'd ever break it.

Fingernails burrowing into my thighs, she rose high on her knees, giving herself over to me as I picked up a ruthless rhythm.

But it was Savanah who was doing the consuming.

Energy crackled as I pounded into her mouth, and I was gripped by that feeling again. The one that promised I was in the exact place I was supposed to be.

There was something about her that compelled me.

Beckoned me.

Something that made me want to gather her up and never let her go.

Take her.

Claim her.

I tried to shun it because Savannah had made it clear what this was.

It wasn't permanent.

It was pleasure.

Release.

Giving in for a moment.

So I gave and refused any reservations that threatened to swell up and invade.

"Fuck…this sweet mouth, Savannah. So good. So perfect. Never have felt anything as good as this. You're going to do me in. Take it, baby."

The words tumbled out like praise as I angled her jaw so I could take her even deeper.

Savannah glowed beneath my words.

Every inch of her sweet, soft flesh glistened. Hair a tangle in my hand. Her single tit still bared from where I'd shoved down her camisole.

I was sure I'd never seen anything more gorgeous than her kneeling there.

"You're the most beautiful thing I've ever seen, stealing my breath every time I look at you."

I needed to be careful that she didn't steal my goddamn heart.

I could scent her arousal, and her nails dug even deeper into my thighs as I let my movements fully take over.

Savannah accepted me as I took her in a way that was close to vicious.

A madness spun through the room.

This possession that wound me into a beast.

Savannah moaned and whimpered while I grunted and snarled.

She pressed her thighs together like it might be enough to staunch this need that I was afraid could never be satisfied.

It was only going to grow.

A growl rumbled in my chest when she swallowed around my cock and took me into her throat.

I thought I might pass out from the feel of it. At this stranger who was coming to mean everything.

Pleasure glowed and gathered. It tracked my spine, a thrill that sped up and down. My balls tightened as the energy coiling in my body gathered to a pinpoint.

"Such a good girl, the way you take me," I told her.

Quickening my pace, I raced for the bliss that waited in the distance.

Severity glinted in the atmosphere. The oxygen growing so dense it was impossible to breathe.

Impossible to see.

Impossible to define this feeling that overwhelmed.

Then those aqua eyes flashed up to me, and I got swept away by the torrent of emotion swimming in the depths.

It was that single look that set me off.

What had that pinpoint of ecstasy splintering out, streaking far and wide and tumbling through every cell in my body.

Paradise.

"Savannah." I grunted her name as I came, my cock pulsing as I poured into her mouth.

She sucked, swallowing every drop, the woman writhing on her knees while she licked me clean.

Shivering because she needed more. Just like I imagined, that intensity refused to fade.

The need keening between us not close to sated.

I swept her up off the floor, and Savannah yelped in surprise as I hiked her into my arms. On instinct, her legs wrapped around my waist. Her center was hot and drenched where it was pressed low to my abdomen.

She rubbed against me, seeking friction.

"I've got you," I promised as she continued to whimper.

I carried her into the bathroom. It was brighter in there, and the girl was lit up in a spotlight as I propped her on the edge of the counter.

Blonde hair wild but it was her eyes that screamed of this mayhem.

I drove three fingers deep inside her.

A delirious gasp raked from her mouth, and her hands flew out to my chest. "Ezra. I need…"

She was so lost to it she could hardly speak.

"I know, baby." I pressed my thumb to her clit, swirling it while

I drove my fingers into her throbbing heat. "Your cunt is so greedy for me."

"Please. I need…"

I knew what she was asking for, but I'd meant it. I didn't think I could handle her pussy hugging my dick. Wasn't sure I'd ever be able to let go if I gave into something so sublime.

If I gave into *this*.

So I focused on what I could give, and Savannah writhed and panted as I wound her tight.

Her body quivered and her thighs shook.

"Come for me, one more time."

That was all it took for her to blow, and her walls spasmed around my fingers as another orgasm rocked her through. Her nails dug into my shoulders as she came and came.

Wave after wave of pleasure.

Her breaths were short and choppy as she struggled to come down from where she'd been soaring, and our hearts were clattering, in sync and completely out of time.

I pressed my lips to the crown of her head, inhaling, filling my senses with mango and cream. "Little Trespasser, what am I supposed to do with you?"

Because I'd been afraid of putting my heart on the line.

And now that I had? I wasn't sure that I could ever go back.

Chapter Thirty-Two

Savannah

I CLUNG TO EZRA PATTERSON LIKE I COULD HOLD ONTO THIS connection forever.

Lost to the comfort.

To the closeness.

To the steady beat of his heart that drummed against my ear where he held me tightly to his chest. To the rhythm of his breaths that panted into the top of my head and stirred through my hair.

It was strange, finding peace in his proximity, especially after I'd laid myself physically bare to him.

Strange, allowing myself to sink into another.

I should be riddled with fear. Alarms going off and sending the barricades high and wide.

What I really should be doing was running. Searching. Focusing on what I'd come here to do.

But I couldn't seem to get myself to let go as we stayed like that until my pounding pulse finally slowed, so utterly distracted by this man that I didn't recognize myself any longer.

Ezra finally shifted, and he peeled himself back, though he didn't go far. He took me by the chin, studying me in a way that left me completely unnerved. Because the man was looking at me like I might be a treasure. "Who knew one sweet mouth could bring a man to his knees."

The faintest smile tugged at my lips. "I told you it was only fair."

"Not fair at all, Savannah, what you did to me." He said it easily, though. Like he wasn't freaking out over what had just happened. Maybe he hadn't been affected the same way as I had been. Except there was something playing in that warm, honey gaze that made me feel like I wasn't in this alone.

"Wait right there." He squeezed the outside of my thigh before he sauntered back out into the bedroom.

Completely buck.

A heaping mountain of muscle, back rippling with strength, his ass cheeks hard and perfectly hewn, indenting on the sides with each step he took.

It turned out Hot Cop looked really good in the middle of the night, too.

Heat spread through my body, and I bit down on my bottom lip like it could tamp out the reaction that blazed. I was in so much trouble because I wasn't sure I'd ever have enough of him.

I didn't know whether to be worried or relieved because I'd thought he'd run the second it was over, but instead, he was smirking over at me as he unwound his briefs from his jeans and pulled them on.

"You should see what you look like right now," he rumbled.

My hands curled around the edges of the counter to keep myself from flying for him and begging for more. Because if we were talking about how someone looked right then…?

That was what was unfair, and I knew I was at a distinct disadvantage.

"And what's that?" I managed a taunting, knowing my hair was mussed and the only thing I had on was that tiny camisole that covered next to nothing. The rest of me was stark naked. It wasn't like I could hide from him, anyway, not when I got the sense he could see straight through me.

"Like the whole reason I renovated this place to begin with."

My heart clutched, squeezing with the sweetness that came rolling off his tongue. This grumbly teddy bear who could go from a demanding savage before he was right back to revealing that soft, sincere soul.

I didn't know which side of him I liked better.

"And why did you renovate it?"

"So I could have something to do with my hands, but I'm thinking this place had a whole different purpose than what I'd imagined."

He lifted his hand and sucked on the fingers he'd just had buried inside me.

I nearly went up in flames.

I did my best to work up a tease when I felt like I was being burned alive. Devoured by a man I'd had no business allowing to touch me.

I ignored the thousand red flags that went up when I couldn't find a speck inside myself that regretted it.

"I'm sure you could have found a better tenant."

He snagged my underwear and my vibrator from the bed and started in my direction. Big body taking up the space. He'd tucked his cock back into his briefs, but it was still at half-mast and perfectly outlined by the fabric. I shifted on the cold granite of the counter, praying for self-possession or even a smidgeon of control.

But it'd all gone missing.

Because I wanted him again.

But this time, I wanted more.

I wanted it all.

Completely. Wholly.

My throat closed off as he tossed the toy into the sink then came to stand an inch from me, and a shiver tumbled down my spine as he helped me into my underwear.

The man was tending to me in a way that no one ever had before. Reaching out, he cupped my cheek and tilted my head back until I was pinned with the full force of his stare.

"No, Savannah, I knew there was a reason I found you that night, and this is right where you belong."

There weren't any storms in the area.

None except for the one that whirled around us.

A hurricane held on the horizon. Lightning crackling at the edges.

Ezra ran the pad of his thumb beneath the hollow of my eye.

Gently.

Another brittle piece inside myself cracked and fell away.

A knot formed in my throat, and it made my eyes sting and my chest burn.

Then I squealed when he suddenly hoisted me into his arms again.

Ezra kept dragging me from one extreme of emotions to another.

From heavy to light.

Though I realized then that every single one of them were positive. That I felt…good. Amazing, really.

My arms flew around his neck, and it was joy that spread through as I looked down at where he grinned up at me as he carried me back to my bed. He tossed me to it, and I bounced on the mattress.

A peal of my laughter danced toward the ceiling.

"Scoot over."

"Excuse me?" Surprise carved its way into my expression, and I pushed up onto my elbows to look at him.

"You don't think I can sleep on a foot of space, do you?" He gestured at himself, all six-foot-five deliciousness of him.

"You want to stay here? With me?"

Oh, it was a bad idea.

Such a bad idea.

The rush of giddiness that poured into my bloodstream was proof of that.

"Yeah, I like the feel of you against me."

Don't make me fall for you, Ezra Patterson.

I should have said it aloud. A warning for us both. But he was already crawling in next to me, and he lifted the covers for me to slide under before he did the same then pulled me tight against the rigid planes of his body.

His arms massive around me, the scent of him invading, his heart a steady beat.

A sigh pilfered free.

Far too contented.

This night a dream.

He shifted us so we were both on our sides, though my head was rested on his bicep, and for the longest time he just…stared over at me with this smile quietly dancing on his lips, his thumb running circles over my shoulder and back.

And that's what it felt like…dancing.

Like we were dancing with the stars. Elevated above reality. Where it was glitter and light and ecstasy.

My attention dropped to the single tattoo on his chest, and I forced myself back into that reality because ignoring it wouldn't make it go away.

I wondered how deeply it would burn me if I touched it. If it might scar me the way it had surely scarred him.

Clearly, I had no self-preservation since I reached out and did it anyway. My fingertips trembled as I lightly ran them over the black-inked art.

Ezra flinched, and his teeth snapped as his hand stopped moving against my skin.

"I'm sorry that you lost her." It came as a whisper as I searched every dip and groove and furrow of his features. Wishing to know him in a way I hadn't allowed myself to know anyone in a long, long time. Wishing he might know me the same, all while it being blatantly clear it'd put me in a position I'd promised myself I'd never be in again.

Only I was terrified that I was already there. On an altar laid out like an offering.

This was probably the worst time for me to bring up the subject, but the evidence of his loss was right in front of me. Square in the face. And I didn't know this part of him. Hell, I really didn't know him at all except for this connection that burned so bright that it made it feel like he was an intrinsic part of me.

When that had happened, I didn't know.

I didn't know when I'd started to care.

But it was there, like binds wrapping around my ankles and wrists, tying me to a man I couldn't keep.

A fool who was secretly wishing that there might be a way that he could *keep* me.

Hold me.

And there was that trust. What I'd sworn to never have for another because people had a nasty habit of taking that trust and trampling it to dust.

It didn't seem to matter right then, though.

Not in this second.

Not in this moment.

Such a stupid girl because this time I was sure my heart would go down in a fiery ball of flames, and there would be no making it out on the other side.

"Please don't feel sorry for me, Savannah." It ground from his mouth like the grinding of stones.

I blinked, searching the shadows that flickered across his face. "Why can't I be sorry for you, Ezra? Feel sorrow for you?"

He already had me feeling so many things, I guessed it only seemed logical that I would feel that, too.

His arms tightened around me, and he brushed his fingers through my hair. A dent was cut so deep between his brow that I had the impulse to reach out and smooth it out.

"Because you're the last person I want looking at me with pity. The last person I want looking at me and thinking that I must be consumed with grief."

A disturbance whirled around him, and I thought it was shame that slammed me on a palpable wave.

"Aren't you?"

His fingers encircled my wrist, stopping me from continuing to trace the lines of the tattoo. I got the impression it was causing him too much pain. Etching the scars deeper. Reopening a wound.

"I'm filled with hate and rage, Savannah, for the ones who took her from this world. At the ones who stole her from my kids and from her family." His voice cracked. "But I have no right to grief."

Confusion bound me, and Ezra blew out a long strain of air. He quietly began to explain, his voice so quiet, like he could hardly stand the idea of anyone hearing what he said.

"Everyone thought Brianna and I were the perfect couple. Inseparable. Two people who just *were* from the instant they came together."

He might have said he didn't have a right to grief, but I could feel it seeping from him.

I eased back a fraction so I could capture every intonation.

The cadence of his words and every innuendo hidden in his expression.

"I met her at Mack's. She was super cool. Cute and sweet."

Releasing my wrist, he twined a lock of my hair around his finger, as if it offered him a distraction from the tension that bound his muscles. "We started dating…more so hooking up, I guess." Air huffed from his nose as he sorted through the memories in his mind. His gaze kept flicking away before it would return to me.

I set my hand on his cheek, needing to touch him, to let him know that I was here for him, and I'd hold whatever he needed to say.

"I liked her, a lot, and when she told me she was pregnant a few months later, we decided we were going to do the family thing together. Get married. Buy a house. I was happy. Really fucking happy because I'd always wanted kids…a whole houseful of them."

A soft smile tugged at his mouth, riddled with the love that he had for his children.

"You have a pretty amazing houseful of them," I told him, my voice rougher than it should be.

But his kids had managed to seep through the cracks, too, every time they were out there in the backyard this last week shouting for me, their little faces so sweet and brimming with excitement as they would fill me in on every detail of the day.

It'd become the best part of mine.

A wash of sadness infiltrated Ezra's expression. "Those kids are my life, Savannah, and I wanted to give them the safest home. One filled with love and security. And things were good for a long time.

But after the boys were born…" Sorrow had him hesitating before he said, "Something inside of Brianna broke."

My heart chugged at the turmoil in his voice, at the regret that intruded on every word. "I don't know if it was postpartum depression or if she'd struggled in the past or it was something brand new, if she was unhappy or what the fuck it was, but her behavior became erratic."

Ezra blinked, and in the depths of those honey eyes was a vat of torment. "She worked as a receptionist at one of the doctor's offices here in town, and it started with her missing shifts…calling in sick. I should have taken it more seriously. Known something was wrong, but I just thought she was tired. I mean, fuck, she had six-month-old twins and trying to keep up with their schedules was exhausting for both of us. But she'd insisted that she wanted to go back to work, and she needed time for herself, which I fully got and respected."

His head shook on the pillow, and I ran my thumb along the stony angle of his cheek, trying to give him whatever comfort I could when it was clear he was barely keeping it together. "She'd began drinking a lot…coming and going all hours of the night…making choices that were dangerous. It wasn't long before she'd started coming up with these outrageous stories, thinking people were after her, just completely delusional and paranoid."

A barbed knot rolled his throat when he swallowed. "I begged her to get help, and she was supposed to be seeing a therapist and taking meds, but it turned out she hadn't been doing either of those things. She kept promising that she would be better, but it turned into this cycle that never ended. We started fighting all the time, and each time that she left me up worrying about her in the middle of the night, I felt the threads of my love for her being ripped away. Close to the end, I found out she was having an affair."

My spirit moaned for him, and a spike of protectiveness rose from the deepest place inside me. Who the hell would cheat on this man?

Shame pinched the corners of Ezra's brown eyes. "And it was no longer encouragement and grace and support that I was giving her, Savannah, but ultimatums. I told her if it happened one more time, I was leaving and I was taking the kids with me."

The loss of faith. I'd felt it so many times. The kind of betrayal that stung in the most excruciating way.

And it wasn't pity that I felt. It was communion. Lost in his sea of suffering. Swept from the safety of the shore and into the turmoil of his past.

"How could you blame yourself for that, Ezra? She was cheating on you. Acting reckless. You were protecting your children. Your family. *Yourself.*"

He didn't deserve that kind of treason.

Ezra hugged me tighter. "No, Savannah." His voice grew hoarse, scraping in emphasis. "Because the truth is my love for her was thin. Flimsy and weak from the start because when I rolled up on her car on the side of the road after she'd crashed three weeks later. I found her completely trashed, there was no sympathy or sadness. It was just—disgust."

The shake of his head was hollow, some of that disgust riding through, then a snort of disbelief huffed from his nose that I somehow felt was directed at himself. "I took my kids to my mom's the next day. She'd always put Brianna on a pedestal. Always was going on about how lucky I'd been to find someone who loved me the way Brianna did. Encouraging me to foster and cherish it. You can be certain when she claimed she loved Brianna like a daughter, she'd meant it."

Regret heaved from his nose. "I honestly think she turned a blind eye because she didn't want to believe Brianna could be up to no good. I couldn't stomach tainting that for her, and I had no fucking clue how I was going to tell her I was leaving Brianna and filing for divorce."

My breath was shallow. Every picture I'd conjured of Ezra's wife, of their past, of their relationship, had gotten smashed into a thousand pieces.

I kept tracing my thumb over the angles of his face while he blinked a thousand times, caught in the memories. "I told her Brianna was going to be working extra shifts and both of us were going to be flat out that week, so I asked her to watch the kids to buy me some time to figure out the best way to handle the situation. My mom had been more than happy to and had suggested we carve out time for ourselves in the middle of it when I'd already known it was over."

"Ezra." I pressed my palm closer to his cheek, trying to hold a piece of it for him.

The agony that rushed from him.

The grief that tormented him.

"Brianna kept begging me for another chance. Promised it would be different, and I told her I hoped to God it would be, that she'd make a change for both herself and for the kids, but it was too late for us. I packed a bag and checked into a motel in Poplar to keep the gossip from spreading through Time River."

"You were still trying to protect her." I searched him, this good, good man. He was. Somewhere, somehow, I knew he was different than any other person I'd met.

Displeasure rode out on a huff. "No, Savannah, I wasn't protecting her. I was too fucking relieved at breaking free." Grimness filled his voice. "She had to have called me at least twenty times a day during that week. I answered the first couple of times, trying to talk her down, but when she started rambling the same paranoid bullshit…I stopped answering. I was just so tired of it. Fed up."

"No one can blame you for that, Ezra." My words were hushed. Desperate. Because I could feel his pain. The way he was bleeding out.

He might not have believed he was suffering, might not have believed he had a right to grief, but I could taste the sourness of it on my tongue.

"No one could blame me, Savannah?" Ezra took my hand and splayed it over the tattoo on his pec, self-loathing filling his voice. "You want to know what this is?"

"Yes. I want to know you." My admission curled through the room, nothing but a plea.

"This was the moment I was fucking some girl I'd met at the bar next to the hotel in Poplar. The moment Brianna called me for the last time. The moment I ignored it because I was too busy seeking pleasure, too busy forgetting her, and she was leaving a message that

222 | A.L. JACKSON

she was afraid. That she was in trouble. I found out two hours later she was dead."

He pressed my hand harder against the brand.

My palm felt singed.

I guessed it really could burn me, that horror that I felt on his behalf.

Sickness churned in my stomach. I couldn't fully imagine the way Ezra must feel.

He continued without stopping. "I failed her, Savannah. I promised to protect her, to stick by her through thick and thin, and I failed her."

I urged him onto his back so I could move to straddle him.

He grunted at the action.

At the nearness.

At this connection that I wasn't sure either of us could understand.

"I'm so sorry, Ezra. I'm so sorry that you went through that. But you have to know that's not your fault."

"If there is one thing I could have stopped, it should have been that."

"What happened to her?" The question croaked from my mouth.

Ezra's laughter was hollow. "She was shot while walking across the parking lot at the bank. It was labeled a robbery gone bad, except none of that ever added up to me. It was more like a drive-by than anything else, so I've always known that designation was bullshit. She'd called me right before everything had gone down, begging me to answer."

"Oh my God, Ezra."

I'd assumed she'd been sick or there'd been a car accident or something terrible like that.

But this...

He lifted his hand and threaded his fingers into my hair where it draped down the side of my face. "I got this tattoo as a reminder of the way that I'd failed her. As a reminder of the way I'd failed my kids. Got it as a promise that I would devote myself to bringing her killers to justice. That I wouldn't look left or right until I found revenge for her death."

Vengeance.

That was the cloud I'd seen so many times haze over his eyes.

"More than that," Ezra continued, "I got it so every time I looked in the mirror I'd remember I didn't deserve to find joy for myself after I'd completely let her down."

He let the rest hang unsaid between us.

He'd broken that promise for me.

I had no idea what to make of that.

"I don't want to be a distraction for you."

His hand fisted in my hair, and he dragged me closer to him, breath to breath as he murmured, "Too late, Little Trespasser."

Then he kissed me again.

Chapter Thirty-Three

Ezra

DARKNESS DRIFTED THROUGH SAVANNAH'S ROOM, AND I kept fluttering my fingers through her hair as we both lay there absorbing everything that had happened between us.

The way I'd touched her and she'd touched me.

Both physically and emotionally.

The confession I'd made about Brianna that I had then sealed with a kiss.

A slow, deep, desperate kiss before I'd nudged Savannah off me and curled her back into my arms, just needing to have the perfect weight of her against me.

I felt like a thousand pounds of shame and grief had been expelled. Present and lingering, but not quite as heavy. Through it, I waited for the guilt to come. For it to hit like another strike of betrayal, confessing Brianna's secret that I'd held for so long.

I'd always felt like I needed to carry it on as some sort of tribute to her name. Hold the piece I should have protected.

Because I'd failed her.

I'd failed so reprehensibly and shamefully, and it'd caused a lifetime of pain and loss for my kids.

I hadn't listened when she'd begged for help. Had turned my back when she'd needed me most.

I wouldn't fail on the last promise I'd made to her when I'd stood over her grave. I would find those responsible. Bring them to justice. Whatever it required.

Tonight, that thirst for vengeance still soaked me through, but it was different, lying here with Savannah like this.

I shouldn't find so much comfort in it, her being here, not when she kept promising again and again she was going to leave. When I knew there was something going on with her. When I knew she was keeping her own secrets.

But there was no putting out the glow that burned in the center of me. A spark in the place where the little trespasser had gotten.

Savannah and I were on our sides facing each other, our breaths mingling in the space that separated us, those aqua eyes swimming with care as she continued to gently trace her fingers over the tattoo like she could assuage the pain.

I took that hand and pressed her knuckles to my lips.

Every rational part of me was aware that I should get up and leave. I was getting attached, and I had no doubt that my kids were, too.

The greedy part of me said fuck it.

I was going to stay.

"What are you hiding from?" I finally whispered into the lapping shadows. Couldn't shake how badly I wanted to know her. Understand her.

Savannah flinched where I held her in my arms. I'd already known she would. Had known she'd fight to keep herself shored up and camouflaged. But there was no not seeing her. Not when she was nothing but a beacon.

This dichotomy of a woman who could make me feel so fucking seen while she thought she didn't deserve the same thing.

"I'm not hiding anything, Ezra."

"Bullshit," I told her. "You think I don't know there's something going on behind those gorgeous eyes? You think I don't see it, the same way as you see me?"

I grinned against her knuckles. "Besides, it's only fair since you know more about me than anyone else. A secret for a secret."

Her eyes creased at the edges, trepidation filling her full, the woman shackled by distrust.

I did my best to kiss it away, lips on the inside of her wrist, her inner elbow, her jaw.

She trembled when I murmured them over the shell of her ear. "I'm here for you, Savannah. You're holding the biggest broken part of me. I promise I'll hold yours, too."

I edged away so I could take in every tweak and pinch of her expression, and I felt like I was getting razed at the knees with the sorrow held in those fathomless pools of blue. The woman sucking me right down. Pulling me under.

"You want to know me?" She blinked over at me.

I took her hand and returned her palm to my tattoo. "Isn't that what you said of me? That you wanted to know me? So yeah, Savannah, I think it's plain that I want to know you, too."

Fear dampened her features. "I don't trust easily, Ezra."

I smoothed the pad of my thumb over the creases that dented her forehead. "I recognized that from the first time I saw you. I'm just hoping there might be a way for you to trust me."

A soft puff of air escaped her nose. It brushed over my bare chest, filling me with her warmth. Covering me in her scent.

Mango and cream.

So goddamn sweet.

"I learned not to trust a long, long time ago."

Pain skimmed across her flesh, and I pulled her even closer, like I might have the chance of locking out that pain. Or maybe just calming it, the way she'd done for me.

She felt so tiny there, where I had her plastered against the hard, rigid lines of my body.

Fragile but tenacious. I couldn't stop myself from kissing along her jaw and down the delicate column of her throat.

Her fingers drove into my hair as she tilted back to allow me greater access. Her words tumbled between a tease and desire. "I never took you for the type of man who employs tactics of manipulation."

A rough chuckle skated free, and I released it at her mouth. "I'm just doing what a man has to do."

Savannah edged back an inch, all traces of any lightness gone and severity on her face. "And why would he need to?"

I reached out and took her chin between my thumb and index finger. "Because he cares."

She blinked. "He shouldn't."

"And sometimes he just can't fucking help it. And don't act like you don't care about me, Savannah. Don't act like you weren't bleeding for me when I told you about Brianna. Don't act like you don't feel *this*, too."

"But *this* is only going to hurt us."

"Probably," I admitted.

Her tongue stroked out to wet her dried lips. "Caring only leaves you devastated, Ezra, and I'm afraid caring about you will end up being the type of hurt I can't take."

"Because you've been hurt so many times before." It wasn't a question. I was just confirming what was written all over her.

Her laugh was hollow. "Everyone hurts me, Ezra. They leave me. They abandon me. They fail me."

They fail me.

Those words cut into me like a dull blade, and I fucking knew that I didn't want to be another person who fell into that category. That I wouldn't fail again.

That this was…different.

Fuck, I didn't know how it'd become so true, but it was.

Protectiveness ballooned inside me, pressing at my chest, the need to wipe the agony from her face. From her eyes. From her heart that thundered against mine.

"Your childhood was rough?"

Unquestionably.

Simply calling it *rough* felt like an insult, but I was hoping to give her a jumping point. A place to start. Even if she only wanted to share a little.

I'd known from the beginning that she was a survivor. A fighter. The kind of survivor who'd clawed her way through the muck to find herself on the other side. Someone who wore her fear like a shield so no one could get too close to inflict wounds again.

Affliction filled the shake of her head, and those locks of blonde strewn with brown tickled across my arm as she stared over at me. Uncertainty rolled through her before she seemed to make a decision, to *trust* me with this.

"My first memories are of the screaming." Her brow pinched deeper. "My mother and father shouting. Furniture breaking and glass shattering. I was probably four years old, and I remember lying in my little bed with my heart pounding so hard, with this feeling I didn't understand at the time, but I know now was fear and anxiety. Even in the middle of it, there was a protectiveness, too."

Her face pinched as she tumbled through the memories. "I remember going to my baby sister, crawling into her crib, and wrapping my arms around her. I don't think I said anything aloud, but I think I was making a promise that I would take care of her. Jessica."

Wistfulness filled her hushed words when she said her sister's name.

It speared through me, her devotion, her love.

"My father finally left one night, the door slamming shut behind him. We never heard from him again." Savannah blinked rapidly. "He didn't even say goodbye. You'd have thought that things might have gotten better after that, but I think in some sick way my father was holding my mother together or maybe she'd lost the one person she'd been taking her cruelty out on because she turned it on us."

Rage skidded through my veins, and I drew her closer, her name my breath. "Savannah."

Sadness shook her head. "She'd yell and scream and hit, and I remember being so thankful when she finally took us and dumped us at our grandmother's when I was seven and my sister was four. We finally had a safe, quiet place."

A bout of solace rolled through me, but it was eradicated in a moment. "Only our grandmother died two years later."

Moisture clouded that storm-filled gaze. "I'd never felt so alone as then, so terrified as when our mother came to the neighbor's house where we'd spent a couple nights and loaded us into her car. I remember how angry she'd seemed. Annoyed by our presence. After that, she kept dumping us different places, with our aunt for a couple months, then with random friends, though inevitably they'd get tired of having us around."

The words seemed to get stuck in Savannah's throat before she forced them out. "Pretty soon, our mother started leaving us with whatever guy she was dating at the time, and they…"

Her throat tremored, and I held her closer. Ugly, uncontrollable rage thrashed in my spirit.

A ferocity blazed through my body and ignited in my fingertips. Searing me with the need to kill.

She swallowed, and she lifted that brave chin the way she did, pushing into a place I had a hunch she never allowed anyone into, either. The words that fell from her mouth were wrought with strain and the type of horror that only existed in the kind of life that she'd lived. "I did everything to protect my sister because she was the only one that mattered to me. It was just me and her against the world, and God, Ezra, were we against the world. Surviving the best that we could. I did everything I could to keep her safe."

Savannah's voice cracked, and I brushed my thumb over the sharp angle of her cheek. Sickness curdled in my stomach.

"No child should ever have to go through that, Savannah."

A tear streaked free. "No, but we did. I was fifteen when our mother left us again. It took a couple weeks before I realized she was never coming back. Her boyfriend saw it as…an opportunity."

She dragged her nails across my chest like she was seeking a way in.

A safe place.

And that's the only fucking thing that I wanted for her.

To give her a safe place.

Savannah's words turned harsh and haggard. "I wasn't going to allow it to happen, Ezra, I wasn't going to stand there weak and pathetic and allow someone to hurt us. To hurt my sister. So I packed the few things that we had, and we escaped that night. I kept us hidden, jumping from friend to friend, just like Jessica and I had done when we were young. But I knew if someone found out that our mother was gone, we'd be put in foster care, and we'd be separated. And that was a fate I couldn't tolerate. I'd promised her that it was just her and me. Forever. We were going to make it together and we didn't need anyone else. Why, when they would just abandon us anyway? Hurt us? We had to fight for ourselves and take care of each other."

More tears fell, and I kept trying to capture them, hold them, so she'd know I'd hold her, too.

How could she trust anyone after what she'd been put through?

And I hated for her...hated every person who'd ever inflicted a scar. Anyone who'd ever let her down. Every single person who hadn't been there for her when she needed it.

"And we did," Savannah wheezed. "Jessica and I made it for years. Hiding in the shadows. We didn't go to school because obviously someone would notice, and I worked two jobs and rented a room from this sweet old lady who I'd convinced I was twenty."

She warred, and her voice dropped even lower. "Once Jessica turned eighteen, I was starting to hope, Ezra. Had started to hope that life was going to turn out different for us. We were going to make it past the abuse and the trauma that we'd been raised in."

She bit the inside of her cheek, and the most gutting kind of vulnerability seeped into her tone. "But history has a way of repeating itself, doesn't it? And I was the fool who thought that things might change. Believed that there were some people who might stand for you because I didn't want to believe this entire world was truly void of devotion and love."

I braced myself for the impact of what she said next, already anticipating the atrocity.

"I opened myself up, Ezra...I opened myself up after I promised myself I never would again, and I loved. I loved a man who promised to protect me and keep me. Give it all for me. He'd encouraged me to get my GED and then helped me chase my dream of becoming a photographer. He was there with me as I took classes, then he helped me get my website designed when I was ready to start my own business."

She inhaled a shaky breath. "I remember the night he struck me so vividly because that single blow hurt worse than any wound I'd ever sustained in my entire life. Because it was proof that no one could be trusted. It was the night I lost the last thread of hope."

A vat of fury dumped into my bloodstream, and I realized I was holding her so tight that it was probably to the point of pain.

But I realized that's what this was. This was pain and savagery and a brutality that made me sick.

My stomach rolled over with nausea and aggression knit me in a fist.

"Fuck, Savannah…" I choked around the anguish. "I can't imagine all that you've gone through. I'm so sorry. If I could, I would race out into this world and undo every wrong that anyone has ever committed against you."

"But you can't, Ezra. There is no erasing this. And Jessica…Jessica was supposed to be the only exception."

Savannah choked over that, and her nails sank into my shoulders as she was pummeled by a deluge of grief.

It crashed over me, too. Saturating my cells and sinking all the way to the core. I pressed my lips to her forehead in an attempt to staunch her misery that was pouring out.

Stagnant and decayed.

"Where is she?" I almost couldn't bear to voice it.

A sob hitched from her throat. "She left me, too, Ezra. She left me, too."

It shouldn't have been possible to get her closer, but I somehow managed it, tucking her into every crevice of my body, covering her like a shield, praying to God I could give her sanctuary from the torment that wracked her as she wept.

"I'm so sorry," I murmured, "I'm so sorry."

I held her like that for a long time before I pushed deeper into the place that called between us. That tether that right then somehow soothed. "And you came here to leave it all behind."

Pulling back, Savannah looked up at me, her face mottled and red from her tears. "No, Ezra, I came here hoping to find my heart."

My own heart thudded an extra beat, like maybe it was hoping to be found, too.

Dangerous.

Because I finally understood. Understood the shields and the walls. The steel barricade she tried to keep around her tender, beautiful heart. A heart that had been battered and torn.

"And you...you keep trying to make me feel things that I know better than feeling," she whispered. I could almost see her begging me to push her away. To prove that I would let her down, too.

"I would never hurt you." It slashed from my tongue. I hadn't needed to give it thought.

"You can't promise me that."

I pressed her hand against the thunder in my chest, and I murmured, "I already did."

Journal Entry

She'd texted me. It was only an address and a time, but I somehow knew it was her the second it came through. I was familiar with the park on the far side of town. There were a couple ballfields and playgrounds on each side, but what made it so peaceful was the big pond in the middle that was surrounded by soaring trees, their branches wide and casting a large canopy of shade.

I'd found her sitting on the sloped hill that was covered in grass, watching the ducks that floated in the placid waters and the children that played on the swing set on the opposite side.

Her arms were curled around her knees that were tucked to her chest, and her dark-blonde hair billowed in the soft breeze that rustled through.

She should have been the epitome of peace.

A picture of it.

Only I'd felt the turmoil roiling from her spirit.

Radiating.

It was haunted and fresh, as if she was trying to escape her pain but kept running straight back into it.

Carefully, I'd eased up before I came to sit beside her, leaving a couple feet between us.

Silence had stretched on for the longest time, though it had felt like I was gaining her trust in it.

Finally, I'd taken the chance and spoke. "I'm glad you reached out to me."

Raspy air slipped from her lungs. "I shouldn't have."

"Why?"

"Because it's not safe."

My ribs had squeezed my heart in the most agonized fist. Because I'd known. Had known it the second that I'd seen her that she was in trouble.

I'd carefully formed my question, praying I wouldn't scare her away. "Why aren't you safe?"

"None of us really are, are we?"

"Not always, no, but some situations are much worse than others." I'd paused, then pressed. "And your situation is dangerous?"

She'd glanced around like she was terrified she was being watched again before she let go of a shaky exhale. "Have you ever just...found yourself someplace you didn't realize you'd gone? Has it ever felt like you woke up one day and you were in a completely different place than you thought you were?"

"Literally or figuratively?"

Caution had filled each word, forming them in a way that I'd hoped wouldn't make her think I was judging her in any way.

"Figuratively, I guess, but now that I'm here, this place looks so different than it was supposed to, so it feels literal." She looked over the waters when she added, "It was a trap."

I blinked through the puzzle of what she was saying. "How so?"

From the side, I'd seen her gnaw her bottom lip. "He was supposed to love me, and it turns out I was only prey."

Dread filled my chest when I looked over at her, and I murmured, "Who?"

I should have known that was what would send her running, but if I was going to help her? If she was in immediate danger? Then I needed to know who she needed to be rescued from.

But she'd jumped to her feet, terror holding her hostage, her attention darting everywhere as if she'd been terrified someone would see her talking with me. "I'm sorry for wasting your time."

I reached for her. "You're not—"

"I have to go."

Without saying anything else, she'd disappeared into the trees.

I'd been torn between chasing after her and respecting her boundaries. In the end, I'd stayed put, knowing if she was ever going to trust me, I had to allow her to talk when she was ready. Otherwise, she would completely lock down.

I can only pray now that she gets to that point soon. Because I'm worried if she doesn't, it might be too late.

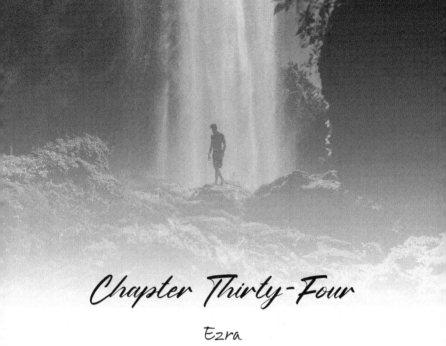

Chapter Thirty-Four

Ezra

I BOLTED UPRIGHT WITH THE NOISE THAT PULLED ME FROM sleep. A straight shock of adrenaline dumped into my veins, and I was instantly on edge as I strained to listen over my heart that ravaged at my chest.

The only sound was Savannah's deep, rhythmic breaths that whispered from where she slept on the mattress at my side, her chest rising and falling where she remained lost to slumber.

My gaze narrowed as I peered through the darkness that held fast to her room. A bare glow from the moon barely lit behind the thin drapes, and it sent shadows scattering over the white walls.

The stillness was so thick that I could taste it.

Ominous.

Sinister.

I didn't know if it was training or instinct, but I knew something wasn't right. I could feel the disturbance that existed beneath whatever had awoken me, and I slowly eased out from under the covers that were tangled around my waist and stood on the plush rug on the floor.

I kept as quiet as I could as I crept across the room to the window that overlooked the backyard, wincing when the floorboards creaked beneath my feet. Still, that silence wept, a shiver that brushed over my flesh and incited a riot inside me.

Carefully, I pulled the drape aside and peered out.

Moonlight spilled from the heavens and cast the lawn in a sheen of silver. The limbs of the massive tree that stood proud in the middle of the yard waved in the breeze, the leaves rustling and shivering through the night.

My house beyond it was still, the porch light I'd left on illuminating the space. My attention hunted over the yard, and I struggled to see into the darkened corners.

That was when I heard it again.

A crunch.

But it wasn't coming from the backyard. It was coming from the front of the guest house. I hurried over to where my jeans had been discarded on the floor. I shrugged into them, the same as I did my shirt.

Savannah stirred behind me, and she blinked in confusion, or maybe it was hurt, as she sat up. I had the imprudent urge to promise her I wasn't going anywhere. That I wouldn't leave her. That I was right there, and *with her* was where I was always going to be.

Only glass shattered and that adrenaline that had been riding through my veins pitched into aggression.

Aqua eyes widened in fear, and I growled, "Don't move, Savannah, stay right here."

I hated leaving her by herself, but I didn't have a choice, and I forced myself to move, attention rapt, fully on guard as I eased forward. At the end of the short hall, I pressed my back to the wall and searched left and right over the living area.

It could be nothing, but I knew full well a person never knew what they were going to come up against, and I sure as hell was not taking a chance with this.

Wasn't taking a chance with *her*.

Savannah whose spirit I could feel toiling behind me. Her anxiety was thick as I slipped through the shadows to the front door. I peered out the window to the side of it, into the glinting rays that danced like wraiths in a playground of darkness.

It was then I caught it. The flash of movement off to the far right on the other side of Savannah's car. It didn't take a whole lot to surmise that it was a person. Dressed all in black like the asshole had been watching too many reruns of *Law and Order*.

Fury billowed up from the fiery depths. Where I'd stored all that hatred for the last year and a half. Because whoever this prick was *knew*. Knew that I was hunting them. Knew I wasn't going to stop until I found whoever was responsible for Brianna, and my gut warned me this bastard had been sent to try to dissuade me from doing it.

They were going to learn tonight that I wouldn't be deterred.

The only thing I really fucking wished was that I had my gun and was wearing shoes, but I wasn't about to let that stop me, either. I had to move quickly before he took off, which didn't give me time to sneak around the side of the house like I would have liked to have done—left me lacking the element of surprise—but it was just the way this was going to have to go down.

I unlatched the lock, flung the door open, and flew out.

Except maybe the fucker was surprised when the whites of his eyes went wide beneath the pale moonlight, though the rest of his face was concealed in the shadows of the hoodie he wore.

One second later, the piece of shit turned and ran.

I didn't hesitate to chase him, unwilling to let the asshole get away, and my bare feet pounded across the porch before I hurtled off the single step and onto the ground.

He darted back down the alley along the outside of the fence that enclosed my backyard. The ground here was rocky and weedy, and sharp spikes dug into the bottom of my feet, but I didn't slow. I raced after the wicked silhouette, my throat clogged with the need to get to him.

To rip the hoodie from his head to find what monster was hidden underneath.

I knew he was related.

Knew he was responsible.

Knew his face would tell me exactly who had taken Brianna from this world.

Hatred and my shame sent me driving faster, harsh breaths panting from my lungs as I sprinted over the craggy terrain. Fucker pushed himself faster, our grunted breaths panted into the air from the exertion of the chase.

I gained on him, my long legs eating up the space and drawing him closer to his demise.

Because I'd end him.

I enclosed, each pound of my feet bringing me closer to him until I finally reached out and got a handful of the back of his hoodie. It ripped, making me lose my grip, but the force of it tripped him up. His arms pinwheeled in an attempt to catch his balance before he toppled forward, and his chest skidded across the pitted ground.

And there he was, the answer to the poison that roiled inside me.

The guy was fairly thick and muscled, but still a fraction of my size.

I reached down with both hands and grabbed the tattered fabric and tossed him over onto his back. Only his arm whipped out as I did.

It was a blur of movement that I didn't anticipate before a blinding pain pierced me in the side. So sharp that my sight glazed over, and I dropped to my knees as a roar ripped from the darkest place inside me.

The creep jumped back to his feet and darted into the darkness of the alley, and a second later, his shadow disappeared around the end of the fence.

Rage billowed from my mouth, and I tried to stand to chase after him. To hunt him down. But the agonizing pain blistering up my side dropped me straight back to my knees.

My hand went to my side, and I pulled it away to find my palm smeared with blood.

Shock penetrated, wrath splintering me through.

The motherfucker had stabbed me.

Chapter Thirty-Five

Savannah

THE FRONT DOOR BANGED AGAINST THE INTERIOR WALL AS Ezra's heavy footsteps pounded across the porch before they faded into the distance.

Gripping the sheets to my chest, I tried to orient myself. To catch up to the fear that consumed. This terror that things had just spiraled out of control.

Funny that five seconds ago I hadn't been afraid when I'd woken to Ezra getting dressed. I'd been struck with a lance of pain, immediately jumping to the conclusion that he was leaving right after he'd promised that he would never hurt me.

My psyche had laughed in my face, demanding to know if I had thought it would be different. Taunting me for falling into the trap of trusting.

People were never who they claimed at the beginning.

They hurt.

They wounded.

They abandoned and they forgot.

It's what they did.

It's what they always did.

I should have expected it.

I just shouldn't have expected it to hurt so bad, but how wouldn't it after I'd shared with him my past? My pain? And I'd been so close— so very close—to telling him why I was really here. That I was looking for my sister. That I didn't believe that she'd just left me.

Only I'd been swamped with the reminder of what had happened with the last person I'd been foolish enough to share it with.

That officer who'd used it as an opportunity to get close to me.

Manipulate me.

I'd known better. I'd known better.

Even after all of that, I had been tempted to tell Ezra.

Somehow, I'd held it back. Because if I trusted him with that? He would have all of me.

And how could I give it to him? After everything this excruciating life had taught me?

But I was allowing Ezra to get so deep. Deeper than anyone before him.

Maybe it'd felt safer to jump to the conclusion that he was sneaking out.

Leaving me behind.

It'd only taken a blink of clearing my eyes to see that Ezra's were close to black.

That his warm gaze was dimmed with destruction.

As if he'd been possessed by another entity completely.

A part of himself rarely seen.

The shattering of glass was what had finally clued me in to Ezra's intentions.

My nerves clanged and clattered as I strained to listen, my ear tuned to where he'd clicked open the front door and slipped out.

Fear pulsed against the determination that flailed in my middle. The part of me that had refused to believe that my sister had left me, the part that cried out that something was wrong, that she was in need. That the journal actually meant something, even though it had never once mentioned her by name.

Terror chugged my pulse in ragged beats. What if whatever danger she had found herself in had just caught up to me? What if the near break-in at the motel hadn't been random? What if I'd brought danger to Ezra? To his children?

My attention darted to the closet where I'd hidden the journal beneath extra blankets and pillows that were stored on the top shelf.

Horror flash-fired. Magnified and turned over. I couldn't stand the idea of him being hurt because of me. Couldn't imagine. Couldn't let it happen.

I tossed the covers off, grabbed my cell from the charger, and ran down the hall. I was still only dressed in my panties and that camisole, but I didn't take the time to worry about it.

I refused the smack of cold that doused my skin in chills the second I stepped out into the freezing air.

None of it mattered when I had no idea what was happening to Ezra outside.

Stalling near the doorway, I listened, unsure of what to do.

Until a roar hit the night. Piercing and cutting into the disorder.

I pushed all the way out the door, and I ran across the porch and out onto the grass before I hit the end of it and the ground became hard. Littered with weeds and dirt and rocks.

I tried not to whimper as sticks and sharp edges of stone bit into the soles of my feet.

I strained to focus, to orient myself to the night that swirled in a disorienting mist. My eyes narrowed as I tried to make out what was in front of me, and a horrified cry jutted free when I realized it was the shape of Ezra on his knees, upright for one moment before he toppled over to the left and slumped to the ground.

Panic squeezed my heart, and I raced to him and dropped to my knees behind him. "Ezra, are you okay? What happened?"

I touched his sweat-drenched forehead, and I tried to lean over him enough that I could see his face. Wide eyes blinked up at me, the whites glinting beneath the glow of the moon.

"Fucker stabbed me," he grunted.

Terror ripped through my consciousness.

"Oh my God." It was a whimper, and my hands shook uncontrollably as I fumbled to lift my phone to dial 9-1-1.

Ezra moaned, and I brushed my fingers through his hair, trying to give him comfort in the second it took for the operator to respond.

"9-1-1, what's your emergency?"

I recognized Pamela's voice. "Pamela," I wheezed. "It's Ezra. He was attacked behind his house, in the alley."

A bare beat of horror flashed through the line before she inhaled and pulled herself together. Good thing one of us had some composure because I was afraid I was going to rattle apart.

I could hear her typing quickly, could hear the harsh quality of her breaths, her professionalism that she attempted to hang onto while worry wobbled her voice. "Police and ambulance are en route. Are you in a safe area?"

I hadn't even thought to look around to see if someone was still lurking in the shadows, and it was fear and protection that filled me full as I rose up higher, making myself as large as I could, intending to be a shield for Ezra if whoever this bastard was returned.

"I don't know," I whispered.

"Go inside," Ezra demanded through a groan.

"I'm not leaving you."

"Go," he grated.

I choked through a disordered laugh, and I ran my fingers through his hair again. There he was, my sweetly overbearing Hot Cop, all grumpy and gruff.

He was going to be fine. He was going to be fine.

"I'm fine." He said it like he'd just heard me silently trying to convince myself of it and was offering me the comfort. "Go inside until we know it's safe."

"I'm not going anywhere, Ezra. Not unless you want me to try to carry you, which I've always thought of myself as strong, but I'm not sure I could lift the likes of you." I didn't allow myself to evaluate the words that escaped.

I was afraid if I did, they might mean more than this instance, and instead I focused on the pelting of relief when I heard sirens suddenly whirl to life.

They were close.

Really close.

Thank God for small towns.

"I would also recommend that you seek safety until the authorities arrive, Savannah." Pamela's instruction was urgent.

"They're already almost here." I could hear the whir of an engine, the siren growing louder as it entered the neighborhood. Not that it would have mattered if they were a hundred miles away.

I wasn't going anywhere.

I wasn't.

"*Dangerous.*" Ezra mumbled it, and I tucked him closer and whispered, "Shh."

I didn't know if I was distinctly lacking self-preservation or what. But there wasn't any amount of *danger* that could get me to move right then.

Red and white lights suddenly jumped through the darkened sky, and a second later, a Sheriff cruiser turned into the alley, followed by an ambulance. The sirens quieted, but the lights continued to flash.

The door to the cruiser opened, and I peered through the blaze of headlights and finally made out the figure approaching.

Samson.

The officer who had come when Ezra had called about the motel break-in. He had his gun drawn as he approached, carefully, eyes hunting through the trees and shrubs to ensure it was clear.

"Perpetrator ran, took a right at Maple," Ezra grumbled, lifting his grunting voice at Samson.

With Ezra's explanation, Samson jogged the rest of the way over. "What the hell happened? Are you okay?"

Samson's attention flashed to me for one single beat, calculating the situation before he returned it to Ezra.

"Find that asshole, and I'll be just fine," Ezra grumbled. "And get these emergency lights turned off. I don't want the entire neighborhood running out here to find their Sheriff like this."

Samson hesitated before Ezra shouted, "Go!"

"Damn, I guess you are just fine." Samson almost chuckled before he ran back toward the ambulance. The driver was just climbing out, and Samson shouted orders at him before he darted around the end of the fence and out onto Maple that ran that side.

A couple seconds later, the flashing lights of the ambulance went out, then the cruiser, too, before three paramedics emerged through the haze of headlights that still burned, close to jogging as they carried their equipment.

A female paramedic carrying a big bag rushed to Ezra when she saw him on the ground. "What the hell happened to you?"

"Some bastard got me with a blade."

"Where?" Worry whipped through her features. No question, they knew each other.

The other two paramedics were right behind. "Fuck, Ezra," one said as he dropped his bag to the ground.

"What bastard am I gonna have to hunt down?" the last said.

Each of them kept peeking at me like they were trying to discern who I was, though each were quick to cover it.

"It's not a big deal," Ezra said, groaning as he sat up.

"Whoa." The woman put her hands out to stop him. "Don't move until we get you checked out."

Ezra placed his hand on his right side. "Asshole got me good enough to knock the fucking breath out of me, but I don't think it's deep. I can stand."

Was he serious?

With him sitting up and the lights shining on him, I could see his white tee was soaked with blood.

Terror coursed through my body.

My hold tightened on him, my voice nearing a shriek. "Don't you dare try to stand, Ezra Patterson. You're going to let these people take care of you."

Those eyes flashed to me, raking over my exposed flesh. They flared when he found that the only thing I had on was what I'd gone to bed in. "You need to get back inside, Savannah. It's freezing."

"I already told you I wasn't going anywhere."

One of the paramedics pulled a blanket from his pack and came around to wrap me in it. "Here," he murmured.

Warmth enfolded me, and I hadn't realized how badly I'd been shaking until I was clutching the fabric around me. "Thank you," I whispered.

"I'm Xavier, this is Everett, and that's Christa."

"It's nice to meet you all." I could barely force it out because introductions seemed a little low on the priority list right then.

"You, too," Christa said before she turned her attention where it should be. "Let's get that injury checked out before you take off trying to hunt down a bad guy, yeah?"

She eased to her knees in front of him, and she dug into her bag and pulled out a pair of scissors.

I pushed to my feet and edged back a little to give them room, but I hovered close. She cut through the fabric and peeled it away, and Ezra hissed as the area was exposed.

The man was a giant sitting on the ground with the headlights lighting him up in a spotlight, his shoulders and chest bare in the bright blaze. I could see the way he vibrated with violence. Without a doubt, he wanted to do exactly what the paramedic had suggested he might.

"It's nothing, Christa."

"Nothing my ass," she shot back as she angled down to inspect it. "You're bleeding like a burst water main over here."

I couldn't do anything but move around to his opposite side so I could see, and my heart fisted when I saw the wound. It was about an inch wide and gaping, blood gushing from it and sliding down his side in fat rivulets.

"As long as it didn't hit any vital organs then it's nothing," Ezra spat.

Christa rolled her eyes like this was expected behavior. "Well, you certainly aren't going to die because it appears to only be about an inch and a half deep, but you are going to need a few stitches."

"Then hurry and stitch me up so I can assist my officer."

Everett laughed. "I'm thinking a trip to the ER in Poplar is in order."

Ezra sent him a surly glare. "I'm pretty sure one of you assholes can handle it."

"We need to recommend that you see a doctor, Ezra," Xavier urged.

Ezra growled. "Not gonna happen, Xavier. Stitch me up."

All three of the paramedics shared a look, and Christa wavered before she said, "Only if you promise you'll stay in bed for the next twenty-four hours. You're going to have to let Samson do the job this time."

Were they actually considering this nonsense?

"Isn't that like…against protocol?" I mean, I was thinking a doctor checking him out and doing the stitching seemed like a solid idea. We needed to know he was really fine. That there wasn't some underlying injury that they were missing out here considering they were doing an examination in the middle of the night, outside, in the freezing cold.

Christa laughed. "This guy right here loves to buck protocol."

She shoved Ezra's shoulder before the three of them stood, and the man had the audacity to grin.

I didn't know what it was about it, but I guessed it was that expression, the one that somehow made me sure he was okay, the one that cracked a hole of relief through the middle of me and allowed the adrenaline to drain away. Only it was replaced by the terror I'd felt when I'd found him falling to the ground.

It welled, thickening my throat and making my stupid eyes burn.

I tried to hold it back.

Contain it.

But there was no stopping it. A sob erupted.

Ezra's expression softened, and he reached out the arm on his injured side, holding his other hand over the wound. "Come're, Little Trespasser."

Crap. Crap. Crap.

I was in so much trouble. So much trouble. Because I knew I was falling when I shuffled forward and again dropped to my knees at his side. But this time the circumstances were reversed, and Ezra was the one comforting me. Wrapping me in that arm and trying to pull me against his hurt side while he pressed his lips to my temple. "Don't worry about me."

Too late.

It was far too late.

I choked over another cry, and Ezra murmured, "I know. I know."

Chapter Thirty-Six

Ezra

MY BEDROOM DOOR CREAKED OPEN, AND SAVANNAH popped her head through the doorway. Her gaze was filled with the same shaky concern she'd been watching me with for the last hour.

My goddamn heart squeezed.

Her hair was a matted mess, her face full of all those severe, striking angles, so sharp they could cut deeper than the wound on my side.

But it was those aqua eyes that slayed as she stood there taking me in like it was the first time she was really seeing me.

Like everything was different.

Like everything had changed.

It had.

I knew it.

I knew it all the way to my soul.

Ten minutes ago, she'd gone to the guest house—escorted by Christa since I sure as hell wasn't going to let her go back there by herself—to change into some actual clothes since she'd been wearing that blanket like a cloak for the last hour.

When Christa, Everett, and Xavier had walked up, I'd had the urge to cover her, protectiveness binding me in a fist of possession. Xavier had caught it and wrapped her in the blanket, thankfully keeping me from snarling at everyone to turn their goddamn heads until I could get her covered because I didn't want anyone to find her in that vulnerable state.

To judge, even though if I was being rational, I knew they wouldn't. I'd known the three of them my whole life and unequivocally trusted them with it.

But there was something about it that had me gritting my teeth.

The whole situation did.

A fresh wave of fury rode through my bloodstream, thoughts snagged on whoever the fucker was who'd been lurking outside the guest house. Outside my house. Someone who'd been scared enough of me getting to him, discovering his identity, that he'd stabbed me.

Fury spun. The need to jump out of this bed and track down the monster was almost overwhelming, though I attempted to tuck it down as Savannah peered over at me in nothing but dread and concern.

I managed a grin. "You don't need to get shy on me now, Little Trespasser."

She'd already invaded.

She eased into my room, and her gaze swept my bare torso where I was propped against the headboard like she needed to make sure I was still in one piece. Everett had just finished stitching and bandaging me up, and Savannah had hovered in the corner of the room the entire time, not wanting to get in the way but refusing to leave.

It was the first second we'd had alone since the stubborn woman had dropped to her knees beside me right after the asshole had taken off, refusing to leave my side even when she knew full well she might have been in danger.

I'd sensed it when she'd shifted, when she'd risen up on her knees and stretched her tiny frame out like a little serpent who wouldn't be afraid to bite.

She'd been guarding me.

Dangerous.

That's what she was. Completely, utterly dangerous to every resolve I had made. Because those resolves no longer existed.

She'd obliterated them.

Slowly, Savannah approached. "How are you feeling?"

"Like I want to chase a bad guy down."

Plush lips dipped down at one side, and the image of her on her knees with my cock in my mouth took the inopportune time to flood my brain.

She crept to the side of my bed. It was so high that the top of the mattress hit her at the waist, and I didn't think she'd ever looked as small as right then. She'd changed into a thin, cream-colored sweater with sleeves so long that she was gripping the ends in her hands, and she'd paired it with black leggings.

She'd swept her mess of hair into a ponytail.

Casual and soft and the best thing I'd ever seen.

"I think I—" She started to speak when there was a tapping at the door behind her, and Samson poked his head inside.

I gestured for him to enter. "Did you find anything?"

Samson's expression was grim. "Not a trace of whoever the prick was, nothing but a few boot prints and the driver's-side window of Savannah's car that was shattered."

Savannah flinched, fear palpable as it ricocheted around the room.

"I want you to get everything you can on those prints."

"We're already on it."

Of course, they were. Samson didn't need me telling him how to do his job because he did it well. But I couldn't seem to stop spitting orders. Not with what was riding on this. Not with what was at stake.

"Thank you," I told him.

He cracked a grin, even though it was brittle. "Don't worry, brother, I'm going to take great pleasure in tracking down this guy."

I didn't want to admit to him that I needed that information for myself. I needed to go this alone. I was the one who needed to get justice for Brianna.

"Just get me whatever you can."

"You can count on that."

Something passed through his expression, and I wondered if he understood. If he got it on some level. Then he gestured at me with his chin. "Now get some rest before Savannah here has my ass for keeping you up for too long."

He glanced at her when he said it with a sly grin on his face.

"I'll make sure of it," she said, clearly not giving a shit that he knew she wouldn't be going anywhere tonight. Nowhere but snuggling next to me on this bed.

He set his hand on the doorknob. "Take care of him. Dude might act like he doesn't feel any pain, but he bleeds red just like the rest of us."

There was an undercurrent to his words, and there was no missing the fact that he wasn't talking about the physical.

Then he dipped out and shut the door behind him.

Sighing, I looked back at Savannah who shifted on her feet next to my bed, anxiety running her through. I figured I should just lay it out. "I've never seen you look so nervous, Savannah Ward. I guess you can see now that you're in over your head."

A frown marred her brow. "What do you mean?"

"It means I've made some enemies."

Surprise clashed with the confusion, and she chewed at her bottom lip. "You think someone is after you?"

"Yeah, honey, someone's after me because I've been after them."

Dread crept into her expression. "Who?"

"I told you that I was hunting Brianna's killers. Everyone else might have written it off, but I'm not about to, and I'm pretty sure whoever these bastards are were trying to send a warning for me to call it off."

I paused, fighting the lump in my throat. "In the back of my mind, I've always thought it was likely a retaliation of some sort. Someone coming back at me for putting somebody behind bars. We've cracked some vicious cells over the years...have taken down some bad guys that went high up. I'm not fool enough to think that didn't go unnoticed."

Alarm flashed across her face.

An incredulous laugh rolled up my throat, and I scrubbed a hand over my face to clear the disorder that blurred my eyes. My sight on this woman, unable to look away, terrified that I should. "It's funny that I brought you here because I wanted to give you a safe place, and I think the only thing I might have done was drag you into my mess. I'm fucking sorry for that."

"You think I might be in danger, being here?" Savannah's voice was a whisper. But she didn't back away. She came closer.

My shrug was full of regret. "I don't know, Savannah, but I can't stand the idea that someone was outside my house, and I can't write it off as nothing when they'd been willing to do this."

I tipped my head toward my side.

"I don't know if I've brought trouble to my door. To you. To my kids."

I choked the last, barely able to speak when I gave voice to my heart. My whole reason.

"But how can I turn my back when my gut promises that Brianna's death wasn't random? What kind of person would that make me, when I already missed the mark when it came to her? I can't just let it go."

Uncertainty had her chewing on the inside of her cheek, and she glanced away for a beat before she returned that striking gaze to me. "What if it was related to what happened at the motel?"

A frown dented between my eyes. "How so?"

She wavered, hesitated, then cleared her throat. "I don't know. I'm probably just being paranoid."

I stretched a hand toward her. "I won't let anything happen to you, Savannah. When I said this was supposed to be your safe place, I meant it, and I'm going to do whatever it takes to make sure that's exactly what you are. Safe. Just like I'm going to do for my kids. Fuck, what if I—?"

The words clipped off because I couldn't bear to say it.

Rage and horror slammed me at the thought of someone hurting them. Affliction beating through me at the idea that something bad could befall them because of the badge that I wore.

I couldn't fail them again.

Savannah climbed onto the bed in the wake of the disorder that banged the walls of my room.

She straddled my waist.

Carefully.

Her touch so gentle as she took me by both sides of my face, tender as she forced me to look into the depths of those fathomless eyes.

I was pretty sure I fell right then.

Into the abyss that was this girl.

I was sure of it when she whispered harshly, "You are everything those kids need, Ezra Patterson. Don't you dare lay here and think for a second that you're a bad parent because believe me, I've seen them, I've known them, and you aren't one of them. You are the kindest, most caring man I've ever met. And those kids? They adore you. They need you. They love you. But your love for them…?"

Her tongue stroked out to wet her bottom lip, and I could hear the drumbeat of her heart battering at her ribs. "That night that I spent here with all of you? I had never witnessed anything so beautiful. The devotion that's here. The safety that rings within these walls. It both broke my heart seeing it and healed it at the same time because it's the first time I'd seen anything like it firsthand."

Savannah's hands tightened on my cheeks. "You made me believe in something I didn't know existed, Ezra. You made me believe in possibility. You made me hope again. And I promise you, you've given all of that to your children."

Devotion clotted my chest. "I won't fail them."

"You won't. You couldn't. Not with the way you love them."

I reached up and fluttered my fingers along that defined jaw. "I won't fail you, either."

The woman hovered above me.

A fantasy.

A dream.

She searched every groove and cut and twist of my expression for the lie.

My palm covered the entire right side of her face. "Stay with me."

She hesitated, then whispered with a smile tweaking the edge of her mouth. "Where would I go? Someone has to be here to keep you in check. You don't seem to be all that great at following directions."

My arm looped around her waist, and I tugged her close, and there was no keeping out the smack of lust that fisted my guts.

I fell into the tease.

The lightness that rained.

This understanding that suddenly billowed through the room.

Safety.

"Are you going to punish me if I disobey?" I teased.

"I might have to handcuff you to me and throw away the key." Playfulness pranced across her lips.

I tugged her closer, ignoring the stinging pain that streaked up my side. "Are you tempting me to run? I'm kind of liking the sound of the penalty."

Taking my hand, she weaved our fingers together and lifted them out to the side. Both of us stared at where we were linked. That energy shivered in the room, and vulnerability seeped into her question. "And when you get tired of me?"

"I think that's the whole problem, Savannah. I'm pretty sure there will be no getting tired of you. The problem is, I might want to claim you forever."

Chapter Thirty-Seven

Savannah

THE BAREST FLUSH OF LIGHT FLOODED THE ROOM AS MY eyes blinked open to foreign surroundings, except I recognized instantly where I was. Recognized the massive man who still held me as tightly as he had when we'd finally drifted to sleep.

An arm as thick as a log was draped over my side, keeping me trapped against his heat, and I couldn't see over the mountain of shoulders where he slept on his side. His breaths were even and long, and his muscled chest rose and fell with each respiration.

I took the opportunity and allowed my fingers to trace over his skin that glowed golden in the first rays of the morning. Over the solid, packed terrain of his beautiful body. My touch trembled over the tattoo written on his heart, terrified that he might completely hold the battered remains of mine.

My fingertips roamed, and my heart clutched in trepidation. In concern. In worry. How could someone have hurt him this way? What if someone really was after him? What if someone hated him enough that they'd want to hurt the ones he cared for?

My spirit clutched at the thought of his children. I wanted to wrap them up and protect them, too, the same way as I wanted to protect him.

I knew he thought I would look at him differently after he'd told me about what had happened between him and Brianna, that I'd think less of him, view him with repulsion and disgust.

How could I have? Not when he'd been hurt again and again. He'd felt the lashes of betrayal. His own trust carved out with a rusted blade. I didn't blame him, even though I knew he blamed himself.

It wasn't like I couldn't feel his devotion. His devotion to Brianna even though he hadn't been in love with her any longer. His devotion to his kids.

And he would fight for them, the same way as I would fight for Jessica.

I was having a hard time delineating what happened last night from her. What if Ezra was wrong and this didn't have anything to do with him but was related to me?

I couldn't stomach the idea that I'd done anything to put these amazing people at risk.

At my motions, Ezra's eyes fluttered open. That warm-honey gaze drank me in through the motes that floated through the room. I'd never noticed how long his eyelashes were until then, the way they framed his eyes in a halo of black.

I reached up and gently brushed my fingertips along the sharp angle of his cheek.

"How are you?" I whispered, my voice still hoarse with sleep.

Pulling me closer, he burrowed his face under my chin and murmured against the sensitive skin of my neck, "Never felt better than waking up with you in my arms."

I should reject those words, but instead, giddiness swept through.

"Don't get used to it, Hot Cop." The tease was out with the impact of it. Lightness filling every hollow and recess of my chest.

Pulling at my lips and tumbling through my spirit.

Ezra propped himself on his elbow so he could look down at me. If it caused him any pain, he didn't show it. Instead, he grinned like a maniac. You'd think the attack hadn't even occurred last night, with the way he was arching those brows and the razzing question played all over his masculine face. "Hot Cop?"

I rolled my eyes. "Don't pretend like you don't know you're hot."

Mischief danced through his expression. "How hot?"

My gaze narrowed. "Digging for compliments, are we, Officer Patterson? Do you really need to hear me say how sexy you already know you are? That I was having a hard time speaking the first time I saw you? That I haven't stopped thinking of you since?"

Possession filled his growl, and in a flash, he had me on my back and pinned by both wrists above my head. His big body hovered and compelled, his weight on his knees that he'd worked between my thighs.

A fortress.

A shield.

My complete ruin.

A gasp whipped from my lungs, and I writhed beneath his heat. Two inches separated us, the man powerful, rugged and gentle and just so much that I didn't know what to do with myself right then.

"Maybe the only thing I need to hear is you screaming my name." He rumbled it a breath from my mouth.

Desire throbbed, and I became very aware of his enormous erection that strained against his underwear.

Apparently, he didn't mind using it against me, either.

Because he angled down enough to rub it against my center. It didn't matter that I had on leggings and he was wearing briefs, the thin fabric didn't come close to stopping the heat that blasted at the connection.

Sparks flashed behind my eyes.

I was also very aware of the square bandage sitting high on the left side of his ribs.

"I'm pretty sure what you have in mind right now is going against Christa's instructions," I wheezed through the desire that was trying to drag me under.

"The only thing I agreed to was staying in bed for the

next twenty-four hours. I might as well reap the benefits of that bargain," Ezra rumbled.

Edging back an inch, he smirked.

Damn him. He really did look good in the morning.

Rolling my eyes, I did my best at suppressing the need that lit a path of fire in my veins. It was really freaking hard to put it out when this man had become the yearning inside me. "The only benefits you're reaping are letting your body heal."

"I think I can multitask."

He rocked against me again. I whimpered. "You aren't fighting fair, Ezra Patterson."

"You know what they say...all's fair in love and war."

"This isn't either of those things."

Or maybe it was. Maybe I was terrified of what saturated the dense, thriving air, what enclosed and pushed at every corner of my being.

Maybe it was also a war, whatever we were fighting. Whatever battle he had to wage. Not to mention the lengths I would go to get to my sister.

"Call it what you want, Savannah," he murmured, "but the one thing I do know is I need you. You say you couldn't stop thinking about me when we first met? It's you who has haunted every single one of my dreams since that night when I found you. Made me want things I promised myself I wouldn't seek for myself. But you...you changed everything, Little Trespasser. You got to places I was never supposed to let you go. And after last night..."

I would have reached out and touched his face if he didn't still have me pinned by the wrists, and my chest arched toward him on its own accord.

No permission.

No self-control.

Somehow, I managed a little of it when I raised my brows at him, and I forced myself to completely ignore what he had been implying. It was much safer that way. "As much as I love the idea of an orgasm in the morning, you were *stabbed* last night."

"It wasn't a—"

"Don't you even say it wasn't a big deal," I said, cutting him off. "Did a knife not penetrate your skin?"

He grunted.

"Are there not stitches in your side?"

Another grunt, that one more yielding.

"That's what I thought."

"I thought what you *thought* about was me." Another smirk ticked up at the side of his delicious mouth. A mouth that had just been on me last night. God, I wanted it there again. This man's lips and tongue were something to write home about, that was if I had someone to write home to.

"You're impossible, Ezra Patterson, now get off me, you big brute. I need to call Dakota and let her know I'm not coming in today."

He frowned. "You don't have to call in for my sake."

"Um, yes, I do. Like I said, you need someone to watch over you."

He grunted, then grinned. "Well, I guess if it means you're going to stay in bed with me all day, I'll call it a bonus."

I pointed a finger at him. "Yeah, we won't be doing that, either."

It was time to put a little space between us. Things had become too intense.

"Now off." Since he had my wrists nailed to the bed, I had to nudge him with my hips.

Bad choice.

Because God, it felt so nice.

A moan got free, and Ezra was looking like he'd just won first-place prize for the best cherry pie.

"I hate you," I mumbled when he finally let me loose, the man chuckling low and sending vibrations across my flesh.

I sat up and started to scoot off the bed.

He ran a single finger down the back of my neck before I could make it all the way off.

Shivers raced.

"No, you don't," he murmured.

Oh, how much I wished I did because what I was feeling in its place was too much.

Too overwhelming.

I hopped off his ridiculous bed that was as big as the man, but I guessed it was required to support a mountain like that.

I felt him shift and start to follow. I whirled around and pointed again. "Don't you dare get up."

He'd already made it to sitting up, the man so gorgeous, wearing nothing but his briefs.

Mounds of bristling muscle and a mile of golden flesh.

"And here I thought I was supposed to be the overbearing one?" He arched a brow.

I crossed my arms over my chest. "Someone has to take care of you."

Damn it.

It was me.

It was me who had to take care of him.

I wasn't sure I had another choice. No chance of walking away.

"I have to pee and I have a little issue to take care of since you refused to do the honors." He gestured at his hard-on with that freaking smug grin plastered on his face.

My belly tumbled.

"And here I thought you were supposed to be the respectful and sweet one," I told him.

"Pretty sure you discovered that is not the case last night."

Heat flamed.

Oh, how much I'd liked it that he hadn't been polite.

"Fine. Go to the bathroom and then get right back in bed."

"Yes, ma'am."

I sent him a glare. "Don't ma'am me."

Chuckling, he stood. I watched him carefully. He didn't wince or recoil, and I was halfway satisfied that he wasn't going to crumble into a broken pile when he strode into the bathroom without lumbering or limping.

I had to fully ignore him since he didn't shut the door, and I rushed to where I'd left my phone charging on the television console across from his bed.

It was only fifteen minutes until I was due for my shift, and I felt bad for just calling now, but it hadn't even crossed my mind when I'd fallen asleep in Ezra's arms last night.

Exhaustion and strain and an unexpected comfort had dragged us into slumber.

Dakota answered on the first ring, like she'd already had her phone in her hands. "Good morning, Snuggle Muggle."

God, she was chipper first thing in the morning.

I was still adjusting to the hours, even though I absolutely loved working at the café. I'd be a liar if I said it wasn't because of the people.

Suddenly nervous, I shifted my weight from foot to foot. "Hey, I hate to do this to you, but I'm not going to be able to come in today."

Silence echoed for a beat before worry came surging through. "Oh no, are you sick? I swear, colds start going around the second the temperatures drop. I'm switching the daily soup to chicken noodle. As soon as it's ready, I'll bring you over some."

"No, that's not necessary." Why was I whispering?

"Then what is it?"

I glanced behind me to Ezra's opened bathroom door. What was I supposed to say? Last night he'd made it clear he didn't want the town knowing about the attack before they had gotten more details, but this was Dakota we were talking about.

They were close.

Family, really.

It felt wrong keeping it from her.

My voice dropped even lower. "There was an incident with Ezra last night."

"What do you mean?"

I wavered, a hand tugging at my hair. "He's okay, but someone was messing around outside his house, and Ezra went out to investigate and…"

"And what?" Panic ricocheted from the other end of the line.

"He only needed a few stitches, but he was stabbed."

"What?" she screeched.

Crap.

This was coming out all wrong.

But what had I expected? That she wouldn't freak out?

"I promise, he's fine. The paramedics were really amazing and took good care of him and then I made sure he was comfortable for the rest of the night, but I just thought it would be a good idea for me to stay here for the rest of the day to make sure he doesn't overexert himself. You know how he is."

"I'll be there in five."

"I don't think—"

The line went dead.

Crappity crap.

I felt Ezra emerge from behind, and slowly, I shifted around. I really should have remained facing the wall. He was in the doorway, taking the whole thing up, the glimmering light streaking in through the window striking over him like a beacon.

That's what it felt like, looking at him.

Like he was a beacon.

A safe passage home.

My *safe place*.

The man was all hulking muscle and tapered waist.

And damn it, his freaking thighs…so gigantic where they pressed against the fabric of his briefs.

"I think you might be drooling, Savannah."

My attention snapped up to his face, and I bit down on my bottom lip. "And I think you might be mad."

A frown marred his brow. "Why would I be mad?"

I danced from foot to foot. "I might have accidentally told Dakota that you were stabbed last night."

He groaned. "You didn't."

"I did."

He scrubbed both palms over his face, wiping away the irritation. "Well, you can count on the troops descending."

"They're already on their way."

"Shocking."

"They love you." I whispered it, knowing what a gift it was. That he had this amazing group who would rally around him. Support him through anything. Drop everything at the mention that he was harmed.

His expression went soft. "Yeah, they do. I was just hoping the word wouldn't spread too fast before I got the chance to tell my mother. Guess I should be thankful the lights and sirens didn't pull her from her house to see what was going on last night. It would have been way worse for her to walk up on that."

"She lives nearby?" I kept pushing. Needing to get deeper into who he was. Know him better.

"Just on the next street."

"I've seen her several times, coming and going."

Affection left him on a puff of air. "She's been my saving grace, helping me take care of the kids after we lost Brianna."

"I'm glad she was there for you. That you had someone you could count on."

The softness in his features dove straight into empathy. "I hate that you've never had that, Savannah. That no one took the time to see the treasure that you are. To cherish everything you are. Adore you the way you deserve to be."

Emotion climbed my throat. Thick and overpowering.

I could feel his tenderness running through me. The need in his touch and the care in his words.

I gestured to the bed, injecting as much easiness as I could into my voice when I felt as if I was standing at the cusp of something magnificent.

Something that couldn't be for me.

Could it? My spirit thrashed with possibility.

I choked it down before it fully took root.

"Into bed now before I force you," I managed.

"You keep making all these threats that I really like." How he went from being so tender to positively dripping sex in a blink, I had no clue. No wonder I'd been begging him for it last night.

I was coming to realize he was everything.

Hard and soft.

Rigid and pliant.

Rough and tender.

Multifaceted.

Each perfect, layered surface coming together to create this amazing man.

"You really are insufferable, aren't you, Officer Patterson?" The words were clogged with emotion.

He growled and took another step forward, and the look on his face tossed me right back into a boiling pot of need. "I'll make you suffer in the best way possible."

I was already there.

Suffering.

Dying to feel him.

His phone rang from his nightstand, cutting into whatever salacious deeds were playing through his mind. "There they are. Gossip travels like wildfire in this town."

"I don't think Dakota would gossip." She had to be the nicest person I knew. As soon as I thought it, I knew that I wholeheartedly believed it. All the way down to my soul.

Her true colors were already showing.

It wasn't an act.

"No, but the word is out to our crew. She wasn't going to keep that from Ryder, and if Ryder knows, then..." He trailed off, his head tilting to the side.

"Are you mad?" I found myself whispering again.

He took another step forward, then another and another until he had my chin between his thumb and forefinger. "No, Little Trespasser. How could I be mad at you? I know why you couldn't help but tell her."

He didn't have to say it.

I was pretty sure it was written on me in broad stripes and bold colors.

I cared about them.

And I cared about him.

There was no longer any denying it.

By the time I'd put on a pot of coffee to brew, there was already a fist battering at the front door. Ezra appeared at the end of the short hall that led to his bedroom, wearing a pair of black sweats and another white tee, one with a Mack's logo imprinted across his chest.

Talk about free advertising. If I saw this man walking around in that shirt? Mack's would be the first place I'd land. But I was already here with him, in his kitchen.

There was no questioning now that I'd ventured into hazardous terrain. Had drifted so off course that I'd lost my way.

My heart panged.

Or maybe, maybe I'd just stumbled upon where I really belonged.

I shoved that reckless thought down and sent the brute of a man a scowl. "What do you think you're doing?"

He arched a brow. "Answering the door before my cousin bangs it off its hinges."

"Absolutely no. What did Christa tell you?"

"I'm not broken, Savannah."

I pointed behind him. "Bed."

"How about the couch? I don't need everyone gathering around me like I'm on my death bed. Besides, there's only one person that I want in bed with me."

The nerve of the man—he went and winked.

"You think you're some kind of charmer, do you?" It was purely exasperation.

A grin split his face. "My mom tells me I'm a pro."

"Fine, you get on the couch, but if Christa catches wind of it, I won't be held responsible."

"I promise she never thought I was going to listen to begin with."

"It seems you come with some kind of reputation," I said as I moved to the door just as he was sitting on the couch.

"My reputation is spotless." He smirked as he put his feet up on the ottoman.

I had to smother a smile, not even knowing what to do with him like this. Hell, did I ever know what to do with him?

I undid the deadbolt and opened the door. Dakota was there with her son, Kayden, hooked on her hip.

Ryder was to the side of her, vibrating with anxiety. His question roiled with the power of a threat. "Where is he?"

I widened the door. "On the couch."

Ryder blew past me. I could tell he was terrified, needing to see for himself that Ezra was okay. Stopping a couple feet from the couch, he loomed over Ezra with his tattooed hands curled into fists.

"Take a breath, man, it was nothing," Ezra told him, his voice placating.

"If someone takes a blade to my cousin, it's not *nothing*," Ryder spat.

"The hazards of being a cop."

"Then get a different damned job."

Dakota cringed from where she was still on the stoop, and she hugged her son closer as she stepped in, the words held below her breath. "Ryder might have come unglued when I told him what happened." She peeked at Ezra then returned her attention to me. "How is he?"

"I honestly think he's fine."

She stepped farther inside, and I shut the door behind her. Kayden clapped when he realized where he was, jumping in her hold as he pointed at Ezra. "Hi, Uncle *Ezwa*. I see you."

Affection stretched wide across his face, Ezra pointed back. "I see you."

I melted a little.

"I'm making coffee. Would anyone like some?" I asked, hoping to break the tension that seethed from Ryder.

"No thanks. I'll have plenty when I get into the café," Dakota said, "and I think my man might be a little hot right now to stomach it."

I cringed. "I'm sorry to let you down today."

Warmth traipsed across Dakota's features. Her high, brown ponytail swished around her shoulders when she shook her head. "Are you kidding me? If you weren't staying here with him, then I'd be the one taking the day off. Don't think twice about it."

"Thank you."

Reaching out, she squeezed my hand. "We take care of each other around here, Savannah."

My heart clenched, and my nod was shaky.

"I'll take one, if you don't mind, since you won't let me off the couch." Ezra's razzing cut into the moment Dakota and I were sharing.

I sent him a look, and he grinned like he was completely innocent.

A buzz fluttered inside, and I kept getting tossed between the severity and lightness that Ezra was trying to maintain.

I dipped my head and rounded the island into the kitchen, rising up on my toes and grabbing a mug from the cabinet where I'd remembered them being when I'd been here for dinner last week. I poured it then carefully carried the steaming cup into the living room.

Ryder sat down on the ottoman across from Ezra.

The guy looked like a dark storm. His black hair was disheveled where he kept tugging his hands through the longer locks, his being whirring with angst.

"Do you have any idea who this bastard is?" Ryder kept his voice low in what I could only assume was an attempt to keep it from Kayden's little ears.

Dakota had sat on the other end of the sectional, and Kayden climbed down and went directly for the toy box under the opposite window.

"No." Ezra didn't hesitate. My heart stalled for a single beat, the same as my footsteps.

Part of me wanted to shout it, tell Ryder that Ezra was keeping a vital piece of information concealed. I was terrified of Ezra being alone against whoever this monster was.

But Ezra had trusted me with it, and I needed to prove that I'd earned that trust.

I gathered myself and walked the rest of the way to him, and I slowly handed him the cup.

Ezra looked up at me. Gaze melted honey. Soft and clearly trying to keep out the trepidation of what had happened last night. When he accepted the mug, his fingers brushed mine.

Fire flashed at the connection.

I inhaled a short breath, and I wondered if a time would come when I would get used to the feel of his touch.

"Thank you," he said.

"We couldn't have you breaking the rules, could we?"

"Never." It was a chuckle.

I sent him the tiniest smile. One of encouragement. One of belief.

I felt the searing burn of both Ryder and Dakota's eyes on me.

I suddenly felt flustered.

Caught red handed.

A usurper.

Standing in a place where I wasn't meant to be.

I needed to clear my head. Take a breath. Straighten out my jumbled intentions.

"I'm going to use the restroom."

I gestured awkwardly toward the children's hall, figuring if I went into Ezra's room, it would only confirm whatever Dakota was thinking. I rushed that way, and I fumbled to close the door behind me. I locked it then turned around. A rush of sudden affection tugged my mouth into a grin when I took in Ezra's children's bathroom.

It was decorated in illustrated pirate ships, a Caribbean theme. I could picture Owen and Oliver in the bath, playing with their little ships and figures that were piled high in a basket next to the tub.

God. They were so sweet.

I went to the sink and splashed cool water on my face.

Get it together, Savannah.

I was here helping my friend.

That was it.

Such a lie, but I figured it was the one Ezra and I should go with for a while.

I needed to be careful before I let myself fall any farther. Before this became too complicated.

Before I wanted to stay.

I needed to remember why I was here in the first place. To find my sister. I needed to train my focus on that.

I could handle this. It wasn't a big deal.

I inhaled a steadying breath then unlocked the door.

A tiny shriek erupted when I found Dakota waiting on the other side. She stuck out her hand and shoved me back into the small space, and she snapped the door behind her.

"I knew it," she whisper-squealed.

My eyes went wide, and my heart jack-hammered at my chest. "That I had to pee?"

Her rust-colored gaze narrowed, though she didn't fight her smile. "Um, that there is a thing going on between you and Ezra."

"A thing?"

"That's right…a thing."

"And what kind of thing might that be?" I crossed my arms protectively over my chest.

"Oh, I don't know, the kind of thing where there's a tension so tight between you two that I can taste it, dosed with an undercut of softness and familiarity that promises you two got naked."

Was I that obvious?

"That's ridiculous."

"Is it?" she challenged.

"Absolutely."

"Yet your cheeks are heated and you're standing there bouncing like a bunny with a fire under its tail." Then she dropped the teasing, and she reached out and tugged one of my arms free from where I had it held like a shield over my battering heart.

She swung our hands between us. "You like him."

I didn't say anything because denying it felt like a betrayal.

"It's okay, you know, to care about him. Ezra's pretty impossible not to care about."

Moisture took that inopportune time to blur my eyes. God, these people had made me weak. Demolished my reserves and annihilated the walls.

"Ezra's just a guy who's been really kind to me since I came into town."

"Just how nice has he been?" Squeezing my fingers, she grinned.

Good lord, she was as incorrigible as Ezra. "Fine…he might have come to my room last night before everything happened and things got a little spicy between us. We didn't even have sex, though. It was nothing."

Her brow rose to the ceiling. "Nothing?"

My teeth clamped down on my bottom lip and the emotion I'd been trying to keep contained flooded out.

"Fine. I like him, okay." Panic laced the revelation.

Like him.

Hah.

Understanding creased the edges of Dakota's eyes. "It's okay to like someone, Savannah."

Except, it wasn't. Because I didn't do that. Not anymore.

"Is it, though?" Desperation bled out with the question.

Dakota watched me with a deep frown. "Loving someone is always scary, Savannah, but even when it's hurt me, I've never regretted it."

Tears blurred, and I felt so stupid, so vulnerable standing in front of her like this. I didn't let these things touch me. But there I was, swamped by it. "And what if loving someone has only ever hurt me?"

God, was I really just going to lay it out like this?

She squeezed my hand again, this time so fiercely that I felt the connection like a band. "Then I say those people never deserved you in the first place. I'd say that maybe you're just too big and bright for them, and you needed to find the ones who would love you for every single thing you are."

A tear got free and streaked down my cheek. I watched it as it dripped onto Dakota's arm. She didn't recoil or shrink.

Instead, her head tilted to the side, her voice bending with emphasis. "You're where you belong, Savannah. Right here with us. And I hope you accept the love we already have for you. And I know you're afraid of accepting that. Of letting us. But we are right here, waiting for you when you're ready."

She stared at me for a beat before she pulled me into a hug.

Hers was fierce and unrelenting.

The one I returned was desperate and pleading.

"Thank you," I mumbled.

"Love is on the house," she murmured back.

She hugged me tight for the longest time before she cleared her throat. "Now we better go check on our men before they come up with some harebrained idea. The two of them are dangerous together."

Opening the door, she stepped out into the hall.

"Our men?" I swiped the moisture from my face and went for the casualness that was getting harder and harder to find. "Don't get ahead of yourself."

Twisting around to walk backward, she dragged me out, a sly grin on her pretty face. "I'm not ahead, Savannah. You just need to catch up."

Chapter Thirty-Eight

Savannah

I SAT AT THE ISLAND, DOING MY BEST TO FLY UNDER THE RADAR while Ryder had peppered Ezra for more details over the last thirty minutes, watching from the sidelines though Ezra kept cutting glances my way, like he needed me to know that he was very aware of my presence.

"And you're sure you didn't get a look at his face?"

"Nothing. It was pitch black out and was impossible to make out anything."

Ryder scrubbed a tattooed palm over his face as Ezra gave him the same answer he'd given him the last fifteen times Ryder had asked.

The front door suddenly burst open, and I jolted since I couldn't help being on edge. Though it was a smile that took to my face when a riot of excitement and clattering feet filled the walls. "Daddy, Daddy, Daddy!"

Their three little voices were distinct, their grins so wide as they barreled into the house like they hadn't seen their father in days when he'd only dropped them off at Caleb and Paisley's ranch the evening before.

"Ah, there are my love bugs." Ezra spread his arms where he remained on the couch.

I winced when I realized no one was stopping the three of them from colliding against his chest.

Ezra didn't seem to register any pain, his own joy riding free as he snuggled them close. "I missed my yahoos. Did you have fun at the Ranch?"

"It was really fun, Dad," Olivia said in her serious way.

Paisley and Caleb stepped through the doorway, along with an adorable little girl with a mess of brown hair and the biggest brown eyes I'd ever seen.

Evelyn.

I'd never met her, but I knew her name.

She threw her arms in the air and came bounding in. "Yes, Uncle Ezra. We had the very best time ever in the world at our sleepover. We made a fort in the living room with all the blankets, and then we went out to the barn when we woke up, and we visited my best horse in the world, Mazzy, but we didn't get to take a ride because my cousins Olivia, Oliver, and Owen don't know how yet, but my mommy said she will teach them really soon if you want her to."

The rush of words spilled from her without pause.

Chuckling, Ezra stretched out his arm for her, too, accepting her into the fold. "I think that sounds like a great plan."

"As if she would have it any other way," Paisley said with a grin as she stepped inside, though concern dimmed her demeanor, questions toiling through her expression.

Clearly, they had kept a tight lip about what had happened last night around the kids, being careful not to let them pick up on anything being wrong.

Caleb vibrated behind her, trembling as hard as Ryder had been, and I glanced out farther to see that Dakota's brother, Cody, was also there. Apparently, word really did spread quickly between these friends, and everyone had congregated to make sure that Ezra was fine.

"That's right, there is no other way because my cousins need to learn to ride so they can always go with us," Evelyn peeped, grinning back at her mom.

"I think it's a really good plan, Dad," Olivia agreed.

"Me, too," Oliver said.

"Me, *fee*," Owen chimed.

Every cell in my body compressed before they expanded. How was it possible these children could be so sweet?

"Well, then it's settled," Ezra said. "I do hope there's a family discount?" He quirked a teasing brow at Paisley.

She rolled her eyes as she strolled the rest of the way inside. "Like I would charge for my sweetums? Who do you think I am, Ezra? A monster?"

His smile was soft. "What you are is the best, Paisley."

"This I know."

Her brow creased, unable to contain the worry any longer.

Are you okay? she mouthed.

I'm fine, he returned.

Her nod was slight before she swept her attention my way. "Hey, Savannah. It's so good to see you again. I see you're putting up with this one?"

Her head cocked to the side. A thousand silent questions rolled from the motion.

What happened?

Is he really okay?

I've been so worried.

And what exactly are you doing here?

None of it was judgement.

"I'm doing my best," I said around the lump in my throat. My response seemed to be the only thing that had clued Ezra's children into the fact that I was there because Olivia whirled around at my voice, and her eyes widened with glee.

"Ms. Ward, you came over? I didn't even have to send you an invitation. I'm really glad you're here."

Sweetness dripped from her as she unwound herself from Ezra's arms and came skipping my way.

Her brothers followed suit, bouncing on their toes as they crossed to the kitchen.

All blond hair and those cherub smiles.

"Hi, Miss Ward! Hi, Miss Ward! I missed you the most!"

Affection spread, a thrill that rolled through my spirit.

My knees felt a little weak when I stood so I could give each of them a hug.

Olivia then Oliver.

And my hugs, they were so tight, clinging to them because I realized I had missed them, too.

Owen was the last, and he looped both arms around my neck and let go of the weight on his feet when I bent over to hug him.

"I a *kowawa.*" He giggled as he swung.

"What, do you think I'm a tree?" I teased through the emotion clotting my voice.

He giggled again. "No way," he said. "You is my S'vannah."

His words struck me from out of nowhere. So hard and unexpected that I nearly wept.

I settled him back onto his feet, and the three kids stood grinning my direction, while I felt the eyes of the rest of the room searing into the top of my head.

I looked up.

Only this time, I didn't get flustered and run.

I didn't seek refuge in the restroom.

Because Ezra was watching me in a way that staked me to the spot.

Tender and fierce and devoted.

Is that what this feeling was? What I wanted it to be?

Devoted?

I jolted when the door opened again, and my attention snapped that way to find Ezra's mother pushing through.

Terror held her expression, and the sparse wrinkles on her face had deepened with worry. Tears she'd likely been holding slipped free the second she saw Ezra sitting on the couch.

Dakota stood, intuitively knowing she needed a private moment with her son. "How about we all go out and play in the backyard?"

"Yes! This is the best idea ever. Only if Miss Savannah is comin', too." Olivia took my hand and beamed up at me when she said it, like we were a team.

Meant to be together.

A disorder of little voices filled the air, and Kayden toddled over and was immediately in the mix. "I wanna play outside! You're it! I gonna swing! Me, too! Me, too."

Olivia tugged at my hand. "Come on, we gotta go."

I glanced at Ezra once more as I allowed his daughter to haul me to the door.

Energy keened between us, alive and humming and stronger than ever before.

It didn't sever.

Even when I turned and helped to usher everyone out.

Chapter Thirty-Nine

Ezra

WITH MY MOTHER STANDING JUST INSIDE THE FRONT door, Dakota, Paisley, and Savannah herded the kids out the back.

Cody, Ryder, and Caleb held back, refusing to go, which didn't surprise me a bit.

They were all itching to get any details about what had gone down last night, or maybe they were set on standing guard over me if the asshole had the balls to come around here again.

But it was the terror radiating from my mother that completely held my attention.

A bout of unease whispered through the air, and I was regretting that I hadn't called her the second I'd woken up this morning. I knew well enough in this town the word was going to get out, and not because Savannah had let the cat out of the bag.

Anxiously, I roughed a hand over the top of my head. "Hey, Mom. I take it you heard."

Her jaw clenched. "Yes, the neighbor told me there was some sort of disturbance in the middle of the night near your house, so I called

Pamela ten minutes ago and demanded she tell me what happened. She tried to play it off, but I knew you were involved. Why didn't you call me?" The words trembled from her mouth.

The rest of my crew retreated into the kitchen area under the pretense of getting coffee, stepping away to give my mother and me a moment.

My mother was the best. As loyal as they came. Her love unending. Protective to the extreme.

Shocker that I'd turned out the same.

She had never taken too kindly to being left out or kept in the dark, though. She'd told me a million times that strong families weren't built on secrets. But some secrets were too big for the pure like her to hold.

I sat forward, hating that she had been afraid. Hating that she stood with hurt smeared across her face. Inhaling deep, I pushed out the best explanation I could. "I didn't call you in the middle of the night because it wasn't a big deal, so there was no reason to disturb you or get you worried."

And because I'd had Savannah to take care of me, and I was selfish enough not to want my mother to interrupt that.

She choked over a cry as she came forward. "You didn't want me to worry? You were *stabbed*."

Shit.

Apparently, Pamela had given her the ugly details.

"It was hardly a flesh wound." I tried to make it a joke, but my mother wasn't having it.

"Ezra…you can't…your kids…they need you."

Grief speared through her features, and I saw what was written on her face. Her fear that my kids would lose both their parents. The loss so fresh even though I knew it would go on in her forever. To her, losing Brianna had been like losing a daughter.

"They aren't going to lose me, Mom. I won't let that happen."

"You can't know that."

A heavy sigh pilfered from my nose. "Yeah, you're right, nothing is a certainty. You and I both know that. But what I can promise you is I will fight with everything I have for them, and that means fighting for me to be there for them, too."

Her attention drifted out the French doors to the sound of shrieks and laughter. Joy in the morning air. No question, my kids were in the middle of that sweet mayhem, having the absolute best time with their cousins.

Satisfaction pounded in my heart that Savannah was out there with them. That she'd stood up to care for them after she'd spent the night caring for me.

"Is that the new tenant?" Mom asked, her voice twisted in something I couldn't quite discern though there was no question it left me unsettled.

"Yeah. Her name's Savannah." I answered it just as quiet.

For a moment, my mother watched.

When she looked back, grief and speculation had knitted her brow. "Are you sure you're ready for that?"

I scrubbed my palm over my face at the blatant insinuation.

The way she laid it out like she'd seen everything that'd gone down in the last twenty-four hours play out in her mind.

I hoped to God not.

The thing was, my mother thought I was heartbroken over Brianna. I wasn't sure I could break her any more right then by admitting the truth.

"We're friends, Mom. She got disturbed with the sirens last night, and she came out to help."

The lie tasted sour on my tongue.

Like disloyalty to Savannah.

Like treason.

Mom didn't seem allayed, but instead came closer, her hand shaking when she touched my face. "I can't stand you going through any more pain, Ezra. Not after what you've already been through."

I reached up and pressed her hand to my cheek. "I'm okay, Mom. I promise. This isn't anything I can't handle. It was likely a thief out looking for something easy to take and he panicked when I had him backed into a corner. We're going to catch the guy, just like we always do."

Agony twisted through her expression. I knew exactly what she was thinking.

We hadn't caught Brianna's.

But we would. I was sure this was one and the same.

"I'm good, okay?"

Reluctantly, she nodded, then she softly smacked me on the shoulder. "If anything like this ever happens again, God forbid, I'd better be the first to hear about it."

"I promise."

She swiveled and pointed between Caleb, Ryder, and Cody. "And don't think I don't hold the three of you responsible for not keeping me in the loop."

Ryder lifted his hand in an oath. "I'm sorry, Aunt Linda. I got distracted racing over here to check that this guy was fine since he didn't bother to call me, either."

Hands pressed to the opposite side of the island, he sent me a pointed look.

Cody clapped him on the back, wearing a giant smirk. "Come now, Ryder, if our brother here needed backup, you didn't think he would call you, did you? He'd call me, then we'd get things taken care of."

Considering Cody was twice as thick as Ryder and just as tall, the dude would come on the scene like a battering ram, not that Ryder wasn't every bit as vicious. Cody was all brute, and Ryder was a scrappy motherfucker who didn't hesitate to take someone out.

"Hardly," Ryder scoffed as he sent the ribbing Cody's way. "What, you think he wants all brawn and no fucking brain?"

Cody feigned a gasp and touched his chest. "The words, Ryder. And here I thought you were supposed to be my best friend. Let it be known that title is still revoked since you started putting those grubby hands on my sister."

Ryder laughed, no concern since the two of them were closer than they'd probably ever been. "Just can't help myself when it comes to her, brother." Then Ryder returned the full force of his attention to me. "And all I'm saying is I think we need a plan."

Caleb smacked his hands together and rubbed them in agreement. "Now you're thinking."

"Exactly my point." Ryder sent a gloating glance at Cody.

Cody laughed low at Ryder using Caleb's words against him. "Such an asshole."

"Nah, guys, I think we'd better leave this one to the professionals," I said with the cut of a warning.

God knew Ryder and Caleb had gotten deep in the bullshit that had tainted their lives, and they were both lucky they were still standing on the other side.

Now that they were past it? No fucking chance would I drag them back into danger.

This? This was on me. And I had to find a way to end it.

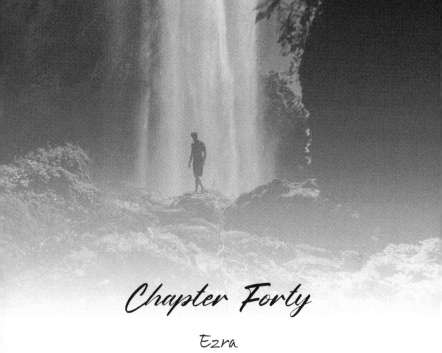

Chapter Forty

Ezra

THE NEXT WEEK PASSED IN A BLUR OF LONG DAYS AT THE station and stolen kisses at night.

We'd dug deep into trying to find whoever had assaulted me. We'd searched my property high and low for any evidence. We had a couple boot prints, but that was like sifting through a haystack the size of the continent. It'd been frustrating to say the least. Tensions had run high. All my officers on edge, desperate to sniff out the threat lurking in our small town.

My relief had been in the evenings, coming home to my kids and seeing their smiling faces, though I'd be a liar if I said I wasn't suffering extreme pressure, terrified someone might come around here again, all while trying to give them the semblance of peace that I was desperate to provide.

The last thing I wanted was for their lives to be caught in turmoil again.

In the middle of all of that were the stolen kisses. They were few and far between, but God, I couldn't explain the relief I felt whenever I got Savannah into my arms. She'd come over for dinner once, the same day after she'd shown up at Olivia's spelling bee and knocked me flat on my ass, though she'd said there'd been no way she could refuse since Olivia had given her another invitation.

The whole time we'd acted like we were nothing but friends in front of the kids, which was painful as all hell. Thankfully, I'd managed to sneak out to the guest house a couple times. Each encounter had set me ablaze, our kisses wild and reckless in those seconds that we'd found.

I'd push her against the wall, and she'd come on my fingers, and I'd beg her to stay in the main house. Trying to convince her it was safer. Telling her that I couldn't sleep knowing she was out there by herself. But she'd refused, stating that it wasn't appropriate, and she didn't want to confuse the kids.

There'd been no mistaking the reservations in her eyes, though, no missing her fear of getting attached, the woman hanging onto the idea that one day she was going to leave.

That this wasn't her home.

It'd become my own fear.

Her leaving.

Because I knew all the way into my soul that I wanted her here.

"I think Miss Savannah is really pretty." Olivia's little voice cut into my storm of thoughts, and I lifted my head from where I was buttering bread for the grilled cheese sandwiches and tomato soup that I was preparing for dinner. She stood on a stool at the sink washing the broccoli that we were going to steam with it.

Not exactly gourmet, but after this week...

Hesitation billowed in my spirit, wondering exactly where my daughter was going with this, wondering if she'd been lost in a stir of these same thoughts and confusions that I'd been prisoner to for the last six days.

She peeked over at me. A sly smile she was trying to hide hinted at the edge of her mouth as she gauged my reaction.

It seemed I had a little matchmaker on my hands.

I contemplated my words carefully before I said, "I think so, too."

"Then you should probably ask her on a date."

She said it so casually.

Like it was a no-brainer.

The obvious direction I should go.

Reservations flooded, all messed up with the idea that it was exactly what I wanted to do.

I'd made all these resolves and promises, sure I'd never touch anyone again after I'd let Brianna down the way I had.

But now? After everything? What was really tripping me up was my kids. The last year and a half had been devoted solely to them and hunting down the ones who'd stolen their mother. Those two things had been the only thing that had mattered. I wasn't sure their fragile hearts would be ready for me moving in the direction my daughter was implying. The boys probably wouldn't understand, anyway, but Olivia...?

I wavered on what to say, then pushed the question out around the knot in my throat.

"That wouldn't make you sad?"

A hint of that sadness did penetrate the room, and Olivia hiked her shoulder to her ear. "I already know Mom can't come back, and you told me we have to be happy in the ways that we can, which I think that's the smartest you've ever been."

I could have chuckled if emotion wasn't clotting off airflow.

"And you think me asking Savannah on a date would make me happy?"

"Yeah. And I think it might make me happy, too." Her voice dipped in vulnerability.

"You know Savannah is only living here temporarily. Time River isn't her permanent home." Fuck, did that ever taste sour on my tongue. Wrong.

A frown marred my daughter's brow. "That's what would really make me sad, Dad."

My heart sank.

It would make me fucking sad, too. Truth was, I thought it might destroy me.

"I know, Livvie. But there are a bunch of things that make this situation complicated." I phrased it carefully, hoping to answer some of her questions without giving her the sordid details.

"Life is complicated, Dad, but we have to do the things that make us happy."

Affection rolled, so thick it pressed hard at my chest. I moved to her and whispered my lips against her temple. "When did my little girl get so smart?"

She rolled her eyes, once again acting like she was going on thirteen and not seven. "Newsflash, Dad. I've always been smart. My whole report card was straight A's, and I won the spelling bee for my whole grade, remember?"

I held the chuckle. "Right, I do remember. That's my Livvie, smart as a whip."

She peered up at me. "Then you agree with me?"

"And what exactly am I agreeing to?"

She huffed like I was hopeless. "That you have to ask Miss Savannah on a date and show her that she really needs to stay here with us forever."

"Livvie…" It was close to a warning.

"Dad, you gotta take the chance or you're going to regret it."

It was right then, with my daughter peering up at me with this look on her face—one of faith and hope and belief—that made this feeling swell. So stark and profound there was no shaking it.

She was right.

I'd regret it if I didn't take the chance.

"Then I guess I'd better ask her, hadn't I?"

"Yes!" she squealed. "See, I knew my dad was smart, too."

She hopped off the stool and blazed a trail to her room. A second later, she was back with her case of markers, stickers, and paper. She climbed onto a stool at the island and spread them out in front of her, dinner completely forgotten.

"What are you doing, Olivia?" Amusement rumbled through the question.

She looked up, brown eyes wide. "What do you think I'm

doing? I'm making an invitation. Sheesh, Dad, you're really clueless at this romance thing. But don't worry, I'll help you."

Five minutes hadn't passed before she was standing in front of the doors that led to the backyard, her sweet little face gleaming when she said, "Let's go."

Chapter Forty-One

Savannah

A CLATTERING OF LITTLE FISTS BANGED AT THE GLASS. My spirit tumbled in my chest, pulsing so fiercely in affection that my lungs ached. It wasn't the first time the kids had come pounding at the door this week. The problem was, each time my reaction to it grew stronger.

The anticipation.

The excitement.

The shock of joy I felt when I'd look down to see their sweet, smiling faces when they'd asked me to come out and watch them play. It had been such a contrast to the way I'd felt all week as I'd searched the town for my sister, randomly driving streets, sitting parked outside the town square where the government buildings were, growing more desperate each day that passed, both feeling like I'd run straight into a dead end and had been led to paradise. Not to mention the way I'd felt when Olivia had shown up with another invitation—this one asking me to go to her spelling bee. As if I'd be the monster to break that little girl's heart.

No freaking way.

That feeling that I had to be there no matter what was probably what should have proven that I needed to stay away. The truth that the only thing I wanted to do was be close to them.

To the kids.

To their father.

If he knew the number of times I'd looked out my window toward their house this week, praying to find him sneaking out and coming to me, I'd be accused of borderline obsession.

I set the rice bowl I'd been eating onto the counter and slipped off the stool, and I padded on bare feet across the wood floors to the door. The sun hung at the horizon line, right above the trees. Pink-spun rays sheared through the branches and leaves, spreading out to warm the small porch in the last whisper of daylight.

It lit the three children in the softest glow, their near-white hair glinting like strands of silver. Their eagerness was palpable as they jumped at the other side of the door.

Affection panged my heart into a rapid, erratic beat.

Turning the lock, I pulled it open, and their voices were no longer muted as they shouted, "Miss Savannah, Miss Savannah!"

"Special delivery!" Olivia sang as she waved a folded piece of paper with stickers all over it above her head.

"We got somefin' for you!" Owen said in his adorable way, bending down on his knees before he popped into the air.

"Wait 'til you see." Oliver jumped even higher at his side.

Olivia shoved it out in front of her for me to take.

"Open it, my S'vannah!" Owen beamed, his gap-toothed smile turned up to me.

Energy whispered on the cool breeze. Warm and right. Soothing and stirring me straight into a disorder. My attention traveled from the kids to the source. Ezra loitered at the edge of the porch. He leaned a shoulder against the pillar, those massive hands stuffed into the pockets of his jeans.

One ankle was crossed over the other.

Hot Cop the epitome of aloof.

Except there wasn't a single thing in his expression that said he was indifferent or impassive.

Severity blazed from the clench of his jaw, though those eyes… they were so freaking soft as they took me in.

A shiver rocked me through, and I gulped down the tumult and forced myself to return my attention to the kids. "What do you have for me?"

"You gotta open it to see because it's a surprise," Olivia told me.

I couldn't keep my hands from shaking when I accepted it. I slid my fingers under the colorful pieces of tape.

"Hurry!" Olivia begged.

An affected laugh left me, and I peeked over at Ezra before I unfolded the note, and my ribs clamped around my heart when I saw what was written inside.

will you go on a date with my dad?

It was decorated with heart stickers, and the check boxes were exactly the same as they'd been in the first two invitations.

Yes. ☐
Definitely. ☐
Absolutely. ☐

Moisture burned my eyes.

"You have to fill out the box," Olivia prodded, and she handed me a pink marker.

I glanced at Ezra again.

His gaze had gone even softer.

Knowing.

My knees wobbled because this wasn't stolen or secret. It wasn't him sneaking through my door so no one else would know.

This was him making a stand.

A statement.

"All right, you yahoos, you delivered the message, now it's time for you to head back into the house like we talked about."

"Do we has to?" Owen groaned.

Affection clutched my chest.

"Yeah, you need to let me and Miss Savannah have a talk."

"If they're going to go on a date, they need *privacy*." Olivia all but scolded them in a whisper as she took the twins' hands, and she took a step to guide them back to the house, only she shifted to look at me from over her shoulder and sent me a wink.

I choked over a surprised laugh, and I watched them prance back across the lawn before they disappeared into the house.

All while an intensity built in the air. A thickness that churned on the gentle breeze.

I finally looked at Ezra.

God, he looked so good in the evening, too.

So sexy it wasn't fair.

He pushed from the pillar, colossal where he stood, the man fully filling my sight as he slowly edged my direction.

Overpowering.

Overwhelming.

All wide shoulders and brimming strength and beating, thrashing heart.

Clearing the roughness from my throat, I waved the letter between us, no stopping the tweak of a smile that pulled at one side of my mouth. "If this isn't a form of manipulation, Ezra Patterson, then I don't know what is."

A low chuckle rumbled out of him, both smooth and raw. "I warned you that my daughter has a way of getting what she wants."

I glanced down at the letter before I returned my gaze to him, the easiness drifting away as I gave into the heaviness that whirled around us. "And this is what she wanted? It was her idea?"

He stepped closer. The air rippled around us. "Yeah, it was her idea."

"Not yours." It wasn't a question.

Ezra reached out and ran his thumb along my chin, tipping it up and sending chills skating along my flesh.

"No. Not mine. Because you and I have been tiptoeing around this thing between us and my daughter is the one who was smart enough to call us on it."

"What are we doing, Ezra?"

It was a plea.

Those eyes flashed before a wry grin tugged at his lips. "We're going on a date, Savannah."

He angled his head toward the piece of paper I held. "It seems you don't have much of a choice, now do you?"

"When?" Would it make me a fool if I begged it? But I didn't think I could hide this any longer, either.

"What time do you get off tomorrow?"

"Three."

"Then I'll pick you up at four. Bring your camera."

Chapter Forty-Two

Savannah

IT WAS EXACTLY FOUR P.M. WHEN KNUCKLES RAPPED AT THE front door. I'd expected him to come to the back the way he always did, and a grin pulled to my mouth that he was obviously making this a special thing.

A bolt of anticipation rushed through me as I took another quick glance at myself in the mirror.

I'd pulled on my favorite pair of jeans and a baby blue lightweight sweater and tennis shoes. I had no idea where we were going or what we were doing, but there was something about the rugged man that gave me the hunch that we'd be outside.

Another roll of anticipation tumbled as I grabbed my camera bag.

God, how deeply my heart had squeezed when he'd mentioned me bringing it yesterday, as if he'd taken away every detail he'd learned about me last weekend and stowed it away.

Kept it as important. Unforgotten in the midst of the attack afterward and the turmoil that had ensued after.

And I guessed that was exactly the way I felt every time Ezra Patterson looked at me.

Like I was important.

Like I meant something.

And meaning something to someone both felt amazing and was utterly terrifying, though I guessed it was the amazing part that had me tossing the strap of my camera bag over my shoulder and doing the same with my purse.

Before I made it there, another round of knocking came from the door. A little louder and harder that time.

My grin came at full force as I undid the lock and swung it open.

Ezra stood on the stoop in a pair of denim jeans and another of his white tees, this one plain, which suited him just fine since the man didn't need a single enhancement or adornment to stop traffic.

Hell, I was considering committing a crime right then for the sake of him handcuffing me. I thought I wouldn't mind at all if he threw away the key.

"Overbearing much?" I tossed out the tease, deciding to forget all my nerves and allow myself to have a good time.

A smirk lit at the edge of his mouth, though that honey gaze flamed as he let his attention drift over me in a slow slide of appreciation. "Not overbearing. Just anxious."

Wings fluttered in my belly. Good God, how was it possible a man could give me butterflies? After everything I'd been through in my life? But there they were, scattering and taking flight.

"And what are you anxious for?" I prodded. The mood was light between us, and I couldn't help but lean into it, loving the way it felt easy with him.

Right.

That didn't mean that energy between us didn't pulse. A connection I was starting to understand existed when two people fit together in a special way.

A magnetism.

A pull.

It was something I'd never experienced before. If you had asked me two months ago, I would have said it was bullshit. Fantasy. A fabrication of romance novels and believers in love at first sight.

I couldn't help but wonder what that feeling had been the first time I'd seen him. If it'd been some kind of fate that had drawn us together. When that awareness had tugged at the deepest, most sacred part of me.

"The thought of spending even one second with you makes me eager." Ezra's words rolled low and rough and smooth, skidding over me on a billow of seduction. "I spent all of last night tossing, thinking of you, of seeing you again, and it only grew with every excruciating second that passed during the day until I finally have you standing right here in front of me."

Oh boy. Was I ever in trouble today. Ezra was not pulling punches.

I was pretty sure the man was set on knocking me out.

A complete TKO because it was then I noticed the small bouquet of tiny purple wildflowers that dangled from his right hand. He followed my line of sight, and one of those soft, affectionate smiles curled his dangerous lips.

"The kids helped me pick these for you. Olivia said it wasn't a real date if I didn't bring you flowers."

Done.

I was done for.

"She knows her stuff, doesn't she?" I barely managed to croak it.

"Oh yeah. She's brilliant, that one. She said going on a date with you would make me happy."

"And is that what you are? Happy?" It was barely a breath.

Ezra reached for me with the hand that held the flowers, taking my index and middle fingers and tugging me closer.

So close that the only thing I could do was gasp, inhaling everything that he was.

Pine and citrus and laundry detergent.

A man.

A father.

Everything that I wanted.

"I forgot what being truly happy was, Savannah, until you came here, and suddenly things don't feel so bleak. So yeah, standing right here, next to you? I am happy, and I have a feeling this day is just going to get better."

"Are you trying to wreck me, Ezra Patterson?"

"I guess I'm hoping you'll meet me there, Savannah, because that's what I've been since the moment I met you."

I forced some lightness into my voice. "Well, we'd better get going then if we're going to make this one of the best days of your life."

Taking the wildflowers from him, I lifted them to my nose, then tucked the little bundle into the front pocket of my bag. "There."

His smile was slow, and he completely threaded our fingers together and brought my knuckles to his lips. "There."

His truck bounced over the bumpy terrain as we climbed the nearly invisible path, following the ambiguous tracks of what appeared to have only been a vehicle or two that had passed over it before.

It guided our way along a steep incline up the mountain.

I sat up high in the seat, watching out the windows as I clung to the little bar on the roof and braced the other against the dashboard.

"Nervous, Little Trespasser?" Ezra glanced at me with a grin.

"I wouldn't be if you'd keep your eyes on the road." Not that it really could be considered a road.

Ezra chuckled. "Seems I have better things to look at."

That heated gaze raked over me.

I snapped in his face. "Eyes on the road, buddy. The last thing I want is for us to go toppling over a cliff."

He returned his attention back out the windshield. Comfort slid into his voice. "You don't need to be nervous, Savannah. This is the kids' favorite place to go when we do a picnic, and you know there's not a chance in hell that I'd risk putting them in danger."

Everything softened, and I loosened the death grip I had on the handle.

Of course, he wouldn't. I knew he wouldn't with me, either.

Trust.

The threat of it trembled around me.

I'd always thought it a curse. A weakness. My gaze traced Ezra's face. Over the stubble that lined his jaw and the creases that marked the corners of his eyes.

I realized I did—I trusted him.

And for the first time in my life, it didn't feel like a burden but a gift.

"Where are the kids staying?" I murmured, overcome with the realization of what I felt right then.

"With my mom."

"I miss them…we should have brought them with us."

He reached over and squeezed my knee. "Next time, Savannah. Today, I want you all to myself."

Next time.

The path shifted to the right and weaved through a copse of trees, their branches covering us in a glittering ceiling before we emerged from the thicket into a clearing.

Ezra came to a stop at the edge of it.

My breath hitched, and I slowly undid my buckle and snapped open my door, no words to be found as I slipped out and took in my surroundings.

Awestruck.

Twilight had barely begun its approach, the very first wisps of pinks strewn in the endless expanse of blue sky as the sun slowly began to dip into the west.

It sat a blazing orb of orange and red.

The woods rose behind us. Dense and deep and climbing the mountain that from this vantage completely disappeared into the heavens above. A canopy that covered and protected.

But what squeezed my lungs was the waterfall to the left. Its source came from somewhere up the mountain, and here, it crashed over the edge of a craggy, jutted cliff, the rocks sharp and spiked, before it dove into a pool below. The pounding of it filled my ears, close to deafening though I swore I could hear a million whispers of the woods at the same time.

The mist that filled the air was close to cold where it brushed across my flesh, and it stirred the oxygen into a swath of water and pine and the earth.

Beyond it, the view tumbled out over the valley, and I could see Time River in the distance.

I shivered, and Ezra eased up behind me and wrapped me in his arms. "Breathtaking, isn't it?"

"It's the most beautiful thing I've ever seen."

His mouth was at my ear when he mumbled, "And I only share it with the most beautiful things in my life."

If the view hadn't stolen my breath, Ezra would have. He would have held it in his hand the same way as he had somehow come to hold my heart.

His arms tightened and his muscles flexed like he felt the need to explain. "I've only brought my children here, Savannah. It's our special place. And now I've brought you."

"How do you make me feel that way? Special?"

"Because you are."

I'd never been that to anyone.

"And you asked me to bring my camera…" I chanced, already knowing.

"Because I heard what was in your voice when you told me about it the other night, and I thought you must miss it, and I doubt there is any other place on Earth that could inspire art more than here."

The camera bag was still strapped to my shoulder, and I unwound myself from his hold and dug my camera out. Releasing the lens cap, I turned to face him, lifted it, and snapped.

Because this place might be gorgeous, but Ezra Patterson was the beauty. The beauty that hadn't existed before he came into my life.

"What are you doing, Little Trespasser?" He grumbled it low, unimmune to the sensation that blistered across my skin.

To what bubbled in my heart and simmered in my spirit.

"You're right, Ezra. I am inspired."

"Savannah." My name was hushed, a warm grumble of praise.

Snap. Snap. Snap.

I kept taking pictures as I circled him, trying to capture his magnificent form at every angle.

My voice was hoarse as I continued to take shot after shot. "You said you'd forgotten what being happy really was until I came here, but I don't think I even knew what it meant until I met you."

Slowly he approached, took the camera, and turned it on me. Since he couldn't seem to be able to tear his gaze from me, he clicked it without looking through the lens, his voice a murmur when he said, "In case you really want to see what beauty looks like."

Ezra went back to the truck and returned with a blanket and picnic basket. I followed him down a short trail to a grassy spot that protruded out with a better view of the waterfall and valley. Here, the trees were farther back, and the heavens were unobstructed above us.

Ezra spread out the blanket and set the basket on top.

"Sit," he said.

"Bossy." The razzing was easy as I sank to the blanket to sit.

He leaned over me, his mouth brushing the shell of my ear. "You don't have the first clue, Little Trespasser."

Each word scraped over me like a rumble of thunder. I shook and the man had the audacity to chuckle as he climbed down the rest of the way and started removing everything from the basket. A bottle of champagne and a fruit tray and some meats and cheeses.

"Are you trying to spoil me?"

He popped the cork on the champagne, filled a flute, and handed it to me. "Has anyone ever done that before, Savannah? Spoiled you?"

My chest squeezed and my head barely shook. "No."

He took a strawberry from the tray and pressed it to my lips. "I think it's time we changed that."

Chapter Forty-Three

Ezra

I**T WAS NO SACRIFICE SPOILING** SAVANNAH WARD **WHEN I WAS** the one deriving all the benefit. She moaned in pleasure every time I lifted another piece of food to her mouth, aqua eyes going wide in some kind of rapture as I fed her.

"You keep making sounds like that and we aren't going to make it through this meal, and it's going to be me who's feasting on you," I warned.

Those eyes flared again, though the edge of that sexpot mouth quirked as she chewed then swallowed. God, I loved that the woman was always at the ready to play and tease, but there was also something deep about her.

Real and genuine.

"You say that like I'd be complaining."

I lifted another strawberry to her mouth, and she wrapped those pouty lips around it and sank in her teeth. Juice dribbled out at the corner of her mouth, and I reached out and wiped it, grumbling, "I didn't bring you out here to get you naked."

Though if she kept this up, I was liable to say fuck it and decide on a quick change of plans.

"And here I thought you were spoiling me?" She feigned disappointment as she swiped her tongue over the remnants of the juice.

My dick stirred in my jeans, but it was a chuckle that slid out as I gave her a slight shake of my head. "You are something, Savannah Ward."

"So you've been saying." She lifted a piece of cheese to my lips. "I'm afraid I might not ever get tired of hearing it."

"Guess I'll have to tell you every day." I bit into the cheese and chewed.

"Every day, huh?" She was back to teasing.

I swallowed. "That's right."

"Ah, there's my favorite overbearing hot cop."

I couldn't do anything but dive for her, knocking her back onto the blanket as I wrapped her in my arms.

Her laughter rang, and it felt like feathers that floated through my chest.

"Oh my God, Ezra, you brute, get off me. You're going to hurt yourself."

I would have all but forgotten about the wound on my side if it wasn't for the need to hunt down the bastard who was responsible.

I grunted at her. "Nah, I'm good as new."

I had her pinned by an arm, and she had her champagne flute lifted in the air to keep from spilling it while she giggled and squirmed below me. I had most of my weight off to the side, though I had her pinned with my arm and shoulder. I thought my mouth was in a permanent grin as I pushed it to her ear. "Say it again."

She stilled and set her flute aside, her laughter tapering off and her breaths turning shallow. "What part?"

"The part where I'm your favorite."

It took her the longest time to answer, but when she did, it was so quiet I could barely hear her, though I felt it all the way to my soul. "You might be my favorite person in the world, Ezra Patterson, and that terrifies me."

I edged back so I could see her. So I could take in the striking, severe angles of her face, the perfect contrast to the softness of her eyes and lips. I traced my thumb along her jaw. "It scares me, too."

We stayed like that for the longest time, staring at each other.

Finally, I shifted to lay on my side and nestled her into the crook of my arm, loving the feel of her cheek on my chest. Her hair tickling my face as the wind blew through.

"Love this," I murmured. "Being up here with you. It feels like I'm being elevated above every worry. Like up here, it can't touch us."

She hesitated, then asked, "Did you find out anything else?"

"No," I whispered at the top of her head. "We're thinking it might have been random. A fluke."

No one really believed it. I had a hunch it had everything to do with my sniffing around, digging for any evidence in Brianna's death. Gut told me someone wanted to shut my questions down—by whatever means possible.

Right then, I didn't want that to touch us, either. Didn't want to think about it. What was to come.

I wanted to relish this moment.

Savannah seemed content with that, too, because she snuggled closer, trying to burrow herself into the warmth my body emitted. The temperature had dropped with the sun's receding, and it was even colder up here with the elevation and the vapor from the waterfall that misted the air.

Our attention was turned toward the sky. It was the deepest blue, streaked with ribbons of blackened turquoise as the last bit of light was sucked away. Stars blinked to life, a scatter across the heavens. Below us in the valley, the lights of Time River had come alive.

Comfort whispered around us. It was the kind of comfort that came from being with someone who was the compliment to you. One who somehow made everything better just by being a part of you.

I pressed a kiss to Savannah's crown, inhaling her shampoo. Mango and cream. God, that was comforting, too. "Thank you for doing this with me."

"It's me who's thankful that you asked." There was no tease in her voice.

Affection curved my mouth. "I guess who we should be thanking is Olivia."

I could feel Savannah's smile against my chest as her fingers plucked along the fabric of my shirt. "We owe her. Big time."

"Yes, we do."

She shifted enough to peek up at me. "She's amazing. All three of them are."

I hugged her closer. "I don't know how I got so lucky to get three kids like them."

"I think they're pretty lucky that they got such a great dad."

"I'm trying to be."

She hesitated, then offered, "I could do a shoot of them, if you'd like? Because they are what's beautiful, Ezra. You brought me out here to be inspired? Their little faces are what inspire me."

My chest tightened.

Fiercely.

In a bid of devotion and turbulence.

"I would definitely like that."

Our words were mumblings. Murmurs that came more from our hearts than our mouths.

"Me, too," she said.

It was strange, having a feeling of just...being. And we stayed like that for the longest time, lying in the stillness as the night deepened around us. It didn't take long before the wind began to howl through the pines, their peaks thrashing, like the woods had become their own entity.

We fell into this perfect silence that didn't require words because I was pretty sure our spirits were speaking for themselves.

I wasn't sure how much time had passed when another shiver rolled through Savannah, and she tried to curl deeper into my side.

"We should probably get back," I said, though I was wishing we could stay elevated above the rest of the world for a while longer.

For a night.

Maybe for an eternity.

But it was cold, and I hadn't thought to bring an extra blanket.

"Is it wrong I want to stay here forever?" she whispered, snuggling closer.

I brushed my lips over her temple. "I thought the same thing myself."

A gust of wind rocked through the trees, and she shivered again.

"But I don't think the best way to end this night is with you freezing to death out in the woods." I let a chuckle wind into the claim.

Nudging her off, I packed our things, pushed to standing, then reached out and took her hand so I could help her up.

I didn't release her when I dipped down and grabbed the basket and blanket with my free hand. Instead, I threaded our fingers together because I didn't want to let go.

We kept peeking at each other as I led her back to the truck. An awareness hummed around us, her smile soft but not close to shy.

I tossed our things into the backseat, and she'd just climbed in on her side when I came back to stand in the open doorway on the passenger side. I reached in to help her buckle.

"What are you doing, Ezra?" Her voice was a tempting play.

I quirked her a grin. "I thought I told you it was time someone started spoiling you?"

And that didn't always mean material things. It often meant attention and care.

"You're pretty good at it, this spoiling thing." Aqua eyes peered over at me.

I brushed a lock of hair back from her face, my thumb grazing her cheek. "Get used to it."

I recognized the things that kept coming from my mouth.

The permanency.

The promises.

The forevers.

I shut her door and jogged around the front of the truck and climbed in. I slowly wound back down the hidden trail, carefully, the lights cutting through the night that had grown thick. Savannah wasn't nervous this time, she just rested back against the seat, her head tilted so she was continuously looking at me.

I reached out and set my hand on her thigh as we drove back to Time River beneath the cover of the stars. Again, no words were needed, there was just that same profound comfort that wound between us.

And when I pulled onto my street, I squeezed her leg where my hand still rested. "I don't want to take you back to the guest house, Savannah."

"Good, because I don't want you to take me back, either."

Chapter Forty-Four

Savannah

THE GARAGE DOOR ROLLED OPEN, AND EZRA PULLED HIS truck inside and shut off the engine. He didn't say anything when he cut me a glance before he got out, but whatever was hidden in that look had me both pinned and vibrating on the seat.

Anticipation twitched through my nerves as I watched him stride around the front of the truck so he could get to my door.

I couldn't move.

I was frozen.

Held to a mounting thrill that bubbled in my belly.

Apparently, whatever quiet we had fallen into on the way home had been the calm before the storm. Tranquil, lapping flames before we were doused in gasoline.

Because the second Ezra opened the passenger door, a frenzy lit.

"Come here, Little Trespasser," he growled, and he hauled me out with those massive arms, and I had no chance to find my footing before he had me pinned to a cabinet.

In the same second, his mouth captured mine.

This kiss? It was blistering.

Searing.

Scarring in a way that made me sure I would never be the same.

His hands were all over me, grappling to touch me everywhere.

I did the same to him.

Wanting to touch.

Taste.

Explore.

I dove into the kiss with everything that I had.

There was no longer any holding back.

Ezra groaned into my mouth as we spun. He knocked into a workbench, and a bunch of tools clattered to the concrete floor. It wasn't enough to slow or stop us.

We were too consumed by this scorching kiss to notice what we were knocking into.

The hood of his truck, a bicycle that toppled to the side, a stack of plastic bins.

We spun and spun as we vied to get closer, hands and mouths desperate, tearing at each other's clothes as his tongue stroked against mine.

Powerfully.

Urgently.

Frantically.

My back slammed into the interior door that led into the house.

He blindly grappled behind me to get to the knob, and the door swung open to the darkness of his house. He backed me inside, his kiss unrelenting. I hit the hallway wall with a thud, and my chest arched in a plea as both of his hands went to my breasts.

"Fuck me, Savannah, what you've done to me." It was a grumble at my mouth, and I felt the severity of it roll through me like possession.

My hands flew to his shoulders to keep from falling, and my knees went weak as Ezra kissed me into oblivion, his thumbs rubbing over the sensitive peaks of my nipples.

"Ezra," I whimpered. He swallowed it down, and without breaking the kiss, he hiked me into his arms. My legs wrapped around his waist.

He palmed one of my ass cheeks while the other wound into my hair.

I rose up high, swept in a frenzy as I rubbed myself against him, my arms around his neck as I kissed him back just as relentlessly as he kissed me.

He began to walk, carrying me through the shadows of his house. He moved all the way through the living room and kitchen, his mouth fervent against mine as he carried me into his room. Lamps burned from the nightstands, his room cast in a buttery glow of decadent warmth.

The air diffused in a glittering gold.

He set me back on my feet, kissing me more, hands on my face as we spun and spun.

Dizzying.

Perfecting.

"Please," I mumbled, not even quite sure what I was begging him for.

I just needed it—I needed him.

He pulled back to stare down at my face with his hands on either side of my neck. "I might not have taken you up that mountain with the intention of getting you naked, but you should know that's exactly what I intend right now."

"I might stage a revolt if you didn't."

The barest hint of a smirk touched his mouth, and he ripped my sweater over my head, mouth descending back to mine as his palms slid around and unclasped my bra.

Tingles spread as he drew down the straps, and he stepped away for one heated instant to remove it.

Ezra reached out and flicked his thumbnail over my left nipple. I bowed. "So fucking gorgeous, Savannah. If you had the first clue what I feel when I look at you. How perfect you are to me."

"No man has ever affected me the way you do, Ezra."

I fumbled at the button of his jeans, but before I could get it freed, Ezra had me hoisted up again and was tossing me onto the bed. I bounced against the mattress, and he approached, a shadow who loomed over me.

My heart pounded wildly.

But it wasn't in fear or reservation.

It was just because I *knew*.

Taking me by the ankle, he undid the laces of my tennis shoe and pulled it and my sock off before he turned to do the same with the other. Then he leaned over me, flicking the button of my jeans and dragging down the zipper.

My hips arched from the bed, rising up to allow him to peel them down my legs. He took my underwear with them, and I gasped and shivered as I lay there completely bare.

Ezra's eyes turned molten, the brown swirling with lust.

"Let me see you," he demanded.

I didn't hesitate. I propped my feet on the bed and spread my knees.

He didn't either. He shoved two fingers inside me. I gasped, hips arching again, the intrusion perfect but not nearly enough.

"You're soaked, Savannah."

"Because I need you."

"That's a good thing because you're about to have me."

Ezra took a step away from the bed, and he knelt and undid his boots before he slowly rose and kicked them off. Without looking away, he flicked the button of his jeans that I hadn't been able to loose, and the sound of him dragging down his zipper echoed against the walls.

A second later, he had his jeans and briefs shoved down around his thighs.

His cock huge and jutting toward the ceiling. The head engorged and throbbing. The veins pronounced.

"Ezra," I mumbled, half delirious, the man so gorgeous where he stood over me, his massive frame covering me in shadow.

His outline was a perfect hedge of protection. Shoulders wide and hulking, his abdomen a landscape of quivering muscles that flexed beneath sun-kissed skin. A chest so solid you'd think the man impenetrable if it wasn't for the softness I knew was hidden underneath.

The man a living statue of carved gold.

"You're different than any man I've ever met, Ezra. I'm not supposed to feel safe with anyone, but I feel safe with you." The admission tumbled from my trembling tongue, and I didn't regret it when I let it go.

It was offered freely.

Truly.

The same as I imparted the next.

"You're everything I couldn't believe existed and everything I've come to need."

That honey gaze softened, and there was something so tender beneath his rigid body when he set a knee on the bed and crawled over me. He used one hand to prop himself up and the other slid beneath my neck. That thumb traced the angle of my jaw as he stared down at me. "And you, Little Trespasser, stole into every place I wasn't supposed to let you go."

Our confessions whispered around us. Tendrils of this connection that wound and claimed.

He shifted and smoothed a palm down the outside of my leg, spreading me wider to make a place for himself between my thighs.

Flames crackled and that energy leapt.

He eased himself down enough to bring us chest to chest. Our hearts flew, a manic beat that drummed at the walls.

"I told you that I didn't think I could handle the feel of you around my cock, Savannah, but what I can't handle is not being inside you for a second longer."

His words provoked a moan from deep inside me. "I need you. I need all of you."

As long as the confessions were flying free, I saw no point in suppressing this one.

Edging back, he dug into his nightstand and pulled out a box of condoms.

"I hope you don't think it presumptuous, but I bought these this week, hoping one day I might get to have you like this. That you'd trust me enough to give yourself to me this way."

God, it was so sweet, the way he looked at me that it shattered through the last piece of the hardened, mangled pieces of my heart.

"I do. I trust you." It was a ragged breath that I issued toward the ceiling.

Praise maybe.

Relief.

Because I knew it, that he would never hurt me. Would never use me the way others had.

He covered himself before he wound back between my quivering thighs.

He eased down onto both elbows, bracketing my shoulders, both hands beneath my head, holding me close. "I promise I will never give you a reason to regret it."

He pushed inside me, slowly, but sure and strong. A possessive thrust that filled me to the blissful brink of pain. So full that I gasped and choked and clawed at his shoulders. "Ezra. I don't think—"

The words clipped off as he nudged in farther. "You can take it, Savannah. You were made for me."

His words flooded my mind. My heart and my spirit. Just as he consumed my body. I whimpered when he finally rocked deep enough that every inch of him was seated inside me.

He stilled, rasping, "Fuck, the way you feel wrapped around me, Savannah. I knew you were going to ruin me. Hope you're good with it, because now I'm going to have to ruin you."

My nails burrowed deeper into his flesh as I angled up to whisper at his ear, "I'm already ruined."

Taking me by the outside of the thigh, Ezra pulled out and sank back in. So deep I was gasping again. His fingers kneaded into my flesh. "Are you good, honey?"

I didn't know why I wanted to weep right then. Didn't know if it was the sheer gentleness of the way he called me *honey*, how he said it like it meant something brand-new, or if it was just the weight of him taking me that had unlodged the last barrier inside.

All I knew was I was mumbling at his shoulder, "You feel so good. So good. So good."

He withdrew and slowly drove back in.

Tingles raced. Tiny flares of pleasure. It wouldn't take much more of him to set me off. Not when it felt like we'd been coming up on this point since the moment we'd met.

The two of us inevitable.

Ezra began to rock over me, harder with each thrust. He grunted each time, filling me deep, taking me whole.

He kissed me as he did.

With a passion only my soul could understand.

Tender and urgent.

"Your sweet cunt, Savannah." He rumbled it at my cheek, and he pushed up on a hand, staring down at me as he moved. "So tight and perfect hugging my dick. Never have felt anything like you. I'm ruined for you."

Those eyes flamed as he took me in, his gaze pure heat as it rushed over my body, gliding down to where we were joined.

He edged his hand between us and rubbed two fingertips over my clit.

I was already close to splitting apart, and it only intensified.

Growing and glowing. Becoming something so immense and overpowering I didn't think there was a way to contain it.

He thrust, swirling and circling his fingers as he filled me over and over.

Slow and possessive and everything.

His muscles bowed and rippled, his skin taut as he moved.

He kept murmuring, "I have you. I have you."

Energy thrummed, crackling and sparking.

And that tension that was all our own filled the air.

Rising and unfurling.

Suffocating.

The man my breath.

"Ezra," I begged, meeting him jut for jut. "Harder. I'm…" I could hardly speak.

Ezra took me faster, his hips snapping as he drove, and his words became nothing more than a growl. "Let it go, Little Trespasser. I can't wait one more second to feel you come around my cock."

And the last thread of my reservation severed and snapped.

Bliss exploded, blinding as it spread, shearing through every cell in my body. I felt like I was soaring and sifting through a new reality. Floating through a new existence. Learning of a paradise that I'd never believed existed.

Safe.

Treasured.

Beautiful.

Loved.

I didn't have time to deliberate the fear it should have evoked.

Because Ezra drove faster, racing to meet me there.

Consuming.

Taking.

Claiming.

"Fuck, Savannah, yes." I felt it when he broke apart. When he came undone. When he met me there.

He clutched me tight as he came.

The man was burrowed so wholly inside me that it seemed neither of us could exist without the other.

Like we might be essential to the other.

And I was afraid it was my heart that had forgotten how to beat without his.

He panted hard, still holding me close as we both came down. Aftershocks pinged between us, a buzz of pleasure wrapping us whole.

Neither of us spoke for the longest time. We just held on tight, refusing to let go.

Finally, Ezra leaned back enough that he could see my face, and the pad of his thumb brushed over my swollen, kiss-bitten lips. His tweaked up at the side.

"Yeah, Savannah, one of the best days of my life."

Chapter Forty-Five

Ezra

I WAS A FIRM BELIEVER THAT IT WAS THE MILLIONS OF INSTANCES that wove and weaved and knitted together the fabric of our lives. It was the innumerable small things that made us who we were. The things that showed us what we were fighting for. Taught us what we loved and the things that didn't really matter.

Uncountable choices that edged us in one direction or another. Shaped us for the good or bad.

But as I lay there gazing down at Savannah, I wondered how many moments in a person's life could be given the title of monumental.

One single instance that changed everything.

One single encounter when you knew you would never be the same.

No question, the days my kids were born were on that list.

Not to mention the stark, gutting tragedy of what had happened to Brianna.

And now I had to believe this moment when I held Savannah had become a part of that, our breaths shallow and our hearts a crashing thunder where they beat at our chests, battling to get to the other.

Or maybe…maybe it had been the second I'd leaned down into the door of her car, and I'd caught those aqua eyes staring back. Maybe that was the second she had reached into my soul and altered my eternity.

Now, her cheeks were flushed and sweat drenched her skin. She smiled up at me, and there was that feeling. Rising up and taking over.

"One of the best days of your life, huh?"

"Oh, yeah, I'm going to give you a couple minutes to recover, and then I'm going to make it even better." I couldn't help the tease, but it was laced with the dense severity that clung to the room.

The energy lulled but more powerful than it'd ever been.

Heat deepened that flush, but she grinned in that sexy, taunting way that had me aching to take her all over again. "You seem so sure of yourself, Officer Patterson."

I growled at her razzing, joy tugging at my mouth. "I thought I told you not to call me that?"

"Oh, that's right, you prefer Hot Cop." Her grin spread. Dazzling and panging through the middle of me.

Growling again, I rolled us over, so quickly that she yelped. She giggled when she found herself straddling me at the waist.

Fuck, she was stunning, that tight little body bare, the dusky pink nipples of her tiny tits peeking out from beneath the fall of dark-blonde hair.

Shoulders delicate and that chin fierce.

"What am I going to do with you?"

She laid her hands flat to my stomach and leaned forward an inch. "I think the more pressing question is what are you going to do *to* me?"

"Wouldn't you like to know."

She attempted to hide her affected smile, and the mood was swinging between us, both light and heavy.

Profound and easy.

"First things first, I'm going to do this." She yelped again when I angled up, sweeping her into my arms at the same second I swung my legs over the side of the bed and stood. I carried her into the attached bathroom, and I flicked on the light above the vanity. I carried her to the counter and propped her on the edge. I ridded myself of the condom then dug into the cabinet, pulled out a washcloth, and ran it under warm water.

I edged back to stand between her legs, spreading her knees and pressing the cloth to that sweet spot between her thighs. She hissed a small sound then whimpered as I ran it over her flesh. "How do you feel?" I asked her.

She hesitated for a second before she looked up at me, no shuttering to her expression, just pure vulnerability. "Shattered."

Monumental.

I pulled her close, my free hand at the back of her head as I murmured at her ear, "Yeah, Savannah, I'm shattered, too."

"I never thought I'd feel like this. I wasn't supposed to."

I eased back, my hand still holding her at the back of the neck. "Sometimes what we think will hurt us most is the very thing we need."

"I didn't come here looking to find you."

A soft puff of air escaped my nose. "No, it was me who found you."

Warmth mixed with her uncertainty, and I pushed into the space where I'd known she'd been keeping me out. "Why did you come here? What were you looking to find? And don't tell me it was because you were passing through and liked the town."

A war went down in her expression, and I could feel every reservation that had held her back since I met her rise to the surface.

The fighter.

The survivor.

The one who'd been failed by every person in her life, so she'd come to rely wholly on herself.

"You can trust me," I murmured. "You don't have to go everything alone, Savannah. Not anymore."

She chewed at her bottom lip, and her attention fell away before she whispered, "You remember I told you that my sister was thriving and doing well after everything that had happened to us?"

My stomach twisted in dread. There hadn't been a chance at missing her devastation when she'd mentioned her sister before. "Yeah."

She blinked a bunch of times like it was difficult for her to process through the memories. "She had been doing so great, Ezra. She had gone back to school, but she really wanted to be a fashion and makeup influencer. She found so much joy in it and was truly happy for the first time in her life."

Torment filled Savannah's voice. "It made me happy, too, because she was the one person I'd been fighting for my entire life, other than myself. The one person who mattered. The one person I'd promised I would protect forever. It was just her and me."

My hand flexed against her neck, hit with the urge to gather her up and hold her. Erase the pain that dampened the happiness that had been lighting her face just a few moments ago. I almost regretted bringing it up, but we couldn't keep this in the background. She needed to know I was here for her, whatever was going on in her life.

This wasn't just me chasing something that felt good.

The physical.

The good times.

This was me committed.

She trembled as her tongue stroked her bottom lip, and her words grew thin. "It was after I left Bryce…"

That time, when my hand flexed, it was because I was fighting the urge to demand a last name. Overcome with the need to hurt whoever had hurt her. But Savannah didn't need me to go on a rampage right then. She needed someone to support her.

Stand by her side.

"I'd never been so sure that it was going to be me and Jessica against the world forever than then. Never so sure that we were the only thing the other had."

Savannah tripped over the confession. "She'd gotten her own apartment during the time I was living with Bryce, which I thought was great because I wanted her to learn to also rely on herself. She was always more…innocent than me. More naïve. But we were still in constant contact. I saw her almost every day and we texted or talked several times."

Her words dipped in a coil of confusion. "She started acting strange. Became more distant. Didn't return my calls and would

disappear for days at a time. I was worried that maybe she was using…
but also…it didn't quite add up to that. I was sure it was something
different."

Savannah inhaled a shaky breath, and I eased closer. I wouldn't
tell her it was okay because it clearly was not.

"It only got worse when I started to press her on it, demanding
to know what was going on because she wasn't acting like the sister I
knew. It only caused her to become more distant. More reserved. Until
one day she sent me a text that she didn't want me in her life anymore."

Her breath hitched and a tear slid from her eye. She didn't try to
hide it. She looked up at me. "But I knew, Ezra, I knew something was
off. I knew it wasn't right. I knew it wasn't really her who was talking,
and when I went to her apartment and found that she'd packed all her
things and left, I knew she was somehow in trouble. That someone
had gotten in her head."

"How long ago?"

"Two years."

Shit. That wasn't good.

"When I made the missing person's report, they'd told me there
was no evidence of anything nefarious, and it wasn't a crime for my
sister not to want to talk to me anymore."

"Have you heard from her since?"

Sorrow shook her head. "No, but I got a clue that she might have
come here. That she might have been living here."

Questions spun through my mind, my investigator kicking in.
"How so?"

She released a disordered breath, a laugh of frustration and disbelief. "It was just…so random. A few months ago, I got this journal
in the mail. It doesn't even mention her by name, but I swear, whoever had written in it was writing about her. A therapist. And why else
would it come to me if it wasn't talking about Jessica?"

Her voice narrowed to a wisp. "It was vague because I think she
was respecting Jessica's privacy, but I also think that maybe this person wanted me to know that something was going on with her. That

she wasn't safe. So I came here to see for myself. To see if I could find any trace of her."

Fuck.

That's what all the sneaking around had been about.

The pond.

The apartment.

The woman putting herself in danger's way.

Alarm howled as I thought of the motel. If her sister was in trouble and someone knew Savannah was trying to uncover her whereabouts?

I didn't like it. Didn't like any of this.

"Did you find anything?"

She almost seemed surprised that I asked it. Like she'd expected me to think she was foolish for trying.

A tremor rolled her throat when she swallowed. "No."

Unease pounded through my blood. "Would you show me that journal?"

She tried to cover her flinch.

"What is it?"

She hesitated.

"You can tell me anything, Savannah."

The laughter she let go of was hollow. Both bitter and haunted. "When I received it, I called the police in Houston to make a report. An officer came to my apartment to get a statement, and he basically laughed at me and said there was no proof that it was my sister. That there was no proof of anything really. No proof of a crime. He said whoever it was sounded like they were only begging for attention, the way I was right then, right before he reached out and tore my shirt."

She inhaled a fevered breath. "I knew exactly what his intentions were. I screamed and fought him off. Told him I had a security camera streaming to my friend's that was capturing everything he was doing. Thankfully, he didn't stick around to check if I was lying or not, which I was. He took off, calling me a cock tease as he left." Hatred whipped off her tongue.

Venom gathered on mine.

Every-fucking-person.

Everyone had let her down.

Tried to use her.

Manipulate her.

I framed her face in my hands and tipped her face up to mine. "I want to track down every person who has ever hurt you, Savannah. I want to undo every fucking wrong."

"But you can't."

"No, but I can be here right now. I can stand for you. I can help you try to find her."

"I don't want to be a burden to you, Ezra. You already have so much on your plate right now."

"You are no burden, Savannah. You're a treasure, and I'm going to prove to you what that means."

"Ezra." My name was a whisper, and fuck, the way she looked at me was like it was the first time she was seeing meaning. The way that aqua gathered on a swilling wave of trust, even though there were still vestiges of doubt floating in them.

It would take time to eradicate it. I knew that. But I would do everything I could to bring her to the place where she understood her life was worth more than bare survival.

"I want you to stay."

I meant it for tonight.

I meant it for tomorrow.

I meant it for forever.

But I knew she wasn't quite ready to hear that yet.

"I do, too." I wondered exactly what she was admitting to herself. She swallowed hard before she tapped her fingers over the raging of my heart. "I'll get you the journal in the morning. For tonight…I just want to be with you. Just us."

I grunted. "I like the sound of that plan."

She squealed when I suddenly picked her up from the counter and into my arms, planning on making good of her suggestion.

Weightlessness swept into the room. Like a huge amount of her own burden had been lifted. This affliction she'd been carrying for two fucking years by herself.

I couldn't imagine how alone she'd felt. The one person who was supposed to be everything to her had abandoned her, too...or worse.

I fought the ball of dread in my throat. Two years was a long damned time for someone to go missing without a word.

I would do everything I could to get her answers.

But for tonight, I would spend it cherishing her.

Praising her.

Showing her how fucking amazing she was.

I carried her back to my bed and set her in the middle of it.

She looked like a temptress there in the middle of the jumble of sheets, hair mussed and completely bare.

"Wait there, I'll be right back."

She frowned, but didn't ask questions, and it took about all I had to leave her there as I ambled out into the kitchen, filled a glass with water, then eased back into the room, figuring she was going to need to stay hydrated with what I had planned tonight.

Savannah was sitting up on the bed, and she'd curled herself in the sheet. It didn't matter that it had only been a minute since I'd seen her, she still stole my breath.

My body locked tight at the sight.

Dick perking up and ready to go again.

She didn't miss the reaction, and those eyes traveled over me.

Slowly.

Deliberately.

Taking in every inch as I approached the bed. I handed her the glass, and she took a deep drink, her delicate throat bobbing as she swallowed. "I could get used to this spoiling thing," she muttered.

"You think me bringing you something to drink is spoiling you?"

"No, my hot cop walking around naked like that is." Her mouth tweaked, and I let go of a low chuckle, half in amusement and half in greed.

"Hmm, and I do hope in this relationship, that spoiling is going to be reciprocated," I teased.

Her eyes flared. "And what kind of relationship are we talking about?"

"One where I get to look at this sweet body whenever I want. One where I get to touch you. One where I get to take you. One where I please you night and day, the same way as you're pleasing me."

I slowly peeled the sheet from her body as I murmured the claim.

Because that's what this was.

A claim.

Savannah trembled, and her entire body bowed as I exposed her. Every muscle in her body quivered in anticipation.

I drew a single finger from her throat all the way down to her trembling stomach. I circled it around her belly button. She whimpered my name, hips bucking in need. "Ezra."

Satisfaction filled my grin, though I glanced at her face when I asked, "Are you sore?"

She husked out a laugh. "In the best way possible."

"Good because I need you again."

Backing away, I fisted myself, stroking my cock once.

"Ezra." It was a thready rasp.

"Do you want me, Savannah?"

Needy disbelief filled her huff. "I think that's obvious."

"Is it?" I taunted. I wanted to hear her say it.

"Are you going to make me beg?"

"Yes."

"I thought you were supposed to be the sweet one." She repeated what she'd told me that one night, though her voice was deep, traipsing into seduction.

I smirked at her as I backed the rest of the way to the couch that sat under the window. I kept stroking myself while she watched.

"Maybe I just want to see you on your knees for me."

I needed her there because that's where she had me.

Savannah angled into a crawl, and she came forward until she was about a foot from the end of the bed before she shifted to her knees.

A goddess rising high.

Muted light diffused over her skin, hair all around her.

"Here I am," she breathed.

There she was.

Lust pummeled me, a need unlike anything I'd experienced before.

"Turn around and show me your sweet ass."

Surprise had Savannah letting go of a shaky breath, but there was no hesitation to it as she complied, and she turned around and got down onto all fours.

Her hips swayed as she gave me the most tempting view of her backside.

"Good girl," I murmured as I stood and moved back toward her, head going light with what she was doing to me. How was it possible she could make me feel this way?

Raging with need.

The call irresistible.

But it was just her. This woman who'd changed everything. Just her *being* was monumental.

She swayed as she waited, her ass in the air, her cunt glistening and throbbing.

I dragged a single finger through her soaked center before I pushed it in deep.

Savannah gasped.

"What I'm going to do to you, Little Trespasser. And I don't intend to ever stop."

"Don't you dare stop," she whimpered.

"Gladly." I grabbed her by both butt cheeks and spread her wide, and I leaned down so I could lick her from clit to ass.

Savannah all out shook, and she emitted this sound that cut me through, her body sagging in with the onslaught of sensation. "Oh God, Ezra."

"I'm going to have you everywhere, Savannah. In every way."

The promise rang in the air, and Savannah pushed back, begging through a rasp, "I'm yours."

Her oath slid through me.

Liquid steel that rushed through my veins.

I angled in, fucking my tongue into her pussy before I lapped down to suckle at her engorged clit. She writhed, pressing back onto my face.

"What do you need, Savannah?" I whispered at her sweet flesh.

"You, Ezra. Just you. I'm on the pill—" She choked it off, like she was terrified of what she was offering.

The trust she was giving.

And I wondered if she knew what that meant to me. That she was here with me in the first place. That after every person who'd let her down in her life, she'd picked me to be the one she allowed to hold her.

I angled my arm around her and urged her upright until her back was plastered against my chest, and I spread my palm out over the erratic pounding of her heart as I leaned in and brought us cheek-to-cheek. "Is that what you want? To feel me bare?"

Her hands spread over mine, clutching me, urging me closer. "I want everything you have to give me."

Easing away, I placed my palm at the nape of her neck and pressed her chest to the mattress, bending her over.

My stomach fisted at the sight.

The vision of Savannah Ward dripping and needy for me.

Ruined.

I was so fucking ruined.

She shifted her hips. "Please."

"Greedy girl."

"Guilty. I don't think I'll ever get enough."

Grabbing the base of my dick, I lined myself up with all that sweet, soaked heat. Another swell of dizziness rushed me when I nudged just the head inside.

Her walls throbbed around me, and I clenched my teeth. "How are you so fucking tight, honey?"

She whimpered as she tried to adjust to me again. "I need you," was the only answer she gave, and I slowly jutted deeper.

Hands on her hips, I took her inch by inch. She squirmed and whimpered, the oxygen thin as that energy whirled about us, making it hard to breathe.

Her pussy stretched wide as she accepted me, my cock filling her so full, her walls squeezing and squeezing.

"So good." I could barely grunt it out. "I knew what your pussy was going to do to me, Savannah. I knew it."

I pulled out slowly, my dick coated in all her slick before I drove back in so goddamn deep.

Her thighs trembled, and she whimpered, "Yes."

I took her by the hips and started to move, driving in and out of her perfect cunt.

The view itself had my balls tightening, and pleasure took to zipping up and down my spine.

"You're perfect, Savannah. So good."

Praise spilled from my mouth. My truth. This girl who'd invaded my world and made it feel like something else.

She jarred forward, a moan ripping free as I was seated to the hilt.

"This one's going to be hard…are you okay with that?"

Her hair dragged across the bed as she nodded. "I'm yours."

And fuck, this feeling swept through me at the profession, so big and bright, a glow at the center of my chest. I took her by both hips, and I began to fuck her.

Possession in every stroke.

But the truth was it was my little trespasser who possessed me.

The one I'd give it all for.

The one I'd live it out for.

The one who had me on my knees.

She started to rock, her body rolling as she met me thrust for thrust.

I reached out and fisted a hand in her hair, arching her back as the other hand smoothed over her right ass cheek. "Such a good girl, the way you take my cock."

A groan rolled her throat, and that feeling rode through my being, something so intense and severe.

She was slick and so hot, growing hotter by the second. I ran my thumb along where we were joined and gathered her arousal.

Air heaved from Savannah when I pressed it to that sweet,

puckered hole that was throbbing just as fierce as the rest of her. I nudged it in slowly, in time with every drive of my dick.

Savannah swayed, her knees going weak, tiny cries toppling from her mouth as I drove her toward rapture.

I could feel it. The way she tightened and the energy heightened. I pushed my thumb all the way in, and she was rasping, "Ezra, oh, yes, I'm going to..."

I slipped my other arm around so I could rub two fingers over her clit.

Savannah exploded.

The girl a thunderclap. A cry erupted from her mouth as an orgasm tore through her body.

She pulsed and pulsed, the pleasure going on forever.

She was still drenched in the aftershocks of bliss when I suddenly swept her up from the bed and carried her to the couch. I sat and shifted her around to straddle me. Her legs were shaking, fireworks going off in her body, but it was the confusion that traipsed through her expression—aqua eyes wild as she questioned the change in position—that fisted my chest.

I brushed back a messy lock from her cheek. "I need to see your face when I come."

The confusion turned to vulnerability, to softness, before it wove right into that trust. She rose up on her knees so I could position my cock at her entrance.

"Show me how good you can ride me," I grunted.

Savannah braced herself on my shoulders, and she sank down hard, ripping the oxygen from both our lungs.

"Fuck," I grumbled. "You feel so nice. So fuckin' nice."

She released a hoarse laugh. "You feel like paradise. Like I'm dreaming."

"Only thing I want to be is your sanctuary."

I spread her wide, running my palms up the inside of her thighs until I was lifting her by the bottom. It shifted the position, and Savannah mewled as I guided her, slow and so goddamn deep. I moved to brace her around the waist with one arm, and I pressed my thumb to that needy bud that was begging for my attention all over again.

Savannah took me like she meant it, her tits in my face as she rode me. I sucked her right nipple into my mouth while I touched her. Her hands dove into my hair, and both of us were panting as the sound of our bodies joining filled the room.

"That's what I want to be, Savannah. Your safe place."

Savannah went off again, taking me with her, my body rocked with the greatest type of ecstasy I'd ever felt.

She quivered and shook while I poured myself into her, coming and coming and coming.

We stayed there, clinging to each other as bliss flickered and lapped, both of us heaving for the nonexistent air as we came back down.

My arm was still around her waist, and I tipped my face up to hers as I brushed back the wild locks of her hair. "I need you to know I've never felt like this."

I needed her to know it was different.

A thousand different emotions fluttered through her expression.

Hope.

Worry.

Reservations.

Love.

I saw it, and I knew it was the one she feared most.

She plastered herself against me, her arms so tight around my neck. "I feel it, too, Ezra, and I'm afraid it's a feeling that's too good to be true."

Chapter Forty-Six

Ezra

One and a Half Years Ago

DARKNESS HUNG CLOSE TO THE GROUND, LIKE THE NIGHT had grown bigger than the sky. His headlights sliced through it like silvered, metallic blades. He was covering the night shift for Samson so he could spend the weekend with his family out of state. Ezra didn't normally mind. But there was something about this night that had set him off kilter. Made him feel like his shaky foundation was getting ready to finally crack completely.

Break in two and fall away.

Maybe he'd sensed it tremble in the sticky summer air. Or maybe it was just that he hadn't been able to get in touch with Brianna before he'd left for work. Maybe it'd all been a premonition as he came up around the bend and his headlights caught the glint of something shiny just off the side of the road.

Apprehension climbed through his cells as he slowed, and he squinted as he peered out the windshield. His stomach bottomed out when he realized it was a car that had skidded while going around the corner and had taken a nosedive into the ditch.

A white car that looked really fucking familiar.

He whipped his SUV off to the side of the road, tossing on his hazards as he jumped out. He went running that way, boots pounding the pavement.

"Brianna?" His shout reverberated around him, terror staking him through. "Brianna!"

He choked over his relief when she came stumbling out from the high grasses that grew along the road, though it was short-lived when he realized she wasn't limping because she was injured but because she was trashed.

Anger climbed up from the place he'd tried to keep buried for the last two years. He hurried toward her, anyway, taking her by the shoulders to hold her up, eyes racing to take her in. "Are you hurt?"

Laughter rolled out of her.

Delirious.

Maniacal.

"Aren't we all, Ezra? Hurt? Isn't that what this life is?"

He tightened his hold on her like it might stand a chance of penetrating. Making contact with the places in her mind she wouldn't let him reach. "It doesn't have to be that way."

She laughed again and jerked herself out of his hold. She stumbled to the side before she spun in a circle and lifted her arms over her head. "It does. It does."

She looked back at him.

"You could have killed someone, Brianna. You could have *killed yourself*." Fury and frustration bled from his mouth.

At least he'd long since stopped allowing her to be alone with the kids. Making more of those excuses to his mother as to why they needed to stay over there while he was away at work. Brianna had gone back to school, Ezra had told her. Night school.

Her mother had been proud, excited for Brianna that she was furthering herself.

How fucking desperately he wished it were true.

Brianna's laughter hitched on a sob, and she staggered back his way, clinging to him. "You have to help me, Ezra. You have to stop them. I tried to help. I tried."

"What are you talking about, Brianna?"

"Don't you see them? They're all around. They can see me. They're going to find me." Her words grew more agitated with each one she released.

Ezra scanned the area. The only movement was the high grasses blowing in the breeze. "There's no one out there, Brianna. No one."

She was so close to him, so close that he could smell her. And Ezra could smell *him*. He might not have known where she'd been, but he knew exactly what she had been doing.

He ground his back teeth in an attempt to keep his cool.

Part of him wanted to demand to know who it was. Did it matter though? Ezra hadn't touched her in months, and the whole time, he'd known, deep down, that it was already over for them, although he felt the fullness of that truth then.

A severing.

A detachment.

And it felt like floating free.

Still, he would stand by her, get her help.

For her sake. For the sake of their children. Because he did care about her. Wanted her safe and whole and healthy.

"I've got to call out a tow truck, then I'm taking you to the ER in Poplar."

Her nails scraped at his chest. "No, Ezra. No."

"You need help, Brianna, and I'm finished covering for you."

"I told you I'm fine." She shrieked it.

"Yeah, and I told you the next time this happened I was leaving, and I was taking the kids with me."

And he'd meant it.

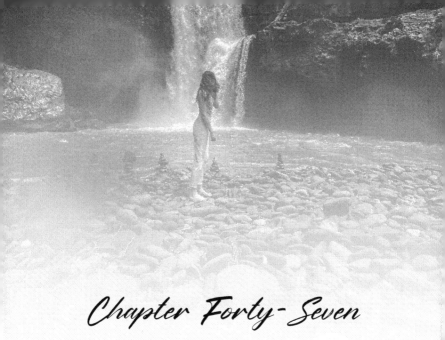

Chapter Forty-Seven

Savannah

WARMTH COVERED ME WHOLE, SKIMMING ACROSS MY flesh and sinking beneath to saturate every cell. Contentment and satisfaction and a pulsing of new hope filled me as I watched Ezra through the morning light that filtered in through the window.

My nails lightly scratched at the prickly stubble that coated his jaw, and he softly traced his thumb over the cap of my shoulder where we lay in silence staring at each other.

Soaking up the perfect moment of when we'd woken at the same time.

Our legs tangled and our hearts slowed in the type of peace I had never felt before.

I was scared of it and desperate for it in equal measure.

The faintest smile dusted his lips. "And here I thought I was the one who was supposed to be spoiling you." His voice was gravelly with sleep. He shifted and brought his palm to my cheek, his thumb caressing beneath my eye. "Then I wake up with you like this, and I feel like a king."

Affection bloomed in my chest, a full-body glow, and my teeth raked my bottom lip. "I like your idea of spoiling."

His mouth tweaked, those honey-kissed eyes gentle. "It seems we have some sort of understanding, then."

"I guess we do."

He drew me closer and nuzzled his face in my neck. "Good."

Joy expanded and pressed, and I could fight it all I wanted, but I was pretty sure there would be no escaping this.

Such a foolish girl who was dreaming about waking up like this each morning.

The one who believed in his care last night.

One who held it like an oath that he would help me find my sister.

Ezra spread a palm over the small of my back and plastered me against every bare inch of him. I gasped when I felt him hard and pressing against my belly, though it was a tease that was rolling from my tongue. "And you call me the needy one."

"Oh, Savannah, get used to it, honey, because there's never going to be any not needing you."

Giddiness flew while a rush of desire tumbled through.

His big palm drifted lower, palming me by the bottom—

The front door suddenly crashed open, and the clatter of little footsteps and a twine of excited voices reverberated from the main room. "Dad...Dad...Daddy! Where is you?" My eyes went wide, and we both flew upright.

"Shit," Ezra rumbled. He barely had time to fumble out of bed, snag his jeans from the floor, and pull them on before his bedroom door burst open. He'd moved so fast that he was already there, grabbing it and holding it partially shut, doing his best to shield the opening.

"I found you!" Owen sang just as Olivia's sweet, eager voice filled the air. "We woke up really early and Grandma said we had to wait until eight so you could sleep in but then we could come over here and make breakfast so we could have a special family morning."

"I wike bweakfast!" Owen shouted it like someone was asking for a volunteer.

"Breakfast is the most important meal we gotta eat," Oliver added.

"All right, give me a minute and I'll be out," Ezra rumbled.

"Miss Savannah?" Surprised curiosity coated Olivia's voice when she suddenly caught sight of me from where she peeked around Ezra's waist.

Crap.

I held the sheet tighter to my chest. Ezra moved to the side and tried to block her view, only to have Oliver poke his head through the other side. "Did you have a sleepover, too, Miss Savannah?"

Mortification burned my cheeks.

"Hey, I asked you all to give me a minute." Ezra's voice had gone stern, and the kids reluctantly retreated, Olivia grumping, "I only wanted to say hi. That's the neighborly thing to do, and I needed to see if she had a good date."

An amazing date, Olivia, an incredibly amazing date, but I'm pretty sure I shouldn't tell you about it while I'm naked.

The second the door clicked shut, I groaned and buried my face in my hands. "Oh my God, your kids are going to be scarred."

A heavy sigh filled the air, and I peeked his way to find him with his back to the door scrubbing a hand over his face. "Sorry about that."

"I'm the one who should be apologizing."

I should have gotten up and went to my own bed early this morning. Hell, I probably should have skulked back to it sometime in the night. Too bad the thought of losing that time with Ezra felt like losing a limb.

Besides, he'd asked me to…stay.

I'd wanted it. God, how much I'd wanted it.

Barefoot and shirtless, he eased back my way, his big feet amazingly light on the floor. Reaching out, he took me by the chin and tipped my head back, forcing me to look at him. "You don't have a thing to apologize for. But I do need to get out there and put out some fires that I'm pretty sure the news of you has started."

Disquiet billowed through my bloodstream. Talk about horrible impressions to make with his mother.

His mother.

Nausea tightened my stomach in a fist. Old discomfort and dis-trust bled through the bliss I'd found myself in last night.

Like he'd read every thought that had gone through my mind, Ezra tipped my chin higher. "It's fine. I promise. Get dressed and come out."

He dipped down and pecked a kiss to my nose, then snatched his tee from the floor and pulled it over his head.

One second later, he was walking out the door.

Slumping back onto the pillow, I stared at the ceiling as I tried to gather up the disorder.

I contemplated hiding out in Ezra's room for the next two hours or maybe jumping out the window and sneaking back to the guest house.

Coward.

What was that going to solve?

So, I tossed off the sheets and hurried to dress in the same jeans and sweater I'd had on yesterday. I used the bathroom then rinsed my mouth with mouthwash I found under Ezra's sink, before I ran my fingers through my matted hair, doing my best to tame it.

I looked at myself in the mirror.

Yep, I still looked like I'd spent the night being fucked by a brute of a man. If you looked close enough, I was pretty sure I had the paw marks to prove it. I was deliciously sore everywhere. My hips and waist where he'd grabbed me, my skin raw and grazed by his stubble, the ache between my thighs that his cock had left behind.

Yeah, sneaking out the window sounded like a pretty solid plan right then.

Blowing out a sigh, I quietly unlatched the door and peered out to the disorder of voices and clanking dishes that echoed from the kitchen. All stealth-like, I crept down the short hall, feeling like I needed to be careful not to step on a landmine.

I peeked around the corner.

Ezra was in the kitchen with his kids. Olivia stood on a stool next to him, chattering away, Oliver was propped on the counter on the other side, and Owen was hanging onto his back and shouting that he was a koala in his adorable way.

Shiny locks of their white hair struck in the bright rays of light that flooded in through the window where the curtains had been fully drawn, their faces alight and their giggles unending as Ezra teased and talked with them as he pulled a big mixing bowl from the cabinet above them.

It was so lovely. So, so lovely that my heart shattered a little again, this beauty unfound.

I didn't know if he'd heard me or sensed me, but Ezra shifted to look at me from over his shoulder.

And his smile…it was slow and adoring.

His attention had the rest of the kids turning to look my way, and Owen slid off his back when he saw me, and he hopped my way with that beaming smile on his face.

"My S'vannah. Is you gonna have bweakfast wif us?"

Affection tightened my chest, the oxygen nearing gone with the overpowering feeling that crashed over me.

"I—"

I started to speak only it clipped off when I noticed the figure who came to a grinding stop at the end of the children's hallway.

Ezra's mother.

I still had never spoken to her, had only caught glimpses of her when she'd been coming and going, except for when she'd come into the house last weekend after Ezra had been injured.

She'd been distraught then, terrified for her son, and we'd ushered the children out so quickly that there hadn't been time for introductions to be made.

Right then, I could tell she was trying to force a smile that just wouldn't come.

Stones toppled in my stomach, the discomfort so stark and bleak as it radiated across the room. I was suddenly having difficulty breathing for entirely different reasons.

I felt like an outsider, standing there.

A usurper.

Clearing his throat, Ezra drew attention back to himself. "I don't think you two have officially met. Mom, this is Savannah. Savannah, my mother, Linda."

I looked back at his mother. She'd managed a smile, but it was brittle. "It's a pleasure to meet you, Savannah."

Except there was no pleasure in her tone. There was only speculation and judgement and a form of surprised distaste so severe that it struck me like a kick to the chest.

"It's nice to meet you, too," I mumbled.

"Miss Savannah had a sleepover with my daddy, Grammy, just like us!" Oliver shouted.

Ugh.

This was the worst.

Humiliating.

It wasn't like her son was a child, but God, she was looking at me like I'd stolen his innocence.

The strain was so intense that it mottled the air.

I didn't know how to handle it. How to put Ezra through it. Not when he kept looking at me in apology. Not when he looked so uncomfortable.

I felt offset. An irregular puzzle piece that I was trying to make fit into this picture.

"Well, I think I should probably go. Give Grandma hugs." She walked into the kitchen.

"Ah, man, don't you want to stay? I thought we were supposed to have a special family breakfast? I'm going to make the most delicious eggs, Grams," Olivia told her.

"You can make me eggs another time," she said, kissing her on the top of the head.

Right. When I wasn't there.

She hugged all the kids, gave Ezra an awkward goodbye, and barely cut a glance at me when she left out the front door.

Oh, but it cut.

I winced beneath the weight of it, then I full-on flinched when the door shut a little too hard behind her.

In unease, I shuffled. "I think I'm going to go out to the guest house really quick."

I needed a second.

To take a breath and clear my head.

A moment to shake off the insecurity that flooded me like a dam breaking loose.

You don't belong.

You don't belong.

You never have and you never will.

I tried to block out the voices.

"Savannah…" Remorse filled Ezra's tone, and he started my direction.

I put up my hand. "It's fine. I'll be right back."

Ezra warred, then conceded with a reticent dip of his chin. I went to the back door and hurried out, thankful I'd thought to grab my purse from his floor before I'd left his room. I used the key to let myself into the back door of the guest house, and I pressed my face into my hands the second I was inside.

"I need you to know I've never felt like this." Ezra's promise rippled through my mind, at odds with the one I'd clung to for so many years. *"It's just you and me, Jessica. You and me because we can never trust anyone else. No one will ever care for us the way we care for each other. They'll only hurt us in the end, but I promise you, I will never fail you."*

I jolted when there was a light tapping at the door behind me. It was relief that hit me, an answer to the questions that spiraled and churned, and I turned, expecting to see Ezra.

Ice slipped down my spine when I saw it was his mother.

She must have heard me going out the back door and then came in through the side gate. Or maybe she'd been waiting.

I didn't know.

The only thing I knew was I was trembling out of control when I went back to flick the lock and reopened the door.

She didn't enter, she just lifted her quivering chin. Pain was there, set deep in her psyche. A brimming of protectiveness and a swelling of desperation.

"I don't know you, Savannah, but I do know my son. And he's vulnerable and weak right now. He might think he's ready to move on, but he's not. Not even close to it. He lost the love of his life. The woman he adored. The woman he thought he was going to spend the rest of his life with. His children lost their mother. The last thing any of them need right now is someone like you coming in here and disrupting their healing."

"Someone like me?" It punched out of me on a wheeze.

Her head barely shook. "Someone who's lost. A wanderer. Someone who will never belong. Someone who runs. Now that is something I can see about you, every time I caught you staring out at them over the last few weeks."

Moisture stung the back of my eyes. I fought it. I fought it with all of me.

I might have been able to hold it together if she hadn't continued.

"And he might think he truly cares about you, but my son is only looking for someone to save since he couldn't save her."

It was those words that pummeled, what had me crumpling in two and struggling to stand. Battered from all sides. I might as well have been on the ground curled into a ball, trying to protect myself as I was being kicked again and again.

Wheezing, my hand shot out to the doorframe to keep myself from falling.

Linda sniffed. "I truly hate hurting your feelings, Savannah. I'm sure you're a nice person, but I think it needs to be said that you will never truly be a part of them. It'd be best if you left now before it causes more pain in the end, for all parties involved."

Without saying anything else, she turned and walked back across the yard, disappearing around the side of the main house and through the gate.

While I stood there gasping. Voices came at me from every direction.

"*Mommy, please, don't.*"

"*Stop crying, you little brat. Do you know everything I sacrifice for you?"* Sharp nails dug into Savannah's shoulders as her mom shook her hard. *"You are pathetic. Worthless. A waste of space."*

I choked around the pain, my chest clutching when a different voice penetrated.

"You don't have to go it alone, Savannah. Not anymore."

My hand curled into my sweater.

"My son is only looking for someone to save since he couldn't save her."

No. It was more. We were more.

"You can trust me, Savannah. I would never hurt you." Bryce touched her face when he promised it.

A lie.

So many brutal lies.

So many promises.

I staggered back into the guest house, and the door drifted shut behind me. Did I want this too much? Did I need him too much? How had I come to rely on someone when I knew better than to ever fully give that trust?

My spirit wept, clawing at my insides, at my heart and my mind.

A toil of confusion and doubt.

I raked at the tears that fell down my face. I hated them. I hated the weakness. The vulnerability.

I sniffled, sucking it down, and I dug into my purse, pulled out my phone, and tapped out a message.

Me: I'm not feeling great. I think I'm going to skip breakfast.

Why did it feel like a betrayal? Like I was stabbing Ezra in the back? Like I was shunning his kids?

Because I cared too much, that was why. I'd gone and put myself in the position I'd promised myself I'd never be in again.

One where I could be hurt. But I'd known it all along, hadn't I? That's where Ezra was getting.

I hurried into the bedroom, frantic, not even sure what the hell I thought I was doing or where I was going.

Away, maybe. To find some clarity. Some space.

I dipped down to grab the duffle bag out from under the bed where I had it stored.

Panicked.

Frenzied.

I started to stand when I felt the presence emerge over me from behind.

Powerful.

Provocative.

The ground shook beneath my feet.

"What do you think you're doing?" Ezra's words were shards.

I did my best to ignore him. To grab the few things littered on the nightstand and shove them into the bag. But my hands were shaking too hard for me to even be able to pick anything up.

"Savannah." His voice curled around me. Raw and severe. "Look at me."

His lure had always been inevitable, the compulsion too great, and there was nothing I could do but slowly shuffle around to face him.

I shouldn't have looked up. But I did. I lifted my gaze to that magnificent brute of a man who was watching me with the tenderness that he always had. But this morning, it was cut in his own fear, in his own frantic desperation as he filled my doorway.

"What are you doing?" he demanded again. Those honey-melted eyes had hardened in anguish.

"I think it's best if I go, don't you?" I shrugged and attempted to make it light. Like it was no big deal. Like this really didn't matter and the thought of losing him didn't have me completely shredding apart. "I mean, it's not like I can stay in your guest house forever."

Ezra growled. A crack of lightning that struck through the room. "No, I don't fuckin' think it's best if you go." He took a step toward me. The air shivered and shook. "Why are you running?"

"I'm not—"

"Don't bullshit me, Savannah. You think I don't know you by now? You think I don't see what's written all over you? You're afraid."

I choked out a disbelieving laugh, and there was no keeping back the torment that ripped from my tongue, my voice louder than I intended. "Of course, I'm afraid, Ezra! How could I not be? Every person I have trusted in my entire life has hurt me, and now you're in the position to hurt me worse than anyone has before you. What do you expect me to do?"

"Stay." He said it without hesitation.

I choked out a brittle sound. "You don't really mean that. You just...you just see someone who needs to be saved, someone pathetic and weak, and once you think you've patched me up and made me all better, then you'll be happy to send me on my way."

The words looked like they impaled him just as hard as they had me when his mother had issued them.

Slaying.

Sundering.

Splitting him in two.

Anger surged in to take its place, and he took another step forward. "Is that what you think, Savannah? That you're a project? A task? Something to make me feel better about myself since I failed my wife?"

He hit every nail on the head. A hammer coming down.

"I just..."

"You think you're not more than that to me? After everything, how do you not know?"

"Ezra." I choked it.

His fist clutched his chest as he angled my direction. "I love you, Savannah. I'm fucking in love with you. So far gone that I can't think straight. So far gone that I close my eyes and it's you I see. In so deep that I'm stuck. I'm stuck on you, Savannah, and that's exactly where I want to be."

He took another step forward, all that bristling strength vibrating in severity. But his touch was soft when he set his palm on my cheek.

Those eyes warmed as he tipped his head in emphasis, his voice dropping to a murmur, "So yeah, Savannah, you can stay forever. With me. With my kids. You just have to decide if I'm worth believing in."

The fingers of both my hands curled into the fabric of his shirt, and I sagged against him. "You are the first person I've believed in for so long, Ezra, and I'm so scared of it. So scared of how much I ache for you. So scared of how much I need you. So scared of how much I love you."

A heaving sigh of relief left him at my words, and he gathered me in his massive arms. He curled them around me as he plastered me against the steady thrum of his heart. He pressed his lips to the crown of my head. "Say it again."

"I love you. I'm in love with you." It whispered free, so quietly, but I swore that it carried through the room.

An echo.

A promise.

And it fell away. The last, mangled piece that had guarded my heart.

I was his.

Exhaling a long breath, Ezra managed to draw me closer, and he started to sway me right there in the room. So softly and slowly as he rocked me back and forth in this slow dance that marked the most profound.

"Little Trespasser, sneaking right into my heart and claiming it." It was a murmur.

"I didn't think I had mine left to give."

His head shook against the top of mine. "No, Savannah. I felt it from the beginning. Alive and beautiful. It was just hidden. I hope here, this will be a safe place where you can let it shine."

I clung to him as he swayed me, and I could feel the edge cut back into his demeanor, though he didn't pull away when he mumbled, "I saw my mom leaving out the side gate, and I don't know what she said to you, Savannah, but I know she said something, and I'm fucking sorry if she made you think you are anywhere but exactly where you belong. But you should know that she doesn't know me the way you do. You see me. You get all of me. I promise you that."

My throat thickened, and I nodded against his chest. "I trust you."

It'd been my breaking point, and somehow, it'd become my healing point.

"Good. Now, we better get back inside before my yahoos tear down the house. They're waiting on you so they can have breakfast."

My spirit flailed, and Ezra eased back enough so he could take my face in his hands. He stared at me, honey eyes molten. "I love you."

Every cell in my body squeezed. "I love you."

His nod was final.

Our permanent understanding.

Then he took my hand and led me back into his house.

The boys were already waiting at the table, and Oliver pounded at the spot next to him, grinning so wide. "You gotta sit right here in your very special spot, Miss Savannah."

"You're here, Miss Savannah!" Olivia shouted at the same time, and she hopped off the stool and came running, barreling straight into me and wrapping her sweet arms around my waist. "I'm really glad you came back."

The confession was buried in my stomach, low and relieved, like she'd been afraid that I wouldn't.

I ran my free hand over the top of her head since Ezra was still holding the other.

"Me, too, Olivia. Me, too."

Journal Entry

She'd been waiting for me behind my office two days ago, hidden behind a veil of ivy that had kept her shrouded. I'd known she was there, lurking in the shadows as I'd produced my key and slid it into the lock. It was me who'd looked around the back parking lot before I'd gestured for her to follow.

She'd been distraught when she'd sat on the couch across from me, her striking face covered in a sheet of tears.

"He's a monster," she'd wheezed. "He was supposed to love me. Protect me. Give me everything that I'd ever desired. Nothing was an impossibility. I just had to stay here in this town and wait for him to rise. Do what he wished. Get on my knees whenever he was ready for me."

Her throat tremored. "I was such a fool. Blinded by his power and his position. Because I had no idea what getting on my knees for him really meant. Not until it was too late."

"But you're free. You're still standing. Walking this town by yourself." I'd tried to convince her of it.

"I'm not sure how much longer that's going to remain true."

"Can't you leave?"

Fear had blistered through her features. "No. He'll find me. I'll be...punished."

Reaching out, I'd taken her by the hand and squeezed. "You have to be brave. Fight him. Tell someone who can help you."

Desperate, her eyes had fallen on me. "Can't you? Can't you help me?"

Could I? Could I be strong enough?

"Meet me tomorrow. I think I know someone who might be able to help."

She promised she would, but she didn't show.

Chapter Forty-Eight

Savannah

"L̲O̲A̲D̲ ̲'̲E̲M̲ ̲U̲P̲."

Ezra was all grins as he helped the kids into the backseat of his truck, ensuring that they were buckled and safe.

"Hurry, Dad, we gotta go!" Oliver shouted, kicking his feet as Ezra was checking on Owen's buckles.

"Hold your horses, Little Man, I'm working on it."

"I *am* going to get to hold the horses. That's why we gotta hurry!" Oliver told him.

"That's right, Dad." Olivia's tone was all of that adorable sass. "We're only going to the best place in all the whole town…Hutchins Ranch! It's a real bar-be-que, Dad, and it's going to be the most fun ever! It's Evelyn's grandpa's birthday today, and he's really old, and we are for sure riding the horses because Evelyn said it's part of the celebration, and you can't say no because that would be really rude."

I held my laughter as I slipped into the front seat, wondering how I'd gone from running six hours earlier to somehow feeling like that puzzle piece fit. Like maybe I'd just been looking at it all wrong. Trying to mash the wrong prong into the incorrect space.

Or maybe I'd just realized that the shape didn't matter. There were no perfect matches. There was just love and understanding and getting someone for who they were.

And God, was there love. So much love that I wasn't quite sure how I was supposed to sit still in it when I kept feeling like I was going to float toward the sky and get lost in the clouds.

"Well, I guess we'd better hurry, then, shouldn't we?" Ezra said.

"Go so fast, Daddy!" Owen made a zooming sound as he shot his hand forward like a rocket.

"But not so fast that you get a ticket," Olivia said, so pragmatic.

Ezra was chuckling as he slipped into the driver's seat, his gaze sweeping to me. Soft and adoring and content. "Well, I sure hope the town Sheriff doesn't get pulled over and get a ticket. Now that would be embarrassing."

He winked.

God, did Hot Cop look so good in the afternoon sun.

Another swell of love came bursting free. Rising up from the depths where this type of feeling wasn't supposed to exist. Now that I'd let it go, there was no stopping it.

I was all in.

Ezra reached over and squeezed my hand, like he was reiterating the exact same thing.

All in.

It was terrifying and beautiful and the most wonderful thing that I'd felt in probably my entire life because I'd never, ever known anything quite like this.

I'd already agreed to go out to Hutchins Ranch today to celebrate Paisley's grandfather's 90th birthday. I hadn't even tried to turn down the invite when she'd come into the café crazy excited about it, demanding that I be there since I was now a part of this extended group, even though I'd yet to meet the man.

Dakota was shutting down the café early so all the employees could attend, but she'd still insisted on not scheduling me for the early shift, teasing me that she wasn't going to be the reason I had an excuse not to show.

Apparently, they'd all thought I was a runner. A hider.

I peered over at Ezra as he glanced over his shoulder to pull out of the garage.

Not anymore.

He grinned.

So damned burly and sexy that my knees quaked.

He put the truck into drive and took the few turns it took to get us out onto the main street before he made a left onto a two-lane road that led out of town and toward the mountains that were even more pronounced in the distance as we headed that direction.

Nonstop chatter and questions and laughing came from the back-seat, loud and raucous and wild, and I realized I'd never felt so at peace.

Ezra held my hand as he drove. I had to stop myself from reaching out to rake my fingertips along that masculine jaw. To keep from touching his lips. His thumb kept brushing over the back of my hand like he was reminding me of the same thing.

He wanted me.

He needed me.

He was thankful I was there.

We slowed and made a right onto a dirt road, driving under a big wooden sign that claimed Hutchins Ranch. There was another newer sign hanging from underneath that boasted Our Favorite Day Equestrian Care Center, the horse training facility that Paisley ran, a special place that had been born of the love that she'd found here with Caleb and Evelyn.

I'd gotten to know Paisley a little more in the times that she'd come into the café. And I liked her. So much. The same way as I couldn't seem but to like everyone I'd met here.

In this place that had come to feel like the home that I thought I would never have.

And I hoped…with Ezra's help…that maybe we could uncover something about Jessica. With everything that had happened this morning, I hadn't gotten the chance to show him the journal before it'd been time for us to leave for the ranch. Faith lifted in my soul, the kind I'd squelched and subdued for so long. Sitting there next to Ezra,

I prayed that too much time hadn't passed. Prayed that somehow she was really here. That it wasn't a fluke or maybe some kind of twisted joke that I'd received that journal.

Above us, the blue sky went on forever, and horses and cattle grazed in the pastures that we passed as we traveled the single-lane, dirt road. Dust flying behind us, we crested a hill, and my breath hitched at the sight.

The ranch was nestled in the valley below. The mountains hugged it at the far side, and there was a river running through. Ezra and I had just been up on that mountain last night, overlooking the glorious view below. I could almost see the spot where he'd held me.

I wondered if our start was written there, a new beginning, a mark in time that had altered our existence, and now that we were down here in the plains, everything had changed.

Buildings dotted the endless acres. There were a ton of barns of varying sizes and shapes that were surrounded by thickets of trees and lower areas of grassy fields surrounded by corrals and fences where more animals grazed.

In the distance was an enormous cabin that rose from the woods on the far side of the ranch, fronted by acres of lawn. It had to be at least three stories high, fabricated of rocks and wood, the pitched roof rising for the heavens.

"Holy…camole." I stuffed down the curse before it dropped free in front of the kids.

"Holy camole, is right, Ms. Savannah. That is my cousin's house, and she has at least ten bedrooms just for herself because her house is really big because her dad is rich and has like a whole billion dollars." Olivia seemed more than happy to explain.

Laughter curled in my throat, and I glanced at Ezra who was grinning. "My cousin does have like a whole billion dollars," he said.

My brow rose in speculation. "I never would have known it."

Ezra chuckled. "If you'd come around here about a year ago when he first showed up in Time River, you'd see a whole ton has changed. He used to waltz around here in his five-thousand-dollar suits, hating the world, grumpy as all get out, and now he's as easy as they come.

I guess that's what happens when you find the one who was meant for you, and they give you the courage to allow who you truly are to come out."

Ezra squeezed my hand again.

I knew it was a silent promise that I could be who I truly was around him, too.

My spirit flew.

"Though I have to tell you that you got the short end of the stick if you were looking for the cousin with the money." Ezra winked.

I had to hold back my laughter, the tease coming easy. "Wait, are you just telling me now that you don't have a whole billion dollars to your name?"

"Sorry to break the bad news." Honey eyes sparked with the ribbing.

"Well, I think you'd better let me out right now then."

"Where is you goin' to go?" Owen asked.

Affection fluttered in my chest, and I shifted in the seat to look at him.

My gaze traced over each of them.

I had been going for light. Playful. But suddenly it was heavy.

My truth.

"I'm not going anywhere, Owen." I looked back at Ezra. "I guess we're just going to have to make do with Sheriff and server's wages."

Ezra's thumb brushed over my wrist. "Ah, I think it's those photographs that are going to see us through."

And there, as we pulled into an open, gravel area where a ton of cars were already parked for the party, my heart just freaking exploded.

Joy.

Pure joy.

"Let's go have some fun, yeah?" Ezra all but shouted.

The kids didn't hold theirs back, voices vying to clamor over the other. "Yes! Let's go! I get to *wide* the horsey first!"

Ezra and I climbed out, and we both went to the back doors to help the children. Owen was on my side, and I unbuckled him quickly.

He jumped out and into my arms, those little arms of his so tight as he wiggled around and squeezed. "I am a *kowawa!*"

I hugged him to me. "That's right…you're my little koala."

I set him onto his feet and took his hand, and we rounded the front where Ezra was standing with Olivia and Oliver.

That gaze washed over me.

Sheer adoration undercut with this possession that churned on that unfound connection.

Warmth spread beneath the heat, the ground trembling beneath my feet.

God, this man had me spun up. He held Oliver's hand in his left, and he reached for me with the other. Energy shivered up my arm at the contact. Olivia darted ahead of us, and we walked with the twins toward the cluster of shade trees that grew off to the side of the lawn where the party was taking place.

I thought the entire town had come. Since Paisley's grandfather had lived here his entire life, it was probably the case.

A couple ramadas and picnic tables were set up on the grass, plus a ton of tables and chairs with blue tablecloths littered the lawn. Streamers and balloons were strung from the trees, and a big banner was hung across the entire area.

Happy 90th, Grandpa Dae!

A man was playing a fiddle on the elevated stage that had been set up to the far side. A dance floor was situated in front of it, and a bunch of children were already trying out their moves on the smooth, wooden surface.

Both the boys broke free of our hold and went running that way, already knowing the other kids who had gathered.

Evelyn was in the middle of it, squeezing the crap out of Olivia, the two so dang sweet in their love for one another.

My nerves rattled a fraction as Ezra and I approached everyone where they were laughing and chatting under the trees.

We were hand-in-hand.

So obviously together.

And on all things holy was this out of character. A thousand miles off base to where I'd been when I'd first driven into this town.

Ezra pulled me closer, his voice a rumble where he angled down to whisper near my ear. "Can't tell you how happy I am that you're here. Right at my side."

"It feels like it's exactly where I belong."

I meant it.

That didn't mean I wasn't shrinking under all the eyes that suddenly shifted our direction and the way the conversations went a little quieter when they realized the town Sheriff was strolling up holding the new resident's hand.

We might as well have had a spotlight on us and a neon light flashing over our heads.

Look who is banging.

I wouldn't care except there was no missing the speculation and pity there, too, like they were all feeling sorry for Ezra who'd had to settle for the runner up.

The consolation prize.

Well, all except for Paisley who squealed when she saw us coming. She threw her arms over her head, her long, white curls bouncing around her shoulders. "Ahh, look who is here! Savannah, get your adorable butt over here and have a margarita with us. We've been waiting for you."

She stood by a frozen margarita machine that was spinning with an electric-green concoction, and there was a bar that was manned by two bartenders off to the right of it. On the opposite end was another table with big glass dispensers filled with different nonalcoholic beverages, a couple different lemonades and teas and punches.

Surrounding her were Dakota, Beth, and Chloe, plus a few other women I hadn't met before.

Dakota's attention dropped to where Ezra was holding my hand, and she pressed her lips together to keep from screaming in excitement, and Beth was literally running in place while swiveling her hips.

Oh boy. I was about to get the inquisition from my friends.

Friends.

Everything thrashed and expanded and swelled.

How was it possible I had those, too?

"Watch out...you're about to get asked about the size of my dick." Ezra's voice tickled at the lobe of my ear, low, rumbly laughter filling it.

"And what am I supposed to tell them? I wouldn't want to make them jealous." No stopping the easiness now.

He angled closer, words dipping with seduction. "You tell them whatever you want, Little Trespasser. The only thing that matters is that you know the cock in question is going to be claiming every inch of this sweet, little body. Over and over. Forever."

He dragged the blunt nail of his index finger from the base of my skull down to the middle of my back.

Chills raced. The man had the audacity to smirk as he took a step back.

"I'm going to go find the guys. Come find me when you want me," he said.

"I always want you."

He reached over and gripped the outside of my thigh with one of those big hands, his mouth at my jaw. "Good girl. That's exactly what I wanted to hear."

Then he walked away, while I stood there panting like a stray dog.

"Um, yoohoo, little miss Savannah, get over here right now." Paisley jolted me out of the stupor, and I hurried over to where my friends were huddled, slinking along like the hundred guests mingling around wouldn't notice me. We all might as well have been in sixth grade with the way we were giggling.

"Oh, Snuggle Muggle, you got all up in that big dick, didn't you?" Paisley didn't hesitate.

Apparently, they didn't need to ask the size. The man spoke for himself.

Dakota swatted at her, her name a chastisement. "Paisley."

Paisley put her hand to her chest, purely innocent. "What?"

"That's a little invasive, isn't it?"

"No topics are off limits between besties." Paisley looped her arm around my waist and pulled me to her side. "Are they?"

Laughing, I shook my head. "No. Never. But I'm pretty sure it was that big dick that got all up in me."

I whispered it so quick and quiet, and a giddy giggle hiccupped out of me on the last.

Surprised, Dakota smacked her hand over her mouth. Beth squealed and Paisley shifted to rock me all over the place while she hugged me. "I knew it. I could see it written all over you."

I'd been worried about how clear that fact was this morning. Right then, I didn't care.

Because I liked this. Loved it really. This…feeling.

The support.

The belief.

The belonging.

And for the first time in my life, I wasn't afraid.

"Is that ever an understatement." Beth took a sip of her margarita. "We could feel it from the second y'all rolled up in Ezra's truck. That man is *whipped*…" She drew it out while she spun an invisible lasso over her head. "Tied. Done for. I mean, did you see his face when he was walking up?"

She waved her hand like she needed to cool off her face. "What I wouldn't give to have a man look at me like that. Like he both wanted to eat you and would stand in front of one of those scary-as-shit bulls lurking around here at the same time."

Beth exaggerated a horrified shiver.

Paisley huffed. "Scary? Those bulls are beautiful. Just ask Daisy Mae over here." She gestured at the cow with two little calves who were hanging out in a grassy, fenced-in area about a hundred yards away. "Penelope thinks so, too." She waved at another cow with a tiny calf following at her side.

Dakota laughed, though her expression was soft as she turned to me and took my hand. "Well, I sure know that look Ezra was giving her." She squeezed my fingers. "I'm just happy Savannah finally caught up to what it really meant because I'm pretty sure he's been done for since the second he met you."

She studied me as she held my hand, and I peeked at where Ezra had gone to sit in a chair next to his cousins and Cody under a tree in the distance.

He took a sip from his beer, though his attention was on me, burning through the cool breeze and lighting me up.

A tether that flamed.

Paisley drew my attention back to her. "Let's get you a margarita and then we need to introduce you to my grandpa, aka, the best man who's ever lived."

"This is such a special day," Dakota said, her gaze on her best friend.

Paisley touched her shoulder. "Thanks to you and your team, it's even better. Thank you for catering all the sides and desserts. I think Grandpa is going to love it."

Dakota looked to where a group of people were gathered in a circle of Adirondack chairs. A fire pit that hadn't been lit yet sat between them. They were all chatting and laughing, but it was clear all their chairs were tilted a fraction to face the older gentleman who was using his hands to tell a clearly very vivid story.

Paisley shoved a plastic margarita glass into my hand, then urged me forward. "Come on, let's go meet the man of honor."

Paisley tossed out hellos and waved at people as we passed, though she didn't slow until we came to the gathering where her grandfather was seated.

"There's my girl," he said, his weathered face crinkling into the brightest smile.

She knelt at his side and pressed a kiss to his cheek. "As if I would ever get far when you are right here."

He chuckled with so much affection that my chest clutched. "You take such good care of me, Paisley Dae. I will never know how to thank you."

"I guess I learned about taking care of someone I love from the best." Adoration poured out of her when she said it.

I knew Paisley had been raised by her grandparents, and their close connection was clear. This love so intense. So different.

But I was seeing it all around me now.

The loyalty I hadn't known.

The devotion that'd seemed figurative.

So out of reach.

And here, in this small town, it floated all around me.

"Grandpa, I want you to meet Savannah. She's new to the area. Savannah, this is my grandfather, Arvil."

"It's so nice to meet you," I murmured.

He smiled a smile that was both welcoming and searching, his grayed eyes brimming with wisdom. "The pleasure is all mine. This one's told me all about you." He patted Paisley's arm. "And it seems you stole the eye of one of our town's best."

I followed his gaze to Ezra who was still watching me, while he still seemed to manage to remain in a conversation with his friends.

"Well, I don't know about that." Gah. What was I supposed to say?

Because every person hanging out in that circle was watching me. I cringed when I saw the mayor was there, too.

"Nice to see you again, Savannah," Jack Harris said. I could have been starstruck that the mayor knew my name, but I was too busy being worried that his advisor was also there.

"You, too," I said around the lump that suddenly formed in my throat, and my attention went racing over the rambling yard in search of Hayden.

I caught sight of him where he was more than a hundred yards away, holding court in the middle of a group of people, everyone seemingly enthralled by whatever he was saying, although the distance was too great for me to make anything out.

My insides shriveled up a bit as I was hit with that unsettled feeling I got every time Hayden was near. That little nudge telling me that he was someone to watch. I just wished I could poke around in his pompous head without having to get too close to him.

At least I had Ezra on my side now, and I didn't have to do it alone. When we got back tonight, I'd show him the journal and see if he could make anything of it.

See if something stuck out to him since he was more familiar with the people and the area.

And I'd ask him about Hayden, ask him to keep a closer eye, check him out.

"Well, I guess time will tell, won't it?" Paisley's grandfather brought me out of the flurry of dread that clamored through my chest, and he winked when I looked back at him. "Ezra is a good one, though, don't you doubt that."

My attention climbed back to Ezra.

Nowhere else to go.

Because this man, he was my safe place.

"I don't."

❧

I glanced in the mirror, blowing the hair out of my face as I washed my hands in the bathroom in one of the outbuildings, then I slipped out into the narrow walkway that ran between the two barns. The party was in full swing to the right, the guests just beyond. Voices and laughter carried on the limbs that whooshed overhead, and I headed back in the direction of where Ezra waited.

Only I stalled when someone stepped out from behind a jut out in the next building over.

My heart skittered, lifted and sank.

Hayden.

I toiled over the options of dropping my head and pushing around him like I didn't notice he was standing right in the middle of my path and going up to him and demanding to know what he knew.

I wasn't exactly…afraid.

Ezra was within earshot, and if I shouted, I knew he would come running.

I just felt…uneasy. Like I was tiptoeing around something unfound.

Both wanting to run and take the chance to look closer at the man who stood in front of me.

But I knew I had to play it careful. I couldn't just demand to know what he knew.

I forced that same feigned smile to my face that I wore every time he came around. "Hayden, hi."

He glanced over his shoulder like he was checking to make sure no one was around. Discomfort pulled my stomach in every direction. Could he be any more sketchy? I could almost read every secret he kept behind his ostentatious smirks.

Only he wasn't wearing one today, and he took a step toward me, his voice so low that it chilled me to the bone. "I've been wanting to get a chance to talk to you alone."

Alone.

I wasn't super excited by the prospect of that. "What about?"

He took another step in my direction. "You never called."

I trembled out a discordant laugh. "It seemed the only reason you wanted me to call was so we could set up a date, and I'm with Ezra now."

I let it hang like a warning.

Ezra would snap this guy in half.

Only I gasped through the shock when he stalked all the way to me, took me by the arm, and jostled me back until we were hidden behind a large tree trunk that shaded both buildings.

It obscured us, blurring the view of anyone going in or out of the restrooms.

"What the hell do you think you're doing?" I fought to keep the panic out of my voice even though each word shook, and I cocked my chin at him in challenge. I would claw my way out of here if I had to.

He planted his hands on either side of my head, and the oxygen punched from my lungs when he had me fully boxed in, his cologne close to noxious when I inhaled.

"I said I wanted to talk to you."

I figured a knee to his balls was an appropriate reaction right about then.

Instinct.

Only I froze when I caught sight of his forearm out of the corner of my eye. Hayden was wearing the sleeves of his shirt rolled up for the first time since I'd seen him, and there was a tattoo exposed on the inside of his forearm that I'd never seen before.

It was the face of a joker, though it wore a crown that dangled from one side of its head.

I was almost positive I'd seen that exact same image before.

Drawn on the bottom of a page in the journal.

My spirit both hit the ground and soared.

Holy shit.

He was involved. Knew Jessica. He had to.

I was stuck. Having no clue if I should run or stay. See how this played out.

Hayden leaned in close, his breath fanning over my cheek. "I—"

Only the growl that came from the side cut him off. "I'd suggest you back the fuck away from Savannah before you no longer possess the ability to."

At Ezra's voice, Hayden jolted three steps back, though it took all of two seconds for his arrogant smirk to return to full force. He laughed and lifted his hands in surrender. "Sorry, Ezra, man. Don't get all spun up. I didn't know she was yours until right now when Savannah told me the two of you had hooked up. I wasn't trying to overstep."

Ezra grunted, and Hayden laughed, clapping him on the shoulder as he moved around the man. "She's all yours, lucky asshole. I'll just be on my way."

"Prick," Ezra mumbled under his breath, shifting to watch Hayden amble down the walkway and back into the party beyond.

While I stood there panting and trying to catch my breath. Ezra eased up, concern etched on his face. "Are you okay?"

My nod was shaky. "I'm fine."

Except it didn't feel like I was. Because this felt like…something. I just needed to check the journal to be sure. Because there had to be a connection.

Chapter Forty-Nine

Ezra

"DON'T EVEN SIT THERE AND ACT LIKE WE ALL HAVEN'T noticed you snuggled up with Savannah." Ryder nudged me in the leg with the toe of his boot, dude sitting there smug as all fuck. "I called that shit from a mile away."

Chuckling, Cody readjusted the brim of his hat as he slung himself back farther on his chair. "Good thing I didn't go after her because my heart would be broken right now."

"Funny, though, that he was *only* trying to help someone out who seemed like she was down on her luck," Caleb jabbed.

I merely shrugged as I took a sip of my beer, not even trying to fight the grin that rose to the surface. I was too goddamn happy to front any annoyance at the barbs they were throwing.

Now Hayden Obermeyer trying to get his disgusting hands on Savannah? That was an entirely different story. Asshole was lucky I didn't rip off his dick and shove it down his throat.

Cody laughed as he hooked his thumb at me. "Asshole is clearly in deep because he's not even denying it."

Savannah took that opportune time to sweep that aqua gaze my direction from where she stood across the yard.

It felt like the air shifted every time she looked at me, and it was a damned good thing I was sitting because otherwise it would have knocked me from my feet. I maintained eye contact with her when I said, "Now tell me why the hell anyone would deny someone like that?"

My crew hooted around me.

"Only a fool, that's who," Cody said, his grin out of control as he looked over at me. "So glad to see it."

The trio of them sobered, like they weren't quite sure how to handle the fact that I was moving on. Thinking they might be treading into dangerous territory, about to rip the scab off a wound that wouldn't heal.

They wouldn't have felt that way if I hadn't kept playing this charade that felt like a bad costume that just didn't fit.

"Yeah, man," Ryder added, taking me by the shoulder from where he sat next to me and shaking me a little. "Makes me happy, too, to see you stepping out and finding joy. Making a new life."

There was sympathy in the middle of it, radiating from all three of them. My stomach soured. I realized it was a secret I could no longer contain, this pretense that no longer made sense to carry. One that was weighing every single one of us down.

"I've been trying to make a new life for a long time. Longer than you all know."

It went silent for a minute as the three of them glanced at each other in confusion. I blew out a sigh. "I know you all think that I lost the love of my life when Brianna died. Truth was, I'd already moved out and was getting ready to file for divorce."

Shock deepened that silence as Cody, Ryder, and Caleb tried to process what I was telling them.

"What the hell, man?" Ryder finally said. "Why didn't you tell us?"

Air huffed from my nose. "After what happened to Brianna? It didn't feel right to tell anyone. It felt like I was dishonoring her memory by repainting the picture you all had of her. But I can't go on pretending that, not when it feels like a disrespect to Savannah. I'm sorry I didn't tell you sooner."

"God, I can't believe this. Talk about a mindfuck," Ryder mumbled, peering my direction like he was looking for a brand-new lie. A frown dented between his eyes. "At the beginning, you always seemed so fucking solid. But if I think about it, I do remember thinking things felt off with you two after the boys were born. I just thought you both were stretched thin with having three kids so small. What happened?"

My head shook, my frustration and anger over the situation making me itch. I'd suppressed it for so long that I think it'd been distorted. That I'd never really allowed myself to feel it. Guilt over what had happened to Brianna had glided in to blot out the memories of how hurt I'd been. The love lost. Every fucking wound that she'd inflicted.

I told them everything I'd told Savannah, the way she'd started acting erratically. The drinking. The staying out until random hours. The lies. The way she'd grown paranoid.

The ugliest part of it that tasted like dirt on my tongue.

"She was having an affair."

"The fuck, man?" Ryder spat, disgust rolling from him as he roughed a tatted hand over his face.

"She'd come back after being gone for days, and I'd smell him all over her."

Always coming in smelling like expensive cologne. Smelling of lies and cheating.

Cody sat forward in his chair, his elbows going to his knees as he looked sidelong at me. Reservations flew through his expression before he came to a conclusion. "I saw her out once…in a park back behind some trees. I couldn't hear what was actually being said, but it was clear it was a heated argument. The type that just didn't sit right, if you know what I mean."

Regret filled his voice.

"It seemed too farfetched for Brianna," he continued. "She'd always seemed so damned cool. I think I talked myself out of it, wrote it off, not wanting what was clearly going on between them to be true."

Unease writhed through my senses. Did I fucking want to know?

"Who was she with?" The question scraped free, anyway.

Cody's head sagged between his shoulders, and he looked to his boots. "That prick Hayden Obermeyer."

A scoff of disbelief gusted out, and my eyes instantly moved to the piece of shit who was across the yard. Disgust roiled. Part of me wanted to cross the space and kick his ass just for the sake of it. The other part knew it wouldn't change a thing. He wasn't fucking worth it.

"Of fucking course," I mumbled.

"I'm sorry, brother. I should have told you, but it seems like you already knew."

"Yup, guess I did."

Caleb was sitting on the other side of me, and he reached out and squeezed my shoulder. "Sucks, man. I'm sorry."

Caleb had never met Brianna. He'd been living in Seattle during the time all that shit had gone down, dealing with his own issues.

"It does suck, but I thought it was time you all knew I haven't been suffering a broken heart."

I'd just been riddled with suffocating guilt since I hadn't been there for her when she'd actually needed me. But how the hell was I supposed to know? Her favorite game had been crying wolf, those wails loud enough to cover up her misdeeds, right up to the point that I couldn't hear them anymore.

Ryder sank back deeper into his chair, gazing over at where our girls were hanging out under the shade of a tree. "It's different with Savannah, yeah?" he asked.

"Yeah, it's different. It's everything."

"Not just a fling?" he asked.

"Hell no." It came out sharper than I intended.

Cody chuckled. "Looks like someone's ready to do a little of that claiming."

"Yeah." Because there was no piece inside me that wanted to deny it.

Chapter Fifty

Savannah

"ARE YOU HAVING A GOOD TIME?" I ALREADY KNEW EZRA was there, easing up behind me where I stood beneath an enormous tree that stretched out over the yard. I was taking in the party from a distance as the evening settled over the crowd. Food and dessert had been served, and the mood had grown light and airy.

Twilight had seeped in and cast the yard in that magical hue that clung to the sky in the last few moments before the sun fully fell away.

The children had spent the afternoon being led around on the backs of ponies, playing games, running, and laughing, while the adults had mingled and conversed and relaxed.

It seemed every ten minutes or so, Owen and Oliver had come racing up to drag me over to see something that they wanted to show me, and each time when I wandered back to where Ezra waited for me with that adoring look on his face I'd been staggered.

Overcome.

My heart overflowing.

Which was why I'd found myself loitering off in the fringes by myself.

Giving myself a moment to absorb it. To soak up this unanticipated new life.

I peeked back at the man who stood behind me.

His handsome face tweaked in a soft, curious smile.

God, he looked good in the fading day.

Hell, I'd come to accept he looked good in every moment. Every second. And I'd never tire of looking at him.

"The best time."

He wound an arm around to my front and pulled me against him. Warmth surged through my body.

"Then what are you doing over here all by yourself?" he murmured where he nuzzled his nose into my hair at the side of my head.

"Sometimes you need to stand back to appreciate the things you've been given. Memorize them."

So they could still be a part of you once they were ripped away.

It didn't matter that I left off the last. I might as well have issued it aloud.

Ezra pulled me tighter, and his breath wisped around me. "And sometimes you have to stand right in the middle of it to know that you truly belong."

Wistfulness fluttered through me, this hope that had sprouted that I kept fighting not to allow my past experiences to taint.

Ezra shifted, rounding to my front and taking me by the hand. "Dance with me?"

Warily, I looked around.

Okay, so maybe one of the reasons I was hiding was because Ezra's mother had shown an hour ago, just when the food was being served. She'd looked like she'd been physically floored to see me, even though she'd done her very best at remaining upright.

Ezra tugged at my hand. "No need to hide any longer, Little Trespasser. I already found you."

The air rippled from my lungs on a wave of love, and Ezra walked backward as he pulled me out from the shadows. He led me beneath the twinkle lights that had been strung up between the trees that were just now blinking to life over the dance floor.

There were a ton of people on it, swaying in time with the slow country song the band played.

He led me to the center of the crowd, and he pulled me close, honey eyes on me as he curled me into those powerful arms. His heart pounded steady and hard, and I rested my ear on the strength of it, listening to the unwavering beat of the man who held me like I was a treasure.

A gift rather than a burden.

One to be upheld rather than trampled.

He shifted and tipped up my chin, that gaze intent. True. "Do you have any idea, Savannah, the way I love you?"

"I think I might be getting the idea."

Affection flitted through his features, and he threaded his fingers in my hair and kissed me.

Kissed me in front of everyone.

In front of the town.

In front of his friends and family.

In front of his mother.

In front of his kids.

And that kiss was only broken by the squealing that suddenly sounded, and we broke apart to find Olivia on the dance floor beside us, clapping her hands and swaying in this gush of excitement that was so strong it nearly knocked me to my knees.

"Does this mean you're my dad's girlfriend now?"

Redness rushed, and I bit down on my lip, caught in a devastating swell of emotion.

As big and as beautiful as the man.

Ezra's mouth tipped up at the side.

"What do you think, Savannah? You want to be my girlfriend?"

It was only partially a tease.

"I think I might like that." It left me on a whispered breath.

Olivia ran forward and wrapped her little arms around Ezra's leg, and she peered up at her father with this look on her face that blew me away. "See, Dad, I told you she might be lonely and needed us."

And maybe it was the first moment when I recognized it, what this little girl had seen in me.

I'd been lonely.

Lost.

My battered heart missing so many pieces that it had never quite beat right.

Ezra looked at me. "And I think we needed her, too."

⌒⋆⌒

"Are you sure about this?" Ezra looked between Paisley and his kids who were watching him with pleading faces, Oliver taking it so far that he had his fingers twined and his hands lifted in a prayer.

The movie they were watching on the lawn with a projector beaming onto a sheet was only halfway finished, and the kids had concocted a plan of spending the night.

"Totally. It's not a big deal at all. I'm going to pop into town early to help Dakota unload some of the catering supplies, so I can definitely get them back to you in plenty of time to get them to school."

"And it's not like my brothers even go to real school, Dad, and I promise I'll go to sleep by 8:30 or maybe just a half an hour late. And it's my aunt and uncle and cousin's house. It's family so it's not like it's even really that fun." Olivia was set on convincing her dad.

He chuckled. "Really?"

"Okay, fine, it's my favorite place in the whole world and I really, really, really want to stay. Please!" Her hands were suddenly lifted in prayer, too, but she'd taken it a step farther and dropped to her knees.

Paisley laughed, her eyes going wide. "I don't know how you're going to say no to that."

"Yeah, my daughter is a master at getting her way."

"Then say yes!" Olivia peeped.

He chuckled again, shaking his head. "Fine. But I mean it, you're asleep by nine, Livvie."

"Yayyyyyy!" She popped back onto her feet and threw her arms around Evelyn. "I get to stay with you!"

"This is the best day of my whole life! Thank you, Uncle Ezra!" Both little girls turned to hug Ezra's legs, and the boys threw themselves into the mix, too.

My chest clutched when they turned to me and did the same thing. "I'll miss you, Miss Savannah, but I'll see you tomorrow!" Oliver told me.

"I can't wait," I said.

Most of the party had filtered out over the last half an hour, and I turned to say my goodbyes to everyone who remained.

Ryder and Caleb and Paisley's grandfather.

"Take care of that one," her grandfather said.

"I will," I promised.

Dakota hugged me tight, her words held so only I could hear. "I'm so happy for you, Savannah. You look…different…and that different looks good on you."

I nodded because I felt it, too.

Different.

But in the best of ways.

Paisley threw her arms around me, swinging me around the way she did. "Thank you for being here. This was so fun."

She looked to Ezra. "Don't worry, I'll have your babies back to you first thing in the morning. You two enjoy that empty house, but make sure you wrap it up by seven tomorrow because they will be coming through the door right about that time."

A slight giggle got free, and Ezra pulled me closer and rumbled, "Oh, don't worry, Paisley, I plan to make good use of that empty house."

Ezra led me to his truck, the man smirking the entire time. He helped me into the cab, then reached in to buckle me, like I wasn't perfectly capable.

"I'm liking this spoiling bit," I told him, my chest so light.

"Have to admit, it didn't take much for Olivia to convince me to let them spend the night. I have all kinds of ways I intend on *spoiling* you tonight."

Tingles raced, and I bit down on my bottom lip to try to contain the need that zipped across my flesh. "You mean like a good night's sleep? I do have to be at work at six in the morning." It was purely a tease.

"I wouldn't plan on it, Savannah." He let his palm glide up the inside of my thigh, and he stroked the tip of his thumb over the seam of my jeans. I whimpered, and he leaned closer, his words rolling low. "You might have to pull an all-nighter."

Then he stepped back and shut the door, the audacity of the man chuckling as he rounded the front of the truck while I sat there squirming. He hopped in and pushed the button to start the powerful engine.

"Just how fast does this thing go?" I basically panted it.

A grin pranced all over his lips. "You heard Olivia earlier. You wouldn't want to have the Sheriff get pulled over now, would you?"

"I'm not sure I'd really mind at this point."

"Eager girl."

"I think we already established that's the way you make me."

"Then we'd better get you home, baby."

He took off down the dirt lane going a little faster than was probably prudent, his hand returning to the inside of my thigh.

Running circles.

Dragging up and down.

Barely brushing the hot spot between my legs.

Teasing, teasing, teasing.

It was the longest, best ride of my life.

And I wasn't sure I was going to make it without combusting right there.

We had just turned onto Manchester in town when his cell rang. He winced when STATION pulled up on the screen. Reluctantly, he pushed the button on his steering wheel to answer. "Hey, Pam, what's going on?"

"I'm sorry to bother you on a Sunday night, but we had a report of a fire over at the city council building. They got it put out, but I thought you might want to check it out. We aren't sure, but Xavier mentioned it could be arson. Looks like it started in a wastebasket."

She seemed to hesitate on the last, like she wasn't sure she should mention it.

"Shit," Ezra grumbled, blowing out a sigh and roughing a hand down his face. The mood immediately shifted, and everything in Ezra dampened in concern. "Who's on the scene?"

"Other than Fire and Paramedic, Samson and Lanie."

"I need to drop Savannah off at the house really quick, and then I'll head over there. Tell them not to leave until I talk to them."

"Okay. Sorry again to bother."

"You know I would have been upset if you didn't let me know."

"Which is the only reason I'm talking to you." A speck of lightness infiltrated her tone before she murmured, "Be safe."

"Always."

Ezra ended the call and his attention drifted to me. This time when he traced his fingers up the inside of my thigh, it was apologetic. "I won't be long."

"It's okay. It's your job."

"But I'd rather be with you." He kept glancing at me as he made the couple quick turns into his neighborhood.

"Me, too, but I understand."

He pulled into the driveway in front of his house, and he dug into the console and produced a key. "For the front door. I'll be as fast as I can."

Leaning over, I set my hand on his cheek and dipped in to quickly peck a kiss to his lips before I pulled back an inch. I lingered for a second, tracing my thumb over the stubble on his jaw. "I'll be waiting."

I felt the twitch of his smile beneath my palm. "Preferably naked."

I laughed, fumbling out of the truck and onto the sidewalk. "Go."

He idled there while I hurried to the door, and he didn't leave until I'd made it safely inside. I flicked on the interior light, and the engine roared as he made a U and headed back the direction we'd come.

Silence echoed back.

So still.

It was weird, being in this house by myself, and I ran my hands up my arms to chase away the chill. I decided to go to the guest house and grab a couple things to keep myself occupied until Ezra returned.

Unlocking the back door, I stepped out, and I ran under the cover of night to the guest house. The chill had lapsed into cold, the month spinning away and nearing November.

I let myself in, and I flicked on the lights.

It felt like a week had passed since I'd been in here, even though it'd just been this morning when I'd fled to the room and grabbed my duffle thinking running was the only thing I could do.

I moved through the guest house and down the short hall to the bedroom, turning on lights as I went.

The duffle was still in the middle of the bed where I'd left it.

I went to the dresser and dug through my pajamas, and I pulled out a pair of lace panties and a matching camisole. Desire buzzed in my belly as I thought of him finding me that way, ready and waiting for him.

I went into the bathroom and tossed my toothbrush and face creams into a toiletry bag. I fought the errant thought that I was being a fool, taking some of my things into Ezra's house like I belonged.

But I did.

I belonged.

My spirit whispered that it couldn't be wrong.

I tossed everything into the duffle, slung it over my shoulder, and headed back into the main room where I went to the cabinet that sat beneath the TV that hung on the wall. I hesitated for only a second before I opened the drawer to dig out the journal where I'd hidden it after I'd had it out the last time.

Ready to share it.

To give it all.

Only my fingers fell against nothing.

Because it wasn't there.

⌒⁂⌒

Two hours passed before the sound of Ezra's truck approaching filled the night. I sat on the edge of his bed, my knees drawn to my chest as I rocked.

Tears wouldn't help, so I'd battled them the entire time, trying not to succumb to the panic that bubbled from the depths. It was difficult though, since the dread was so thick I felt like I was being strangled.

Oxygen missing from my lungs, every breath haggard and harsh as I tried to inhale.

I listened to the garage door open then close, the opening of the hallway door and thudding of Ezra's heavy feet. I wondered if he could feel the disorder clamor through the air, the fission of desperation and fear that crackled through the quiet stillness of the house.

Because his approach was slow. Cautious before he stood in the doorway, his jaw locked tight.

"Did you find anything out?" I forced the question up my throat, though the words came out like they'd gotten flayed on the way up. Cut into shards.

"By the looks of you, I don't think the city council building is what I need to be concerned with right now. What happened?"

I blinked, and a tear fell, like it was free to fall into the safety of who Ezra was.

"Baby," he whispered, and he was in front of me, my face in the surety of his hands. "Tell me what's going on."

I gulped around the razors, hating the weakness. The way I felt like I was falling apart. But it was my one link. My one hope. And someone had stolen it. Just like everything was stolen from me. And if someone wanted it, knew about it, and had come to take it? Then that meant my sister was truly in the trouble I'd feared she'd been in all along.

"The journal…I went to get it so I could show it to you, and it was gone."

Every muscle in his body went rigid. Wired in protection. I could see his mind so clearly spinning through the possibilities.

And I knew we both were there, thinking about the near break-in at the motel and then about the person who'd been lurking outside the guest house—someone who'd been so desperate that they'd stabbed him.

Both of us had knitted the incidents together as if they were one.

"Where was it?"

"In the middle drawer in the cabinet below the TV. Hidden under a couple magazines."

"Stay right here."

Ezra stormed from the room, leaving a wake of rage behind him. The back door slammed, and I slipped off the side of the bed. I paced the room as I waited for him to return, part of me wanting to go help him, but the other already knew it wasn't any use. I'd already searched every inch of the guest house before I'd finally retreated in here.

I knew he hadn't found anything either, with the way the atmosphere dimmed and darkened when he returned, the way regret and fury were set deep in the lines of his face. "I didn't find anything. Not the journal or any indication of someone trying to break in, either. Were the doors locked when you went out there?"

My nod was wary. "Both front and back. I checked."

"Fuck," he spat, looking to the ground for a beat before he was moving for me. A flash of lightning that struck in the room.

Energy powerful.

Potent.

I swayed beneath it, caught in his wave. He looped his arm around my waist, towering over me as his other hand held me by the back of the neck. "I won't let anyone get to you, Savannah. I promise you."

"What if someone has her? What if someone has hurt her? What if someone is trying to stop me from finding her?" Terror poured out. It was everything I'd held for years, amplified a million times once I'd received the journal.

Brown eyes flared, and that warm honey brimmed with fire. "We'll find her. You and me and my team. We're going to find her. I'll hunt for her, Savannah, high and low until we know exactly what happened to her. Until this piece of your heart has been restored."

Ezra gathered up my hand and placed it over the ravaging thunder at his chest. Over the spot where he'd marked himself with his wife. Where he'd believed his mistakes would forever forbid him to love again. His error too great.

"Because you are my heart." His voice ground in emphasis.

"I can't put you or the kids in danger, Ezra. I—"

His mouth crushed against mine, cutting off the words he knew were coming. His promises shutting down my fears.

I have you.

I love you.

I will fight for you.

"Don't say it, Savannah. Don't say you're not worth it when you are worth everything. Don't listen to the lies you've been fed. Listen to this truth."

My palm was still flat against his heart, and Ezra had me bent back, keeping me from falling.

He was asking for my surrender. For me to fully give. To trust.

"Ezra," I mumbled against his mouth.

I wanted it.

To completely give.

Because I believed in his love.

I believed in him.

It was the rest of this vicious life that had proved time and again that it couldn't be trusted. The ground always falling away.

He deepened the kiss.

So powerful I gasped at the intensity of it.

At the intensity of him.

His tongue tangled with mine. Warm and wet, and heat streaked down my spine.

"I promise you, Savannah. I promise you everything I have to give."

374 | A.L. JACKSON

I kissed him back with as much as he was giving me, my nails raking over his shoulders and trying to find a place to sink in. "I love you."

"So goddamn much," he murmured back. He stepped back long enough to rip my sweater over my head. He tossed it aside and dove back in, kissing me mad as he backed me toward his bed.

Dizziness spun. My senses both heavy and light. "I love you," I mumbled again.

I'd say it forever. For all of my days. Whatever that meant.

"You're mine," he growled against my mouth, and when he edged back to drag his shirt off, I knew this was going to be a claiming.

He needed me just as desperately as I needed him.

His skin glowed golden beneath the hazy lights that burned from the nightstands, his shoulders so powerful and wide.

His big body cast imposing shadows across the room.

This beast of a man who fought to consume me.

He dove back in, his kiss unrelenting, and without breaking it, he picked me up by the waist and set me on the edge of his bed. He wound himself between my legs and pushed them wide. We were both still wearing our jeans when he ground himself against my center.

Flames erupted.

"Ezra."

He moaned at the contact. "Savannah, baby."

Heat streaked, and the man's hands rushed to find every inch they could touch. Racing my back. My sides. My breasts. Pushing against my trembling belly until I fell back against the bed.

He jerked the button of my jeans open, and I whimpered as he yanked them off. Cool air blew across my heated flesh. My panties and socks were next, and all of three seconds later, I was completely bare.

He dipped down and licked my core, his tongue stroking deep.

Pleasure sparked.

"What I'm going to do to you, Savannah."

"I want it all. Everything you have to give."

He stepped away and ridded himself of the rest of his clothes, and he pushed to his full height, towering over me, filling the room, filling my heart.

Trust and need and belief.

It pooled and poured.

"I need you," I muttered.

My truth.

My truth.

His gaze flamed before he leaned down and ran his nose up the inside of my thigh.

I bucked toward him. "Please."

And I'd never felt so alive as right then.

Whole.

Perfect.

"Do you trust me?" Ezra rumbled.

"Yes." I answered without hesitation.

"Good girl."

Chapter Fifty-One

Ezra

Good girl.

This fucking perfect girl who had no idea what she'd done to me.

Stormed into my life and infiltrated all the hidden places.

Sparked to life what'd gone dead.

My little trespasser who'd gotten in so deep.

I edged back, my stomach in knots and my cock jutting for the sky, eyes on her as she squirmed anxiously on the bed.

Dripping wet, her pussy throbbing.

I pushed two fingers deep inside her.

She gasped and pushed up on her heels, lifting her ass from the bed. "You want me begging, don't you, Ezra Patterson?"

"Not gonna lie, I like you wet and pleading."

"That's right where I am."

I stroked myself once, from base to tip, before I stepped forward so I could drag my aching head through her center.

Pleasure sparked at the base of my spine, and my teeth ground in restraint. "You're mine, Little Trespasser."

I drove my dick into her pussy in one quick thrust.

Air ripped from her lungs. My name was mangled in the middle of it. "Ezra, oh God."

Her legs trembled around me as she adjusted to my size.

"So good, honey. What you do to me," I rumbled low.

It was close to a scoff that fell from that sexpot mouth. "It's what you do to me. I've never wanted anything more than I want you. Have never…"

She trailed off.

But I knew it. I knew it'd never felt like this because it'd never felt like this to me, either.

This sense of perfection that rolled through me when I was seated deep inside her.

Owning her.

Possessing her.

Claiming her.

I fully withdrew and she whimpered. "Don't tease me," she begged.

"Do you trust me?" I asked again, and that aqua gaze was on me, searing me through, sucking me under.

"You're the only person I do." Vulnerability seeped into the words, her confession rising into the air, stealing my breath.

My heart.

My soul.

My days and my truth and my devotion. They all belonged to her.

"Off the bed and turn around."

She complied without hesitation, eyes on me as she slid off and onto her feet, her small tits peeking out from beneath the fall of her hair.

Long, long locks, blondes mixed with every shade of brown.

The woman so fucking pretty she hit me like an arrow to the chest.

She watched me as she turned around, her breaths shallow.

Stepping forward, I kissed across the cap of her shoulder. "Let go, Savannah. Believe in me. Let me hold you. Let me keep you."

"I'm already yours," she whispered into the lapping light that curled around the room.

Reaching over, I opened the drawer of the nightstand and pulled out a tube of lube. "I told you I was going to claim every piece of you, Little Trespasser, the way you claimed me."

I palmed one of her butt cheeks, and she bent over, her hands going to the mattress while she trembled and shook. Anticipation blistered from her flesh.

"Do you want it? Do you want me?"

"I'm yours."

Everything expanded, and I splayed my hand over the small of her back, thumb stroking her spine.

Softly.

Gently.

An oath that I'd take care of her.

Treat her right.

Love her the way she should have always been. I coated my fingers with the lube, and the air heaved from her when I slid them down the cleft of her ass, two fingers finding that sweet, puckered hole.

She moaned, but pushed back, welcoming me.

"Do you want it to be my cock taking you this way? Where do you want me, Little Trespasser?"

"I want you everywhere, Ezra. I trust you. I trust you."

A growl clamored in my chest.

I covered my dick in the lube, and I positioned myself before I barely nudged the tip inside. Her head swept from side to side, the woman sagging at the pressure, at the need, at the flicker of pleasure.

"I'd never hurt you, Savannah. Your pleasure is mine."

I slowly began to fill her.

Carefully.

My hands smoothed over her butt cheeks, kneading and massaging while my cock sank deeper and deeper into her ass.

She pushed back again. Desperation tumbled from her lips. "How does it feel like this? It's so good. I need… Harder. Deeper. Show me what it's like."

I knew what she was asking.

What she was giving.

Trust spilled out into the room, mixing with the desire, the need that sparked and lit behind my eyes as I slowly began to rock inside her.

She hugged me so tight. So fucking tight that I thought I was going to lose it, come undone in five seconds because she felt so goddamn good.

"So good, Savannah, so fucking good, taking you like this. Your tight ass. Your sweet body. What you've done to me. I'm going to spend the rest of my life giving it back to you. Showing you the treasure that you are. How fucking good you are. How important you are. How it feels like my heart is getting squeezed in two every time I look at you."

She gasped and shivered as she began to rock in time, taking me deeper with each rush of her body as she angled for me.

Body begging.

Like she couldn't get enough, either.

Wanting more.

Needing more.

"You were made for me," I told her, words grit.

"I know. It wouldn't feel like this if I wasn't. If I wasn't yours and you weren't mine."

Pleasure hazed over my vision, ecstasy nearly bringing me to my knees with every stroke.

I took her left leg and hooked her knee on the bed, spreading her wider so I could take her even deeper.

She gasped and wheezed, and her fingers dug into the sheets. "I need…I…"

I slipped my arm under her leg so I could get to that throbbing little bud that I knew would set her off. What I wasn't expecting was for her to shatter the second I touched her, the woman shuddering and shaking as an orgasm rushed her like a landslide.

Sending her flying.

I could almost see the sparks light across her skin.

The way she glowed.

The vibration of her orgasm rocked through me, bigger than anything I'd ever felt.

She just kept going.

Pleasure rolling and rolling.

Hers and mine.

Mine.

I knew it.

Knew she was made for me.

My match.

My heart.

I pulled her up against me, her chest to my back as I picked her feet off the ground, holding her weight as I drove into her so fucking deep.

She throbbed around me, hugging my dick so tight that I couldn't take it any longer.

I split.

Broke apart.

Bliss pounded through me as I came, and her name ripped from my tongue as I poured into her.

And together we were shattering the stars. Rising above the heavens. Floating somewhere that shouldn't exist.

I was probably gripping her too fucking tight.

But I couldn't let go.

I wanted to hold her.

The claim of my soul.

Forever.

I buried my face into the fall of her hair while we both stood there gasping and shaking. Our skin drenched in sweat. Our bodies one and our hearts beating in the perfect time.

"Forever," I whispered near her ear. "I will love you forever."

Chapter Fifty-Two

Savannah

"**A**RE YOU AS READY AS I AM FOR THIS DAY TO BE OVER?" Dakota blew her bangs from her forehead as she bustled behind the counter where I was making a couple of her famous strawberry iced teas. She carried a tray of freshly baked cookies to stock in the display case, and the scent of coconut and almonds saturated the air as she passed.

I was never going to get used to how delicious it smelled in here. I swore, she had my stomach rumbling every time she came up with a new recipe.

"Don't get me wrong," she continued as she used tongs to transfer the cookies into the display case. "I love a good Sunday afternoon party, but I had one too many margaritas last night, and this girl is dragging. Five o'clock came early. But you, my sweet Snuggle Muggle, look like you've barely slept. Tell me Ezra kept you up all night."

She quirked a teasing brow at me from where she was knelt at the case.

I choked out a little laugh. It was the truth. I'd barely slept. Ezra knew there was no chance of me settling after the journal had gone missing, so he'd kept me distracted in the best of ways. And in those few moments before dawn when we'd finally flopped exhausted onto his bed, he'd curled me in his arms from behind, holding me while I'd barely drifted, a thousand silent promises whispered into the tranquil air.

"He might have kept me up for an hour or two."

"An hour or two? I know a marathon when I see one."

My laugh was deeper, the memories of last night whirling through my mind and sending my belly quivering. "Okay, I might be going on an hour."

She giggled. "Well, I do hope you aren't complaining. If the way Ezra hauled you out of there last night was any indication, he made it well worth your time."

"I'm pretty sure Ezra is worth every second."

The off-handedness she'd been wearing slipped straight into sincerity, and she straightened as she came my way. "I know it was scary for you…opening yourself up to his love…but I'm so thankful you know what it means now. That you know what it's like to be loved by someone like him."

"I never knew anything like it before," I admitted.

"I know. And you could have rejected him. Shut yourself off to it. But even after everything you've been through, you were still brave enough to try. To take that chance."

I did. I took it. And I'd fallen. Fallen so hard.

Unease flitted through my senses, my stomach sick with the idea of losing it.

"It's worth it," Dakota whispered as she passed, squeezing my arm as she did before she disappeared back through the swinging doors.

Shaking myself out of it, I grabbed my customers' refills and carried them to their booth. "Here we are, two strawberry teas. Anything else I can get for you this afternoon?"

"No, we're stuffed. Just our bill."

I dug it out from my apron pocket and sent them a warm smile. "Here you go."

"Thank you."

"Any time. Let me know if you need anything else."

I turned to head back to the kitchen, though I slowed when I saw the single person sitting on a stool at the counter, which was part of my section today. We were a couple hours after the lunch rush, so things had cleared out, that lull that always happened before shift change with the dinner staff.

Awareness flickered then tipped into trepidation as I took the man in from behind, wearing slacks and a long-sleeved button down, his tie loosened at the throat. Hayden Obermeyer looked a little more disheveled today, though, his impeccably styled hair a smidgeon off, like he'd been dragging his fingers through it then tried to pat it back down, and his jaw showed signs that he hadn't taken the time to shave today.

I attempted to tamp down the anxiety that flared, my nerves rising in a discordance that clanged against my consciousness. I couldn't believe he'd come in here after Ezra had chased him off yesterday evening.

The man had balls, that was for sure, or maybe a death wish.

Either way, he was in my section, and I cleared the knot from my thickened throat and pasted on one of those feigned smiles that used to be normal before my joy had become real.

"Welcome." I wondered if he recognized there was zero welcome in my voice. I set a menu in front of him. "What can I get you to drink?"

I could see his smile was faked, too. Far too wide and showing off those straight, gleaming teeth. They might as well have been fangs.

"A mocha."

I dipped my chin. "Sure thing."

I went to work, watching him from out of the corner of my eye as I filled a tall mug with coffee then stirred in the chocolate and topped it with whipped cream. I was unable to stave off the shaking of my hand when I turned and set it in front of him.

"What else can I get you?" No question, he heard it tremble. Part of me wanted to run from the nausea that churned and the other wanted to throw myself over the counter and take him by the throat and demand what he knew about my sister.

He knew something.

He had to.

I might not have been able to check the journal, but I knew the tattoo he had hidden under his shirt sleeve was the same.

And that journal? It was gone. Was he the one who'd taken it?

Unease wound while I waited for his answer, half thinking I should call Ezra to come over here but also knowing it was ridiculous considering there were a hundred people around me.

"I made a mistake." There was something about the way he said it that lifted the hairs at my nape.

"A mistake?"

"A huge, fucking mistake."

Apprehension clawed at my spirit. "What do you mean, a mistake? Backing me into a corner at the Ranch?"

I said it as almost a challenge.

He scoffed. "No, Savannah…I made a mistake getting you involved. This all went…wrong. It wasn't supposed to work out like this."

He suddenly stood, and my hand shot to the counter to steady myself, caught off guard by the abrupt movement. I glanced around for a weapon. Anything to use if he came at me.

Instead, he casually dug into his pocket to get his wallet as he spoke, though his words were quieted so only I could hear. "You shouldn't be here. You need to leave this town. Forget you ever came here. Forget what you think you know." He tossed a twenty to the counter before he leaned my direction, voice held with the warning. "Before you find you can't leave."

He left without saying anything else, while I stood there gaping. Shock scalded me from the inside out. A sticky fear that clamored and pricked through my bloodstream.

My mind was a muddle of questions and confusion.

Truths and doubts and perplexities.

Because he knew. He knew. Of that, I was certain.

But why would he warn me? Why…why did it seem like he was the one who was suddenly afraid?

Everything was off.

So off.

But I knew he was the one who held all the answers.

Jessica. My sister. She needs me.

It was enough to snap me into action, and I fumbled to get the ties of my apron loosed as I hurried through the swinging door to the kitchen and to the employee lounge to get my purse. I slung it over my shoulder, and I barely took the time to poke my head into Dakota's office. "I'm sorry to bail early, but I've got to go check on something."

Worry jumped into her expression as she looked up from where she sat at her computer. "Are you okay?"

"I'm fine…I'll…I'll text you later."

I flew back down the hallway with Dakota calling behind me, "Savannah?"

I didn't slow. I pushed back through the swinging door, dodging a few people as I hurried through the restaurant and store before I was pushing out into the afternoon sun. I ran toward my car parked across the lot, clicking the locks and jumping inside. I rooted through my purse to find my phone, and I dialed Ezra's number as I backed out.

It rang four times before it went to voicemail.

He'd told me before I left this morning that he was going to call in for a meeting with the mayor to talk to him about his concerns about Hayden after I'd told him my suspicions. The way my gut coiled in foreboding every time he came near. The way he had a tattoo that I didn't believe for a second was coincidence.

The proof of it was in that journal.

He was likely in the middle of that meeting, so I left him a rushed message as I peeled from the parking lot. "Ezra, hey, I left work early. Hayden came in. He gave me this vague warning, telling me I should leave town. And I know I told you that I thought he might be responsible, but I…" It hit me like a deadbolt clicking into place. "I think he was trying to scare me away."

But that meant my sister…she could be right here.

Alive.

I refused to believe the alternative.

Hope weaved through the panic, a frenzy that lit a path of desperation through my bloodstream. Pounding hot, a thunder that raged. "She has to be here. I have to find her. I'm…"

My eyes went wide when I saw Hayden driving in the opposite direction, his Maserati that was outrageously out of place in this town standing out in the few cars that passed by going that way.

And there was nothing I could do. I checked that the path was clear before I made a U-turn and got in line behind Hayden, two cars down. "He just passed me heading the other way. I'm going to try to talk to him. I'll text you where I'm at."

I needed answers.

I needed to find my reason.

I *needed* my sister just as sure as I was certain that she needed me.

I kept pace with Hayden as he drove down Manchester, though I made sure to remain a couple cars behind him so he wasn't aware he was being tailed. The last thing I wanted was for him to try to ditch me. As it was, I doubted much the answers I was seeking were going to come all that easily.

He made a left up ahead, and I stayed back, waiting a few seconds before I followed. It was a neighborhood of nicer houses, larger than those in Ezra's area on the opposite side of town. Most were two story and sitting on sprawling lots, fronted by manicured lawns and trimmed, perfect trees.

I kept my distance, his glittering black car a speck that gleamed beneath the sunlight that blazed from the sky. He made a right, and I held my breath, praying I didn't lose him.

I thought I had when I finally made the turn and began to crawl up a winding road. Here, the houses were even larger, tucked way back and hidden by the dense trees. Some were concealed by towering walls that were protected by gorgeous, wrought-iron gates.

My heart hammered, my pulse so heavy that I felt it pressing up beneath my skin. I finally spotted him up ahead, rounding a bend that curved to the left. The trees soared, their branches stretching out to cover the road in a hedge of shadows. Rays of light speared through, flashing against my windshield as I inched forward.

I slowed even more when I realized there were no longer any houses on either side, and I eased to a stop where I was shrouded by flowering bushes that hugged the road. I peered through them, watching as Hayden reached out his window to punch a code into the single gate that sat like a fortress up ahead.

It opened and he drove through, one second before the gate closed behind him.

"Crap," I muttered, glancing around, wondering what the hell I was supposed to do. I'd come here for this sole purpose. Not to cower and wait.

But to find my sister.

I clicked open the door and slipped out, trying to keep my feet from crunching as I crept along the road toward the fence line that almost completely blended in with the scenery.

My attention caught on a glimmer flickering to the right, barely visible through the trees.

A ripple of silver against a vat of black.

A pond.

A pond.

I'd scoured the map, searching for each one in the area, which was why I'd ended up five miles out of town camping out next to the one on Mr. Landers' property.

I was certain this one hadn't been marked.

Apprehension gusted, awareness full, as if the air was suddenly saturated with depravity. The raven cawing as it flew overhead an omen.

My stomach twisted and my chest felt too achy and tight.

I could just feel it—this was bigger than I was prepared for. Dangerous.

You no longer have to go it alone.

I hurried back to my car so I could try Ezra again. I opened the door and leaned in to grab it where I had left it in the center console, only I froze when I heard the snap of a twig off to the side.

Frigid cold streaked beneath my flesh, and I gulped as I shifted a fraction, then I breathed out in relief when Samson stepped out from the woods.

"God, Samson, you scared me."

He must have already been out here scoping the area, picked up a clue, an indication from when Ezra had been stabbed.

"You shouldn't be out here, Savannah," he said as he approached.

"I know," I told him, turning back to reach for my phone. "I was just calling Ezra. Who lives here? I think my sister—"

He was suddenly there, right behind me, his hand ripping my head back before he smashed my face into the edge of the roof of my car.

Pain splintered out from the point of contact.

Cracking.

Fracturing.

Agony.

Agony.

Splitting me in two.

Blood gushed, running down over my eyes in a hot river, falling like tears down my cheeks. I struggled to remain coherent. To fight. I flailed, catching him with my elbow in the chin.

It didn't do anything to stop him, he just yanked harder at my hair, sending spikes of torment stabbing into my brain.

He pushed his mouth to my cheek. "You stupid bitch. I warned you. I warned you both, but neither of you were fucking paying attention."

Then he bashed my face against the frame again.

Chapter Fifty-Three

Ezra

"GODDAMN IT." I TOSSED MY PHONE TO THE TABLE AFTER trying to call Savannah for the hundredth fucking time. It wasn't like I hadn't expected it to go to voicemail, but I'd been praying for a miracle.

Praying that she'd suddenly answer, and in that throaty, sexy voice, she'd accuse me of being overbearing.

I'd take that title a million times over if it meant she was safe. If it meant she was whole. If it meant I got to hold her in my arms tonight and she knew it was exactly where she belonged.

I scrubbed a palm over my face like it might stand a chance of breaking up the terror. The clot of mayhem sending rage scattering through my cells. Fury that blotted out reason and sight.

We'd hunted all over the fucking town for her. For Hayden.

I had every hand on deck, each officer covering different sections of the town and extending all the way out through the county.

Lanie out east covering the rural neighborhoods and farms.

Bryant downtown.

Maliq taking the west quadrant in the more industrial area and the homes surrounding it.

Samson was out in Crestwood Village and beyond.

While I'd driven like a madman down every single road and alley, trying to pick up a trace.

None of us had come up with anything.

It was like she'd fucking disappeared out of thin air.

My chest clutched so painfully I was sure my heart cracked right down the middle.

This couldn't happen. I wouldn't let it. I had to find her. I had to.

I ripped at my hair as I paced the area between my kitchen and the dining table, turned and strode the other direction before despair had me stopping.

Faltering.

Just fucking lost. My world that had finally felt like it was coming to life going bleak and dim.

Ryder stepped up from behind, and his hand went to my shoulder in a show of support. "We're going to find her, brother."

My crew had shown at my house fifteen minutes ago to join the search.

Caleb and Paisley.

Ryder and Dakota.

Beth and Cody.

I had a map spread out on the table, this one larger than the one we'd used at the station. We'd each been assigned an area, and I'd given them implicit instructions to stay in their cars and contact me, no matter what they found. The last thing I was willing to do was put them in the line of fire, but I couldn't deny their demand to help, either.

They all loved her, too, this woman who had slipped right in and become a part of us.

Paisley had picked up my kids from the after-school program, and we were just waiting on my mother to get here to stay with all the children so we could head out.

Each one of my officers were still on the hunt, instructed to report back if they picked up on anything at all. A hunch. An innuendo.

I didn't fucking care.

Just as long as we found her.

I felt like shit that I'd sent the kids to their rooms, but I hadn't wanted them to overhear the conversation. Didn't want them to hear the hushed urgency that had lashed from my tongue as my friends and family had gathered around me. As I'd run down the list of shit that occurred over the last few weeks.

The attempted break-in at the motel.

Whoever had been outside the guest house.

The journal that had gone missing.

They'd picked up on the panic, though. I knew it. I could feel their own turmoil radiating from their rooms.

"We will, Ezra. We'll find her. We have to." Dakota's brown eyes were misty as she stood there, wringing her fingers together.

I'd had back-to-back meetings, one I'd personally called with the mayor to talk about my concerns over Hayden, and another right after with the Fire Chief.

I should have checked my goddamn phone, but I'd gone from one to the other and hadn't pulled it out of my pocket. I'd had two messages waiting for me…one from Savannah saying she was following Hayden and another one from Dakota who'd been worried about her friend who'd taken off suddenly before her shift had ended.

Her friend that none of us had heard from since.

There was a light tapping at the door before it creaked open and my mother stepped through. I was still angry with her, but I didn't have time to deal with that right then. I grabbed my phone and stuffed it into my back pocket. "Thank you for coming," I told her as everyone stirred, preparing to leave.

"Of course."

"Lock the doors and don't let anyone in unless it's one of us."

Warily, my mother nodded, unimmune to the tumult that twisted through the atmosphere. I was heading for the door when the little voice hit me from behind. "Daddy."

Olivia.

Using that timid, sweet tone that she only used when we were alone.

Grief clutched my insides. I couldn't handle her precious heart being crushed again.

I fought the burning that raced the back of my throat, trying to act like I had it together when I was falling apart as I turned to her where she stood at the end of the hall.

Her blonde hair was in a messy braid, and she was wearing the same pink dress she'd had on this morning when she'd left, but her spirit was different. Marred by worry and fear.

"I need to go right now, Livvie. I'll be back soon. I promise." Regret filled my tone.

"But I need to talk to you."

"I can't right now. I have to—"

Tears streaked down her cheeks. "Daddy, please."

I cast a glance at everyone who was waiting.

"Go on, brother," Cody said. "We'll all load up and head out."

I dipped my chin, and I followed Olivia into her room. She shut the door behind her. I could feel her nerves raving, the way she was trembling, her soul shaken.

I dropped to a knee in front of her. "Sweet girl, I know you're scared right now, but I need to go and find Savannah so I can bring her home to us. You don't have to be afraid."

I prayed to God it wasn't a lie.

She pressed her lips together and looked away. "I think I did something really bad."

Guilt tinged her cheeks a mottled pink.

Fuck, I hated that I didn't have time for this. That I felt hope ticking away.

"It's okay, Olivia. Whatever you did, we'll talk about it later."

Her head shook. "I didn't think I was stealing it. I just thought…I just thought it was Mommy's because I gave it to her for Christmas and we never found it before, and I thought I should keep it with the album you gave me with all our special pictures."

A frown carved itself deep between my brow. "What are you talking about, Livvie?"

She blinked through the tears that wouldn't stop falling. "The journal in Miss Savannah's room. I was just looking for a marker and a piece of paper when she was taking a shower so I could leave her an invitation so she could have dinner with us forever and never be lonely again, but I found Mommy's journal and I took it. I didn't mean to steal it."

Dread sank like a stone to the pit of my stomach.

I took her by the outside of the arms. "Where did you find it?"

"In the drawer under the TV. I'm really sorry, Daddy. I didn't mean for Savannah to get lost."

I smoothed my hands up and down her arms, like it might be able to soothe us both. "It's okay. It's not your fault, Olivia. I promise, it's not your fault. But I need you to show me that journal."

Sniffling, she turned away and got to her knees beside her bed. She shoved her hand under the mattress and box spring and pulled a journal out from where she'd hidden it. Shame clung to her as she slowly brought it back to me, her head tipped down.

"It's okay," I promised.

But it wasn't.

It was not okay.

I skimmed through the pages.

Diary entry after diary entry.

Note after note about a beautiful young girl who'd gotten wrapped up in a powerful man and had lost both her innocence and her freedom. A spiral of misdeeds and manipulation. A therapist who'd tried to save her.

Only it was all written in Brianna's hand, and my wife had not been a therapist.

It started off sounding sane. Legitimate. As if she were truly trying to help this unknown person out of the wickedness that had taken her hostage.

Only the mindset spiraled and became so perfectly in sync with the delusions that Brianna had cast, her handwriting growing more frantic the more words that she'd written.

I told her to run. To get away from this place. It's not safe. It's not safe. I think he knows. She told me she loves him. I love him, too. I love the cuts he makes on my flesh. I love the way he kisses me. How could it feel so good when it hurts so bad? It's time. It's time. He wants me but he'll never keep me.

I kept flipping through the mayhem of her mind, the words slipping into crude slashes and shapes.

Random numbers.

Time stamped over a river.

A drawing of a pond in the middle of a stick-tree forest.

On the last page was a road leading to a gated dead end, a big, square mansion on the other side.

It's too late. It's too late, was carved deep into the page by a pencil.

My heart dropped to the floor.

Because I knew exactly where they were.

Chapter Fifty-Four

Savannah

BLINKING MY EYES OPEN FELT IMPOSSIBLE, LIKE COMING UP from the darkest waters where everything was blurred in an abyss of nothingness, and as I floated to the surface, pain began to stab and slash and flay. I fought my way through the murky depths that would be so easy to drown in, accepting the agony because I refused to give up.

Not when I'd come here to fight.

Still, I felt like the life was being squeezed out of me when I finally pried them open to the blurry haze of the darkened room. My face was throbbing so badly that it felt like it might burst from the pressure, the pain in my head splitting.

It was a foreign place that murmured of foulness and greed. There were no windows or natural light, just the jaundiced glow of hazy lamps.

My eyes were nearly swollen shut, and I wanted to weep in agony as I forced one open so I could make out my surroundings. It was a massive, rambling room, though the ceiling was low. Decorated as if it hailed from another era. Thick tapestries and dark velvet couches.

Luxurious in a way that could so easily leave you glamoured. Several round tables were situated about, and an ornate mahogany bar that was fronted by high-backed leather and wood stools sat on the wall on the opposite side of the room.

No question, it was a place for entertaining.

Even in it, I could sense the earth all around, almost smell the dirt that surrounded me on all sides.

A basement, I was sure.

I took stock of myself.

I was bound by the wrists and ankles, lying in the center of an enormous bed that was just as posh as the rest of the room. A deep purple duvet was below me and oversized pillows were piled against the elegant headboard.

I wondered idly if they cared that I was bleeding all over it or if that was part of the fun.

I suspected the last.

Honestly, I was sure of it as my mind played through the journal entries I'd read a thousand times, trying to decipher them. Trying to make them add up to evidence. They'd gone from insightful and caring and objective to so chaotic and disturbed that I'd questioned their validity as many times as I'd believed they had to mean something.

But I recognized it now, the fragments of facts mixed with the pieces that still didn't fit.

It'd been enough to bring me here, and I was terrified it was all going to have been made in vain.

The hope I'd found now lost.

I tried to move, and an ulcerated moan rolled up my throat without my permission, pain splintering through every limb of my body. Everything ached and throbbed. I was pretty sure I had to have been dragged down here. Like I was garbage and something to be thrown away.

I tried to clamp off the sound and not to draw attention to myself, and I did my best to pay attention to the words of the two men who were across the room, off to the left of the bar.

Samson and the mayor.

Shock whirred through my pounding brain. The mayor? He was the one who'd had my sister? I locked down on the cry that wanted to erupt from my soul. One begging to know where she was. If she was okay. If she was here.

And Samson…

Bile burned in my throat as I watched the two that I'd so easily trusted. Jack Harris angled toward Samson, his words the sharpest blades that cut from his tongue. "Did you get her car hidden behind the walls?"

"Of course, I got it inside. But Ezra is looking for her high and low. I reported back that this area was clear, but I know him well enough to know that's not going to stop him. He'll hunt every inch of this fucking state until he finds her."

"Then they've all got to go."

My eyes rammed closed, like it might hold the strength to block the impact of his command. The sickness of what he intended. I couldn't handle it, putting Ezra in the path of danger, and there was no missing the peril that lurked all around.

Samson let go of a dubious laugh. "That's a tall fucking order. You want to take out the fucking Sheriff? I'm afraid you're digging a grave deeper than you're going to be able to climb out of."

"I'm the mayor." Jack Harris smacked himself across the chest. "The fucking mayor. And you know what is riding on my shoulders."

"And if you hadn't been so goddamn obsessed with Brianna, you wouldn't be in this situation. I tried to get that journal back, but I got headed off every-fucking-time, both at the motel and at Ezra's place. You're fucking lucky Ezra didn't see my face that night in the alley."

Brianna?

Ezra's wife?

And it had been Samson at the motel. Samson who'd stabbed Ezra.

Nausea turned over my guts.

The mayor turned to face the room, and I could barely make him out as he rubbed his hand over his chin, his head cocked down as he contemplated.

But I could feel it.

The arrogance. The disgust and disbelief written into his pompous demeanor, as if he had the right to anger.

As if he wasn't responsible.

I tried to remain as still as I could, wishing I could disappear into the shadows.

He laughed a hard sound, and his attention moved to the far wall to my right. "I should have known you were nothing but a worthless fuck."

He crossed the space, his dress shoes clacking on the shiny wooden floor. A smack rang out followed by a long moan.

Surprise jolted me, and my head tilted all the way back so I could peer into that side of the room, unable to keep myself still any longer.

Oh my God.

Hayden was on the floor, bound the same as me, though a gag had been stuffed into his mouth and taped in place.

"You did it, didn't you? You're the one who took the journal? I should have known, but it wasn't until this afternoon when Ezra Patterson came into my office to voice his concerns over you that I knew who was responsible. You sent it to her sister, didn't you? Brought her here? What did you think you were going to achieve?"

Hayden frantically shook his head, and a garbled sound rose from his throat.

Jack Harris cracked the back of his hand across the side of his face, and his voice lifted in a depraved shout. "I said, what did you think you were going to achieve?"

Hayden thrashed where he was bound.

Jack reached out and tore the masking tape free, and I cringed at the sound of ripping skin. He knelt in front of Hayden, going still, the words deathly quiet. "Answer me."

Hayden laughed. A choked, bitter, resigned clank that hit the atmosphere like a bomb.

"Because I didn't sign up for this. Because you're a twisted fuck who deserves to be exposed. Because I tried to convince Brianna to tell Ezra what was happening, but she was so spellbound by your bullshit that she couldn't see what a goddamn monster you are. I sent it to Savannah thinking she would give it to the cops, and they'd discover the sickness of what you've been doing down here. Most of all, I did it because I can't sit idle and watch you hurt these girls for a second longer."

Hayden bit out every single one of the words.

"Good, you don't have to."

The mayor stood, pulled a gun from inside his suit jacket, and fired.

I didn't know what was louder. The sound of the gunshot or the scream that lacerated the air.

My scream that I couldn't contain.

Horror taking me over, terror surging and sending me flailing back. I ripped and tore at my bindings when Jack Harris turned his sights on me, and my heels dug into the mattress and pushed me up against the headboard.

No, no, no.

He slowly crossed the room until he was standing over the bed. Reaching out, he dragged a single fingertip down my cheek. "It's a shame I can't keep you around. I've had so much fun playing with your sister."

Whimpering, I reared back from his touch, nausea churning in my guts, my heart hemorrhaging.

Jessica. Jessica.

"What did you do to her? You fucking monster, what did you do to my sister?"

"Go get them." He wasn't talking to me, even though he remained staring down at me when he spoke. He was speaking to Samson.

Samson, who hesitated before he turned and disappeared through a door to the left of the staircase.

Dread weighed and pressed, and I was barely breathing by the time he returned with three young women. They shuffled in with their heads bowed, each wearing a loose beige linen dress.

I gasped when the one in the middle looked up.

My sister.

Her face gaunt and at least twenty pounds underweight.

And I didn't know if it was relief or grief that speared through me at the sight of her, the way my ribs felt like they'd just been rended apart and my heart was bleeding out in the middle of it. The only thing I was certain of was Jessica and I were feeling the exact same things.

Relief.

Grief.

Sorrow.

Regret.

Because I thought we both knew there was no coming back from this.

"Bring them," the mayor demanded.

Samson shoved them forward. "You sure this is the direction you want to go?" he asked.

"I don't see another choice. We've been compromised, and we have to clean up the mess Hayden created. We'll start fresh. Take care of the girls first, and we'll deal with the Sheriff later."

No, no, no.

I didn't even realize I'd whimpered it aloud.

"Oh, yes," Jack murmured.

Samson nodded, taking it as a final command. This bastard who Ezra had trusted. Someone who was supposed to care for the town and its people.

He forced all three women to their knees. They whimpered, though I thought they must have learned a long time ago not to fight because they went willingly.

Without a struggle.

Not me.

When Samson grabbed me by my bound wrists and yanked me off the bed, I kicked out with trussed feet. They struck Jack Harris in the stomach, hard enough to knock the air from his lungs, and I flailed, fighting against Samson's hold as he shoved me to the ground.

I tried…I tried to break free, but I was already so battered that I wasn't even sure I'd be able to stand, let alone fight off this man while I was tied.

From behind, Jack Harris took me by a fistful of hair and pushed the barrel of the gun to my temple. "You stupid bitch. You should have stayed home where you belong and left your sister where she did. You and Brianna both, trying to interfere. It broke my heart, killing her. But you?" He leaned in and uttered close, "I'll take pleasure in it."

Jessica whimpered where she was lined up one down from me, the four of us on our knees. I didn't know the other women. I didn't know their stories. I didn't know their pains or their failures. Their hopes or their dreams.

And I wondered if they'd felt alone like Jessica and I had.

Abandoned.

Only themselves against the wicked world.

But I guessed that wicked world had just caught up to all of us.

Jack Harris cocked his gun before an earsplitting bang exploded in the room.

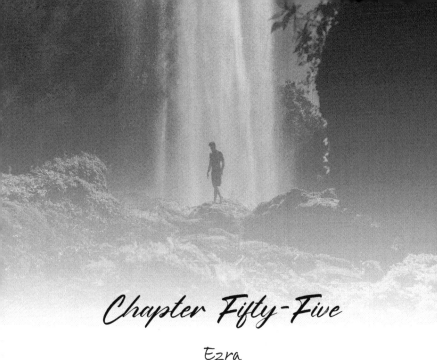

Chapter Fifty-Five

Ezra

I DROPPED DOWN ON THE OTHER SIDE OF THE STONE WALL THAT surrounded the mayor's estate, hitting the ground in a crouch, eyes scanning through the bare light that remained. The sky was drawn in the darkest blue, a knitting of indigo and slate, the first stars dotting the heavens that felt too fucking far away right then.

My heart pounded so loud that I was sure this bastard could hear me coming from a mile away, though I didn't sense any movement as I searched through the shadows that blanketed the exterior of the mansion.

Three stories tall.

At least that's what I'd always believed.

Until I found the drawings at the back of the journal that stated otherwise.

This asshole had a secret basement.

Cody slipped over the wall behind me, landing hard.

Ryder and Caleb hit the ground beside him.

"There's still time to turn back," I grumbled, knowing what we were likely up against, and every cell in my body rejected the idea of putting them in the line of fire.

"Not going to fucking happen," Ryder spat low. "You've been at our sides when things got rough, and you can be sure we're going to be at yours."

The rest of my officers were on their way, ten or fifteen out, all except for Samson who I hadn't been able to get in touch with.

And this couldn't wait. Every second felt like hope was ticking away.

Rage burned through my insides, adrenaline thudding hard through my veins, my throat so goddamn tight as I pulled my gun from my holster.

Cody, Ryder, and Caleb pulled out theirs, too.

I didn't even pretend like I wasn't breaking a thousand rules, having them here like this, their weapons drawn.

But you know what is said when it comes to desperate times.

"Yeah. Thought we already established who you'd want taking up your back when you're in trouble, and here I am," Cody joked, trying to keep a lightness that none of us felt. "Now let's go get your girl."

We didn't hesitate. The decision was made. From that second, we were all in. We spread out, keeping low as we crossed the sprawling yard, checking each direction.

Stillness echoed back, no sign of movement, no sign of life.

That didn't mean I couldn't feel it, that turmoil that thrashed and convulsed. A violence that held fast to the air.

And I prayed...I fucking prayed that we weren't too late.

We all hit the front wall, pushing our backs against it, our ears tuned, listening for any sound.

Nothing.

We moved to the front door, our breaths shallow and hard, panting as we looked at each other.

This was it.

I stood and punched in a set of numbers I'd found next to the drawings into the pad at the side of the door. I held my breath, then heaved it out when the lock gave, spinning open and disengaging the security system.

"Thank you," I mumbled under my breath.

To Brianna, I guessed.

She'd cast so many wrongs, but she'd led me here.

I pushed inside, my gun drawn, and I swiveled from left to right as I searched the entry room.

An eerie stillness echoed back, and I edged forward, attention darting in every direction.

The house was as old as the town, in Jack Harris' family for years, though he'd had it remodeled. Everything was sleek and contemporary lines.

My crew came in behind me, coming up to my side, like they promised.

"Now where the fuck is this kitchen?" Ryder grumbled.

It was also in the journal. The diagram leading us to the kitchen where there was a room hidden at the back.

We wound around an over-the-top dining room, the whole time vigilant, on edge, breaths so shallow we were hardly breathing, keeping our footsteps quiet as we moved.

"Jackpot," Cody said as he looked through a doorway.

The kitchen reeked of arrogance, this fucker living like royalty, and I knew he'd come from money…but this? I had a sense Jack Harris' greed went so much deeper and darker than any of us knew.

Well, no one except for Brianna.

We eased through the kitchen, and I went directly for the door tucked off to the side of a built-in refrigerator.

I opened it and stepped into what looked like a butler's pantry.

I moved right to where a rug had been shoved aside, revealing a hole in the floor, covered by a slat of wood.

I reached for the hook and lifted it to reveal a staircase that led down into the bowels of the house.

My stomach fisted.

Red-tinged lights lined the steps, lighting the way to the sickness below.

I knew it, without question, that she was here.

I could feel the energy that flailed in the atmosphere. That connection that called. The lure that had led me to her from the start.

The four of us quieted our feet as we edged down. Deeper and deeper. Far below where a typical basement would lie.

Finally, we came to another door.

It was locked, but this one didn't have a code.

I glanced back at my crew. "Stand back," I said before I fired.

Fired and fired until the wood was splintered, and I lifted my foot and kicked in the door as I hurried to change the mag on my gun.

We burst inside, smoke clouding our vision. It took a second for it to clear enough that I could make out the enormous room.

All the way across it, I found that Jack Harris had whirled around and had a gun pointed our direction.

But it was Samson standing there with his own gun drawn that nearly had me stumbling. Mind so mucked that it took me a second to realize he hadn't gotten there first but instead was involved. I knew it with the way he stood next to the mayor. The way something vile slid into his features.

Betrayal split me through.

But I didn't have time to let it affect me, not when I saw the four women who were facing away on their knees on the floor.

Savannah was on the right.

Rage blistered, a firestorm that consumed all thought.

"Motherfucker," Cody wheezed as he took in the scene, while Ryder and Caleb toiled, antsy to let loose as we caught up to what clearly went down in this room.

I tried to keep it together when Jack Harris took Savannah by the hair. Not to go running across the room to get to her.

I had to play this right if I was going to get everyone out of here alive.

My jaw snapped in restraint as he jerked her around, and she cried out as he dragged her across the floor to position her in front of him, still on her knees.

I nearly pulled my trigger on the bastard when I saw her face.

Bloodied and beat to shit. Her eyes nearly swollen closed. The dress she wore ripped and tattered.

Her sorrow was so stark and deep that I nearly choked on it. Like she'd already accepted this fate, thinking life was going to let her down once again.

Not this time.

I refused to let it.

I forced out the words through clenched teeth. "Put your gun down and get on the ground."

My attention kept jumping between Jack and Samson. They were outnumbered, but that didn't mean us taking them out wouldn't come without casualties.

I was a damn good shot, but so was Samson.

Jack Harris laughed this cocky, deranged sound as a sneer hit his face. "Have you forgotten who you're talking to?"

My scoff slashed like razors. "It seems I never really knew who I was talking to, did I?"

"Well, we all have our little secrets, don't we? Just like your sweet, little wife."

This asshole was trying to bait me.

"Sure. And it looks like your secrets are going to put you behind bars for the rest of your days."

Justice for Brianna was right there, dangling out in front of me. What I'd promised. I just hated that she'd allowed this monster to invade her mind, but I was pretty sure after reading that journal, she hadn't had much choice in the matter.

She'd been manipulated.

Her vulnerabilities and paranoias used against her.

He snorted. "I don't think that's how this is going to play out, Ezra. I mean, it's a true shame you and your friends here had to trespass on my property." He waved his gun toward my cousins and Cody. "Threaten me for my family's wealth."

He tsked sadly. "I was just trying to protect myself and the heirlooms I keep here. Luckily, Samson got here just in time to save my life. Unfortunately, that meant having to take all of yours. The town will be shocked. But they'll come to understand, though. It's not like your friends here haven't always been trouble."

Rage trembled, and my arms fucking shook, and I had to fight with all I had to keep myself steady. To keep from coming unhinged. To keep from running across this room and putting a bullet in his brain.

"Everyone will know it's bullshit. The rest of my deputies are already on their way. Hell, they're probably pulling up as we speak. It's not going to happen, Jack."

I snarled it.

"So why don't you put down your gun. You, too, Samson."

I jutted my chin at him.

"I'm sorry, boss, but I'm afraid I can't do that. You should have moved on and dropped it when I told you to."

Before I had time to react, he yanked one of the women in front of him. She cried out as he dragged her against his body, terror ripping through the room, a shockwave of horror.

He lifted his gun and put it to her head.

"All of you on your knees or this bitch is going to lose her brains."

Visions slammed me. Arriving on the scene after I'd gotten the call that there'd been a shooting in town. Unaware it was Brianna until I'd run up and found her splayed at an odd angle on the pavement. Blood pooling around her.

It was him. Samson had killed her. And I knew it was what they'd intended here, and there wasn't going to be any coming out of this basement without spilling more. Theirs or ours.

We only had one moment. One chance to make this right. To show them they were worth more than whatever this deviant had convinced them of. They were worth it all.

My attention was on Savannah as those thoughts flashed through my mind. Even though her eyes were slits, that aqua stared back. Swimming with terror, though beneath it, there was more.

Our connection keening. Awareness thrumming through the space.

And I hoped she knew I'd meant every word. That I'd meant every touch. And that right now, no matter what, she knew she was not alone.

I'd give it all.

Because I loved her.

Forever.

I made the move before either of these fuckers could anticipate it. I ran forward, firing two shots just above Samson's head, low enough that it would send him ducking but high enough there was no chance that I would hit the woman the bastard used as a shield.

Surprise sheared through Jack Harris' face as I came running across the room, the asshole stumbling back in shock, unprepared. Savannah took the opportunity, and she threw herself to the side, only I saw out of my periphery what she was throwing herself on.

One of the other women. Young. Blonde hair. She cried out a mournful sound, and I knew it was her sister.

Only my attention remained there a beat too long, and Jack had regrouped, and he swung the gun around in Savannah's direction.

Savannah who was awkwardly spread out over her sister with her arms and legs bound.

A shroud.

A shield.

Protecting her the way she promised she always would.

I hurtled for Jack, feet pounding as I ran his direction, firing as I went.

He whirled back at me at the exact same time, pulling his trigger, too.

Gunshots rang out from every side.

So loud. Disorienting. Deafening.

Though I barely felt them as they pierced my skin.

I just kept going. Barreling into him, colliding with the beast and taking him to the ground. We rolled, both trying to pin the other. He got on top of me, but I managed to shove him back enough so I could let go of two more shots right into his chest.

His eyes went wide before he slumped forward, and I grunted as I tossed him off, gasping as I tried to orient myself to the mayhem.

To the shots and chaos that had rained before everything had gone deathly quiet.

The utter silence that rang out before soft whimpers started to rise into the dusky, smoke-laden air.

That heavy air wheezed into my lungs, and I felt disoriented. Lightheaded. Though I forced myself to sit up and stagger to my feet. I pressed my hand to my side where blood was gushing as I squinted, scanning the area.

Caleb stood over Samson, his gun still pointed his direction, even though Samson was sprawled out, facedown.

Dead.

Cody had come to stand over Jack who was in a similar position, and he nudged him with the toe of his boot to make sure he wasn't moving.

Ryder had crouched in front of the girl Samson had used as a shield, the woman bleeding heavily from the arm.

And Savannah.

Savannah wept where she was now sitting up, still bound, tears sliding down that striking, unforgettable face.

I dropped to my knees in front of her. I reached out and touched her cheek.

Love rushed out as I was slammed with relief.

She was safe.

"I found you," I managed to force out. That time, I knew exactly why it came out sounding like it meant something.

This woman who I'd discovered hiding in the woods.

My little trespasser.

"I found you."

Then I slumped to the side.

Chapter Fifty-Six

Savannah

I FOUND YOU. I FOUND YOU.

A scream tore from my soul as Ezra fell. Blood poured from his abdomen.

I flailed to get loose of the ropes around my wrists and ankles.

So I could get to him.

Hold him.

Jessica was suddenly in front of me, her fingers frantic as she started to rip at the bindings, her head lowered as she kept mumbling, "I'm so sorry. I'm so sorry."

I had so many questions. So much love and hurt and sorrow. So many things that needed to be said, but I couldn't say anything once she freed me.

My only instinct was to get to Ezra. I scrambled to his side, my trembling hands touching his face, his lips, his jaw. "Ezra. Please. Open your eyes."

I found you.

I found you.

I pressed those trembling hands low on his abdomen and to the side. Blood seeped between my fingers.

"Ezra, please, you're going to be okay. Please be okay."

A flurry suddenly burst around us again as footsteps and voices clashed as more officers ran into the basement. It seemed to snap everyone out of the shock, and the room was instantly riddled with the cries of the women who'd been held here, taking in the carnage strewn around the room.

Cody, Ryder, and Caleb rushed up, skidding to a stop when they came to hover over us.

"Fuck."

"Get the paramedics in here."

"Hurry, please!"

Their voices drifted through the bleary haze that blurred my sight.

But this overbearing, beautiful man was the only thing I could see.

My love.

My forever.

My safe place.

Chapter Fifty-Seven

Savannah

LOVING HAD ALWAYS BEEN MY GREATEST BURDEN. WHAT HAD hurt me the most because loving had only left me hollowed out. Those vacancies, the wounds, the hurts driven so much deeper because it was never offered in return.

The echo of it had only amplified the emptiness.

Yet, I'd given myself fully to my sister. My devotion. My love. My everything. I'd shored up the rest, guarded myself from caring at all costs because I'd never believed I would find a person worthy of the gamble of being hurt again.

It was so much better to go it alone than to risk the pain of losing.

But I wasn't alone where I sat in the waiting room of the hospital in Poplar where Ezra had been taken. I was surrounded. Surrounded by this care and love and concern that I'd never known.

True and real and resolute.

Dakota held my hand on one side and Paisley the other, and Beth had pulled up a chair in front of me and was rubbing my knee.

Caleb, Ryder, and Cody were there, too, though they were stalking back and forth across the room, unable to sit still, the adrenaline still clearly ticking through their systems, the bedlam they'd been partner to trembling as shock through their veins.

We knew the FBI was on their way and they'd be questioned soon, and a raid had been ordered on Jack Harris' property. Samson and Jack Harris were dead. Unquestionably, their misdeeds had gone deep and dark. Stretching far and wide.

The three women were safe, currently admitted to this hospital until it could be determined what type of care they needed, including my sister. My sister who I hadn't been allowed to speak with yet, though I wasn't sure I could even handle it right then. Not when it felt like I was being shredded while I waited for news on Ezra.

"It's been too long." I scuffed around the torment.

Dakota squeezed my hand. "I know it feels like a day has passed, but it's only been an hour since they took him back. He's going to be okay. Ezra's way too big and bristly to let a little bullet take him down."

She stumbled over the levity that she tried to force, the words hitching.

I sniffled. Ezra, my massive, mountain of a man. So rough and burly. But he was so soft underneath. Too soft. Too good. And I'd seen his intentions written all over him before he'd surged forward.

His promise.

The sacrifice he would make.

The door slowly swung open, and we all anxiously looked up, hoping to see the doctor with an update. Instead, Ezra's mother stood at the threshold, her face a mess of torment and tears.

Dakota's mother had gone to stay with the children so Linda could come here.

My spirit crashed against my ribs. She'd been so terrified of me hurting her son, but neither of us had truly understood the extent of where this would go.

Guilt blazed across my chest.

Searing.

Scoring.

Linda stumbled forward, hardly able to stand. I winced, though I

414 | A.L. JACKSON

didn't lower my head. I just looked at her with an apology that would never be good enough.

"Have you heard anything?" she pressed through the anguish.

Paisley stood, her voice soft. "No, not yet, but he's only been back there for about an hour. Here, sit."

She gestured to the chair next to me.

Linda sank onto it. Grief billowed and blew.

"I'm so sorry," I whispered out into the room.

From my periphery, I saw her slowly shake her head. "My son loves his job. He loves protecting Time River and the people in it."

Shock jolted through me when she reached out and took my hand. "And I was too blinded by my own sorrow and loss over Brianna to see what Ezra really felt—not until I saw him last night on that dance floor with you. It was so plainly clear to see what he *really* loves. And what he really loves is you. So it's me who's sorry."

I squeezed her hand back. "You were right about me. I was a runner. Afraid. Terrified of being loved and of loving back. But your son…he proved to me that I didn't have to be. That loving is worth it."

Even if you lost it in the end.

We sat like that together for the longest time while we waited.

Finally, the door swung open again, and our attention jumped that way.

A nurse stood in the doorway.

I rocked forward, desperate. My spirit pleading and praying.

She smiled. "Someone is awake and demanding to see you."

She was looking at me when she said it.

Heart in my throat, I hurried down the hall to room 3B, hands shaking like mad as I rushed through the door. Only I stalled out the second I stepped into the room and saw the beast of a man propped at an incline on the bed.

I was frozen.

Held.

Emotion so overpowering that I couldn't stand in it, and a swell of lightheadedness slammed me.

I was struck with too many things.

Relief.

Love.

Horror at what he'd been through. At what might have happened.

My eyes raced to take him in. Tracing over every deep-set line and masculine angle. So big in that small bed that he looked like he was going to crush it, my sweet beast of a man whole and alive.

Tears blurred and my spirit thrashed.

A smile hitched at the corner of his mouth. "Get over here, Little Trespasser."

Joy left me on a yearning cry, and I flew across the small room, aching to throw myself on top of him. I settled for grabbing his giant hand in both of mine and pressing his palm to my face. I planted kisses all over the surface. Inhaling everything that he was.

Citrus and pine. Love and loyalty.

My home.

My safe place.

"What were you thinking? Storming in there like that?" Desperation abraded the words. "That was a little overbearing, don't you think?"

I struggled to make it a tease. To make it light.

It croaked out, instead, and the latent fears tumbled out with it. "I could have lost you. Your kids could have lost you."

Shifting his palm, he set it on my cheek, and his thumb softly stroked as he looked at me with those warm, honey eyes. "And I could have lost you."

His return was thready, harsh and cut with emphasis.

His head angled farther to the side as his gaze ran over the wounds that littered my face.

His eyes flicked back to mine. "Do you think I really would have waited one second, Savannah, knowing you were in that basement? Do you think I could have turned a blind eye? Pretended my heart wasn't already in there with you? I would never abandon you. Would never leave you."

Tears fell harder.

"You are worth every sacrifice," he continued in that gruff voice, "but I wasn't about to let that bastard steal you from me or me from you, either. This wasn't going to be our end. Because we belong together. You, me, and the kids."

I clung to his hand, pressing it tight against my cheek, needing to feel his pulse against my skin.

"Don't you get it yet, Little Trespasser? You are my forever. For as long as you'll have me."

"I'm afraid you're stuck with me, Hot Cop." My smile was soggy.

Ezra grinned. "I do have to say I like the sound of that."

Chapter Fifty-Eight

Savannah

"HEY," I MURMURED AS I STEPPED INTO THE DIMLY-LIT room. My footsteps were tentative. Hurt radiated from my soul like it had become a physical, tangible thing, banging against the walls, magnifying as it bound with the stark, gutting relief of seeing my sister sitting against a pillow in the hospital bed.

She looked so different. Worn. Parred down to the shell of the girl I remembered. One who'd seemed so vibrant and ready to tackle the world.

I should have recognized that her wounds had been carved deep. As deep as mine. Our scars had just manifested differently. Where my tattered heart had become a steeled barricade that I'd refused to let anyone through, hers had ached to be filled, to be seen, to be held and adored, though that need had been distorted by the abuse that had been inflicted.

I hadn't seen how vulnerable it had left her.

Her chin trembled as she fought the emotion. A sob ripped free, anyway. It fractured my hesitation, and I rushed across the room and wrapped my arms around her shoulders.

Relief pummeled.

Swell after swell as I sat there holding her while she wept. While I wept.

We stayed that way for long minutes. As if I held her for long enough it might make up for the times that she'd been alone. Make up for what she'd gone through.

"I'm so sorry." She gasped and choked over the only words I'd heard her say since we'd found her in that basement.

I pressed my lips to her crown, my words a haggard whisper. "I'm so sorry, too."

"How could you apologize, Savannah?" she choked, clinging to me. "You've always taken care of me. Been there for me."

"I tried to be there for you, Jessica, but I understand now I couldn't be everything you needed."

"You are the one person who has ever fought for me. Stood for me. And I did *this*."

I edged back, my head angled as I took her by the hands, staring at her beautiful face that I'd been terrified I'd never get to see again. "But I think I did it so fiercely that I blocked you off from the rest of the world. You were searching for what was missing while I shamed you into thinking you shouldn't need it. It created a wedge between us, and *I* am sorry for that."

A quiet understanding rippled between us, and I sniffled and tried to dry my face as I eased back a little. "Do you think you'd be able to talk about it? I don't want to push you."

We'd gathered fragments and scraps over the last day, but there were so many gaps that didn't touch, and we knew Jessica was likely the only one who could fill them, whether if that was today or months down the line.

Jessica grabbed a tissue, and she blotted her eyes. "If only I would have talked to you from the beginning. You would have seen Jack Harris coming from a million miles away."

Anger pulled at my insides as she mentioned his name, and she dipped her head, gathering herself as she dug around to find strength, though her voice was still little more than a whisper. "I met him at a function in Houston. It was one of those trendy parties I loved, everyone dressed to catch the eye of everyone there, wanting to be seen. Only I caught the eye of Jack Harris."

Her inhale caught in her throat, and her attention dipped to her lap before she peeked back at me. "God, he was so charming, Savannah. So handsome. Rich. Powerful. And he was looking *at me*."

A tear got free from the corner of Jessica's eye as she continued. "He took me to dinner the next night, and that was all it took to get caught up in him. A whirlwind that I couldn't find my footing in. He showered me with gifts, took me to the most expensive restaurants, filled my closet with every designer label I could ever desire. I thought, 'how could I get so lucky?'"

The laugh she let go of was haunted, a hollow clang of regret. "I thought everything was perfect, except he told me we had to keep our relationship under wraps for a little while since he was going to be running for Congress and I was so much younger than him. He promised to marry me after that, but for the time being, it had to be our secret. I mean, how could I be such a fool, Savannah? Fall for that? But I did."

Pain lancinated my heart because I understood why. She'd been empty and desperate for someone to fill those vacant places her childhood had left behind.

"You believed it because you deserved all those things. He's the one who manipulated you, Jessica. He's the one to blame."

She blinked through the memories, swallowing hard before she pressed on. "He'd travel back and forth to visit me before he finally asked me to move to Time River so we could be together. I was so happy. I thought things were finally going to change until he told me it still had to be kept under cover. No one could know. And there was a part of me that knew it, Savannah—this place inside me that revolted against it again—that warned me something wasn't right. And still I went with it because no one had ever made me feel that good. So important. So beautiful. Like I was cherished."

Regret tipped her mouth all the way down on the right side. "So, I texted you and told you I didn't need you in my life anymore.

It destroyed me, severing our connection. It was the biggest mistake I ever made, shutting you out."

"It broke my heart, too."

"I know. I knew it would. And still I went along with it."

She paused, then said, "I moved the next day. When I got to Time River, I was upset, expecting something much more glamourous, but he told me to trust him, that everything was going to work out the way he'd promised, and he put me up in this gorgeous condo."

My stomach twisted. The condo that had been in the journal.

"He'd visit me there most days, sneaking in at all hours, since God forbid, he be seen with me, until he finally asked me out to his place one night. And there I was again, the fool who thought he was finally going to make me a real part of his life."

Bitterness filled her voice. "Only I wasn't the only woman there."

She paused, processing the hurt.

The pain.

Her shame was sharp and clotting the air.

I reached for her hand. "It's okay, Jessica. I'm right here."

She sniffled, but she kept her attention on me as she murmured, "My heart cracked right in half, Savannah, yet somehow...somehow that bastard still managed to convince me to go with them to his room. He'd said nothing could bring him greater pleasure than having the two of us together."

Her gaze tripped to the wall, to the floor, then back to me. "When Jack was out of earshot, she'd squeezed my wrist so hard that I'd thought she would draw blood. Her words had been rushed and quieted as she'd urged me to leave. She'd told me to run far away and never look back. And I let jealousy get in the way...thinking she was trying to get rid of me so she could have Jack to herself. A fool who didn't listen."

Sorrow bottled in my chest. "Brianna?"

My mind still reeled with the truth. I'd been filled in on the link with the journal. Told that my sweet Olivia had taken it, not understanding what it meant. And here I'd been searching Ezra's ex's journal for months and had no clue.

Sorrow filled the quiver of her chin. "Yes, Brianna."

Jessica paused, warring through the images that I could see plagued her mind. "It started out with only the two of us. Usually in his room. Sometimes at my condo. He'd take turns with us or sometimes watch us together."

Her head shook in guilt. "I didn't know Brianna was married, Savannah. Not until we were a few months in. I was stunned, unable to wrap my head around the fact that she had this double life. But she'd been just as swept up in Jack as I had been. Too blinded to see what she was sacrificing for the chance to be with him."

My spirit felt like it was getting beat up on all sides. Grief slamming me. For Jessica. For Ezra. For his kids. It was also there for this woman I could never truly understand, but I had to believe she'd been just as manipulated as my sister had been.

Jessica's attention dropped to her lap, and she pulled her hand from mine and started to fiddle with the tissue, her fingers trembling so hard I could feel them shaking the bed. She peeked up at me from beneath her bangs. "Being with Jack was more pleasure than pain, but he was into that, too. I…" She paused, then rushed. "I found I liked it. It was exciting. Exhilarating. That was until he started taking us down to his basement. That was when the pain became a real, terrifying thing. It wasn't until then I started to realize I'd gotten myself into a situation I wasn't sure I'd be able to get myself out of. One that so many times I felt like I didn't *want* to get out of."

I squeezed her knee, my voice soft. "Because you loved him."

Jessica wheezed. "Yes. Brianna did, too. But soon there were more women…more men."

I felt the barrage of remorse that battered my sister's soul. "Brianna had been with him the longest and he loved her the most. He gave her the most freedom. He almost seemed to like that she would go home to her husband and then come crawling back to him. She wasn't well, though, her mind."

She peeked at me as if she felt guilty for offering the secret.

"Like any of us could really be in that situation. He preyed on it. Preyed on those of us who could be easily manipulated and trained."

Sadness pulled at her mouth. "But Brianna…her mind was so broken. I didn't realize it until Jack started keeping us down there for days at a time. I never knew who she was going to be when I saw her."

Anguish pulled through my senses. God, this was unbearable, listening to what they had been through. Horror curled through me. For all of them. I couldn't help but feel anger toward Brianna for the hurt she'd caused Ezra and the kids, but how could I blame her for something she likely couldn't control?

Jessica's head shook in confusion, her eyes narrowed as she fell back into that time. "There were times when she would act like everything was normal, like we shouldn't be concerned about what was happening. Other times, she'd…"

Despair pinched Jessica's face. "She would be in a frenzy, muttering that they were coming for us, that they were going to kill us. I'd ask her who, and she'd only beg me to leave while I still had the chance. It was like she was paranoid, but didn't she have every reason to be?"

Jessica lifted her gaze to me when she asked that. Like she was begging me to understand.

Then she gave a harsh shake of her head. "If I would have listened, gone to someone, told them what was happening…"

Reaching out, I pried her hand from where she was shredding the tissue. I squeezed it in emphasis. "You were blinded, too."

The shake of her head slowed in sadness. "That doesn't make it okay, though, does it? That I was so wrapped up in a man that I'd turn a blind eye to what was happening? I'm just as responsible, Savannah."

"No, Jessica, you're not." But I knew I could tell her it a million times right then and it would likely not make an impact. It was going to take time for her to work through what she'd been through. Time and help and care to work through the trauma that scarred her soul.

My sister let go of a soft though incredulous sound, sniffling around the tears that kept falling. "Brianna used to hide in the corner, frantically scribbling in this journal."

She trailed off, her attention dipping to our joined hands before she continued, "She left it sitting out, once, and I read it. She'd written in it like she was an entirely different person. A therapist. I knew it was me she was writing about. She had written about all these different places where I'd actually run into her around town in the past, though we'd ignored each other each time because we couldn't take the chance of being seen together. Jack wouldn't stand for it. I think…I think it was her way of wishing she could have stopped me from getting involved."

Jessica choked over a sob that suddenly rolled her throat. "I thought she was crazy, Savannah, but I sometimes wonder if she didn't know more than all of us. If she hadn't already seen somewhere deep in her chaotic mind what was getting ready to happen and she was trying to save us from it."

Her lips pressed thin as she attempted to keep them from trembling. "Because it didn't take long for things to spiral with Jack. For things to become more depraved."

"Jessica." I whimpered it, wishing I could hold all of it for her. But the only thing I could do was be there. I balled her hands in both of mine. Squeezing so tight in silent encouragement.

"There were so many men, Savannah." Her brow pinched. "Powerful men. Oh, but Jack made sure to create this world where he was the most powerful one. He was the supplier of the depravity, but in it, he held those men's secrets, and he was going to use them to rise to the top. I'm certain he was blackmailing them. His sordid desires were met in every direction. Gaining wealth, pushing forward his ambitions, and that rush of power he got when he inflicted pain. And that pain got worse and worse. We'd all become basic prisoners. Subject to Jack's beck and call and every whim. And those whims…"

I held tighter.

Jessica looked up at me beneath the lock of hair that fell in her face. "Those whims became horrible, Savannah. We were tied up. Forced. Used. Nothing but playthings and entertainment."

Her words got tangled as she forced out the next. "Brianna snapped one night… She started screaming that she was going to expose every person there. Screaming that she was going to go to her husband who was the Sheriff and give every single name. Out them all. Jack had laughed, humoring her, like she wasn't anything to worry about."

Sadness hitched on the shaky breath Jessica inhaled. "When Jack wasn't paying attention, she grabbed me the same way she'd done that first night...her nails cutting into my skin as if she was trying to get through to me. She said she was going to run, and she wanted me to go with her. She was going to empty out her bank account, take off, and start new. But not before she let her husband know what Jack was doing. She was dead the next day."

Grief blurred my eyes, my heart torn in a thousand directions. "Who killed her?"

"Samson."

God. Disgust lined my insides. Ezra had speculated that it had to have been him, but knowing it?

She chewed at the inside of her cheek as her head bobbed through the disorder. "Samson never participated, but he was on the payroll. There to cover tracks. To make sure no one picked up a trace of what was happening. An insider so Jack would always be one step ahead of the authorities."

"And after Brianna was killed, Jack didn't let you leave?"

It was all clicking together. These sick, twisted pieces. I'd seen so much cruelty in my life, but this? It went so much deeper than I could have imagined.

"I was never allowed to leave the basement again." Her words quivered as she was taken back to the horrors that she'd just been freed from. "Brianna was the example of what would happen to us if we ever tried. Jack had me right where he wanted me. Reliant. Weak. No one having a clue where I was. No one to know I'd gone missing. It was the exact same thing he'd done to the others."

Jessica blinked slowly, wading through a reality she wished hadn't existed. "I don't even know how long I'd been down there when one of the men came to me. He asked me who I trusted most...who would fight to find me...and I gave him your name."

"Hayden. He sent me the journal."

Guilt burned through my spirit. God, I'd been so wrong about him, and he'd been killed for it.

Killed for trying to save my sister and the other women down there.

If I'd done it differently, would he still be alive?

Sorrow cut me in half. I hated it, wished I could go back and do it all differently. But I guessed all of us would have done it differently if we'd really understood what was happening. But this cesspool had been so deep and ugly that there'd been no logical, prudent way to move through it.

Jessica's nod was slow. "I knew the first time he came down into the basement that he wasn't like the others. He seemed...shocked. Completely shocked by what was happening down there. He never participated. I got the sense he was a prisoner every bit as much as me but in a different way. Jack had that way about him. Keeping every person around him under his thumb. Either terrified of what he would do or so swept up by his promises that you didn't realize what was happening until it was too late."

I set my palm on her tear-stained cheek. "Jack is gone now, and he can't hurt you anymore."

She curled her hand around my wrist. "Because you never gave up on me. You fought for me. You saved me."

My head shook, and I was barely able to push out the words through the emotion. "I could never forget you, and I will fight for you for all my days. I promised you before and I'll promise it again. You can always trust that."

She inhaled. "I should have listened to you all the times you told me not to trust anyone but you."

Love billowed, a flood that ran just under the surface of my skin. Covering me like a shield. "I think we were just trusting the wrong people, Jessica."

Her blue eyes flicked back and forth across my face. "You seem different."

"I am different."

"The Sheriff?" she asked.

My nod was slow. "I came here looking for you, Jessica, and I am so thankful that I found you. So thankful. But I also found everything that I never knew that I needed. I found my heart."

"I guess the only thing we can be thankful for is that something good came out of this mess. That you found joy."

I had to think Ezra might have found me anyway. That someway, somehow, our paths would have led us to each other.

That we would have collided.

It seemed impossible now that it would have turned out any other way.

Another tear slipped down Jessica's soaked cheek, and I hesitated before I asked, "Did you decide what you're going to do?"

She wavered for a moment, before her voice filled with both hope and uncertainty. "I'm going to go to the facility that the social worker suggested. Heal the best that I can. Learn how to stand for myself. After that, if you'll forgive me, I'd like to be wherever you are."

"There is nothing to forgive, Jessica. And this is my home now. With Ezra and his kids. And I'll be right here waiting for you. Whenever you're ready."

Chapter Fifty-Nine

Ezra

"DADDY, DADDY, DADDY!"

I'd not even fully stepped through the door of the house before I was hit with a barrage of little voices calling me by my favorite name. All three kids hopped up from the living room floor where they were playing a board game with their grandmother.

Faces so full of joy at seeing me that it struck through me like a rod of lightning.

A stake of belonging.

They came flying my way, arms above their heads as they raced across the living room.

I knelt, ignoring the stabbing pain that lanced up my side. The only thing that mattered right then was holding them.

"Careful," Savannah said, voice soft where she stood at my side, carrying in the bag that she'd brought me so I could change into regular clothes after I'd been discharged from the hospital.

Olivia skidded to a stop, and she grabbed her brothers by the hands. On a dime, the kid turned into caretaker mode. "That's right.

Dad got an injury, and we have to be really cautious and make sure we don't hurt him any more than he already got hurt."

"Is you hurt, Daddy?" Owen asked in his sweet way. He was held in place by his big sister, though his little body drifted my way as he peered at me.

Reaching out, I ran my palm down his cheek. "I'm just about all better. Give me a couple of days, and you can start climbing all over me again."

"'Cause I'm a *kowawa*."

"That's right."

"And then we can play football!" Oliver shouted, jumping from one foot to the other and throwing a fist in the air.

A chuckle rolled free. "You want to play football, huh?"

"Daddy, you know I gotta do a blitz, and I'm going to do a blitz on you!"

Savannah laughed at my side. A throaty, beautiful sound that wrapped me in a comfort unlike anything I'd ever known. When I glanced up at her, I caught her gazing down at the four of us, affection so stark on her stunning face that I felt myself sway to the side.

Heartstruck at the sight of her.

I'd thought she'd have no idea what had hit her, but it was me who'd been slammed.

Knocked off my feet. Everything I'd thought I'd known stolen. Taken and reshaped.

Little Trespasser owning all of me.

"Don't worry, Dad, I took such good care of my brothers while you were in the hospital so you and Miss Savannah wouldn't have to worry one bit." Olivia drew my attention back to her. "I made dinner three whole times, and it was so good. Just ask Grandma. She said I was a natural like my auntie Dakota, and I bet I can even work at Time River Market & Café when I grow up if I want to, but maybe I think I should be a doctor instead so I can take care of you."

Love pulsed. A swarm of it that covered the room in a swath of devotion.

"You're pretty dang good at everything you do, Livvie-Loo. I'm thinking you can be whatever you want to."

The kid beamed, and I spread out my arms. The three of them stepped forward, way slower than they'd come at me, and I curled them into my hold, breathing them in, so thankful that I was here with them today.

No question, it could have turned out differently.

I was still all fucked up in the head, trying to wrap it around what Brianna had done. What she'd been embroiled in. More had been uncovered in the three days I'd been in the hospital, and while my officers had gone through Jack Harris' belongings, evidence had been found that Brianna had been involved with him before we'd met.

He'd kept a bunch of her things. Trinkets. Pictures. Letters. More journals. Some confessing her love for him. Others filled with thoughts and ideas that were erratic and detached from reality.

It seemed she'd broken things off with him when we'd first started dating. Looking for stability, I guessed. Normalcy. Joy. Contentment. But I guessed the power he held over her was too much, a force too great, and once she'd hit that spiral, when she'd stopped seeking help, she'd been lured right back to him.

It broke my heart. Not for myself. But for her. For our children. Hating the fact that I hadn't known how to help her. Hating that I hadn't recognized the full scope of what she was going through. Hating that I'd let my anger and frustration drive a wedge so deep between us that I couldn't see when she really needed help.

I'd wanted justice for her, but I wasn't sure that was truly possible. What she'd lost was so much greater than just putting Jack in the ground. It was a life that could never be reclaimed. Memories with her children that she was never going to have.

I'd failed her and I'd failed my kids, and I'd do anything to go back and make it different for them. Give my kids the chance to grow up knowing their mother. But the only thing I could do now was be there for them, with all of me, giving them everything I had.

I peppered a bunch of sloppy kisses all over their faces, making them giggle and squirm as I held them tight against me.

"Eww, Dad, that's so gross!" Except Olivia couldn't stop the riot of laughter that rode out, happiness spun in the middle of it.

And she and her brothers gave me those sloppy kisses right back.

"Miss Savannah needs kisses, too." Oliver yanked at Savannah's hand, and those aqua eyes trickled over us.

There were no longer any barriers there. No longer questions or reservations. She knew right where she belonged.

She climbed to her knees, and the boys basically attacked her, jumping all over her, arms around her neck, smacking kisses all over her precious face, the bruises that had marred it finally beginning to fade.

She was laughing, kissing them back.

Giggles rang, filling up this house with every bit of the love it deserved.

I leaned over and planted a giant one on her cheek, and my grin was unstoppable when I pulled back. "How many kisses do you think Miss Savannah needs?" I asked my kids, never looking away from her when I issued it.

"A bazillion." Oliver threw his hands overhead, all his fingers spread wide.

Olivia, my little sassy pants, scoffed. "That's not even a real word."

Then she snuggled up to Savannah's side and kissed her cheek. "But I think she needs a whole lot."

⁓

My mother had tried to slip out before dinner to give us space.

Privacy.

Savannah had stopped her and asked her to stay.

We'd all shared a meal together. Laughed. Joked. Gave thanks because Savannah and I had learned to be grateful for every day.

My mother had left soon after, but not before hugging each of us. She'd whispered how much she loved me as she curled me in a fervent embrace, had told me she was so thankful that I was whole. That it was over. That I'd found my heart.

Then she'd turned to hug Savannah, and the words they'd shared had been hushed, but there was no missing the bond they were forming.

Once my mother had left, I'd insisted on doing dishes, even though Savannah had *insisted* I didn't, the woman fretting over me, worried about my healing wound. Thing was, I didn't think I'd ever felt so good. So right. Like my forever and hers had perfectly aligned.

I finished wiping off the counters before I sauntered down the hall to the lilting of voices.

I moved to the twins' doorway, breath getting knocked from my lungs as I took in the scene. Oliver and Owen were on their beds, cackling like the little yahoos they were while Savannah read them a story.

She was on the floor.

A siren where she sat in the middle of them.

A five-alarm fire raging in the room.

Legs curled beneath her as she changed her voice, rising an octave then dipping to a low baritone as she shifted between characters.

I couldn't wait to spend the rest of my days standing in her flames.

"The end." She drew it out like it was the best part of the book.

"Do it again!" Owen begged.

Apparently, he didn't agree.

A soft giggle rolled from Savannah. "I've already read it twice."

"*Fee* is my favorite." Owen held up three chubby fingers.

With a tender laugh, she returned to the first page and started again, and when it was finished, she climbed to her knees. She crawled first to Oliver where she lifted up his covers. "In you go, my sweet boy."

He slid under, and she pulled his blanket to his chin then pressed a kiss to his nose. "Sleep tight."

"And I won't never let the bugs bite!"

"Never, ever." She touched the tip of his nose where she'd dropped a kiss, then she moved to Owen's bed. "Your turn."

"Do I has to?"

"Yep, it's already past your bedtime."

"Oh, man." Reluctantly, he crawled in, and when she went to lean over him to peck a kiss to his nose, he took her face in both his little hands. "Night-night, my S'vannah."

Tenderness rolled through her being.

"Night-night, my sweet Owen."

Standing, those aqua eyes swept toward me. A flash flood. A torrent. I'd gladly stand there and drown in it. "Your turn," she murmured.

I ambled deeper into the room, brushing her hip with my fingertips as I passed, and I tucked my boys in, that gratefulness overflowing.

"I'm so glad you got *aww* better, Daddy," Owen told me.

"That is because our daddy is so big like a tree and so strong, right, Daddy?" Oliver asked me.

My chuckle was slow. Adoring. Filled with the remnants of the tragedy we'd been through and with the faith that we could finally put all of this behind us. "I was just fighting for the things I love most."

"That's us, right?!" Oliver enthused.

"That's right, buddy. All of you...you're what I love most."

I tucked them the rest of the way in, brushing kisses to their temples, then I pushed to standing and moved across their room. I got lost in that gaze as Savannah took me in from where she leaned against the wall. Caramel waves rolling around her shoulders, the woman wearing a pink jumpsuit, pouty lips tipped in the softest way.

Energy thrummed, though tonight, it was quieted, coming at me like the tranquil flow of a rising tide.

I took her hand when I got to her and led her out, flipping off the boys' light and shutting their door part way before we crossed to Olivia's room.

She was in the middle of her bed with paper, colors, and stickers strewn around her. "What are you doing, Livvie-Loo?"

"I'm making something really important, but it's a secret, so you have to wait right there."

Savannah glanced at me. Gentle amusement played through her features.

My chest tightened. Fierce, fierce love.

It was so much more tonight. More than anything I'd ever felt.

"All right, but you need to finish up. It's past your bedtime."

"Yeah, yeah, yeah, I already know, and I might as well not even try to talk you out of it because you're just going to say, 'Don't even try it, Livvie.'" She mimicked my voice as she started cleaning up her things.

Once she had everything in the pink box, she scrambled off the bed, slipped it onto the shelf under her little white desk, then hopped back under her covers. She looked across at us. "You may now enter."

A chuckle loosed, a vibration in my chest, and I shuffled across the floor and bent to kiss her forehead. "Goodnight, sweetheart."

Her smile was soft as she peered up at me. "Goodnight, Daddy. I'm so glad you're home."

"It's the only place I want to be."

I could feel Savannah behind me, her presence profound, filling the voids. She edged around and wrapped Olivia in a big hug. She started to release her, but Olivia hung on, not letting her go. "I love you a whole lot, and I hope you stay with us forever."

Savannah froze, emotion crashing as she clung to Olivia just as tightly, before she edged back so she could stare down at my daughter when she murmured, "I love you with every piece of my heart, Olivia, and I don't want to be anywhere else."

"Good, then you have to eat dinner with us every single night."

An affected laugh escaped Savannah. "That sounds like a really good plan."

Savannah stood, and I threaded our fingers together and led her out. I paused at Olivia's doorway and glanced back. She was grinning our direction. "Goodnight, Livvie."

"Night, Daddy," she whispered.

I flicked off her light and started with Savannah back down the hallway.

"I do hope you're planning on walking straight to your room and getting into bed. You need to rest," Savannah said.

I angled my mouth toward her ear. "Oh, I plan on heading straight to bed, but *resting* is not in that plan."

I turned, walking backwards as I guided her through the house and down the short hall into my room.

Suspicion twisted her brow, though it was playfulness that edged those pouty, full lips. "I'm pretty sure what you have in mind right now goes against the doctor's orders."

I edged around her so I could shut the door. The lock clicking into place reverberated through the room.

I swiveled back to face her. There was no missing the way Savannah warred with the desire that clashed with her need to take care of me.

"I think she already knew I wasn't going to follow them," I said as I started backing her toward my bed.

"You need to rest," she contended, right as she was boxed in against the high mattress. A shaky wheeze left her when I curled my hand around the back of her neck.

"What I need is you." The words were hoarse, and I let my hand wander along her side until I was gripping her by the ass. I yanked all that softness against the hard planes of my body. Fire erupted between us, that connection burning bright.

"You aren't fighting fair, Ezra Patterson," Savannah whimpered.

"You know what they say…all's fair in love and war." I rumbled it down the delicate column of her neck, going back to the first night she'd spent with me.

Needy fingers curled into my shirt, and she tipped that sharp chin up to me.

"And this is love." Her words climbed through the atmosphere. Taking possession.

"It's love."

Love. Love. Love.

I felt the moment she relented, and Savannah kept peeking up at me as she helped me undress, carefully peeling away my shirt. A tremble rocked her through when it exposed the bandage that sat low on my right flank. The bullet had entered just below my vest. Another had grazed my hip. I'd bled like crazy, but it'd missed any vital organs, which had saved my life.

I knew there was a piece of her that blamed herself. Thinking she'd brought this into my world. But Jack and I would have met the same way at some point in time. The same as I would have sniffed out the wickedness that lurked in Samson. Sometime, someway, I would have uncovered their secrets.

But even if I'd had no connection to them?

I would have gladly stood in the line of fire for her.

Always. Forever.

"I'm okay, honey. It's over." I said it softly. Like it might stand the chance of being a balm.

"I was so scared," she whispered into the shadows that danced along the walls of my room.

"Me, too, but it's just you and me now. I'm right here, and neither of us are going anywhere."

I peeled off the sweatshirt she wore. She wasn't wearing a bra underneath, and those pert, tiny tits peeked out beneath the fall of her hair. I brushed a knuckle over a taut peak. A whimper wisped from between those plush lips, and I captured her mouth and swallowed it.

Drank down the greedy sounds that slipped from her tongue.

She peeled me out of my jeans then shimmied out of her sweatpants, leaving both of us bare.

"Lay down," she muttered, giving me a slight nudge, and I climbed onto the bed. I leaned against the headboard, never taking my eyes off her.

From the side of the bed, she took me in, that gaze sweeping, devouring where I was sprawled out, ready for her.

My cock stony and hard. Blood boiling with need.

"Come up here and let me have that sweet cunt."

Lust flash-fired. Ricocheting.

Though she remained careful as she climbed onto the bed, and gingerly, she came up to straddle me. Her hands went to my shoulders while her weight remained completely on her knees.

A goddess eclipsing sight.

I palmed her hip. "You have me, Savannah."

I told her that same thing so many times. That I had her. That I wouldn't hurt her. And I knew she wouldn't hurt me, either.

Trust burned between us.

She gripped my dick and positioned it at her entrance. So slowly, she sank down.

Consuming me.

Owning me.

Claiming me.

"Fuck me, Little Trespasser. You feel so good."

"So good." She breathed it as she seated herself fully.

I let a smirk ride to my mouth as my fingers burrowed deep into her hips. "Exactly what the doctor ordered. You are the best kind of medicine."

Savannah choked out a laugh, one that was half a moan as she slowly began to ride me, though her confession rang with severity. "And you are my remedy."

"Sounds like we're just better together. I might have to handcuff you to me and throw away the key."

Affection skimmed and spread through her expression as she thought of the way she'd teased me that first night, though this time when she took my hand and weaved our fingers together and lifted our hands out to the side, I reached under the pillow and grabbed my cuffs that I'd hidden there, and I shackled our wrists together.

Savannah laughed a surprised sound. "Ah, there he is…my Hot Cop giving into his overbearing ways."

I tugged her closer, a grin stretching across my mouth. "Sorry to break it to you, Little Trespasser, but you're mine, and I claim you forever."

Epilogue

Savannah

MIST SATURATED THE CRISP SPRING AIR, THE SOUND OF the waterfall rushing over the cliff and crashing into the pools below filling my ears. That and the shouts and howls coming from the children where they played in the woods. Their father's booming laughter thundered through the air as he chased them, the rambunctious game of hide and seek making them shriek with delight.

I snapped picture after picture, capturing the joy on their faces as they played.

As they loved.

As we spent this glorious Saturday together.

Six months had passed since this little family had changed everything. Since they'd shifted my foundation and built something brand new.

Once Ezra had come home from the hospital, I'd never left their house.

It'd become mine.

I'd never dared to dream of having a family. Of having people I would fight for just as fiercely as they would fight for me.

But sometimes all it took were a few special people to show you what it was like to be cherished and how fulfilling it was to get to cherish them back.

I was whole.

So full of joy that it was hard to process most days.

I aimed, snapping picture after picture as Ezra gently tackled Oliver onto the blanket that served as home base.

"I made it before you even got me because I'm so fast!" Oliver shouted.

"Dang it, I just missed you." Ezra feigned a pout.

Owen came barreling in from behind and threw himself on top of them, and in an instant, they were embroiled in an unruly wrestling match.

Olivia couldn't help but join in, too. "Doggie pile!"

Finally, Ezra shifted, sitting up and taking the kids into his arms. He muttered something under his breath, and all four of them shifted to face me.

Snap. Snap. Snap.

I couldn't imagine anything more inspiring than this. Taking pictures of the people I loved most, even though I found a great amount of purpose in my new business.

A Moment in Time Photography.

As much as I'd liked working at the café, my spirit had always ached for something different.

And I loved it, getting to capture the most treasured moments of people's lives.

And this moment, it felt like one of my greatest *treasures* as I caught every exuberance on their perfect faces.

Bright, bright light.

Belief.

My hope.

My heart.

Ezra whispered something in Olivia's ear, and she climbed out of his arms and scrambled to her backpack that was sitting next to our picnic basket. She pulled something out and the boys hopped up, too.

"Miss Savannah, Miss Savannah, we got something special for you!" they sang as they came running my way. Olivia held onto a folded piece of paper that had a bunch of stickers on it.

My chest expanded. They were always bringing me notes, making me feel like the most important person in their world. "What do you have for me?"

Behind them, I saw Ezra slowly climb to his feet, those honey eyes covering us with warmth.

"You have to open it to see, but it's the most special surprise, and I can't even wait," Olivia peeped. "I made it a really long time ago to save for the most important day."

"Hurry, hurry!" both the boys shouted, pushing in close.

I peeked at Ezra who was slowly advancing, his big body filling my eyes.

That connection throbbed.

His spirit filling my soul.

My fingers trembled as I loosed the pink pieces of tape and unfolded the paper.

Inside, was another invitation.

This one inviting me into forever.

will you marry our daddy?!?!

Heart stickers decorated every inch, and beneath it were three check boxes.

Yes. ☐
Definitely. ☐
Absolutely. ☐

Emotion raced and rushed and infiltrated every cell.

So beautiful I couldn't speak.

I could only look to Ezra who'd dropped to his knee. All the kids rushed over beside him to do the same, and I pressed my hand to my mouth as my eyes bleared.

Olivia pulled a marker from her pocket. "Here, you have to mark your answer."

I took it, and the laugh that bubbled out of me was saturated in bliss when I saw the ring that was attached to it, dangling from a pink string.

"What do you say, Savannah Ward? Will you marry me?" Ezra rumbled in that low, grumbly voice, the hint of a tease undercutting it. "You know my daughter has a way of getting what she wants."

I gazed down at their sweet, eager faces.

At my life.

At my family.

At my forever.

And I took the marker and checked the box.

Absolutely. √

The end

About the Author

A.L. Jackson is the *New York Times* & *USA Today* Bestselling author of contemporary romance. She writes emotional, sexy, heart-filled stories about boys who usually like to be a little bit bad.

Her bestselling series include THE REGRET SERIES, CLOSER TO YOU, BLEEDING STARS, FIGHT FOR ME, CONFESSIONS OF THE HEART, FALLING STARS, REDEMPTION HILLS, and TIME RIVER.

If she's not writing, you can find her hanging out by the pool with her family, sipping cocktails with her friends, or of course with her nose buried in a book.

Be sure not to miss new releases and sales from A.L. Jackson - Sign up to receive her newsletter http://smarturl.it/NewsFromALJackson or text "aljackson" to 33222 to receive short but sweet updates on all the important news.

Connect with A.L. Jackson online:

FB Page https://geni.us/ALJacksonFB
A.L. Jackson Bookclub https://geni.us/ALJacksonBookClub
Angels https://geni.us/AmysAngels
Amazon https://geni.us/ALJacksonAmzn
Book Bub https://geni.us/ALJacksonBookbub

Text "aljackson" to 33222 to receive short but sweet updates on all the important news.

Made in the USA
Columbia, SC
13 March 2024